Anne Bennett was bo. in the Horsefair district of Birmingham. The daughter of Roman Catholic, Irish immigrants, she grew up in a tight-knit community where she was taught to be proud of her heritage. She considers herself to be an Irish Brummie and feels therefore that she has a foot in both cultures. She has four children and five grandchildren. For many years she taught in schools to the north of Birmingham. An accident put paid to her teaching career and, after moving to North Wales, Anne turned to the other great love of her life and began to write seriously. In 2006, after 16 years in a wheelchair, she miraculously regained her ability to walk.

Visit www.annebennett.co.uk to find out more about Anne and her books.

By the same author

ANNE BENNETT

Keep the Home Fires Burning

HARPER

Harper
An imprint of HarperCollins*Publishers*
77–85 Fulham Palace Road,
Hammersmith, London W6 8JB

www.harpercollins.co.uk

Published by HarperCollins*Publishers* 2010

3

Copyright © Anne Bennett 2010

Anne Bennett asserts the moral right to
be identified as the author of this work

A catalogue record for this book
is available from the British Library

ISBN-13: 978 0 00 735919-6

Set in Sabon by Palimpsest Book Production Limited,
Falkirk, Stirlingshire

Printed and bound in Great Britain by
Clays Ltd, St Ives plc

Mixed Sources
Product group from well-managed
forests and other controlled sources
www.fsc.org Cert no. SW-COC-001806
© 1996 Forest Stewardship Council

FSC is a non-profit international organization established
to promote the responsible management of the world's forests.
Products carrying the FSC label are independently certified
to assure consumers that they come from forests that are managed
to meet the social, economic and ecological needs
of present and future generations.

Find out more about HarperCollins and the environment at
www.harpercollins.co.uk/green

This book is dedicated to my youngest and second granddaughter, Catrin Louise, who was born on 28th July 2010 and who has already given us all great joy.

ACKNOWLEDGEMENTS

There are a great many people that I must also thank for getting this book on to the shelves at all. Those of you who read my website will no doubt be aware of the traumatic year 2009 was, and the start of 2010 was little better. In the spring my lovely husband Denis, who is always such a support to me, developed double pneumonia and pleurisy and was very ill for some time. His illness inevitably greatly affected my life, and therefore my attempts to write a book during this time. I have in the past referred to the team I work with as my security blanket and they reaffirmed that title in their unrelenting concern and sympathy for me as I battled on with the manuscript. And so my heartfelt thanks go to Susan Opie, who virtually took the whole thing apart and then helped me re-assemble it, and to Judith Murdoch my agent who also gave me such staunch support. At HarperCollins, thanks go to my editor, Victoria Hughes-Williams and my publisher, Sarah Ritherdon, both of whom were extremely sympathetic. Thanks to Yvonne who copy-edited the book and Amy Neilson, who will help me promote the finished product. I must also thank Judith Evans who started me off with HarperCollins in the first place and Peter Hawtin who listened to what I had to say and acted on it. Grateful thanks go out to the both of you.

My family, as always has helped me a great deal. My eldest daughter Nikki and her husband Steve have been terrific, and the children too – though officially Briony is a child no longer and even Kynan has reached his teens. My son Simon and his wife Carol are also a great support to me, and so are eleven-year-old Jake and nine-year-old Theo. Beth is still at home and was a big help when her father was so ill, as were Tamsin and Mark, who live locally. You will see that the dedication of this book is to Tamsin's baby, Catrin Louise, who was born on 28th July 2010. She is truly wonderful and perhaps a new birth is a good omen of better days ahead for us all.

I value all my friends who are always there for me when things got tough; those I have had for years that I see as often as I can, those of you I meet each morning while dog walking, and my writer friends that I try and see once a month.

However, all this would be of no earthly use at all if you, my loyal readers, didn't buy my books or borrow them from the library, so a sincere and wholehearted thank you for that. And thank you too for the letters and the emails that you send. I read them all and truly appreciate every one of you.

ONE

'I was speaking to Fred Shipley after Mass this morning,' Bill Whittaker said as the family sat around the table that early April morning, eating their large breakfast. 'You know, from a few doors up?'

His wife, Marion, nodded. 'I know him. Ada's husband. They have a son in the navy.'

'So he was saying. He claims they're getting all the ships into tiptop condition and more are being commissioned. Not that they tell the men much, but apparently they're recruiting nineteen to the dozen, only it's all hush-hush at the moment.'

'Why?'

'At a guess I'd say that they don't want to start a national panic. Now, you're not to fret about this, though maybe it is better to be semi-prepared, but I am beginning to wonder if Chamberlain was wilier than we gave him credit for when he came back from Munich waving that piece of paper last September, declaring that there'd be "Peace for our time".'

'In what way?'

'Well, I'm wondering if all that talk of appeasement was just a ploy so that we could get ourselves on a war footing should the need arise. I mean, can you see a man like Hitler being satisfied with just Austria and Czechoslovakia? And just at the moment he has plenty on his side, with the Fascist Franco winning the war in Spain, and Mussolini in charge in Italy. And Stalin seems to be another brutal dictator.'

Marion let her eyes settle on her family grouped around the table listening to her husband. Her elder three children looked very like her, with their hazel eyes and light brown hair, her handsome elder son, Richard, tall for fifteen. He had been apprenticed in the brass foundry, where his father worked, for almost a year now, Sarah, her beautiful eldest daughter, would be fifteen in October, and her mischievous second son, Tony, was just turned nine and sometimes one body's work to watch. The identical twins, Miriam, who was known as Missie, and Magda, looked the spit of their father with their dark eyes and dark hair, and would be seven in June.

Suddenly Bill's words seemed to threaten all Marion held dear, and she shuddered as she said, 'Europe doesn't seem to be a very safe place at the moment.'

'It isn't,' Bill answered grimly.

'But, Bill,' Marion's eyes looked large in her pale face, 'surely no one wants war, certainly not after the last lot.'

'No sane person wants war at any time,' Bill said. 'But Hitler isn't sane, is he? You remember that rampage against the Jews that we heard about on the wireless last November? Would any sane man authorise that?'

'Oh, I remember it well.' And without thinking of the children listening, Marion went on, 'The night we heard about it was a filthy one too, cold and windy with rain lashing down, and I thought, what if it had been us thrown out on a night like that, like those poor Jews were?'

Magda's eyes were like saucers. 'So why was Jews thrown out then?' she asked.

Tony suppressed a sigh, but he could cheerfully have murdered Magda. She never would learn that once adults realised you were taking an interest in what they are saying, they either clam up or send you away.

Marion bit her lip and looked straight across at Bill. He mopped the last of the egg yolk up with his bread before he shrugged and said, 'These are strange times. Maybe it is better that they know what happened.'

Marion really thought Tony and the twins too young to know the full horrors of that night, yet they looked the most interested, but it was Sarah who said, 'Please tell us the rest? You can't leave it there.'

'All right,' Marion said. 'The people attacked and thrown out of their homes that night were Jews in cities and towns all over Germany. Even

3

the broadcaster on the BBC was shocked at the level and scale of violence. Storm troopers, members of the SS, and Hitler Youth beat and murdered even women and children.'

'Yes,' said Bill, accepting another cup of tea from Marion. 'It went on for three days in some places. One observer claimed the sky had turned red with the number of synagogues that were alight, in case the persecuted Jews tried to take refuge there, and the Germans called it "The Night of Broken Glass".'

'But why?' Richard asked.

Bill sighed. 'Many German Jews had been rounded up and dumped on the Polish border, each with all they could carry in one suitcase. One young Jewish boy living in Paris heard that his own family had been evicted in that way and he bought a gun and killed a German Embassy official. This was the German response.'

'Gosh,' Richard said. 'I don't suppose he ever thought the Germans would react like they did.'

'No,' Bill agreed, 'I don't suppose he did.'

'What happened to the Jewish people when it was all over?' Sarah asked.

Bill shrugged. 'Many died, some were arrested, others just disappeared, and it was said that a lot committed suicide – in despair, I would imagine – and who in God's name could blame them?'

'Did anything happen to Germany for doing such awful things?'

'Most of the other countries said it was dreadful

and barbaric, and America did recall their ambassador, but that was all.'

'It was a terrible thing to do,' Sarah said.

'Yes,' Marion said heavily. Then: 'And we could talk about it till the cows come home and it won't change a thing. Meanwhile, if you've finished, Bill, I could do with clearing away because I need to get the dinner on. Sarah, will you give me a hand?'

Sarah smiled to herself as she collected plates, for it wasn't a question. She was the eldest girl and so it was her lot to help her mother. She didn't really mind because her mother was a very good cook and she learned a lot by watching her.

As they rose from the table Bill saw Richard's eyes on him and knew he would have liked to talk some more. However, he knew when Clara Murray, Marion's mother, came to tea, as she and Eddie, Marion's father, did every Sunday. She would likely have an opinion on the world's unrest. She did most weeks – and her views, on any subject, were delivered in tones that would brook no argument.

Bill disliked her intensely and, he knew, so did the children, so every Sunday afternoon, just after one of Marion's succulent dinners, unless it was teeming from the heavens, he tried to keep Tony and the twins away from their grandmother for as long as possible.

*   *   *

A light breeze scudded the clouds across the blue sky where a pale yellow sun was trying to shine as Bill, Tony and the twins stepped out into Albert Road that afternoon.

'Well, where do you want to go?' Bill asked.

The children looked at one another. They knew if they turned right and went to the bottom of the street then they would be at Aston Park, which they liked well enough, but if they turned down Sutton Street and into Rocky Lane they would come to the Cut, which was what Brummies called the canal. Their father had told them once that Birmingham had more canals that Venice, and whether it had or not, the children loved to see the brightly painted barges decorated with elephants and castles, and so they said as one, 'The Cut.'

'Right you are then.' Bill strode down the road holding a twin by each hand, while Tony ran ahead like a young colt. The sun peeping out from beneath the clouds made even the water in the mud-slicked canal sparkle and the paintwork on the boats and barges gleamed. The Whittakers wandered along the towpath towards Salford Bridge. These days the barges had small motors to drive them, but Bill said when he was a boy they had been horse drawn: 'Big solid horses with shaggy feet.'

'Like the one the coalman has?' Magda asked.

'The very same. They're called shire horses and are built for strength and stamina, not speed. Now, when they would come to a tunnel, the men and big boys would have to unshackle the horse and walk the barge through with their feet. It was called "legging it".'

'And I suppose the horses had to go over the top?' said Tony.

'That's right. A younger boy or a woman or girl would lead it over to meet up with the barge on the other side. It was a grand sight to see, but motorised barges make life much easier for them.'

'Faster too.'

'I don't know if it would be that much faster, Tony. A barge isn't allowed to go at any great speed anyway. They're not built for it.'

'No,' Tony said, 'they're not, but I wish I'd seen the horses pulling them, anyway.'

'And me,' said Missie, as she gave a sudden shiver.

'Are you cold?' Bill asked.

'She can't be cold,' Tony declared. 'It ain't the slightest bit nippy and them kids don't seem to think so either.'

He was referring to the bargee boys. They were brown-skinned, often scantily dressed and bare-foot, and they didn't seem to feel the slightest chill as they leaped with agility from boat to boat or out onto the towpath to operate the locks.

Tony watched them with envy. 'Wouldn't that be a grand life, Dad?' he said. 'Just to do that all day long. I'd never get fed up of it.'

Bill smiled as he turned back along the towpath. 'I think you would, son,' he said. 'It's not that

7

fine a life; I think a fairly hard one, for the children at least. Many of them never have the benefit of a proper education, with them moving up and down the canal the way they do.'

Tony looked at his father in amazement. 'I wouldn't care a whit about that,' he maintained. 'A life like that would suit me down to the ground.'

Bill let out a bellow of laughter. 'I think, Tony, that you and school are not the best of friends.'

'No,' Tony said. 'I hate school, if you want to know. Everyone does, don't they?'

'No, they don't,' Magda contradicted. 'I don't. I like school. Don't you, Missie?'

Missie nodded as Tony said disparagingly, 'That's because you're still in the infants. You wait till you're in the juniors in September. You do summat wrong, or don't do your work right or quick enough, and they hit you with a big cane, or bring the ruler down on your knuckles.'

'How many girls does that happen to?' Bill asked with a sardonic grin.

'Well, not that many, I suppose,' Tony had to admit. 'They seem to have it in for boys.'

'That's because boys are always playing up,' Magda said.

'And you don't, Miss Goody Two-Shoes?'

'No,' Magda said. 'I don't like being yelled at, and really the only person who seems to do that all the time – to me anyroad – is Grandma Murray.'

'Don't take that personally,' Bill said. 'She seems to have it in for a lot of people.'

'But it's not fair,' Magda said. 'The one she should tell off more is Tony, but he always gets away with it, just 'cos he's a boy.'

'Can't help that, can I?' Tony said with a cheeky grin, and Bill had to compress his lips to stop himself from smiling.

'Come on, stop bickering,' he said, 'it's time to head home. If we're late we'll all be in for the high jump.'

Magda gave a grimace in her sister's direction because the twins knew exactly how it would be when they got home. As far back as they could remember, their grandparents had come to tea on Sunday. It was always served in the parlour, the room their mother set such store by, like she did about the piano. Sarah had told Magda and Missie their father thought the piano a waste of money, for no one had ever learned to play it, but their mother had wanted the piano because she said none of their neighbours had anything so fine.

'Why does that matter?' Magda had asked.

Sarah shrugged. 'I don't know why,' she'd admitted. 'It just does.'

It was very confusing to both girls but, as Missie said, grown-ups often did odd things, and Magda had to agree.

All the furniture in the parlour, like the piano, was big, dark and gloomy. On Sundays it all had to be moved about to accommodate everyone. Six days a week, the big mahogany table would be set in the bay window behind madras net curtains.

It would be covered with a dark red chenille cloth, with an aspidistra in a decorated pot in the centre of it. Either side of the table were two straight-backed dining chairs with padded seats, and two more dining chairs stood either side of the matching sideboard.

The picture of the Sacred Heart of Jesus, in which Jesus held one hand to his heart dripping with blood in his open chest – a picture that always made Magda feel queasy – hung on the wall above the fireplace. That was surrounded by marble tiles and protected by a brass fender. In front of it sat the dreaded horsehair sofa.

However, on Sunday afternoon, the aspidistra would be placed on the sideboard and the chenille cloth changed for one of Nottingham lace. In order that the table could be pulled out with the four padded chairs round it and two wooden ones brought out from the kitchen for Sarah and Richard, the horsehair sofa would be swung in front of the piano. And every Sunday the twins had to sit on it in silence and wait for the adults to finish eating before they could have anything, because their grandmother said it would put manners on them.

It was just like that when they went in that day. Marion and Sarah were carrying things to the table in the parlour where the children's grandparents were already sitting, but Tony was nowhere to be seen. He had been with them as they walked back home and when they went in through the back gate, but between there and the back door he sort of melted away and Magda knew he had gone over the wall again. So did Bill, and he couldn't blame the boy, nor had he any intention of going after him. As soon as he had started doing this, a year or so ago, Marion had said that he should discipline him. 'For what?' Bill had said angrily. 'For refusing to sit still and silent for as long as it takes us to eat our tea on a Sunday, and all because that's what your mother wants? It's bad enough for the girls but Tony would never be constrained that way and you know it. It would be more trouble than it's worth.'

Marion knew that Bill spoke the truth and she would spend the whole of the meal telling Tony off, so she had said nothing more. Every week Tony got away with it, as far as Missie and Magda were concerned.

'No Tony again, I see,' Grandma Murray remarked as the girls settled themselves on the sofa 'Ah, well, boys will be boys.'

Grandma Murray was fond of sayings. One she usually directed at Magda was, 'Little girls should be seen and not heard.' Magda often wondered if there had been a similar one she attached to grown men because Granddad Murray never seemed to say much more than please and thank you at the table where his wife held sway, and even her father was less talkative at Sunday tea.

'Magda, if I have to tell you again about keeping those legs still I might be forced to administer a sharp smack across them,' her grandmother suddenly snapped, and Magda realised that they were waggling again, just as if they had a mind of their own. She fought to gain control over her wayward legs because she had felt the power of her grandmother's slaps before.

She heard her father's sharp intake of breath clearly and saw his lips pursed together and knew he was vexed. If her grandmother were really to smack her then it would probably result in a row, as it had done in the past, and that was worse than any smack.

She knew her father didn't like the fact they had to sit there every Sunday he'd said to Marion angrily and watch the adults devouring all the dainty sandwiches, crisp pastries and feather-light sponge cakes that Mommy had spent hours preparing, because she'd heard him arguing with her mother about it. 'It's unfair to them,' Magda had heard him protest angrily after their grandparent had gone home. 'They're only children and its ridiculous to have them sitting there each Sunday like a pair of bloody bookends.'

Bill Whittaker, however, knew only the half of it because, as the adults ate, the horsehair pushed through the fabric of that sofa and through the twins' clothes to attack their legs and buttocks like thousands of sharp needles. That was why Magda swung her legs and shuffled about, to try to ease the torment that Missie seemed better able to bear.

Missie was always neater and tidier than Magda was as well, as her mother and grandmother were always reminding her. She stole a look at her twin sister. There she was, sitting as if she were made of stone, with her pristine Sunday clothes still neat and tidy, and her dark ringlets shining in the sunlight.

Magda knew her hair wouldn't look like Missie's. Each weekday, the two of them had their hair in plaits because of the risk of nits at school, and Magda would marvel that Missie's plaits never came unravelled and she never lost her hair ribbons. Magda's kirbi grips, too, seemed to develop a life of their own and would fling themselves recklessly from her tangled locks, to be trodden underfoot and lost for ever.

On Saturday night, however, after their bath, their newly washed and still damp hair was twisted into rags so that they would have ringlets for Mass on Sunday morning. This worked with Missie, but sometimes Magda's hair wouldn't co-operate. Her mother was always saying that she couldn't understand it. Magda couldn't understand it either, but she knew it was no use saying so.

Marion hoped that war talk wouldn't dominate the tea table but, surprisingly, it was her father who said in a break in the conversation, 'They've recalled the Territorial Army from overseas. A bloke at work told me that his son was in France and had to come home.'

'You never told me this,' Clara complained.

'I'm telling you now, aren't I?' Eddie said mildly.

13

'Tell you summat else as well. They've begun a call up of men aged twenty and twenty-one.'

'Christ! That's it then.'

'Good,' Richard said. He looked at his parents as he went on, 'What you told us this morning about The Night of Broken Glass made me feel sick. It's hard to believe that people could be so cruel and heartless, and Hitler's long been picking on the Jews. One of the Jewish apprentices told me that they hadn't been able to go to school for ages before they came here.'

'That would suit Tony then,' Bill said.

'Don't think much of what they tell me would suit anyone, Dad,' Richard said. 'You wouldn't credit some of the things they say happen. I thought that maybe they were exaggerating a bit. Now I'm pretty certain they're not. They had to leave their parents behind and haven't heard a word from them since.'

Clara had been astounded at Richard speaking so forcibly, but she recovered herself enough to say, 'We are talking about Jews. They are little better than heathens – and don't forget they killed Jesus Christ.'

'Not these particular Jews,' Richard said with a pitying glance at his grandmother. 'That happened nearly two thousand years ago, and they worship the same God as you. But, just as important as all that, they are people, the same as us, who feel the same hurt and pain. Someone must stop Hitler.'

14

'It very much looks as if we're getting ready to do just that,' Bill said.

His words hung in the air and there was nothing anyone could say for a minute or two, the atmosphere was so highly charged.

In the end Marion said, 'If we have finished shall we go into the other room and let the children sit down? I'm sure they're more than ready for it, and we can have another cup of tea in there if you'd like one.'

Clara got up from the table, grumbling about being shooed away before she was ready, and glared so malevolently at the twins that Magda said afterwards it was as if she was begrudging them every mouthful.

Tony came sidling in as the adults were leaving the room. Magda could never understand how he timed it that well. She was so mad at the unfairness of it all and her brother's smugness that she gave him a hefty kick under the table with her stout shoes and heard his yelp of pain. She thought it worth the reprimand because it managed to wipe the smirk off his face for once.

Despite the lovely food they had on Sunday, Magda often felt that it was the very worst day of the week, not only because of her grandmother's visit, but also because of the clothes she had to wear for Mass. Marion often despaired of getting Magda to behave in a more ladylike way and the difference between the twins was more marked on

Sunday, when they dressed in their best clothes, than on school days when they wore more service-able clothes in navy or grey. Today they wore matching lace-trimmed dresses decorated with swirly patterns in pastel colours, with lace peeping out from the hem, and Magda knew that when they undressed for bed that night, Missie's would be little different from when she had first put it on, while her own would resembled a limp rag.

'It's just as if, as soon as she's dressed in her good clothes, muck in all its various forms flings itself onto her,' Marion said to Bill later that same evening after the twins had gone to bed. 'And she is so clumsy on Sundays. She seems to drop or spill nearly everything given to her and so that ends up on her dress as well. My mother always has something to say.'

'Huh,' Bill said. 'That's no surprise. She never has a good word to say about Magda anyway.'

'She does seem to have it in for her all right,' Marion conceded.

'And have you thought that Magda might soil her clothes more because she is trying too hard? Her nervousness makes her more clumsy, especially with your mother around.'

'I never thought of it like that before.'

'Well, I've just been up to them,' Bill said, 'and their dresses are hung on the chair by the bed, so how about saying nothing more to Magda tonight, especially as your mother gave her a real roasting about the state of her clothes already?'

16

Marion knew that Bill had a point, so when she went to say good night to the girls she took the dresses without a word, though she knew she would have her work cut out getting Magda's dress respectable enough to wear the following week. Magda, expecting some reprimand, was surprised when none came.

'Have you both said your prayers?' their mother asked, and the twins nodded solemnly.

'We said them with Daddy,' Missie said.

'Well now, don't you be talking half the night either,' Marion said as she tucked them both in, gave them each a kiss and turned out the light but left the landing one on so that there would be a dim light for Sarah to get undressed by. 'Remember you have school in the morning.'

Magda couldn't believe she had got away so lightly and neither could Missie. 'Maybe it was because Grandma told you off so much?' Missie suggested.

'Shouldn't think so,' Magda said. 'She has told me off lots of times. Maybe Mommy just thinks I'm a hopeless case.'

'Well, Grandma might too eventually.'

'She won't,' Magda said. 'I heard Daddy say that she'll still be giving out when they nail her coffin down.'

Missie giggled.

'I don't think I was supposed to hear,' Magda said, 'but he really doesn't like Grandma any more than we do.'

'Does anyone?' Missie answered. "Cept Granddad and Mommy, I suppose.'

'Well, I don't blame anyone for not liking her,' Magda said.

'Nor me,' Missie agreed, and the two girls fell to discussing just how horrid their grandma was, so that when Sarah came to bed the two girls were wide awake.

'You two should be asleep by now,' she chided.

'We were talking about Grandma Murray,' Magda explained. 'I think she's a witch. She looks like a witch. Everything is long and pointed, like her bony fingers and her nose, and she's got no proper teeth, just brown stumps.'

'And she always wears black as well,' Missie put in.

'That's because she lost all the babies and that,' Sarah said as she took the grips out of the bun holding her hair in place. Her hair cascaded down her back and she brushed it out with the big wide brush. 'Mom told me and Richard ages ago.'

'Tell us then.'

'It's time for you to go to sleep.'

'Oh, go on, Sarah,' said both girls together.

'All right,' Sarah said, winding her hair into one plait with a speed that the twins always envied. She secured her hair with a band and padded across the room, saying as she did so, 'But budge over then. I need to get into bed first.'

The twins moved across to make room for their sister and she turned off the light and got into bed between them. With the three of them all tucked in together and the darkness settling around them, Sarah said, 'Mom said Grandma Murray had ten children altogether and one by one most of them died.'

'What of?'

'Some from diphtheria, Mom said, and others from TB.'

'And was they all babies?'

'No,' Sarah said. 'Mom said they were mostly children, only there was a baby who died in her cot when she was only little and they never found out why. Anyroad, in the end, there was only four left, Mom, Aunt Polly and the two eldest, Michael and Owen. Then Owen and Michael decided to try their luck in America, only Michael didn't make it and when Owen wrote and told them of his death Grandma Murray pledged that she would wear black until the day she died. Mom always said that his death had affected her most, for he had been her first-born and the seventh child of hers to die, and then his body had been tipped into the Atlantic so she didn't even have a grave to visit.' Sarah let the twins reflect on this for a moment or two and then she said, 'Now you've got to admit that that's really sad.'

'It is,' Missie agreed slowly and then added, 'And with anyone else I would feel very sorry for them, but Grandma's hard to feel sorry for, and she can be so nasty at times.'

'Mom always says that we have to make

allowances,' Sarah said. 'Point is, though, I don't see how shouting and going on like she does can help anyone cope better.'

'Nor me,' Magda said. 'And I still don't like her much.'

Missie shivered. 'Nor me, and she scares me as well.'

'She don't scare me,' Magda declared stoutly. 'I won't let her scare me.' But she said it as though she were trying to convince herself.

'Well, whatever you think about her, let's stop talking about her now and go to sleep,' Sarah advised. 'Or Mom will be up to see what we are gassing about, and I'm bushed and don't want to talk any more.'

Neither did Magda, who was suddenly feeling very sleepy, and beside her she heard Missie give a yawn and the three girls snuggled down together and were soon all fast asleep.

TWO

Afterwards, Marion thought it was from that weekend that the mood of the country changed subtly, as most people realised that the war no one really wanted was moving closer. Bill told her of the shadow factories springing up alongside legitimate ones, making military equipment and vehicles. In Birmingham the gun trade was booming. These sorts of things weren't reported but, as Bill said, you can't stop people talking, and word got around.

'Personally I find it reassuring,' he said. 'If we do eventually go to war, then I'd like to know that the Government has been making plans for it.'

Only a week or so later Marion's sister, Polly, popped round to announce that her two elder boys, Chris and Colm, had got jobs in Ansell's Brewery on nearby Lichfield Road, taking the place of two boys just a little older, who had been conscripted. Polly's sons were sixteen and fifteen, and had not had jobs since leaving school. Marion was glad that the lads were working at last and hoped that would make life easier for her sister.

Polly was married to Pat Reilly, who was a wastrel. If he had got work of any kind and looked after her sister properly, Marion might have forgiven him for taking her down when she was only sixteen, but he hadn't done that. Polly's house was little more than a stone's throw from Marion's, yet it was part of a warren of teeming back-to-back houses and as different from where Marion lived as it was possible to be.

When Polly had married Pat they had had nowhere to live but with Pat's riotous family, but a little after Chris's birth, a scant three months after the hasty marriage, they had acquired the house. Marion thought it little more than a slum. Entries ran down at intervals from the street to a squalid back yard, onto which Polly's house and five others opened directly. The yard, usually criss-crossed with washing lines, housed the brew house where all the women did their washing, the tap outside it however, which froze every winter, had been the family's only source of water until it had been piped into the houses just a few years before. Even now, Polly shared with two other families a miskin, where the ash was deposited, a dustbin, and a lavatory, which was situated at the bottom of the yard.

The house itself consisted of a scullery, which was little more than a cubbyhole at the top of the cellar steps, a small living room, a bedroom and an attic. Attached to Polly's house was one just the same, which opened onto the street. There was a smell about the whole place: the smell of human beings packed tightly together, the stink of poverty and deprivation mingled with the vinegary tang from HP Sauce halfway up Tower Hill just behind them, and the yeasty malty odour from Ansell's Brewery on the Lichfield Road, and you heard the constant thud of the hefty hammers from the nearby drop forge.

Marion blamed Pat for not working harder to get a job so that he could lift the family into something better. She thought Polly was far too easy on him and that she should tell him straight to steer clear of the pubs until he found employment. Polly, however, claimed he did try to get work but all the jobs he could get were casual or temporary, and that a man had to have a drink now and then.

So now Marion said to her sister, 'No chance of Pat getting set on there, then?'

'He did ask,' Polly said, 'but it was young fellows they were after. Anyroad, I don't think it would do Pat any good to be working at a brewery. He might be tempted to taste the wares.'

'He'd not reign there very long if he did that.'

'He did ask the lads if they ever got any free samples.'

Marion wasn't surprised at that. 'He would.'

'Anyroad,' Polly said with a grin, 'while they don't actually give free samples, each worker gets

23

a docket for two pints of beer a night. Colm and Chris won't yet, of course, because neither of them is eighteen. Chris said when he is, he will give his dad his allowance, but I said he might be in the army when he's eighteen so Pat may have to do without his beer.'

'Yes,' Marion said. 'Worrying times, these, to have boys the age they are. I tried to get our Richard interested in the joining the Territorials. They're looking for recruits and they might have taken him next year when he's sixteen. Thought it might keep him out of the regular army for a bit, but he wouldn't hear of it. He said until he is old enough to enlist he'll do his bit in the brass foundry.'

'My lads are the same,' Polly said. 'They said that Ansell's will do till they are eighteen and then they both want to join the Royal Warwickshires. The brass foundry is probably making summat for this bloody war everyone is certain sure is coming our way, anyroad. Pat says a lot of firms are doing that now.'

'It is. Richard said they're getting new machines in soon, and new dies fitted to the old ones, and all work then will be war related.'

'All this talk of war is scary,' Polly said. 'Pat seems to think that it's inevitable.'

'So does Bill.'

'Makes you wonder where we'll all be in a year's time.'

'Maybe it's a good job we can't see into the future.'

'I suppose,' Polly mused. 'Funny how life turns out. You always seem to fall on your feet, though.'

'That's not really fair,' Marion said. 'A lot of my good fortune is because I married Bill and he has a good job.'

'Yeah,' said Polly. 'And you kept your legs together till the ring was on your finger, though if I hadn't been expecting, Mammy and Daddy would never have agreed to me marrying one of the Reillys.'

'Maybe not,' Marion said. 'But that's not really any excuse for . . . Look, Polly, when I spotted you staggering down the gravel drive carrying the bass bag you had taken with you into service that afternoon in June 1923, the blood ran like ice in my veins.' She still carried that mental image with her. Her sister had always had more meat on her bones than she had, and her hair veered more towards blonde than brown, but apart from that they were very similar and both were pretty girls. Polly had just a dusting of pink on her cheekbones, a cluster of freckles below her eyes. That day, though, her face had been bright red and swollen with the tears she had shed and her hair falling over the face, and even her straw bonnet had been askew.

Polly nodded. 'You knew what it was all about then, didn't you?'

'Course I did,' Marion said. 'That's about the only reason that anyone is dismissed from service. Tell you, I was almighty glad that promotion to lady's maid meant I had a room of my own and I could grab you before you alerted the house, and hide you away in there.'

'You nearly shook the head from my shoulders.'

'Can you wonder at it, Poll?' Marion demanded. 'I wanted you to say that you weren't in the family way. I would have been so pleased that day to have been proved wrong.'

'I never remember feeling so miserable,' Polly said. 'And you went wild when you knew who it was I'd lain with. And he didn't take me down, not really. I mean, he didn't make me or anything.'

'Be quiet, Polly,' Marion said, genuinely shocked. 'Have you no shame? Don't talk in that disgusting way. Did you at no time think of the consequences and that your disgrace and shame would taint the whole family?'

'No,' Polly said. 'Not then I didn't. I loved Pat, see. I wasn't really a bad girl.'

Marion knew she wasn't. Polly didn't have a nasty bone in her body, but she had been very gullible then, and anxious to please when she was younger, and, Marion had to admit, hadn't changed much. Polly had always wanted to be liked and probably still did.

There was only one answer, one way out of this terrible dilemma. 'Well, Pat Reilly will have to be made to marry you, that's all,' Marion had said, but even as the words were out of her mouth she knew what Polly's life would like, married to such

26

a man. She doubted she'd ever have a penny piece to bless herself with and a houseful of babies before she was able to turn around.

'I never minded marrying Pat,' Polly said, and added a little defiantly, 'and he didn't have to be forced either. Despite everything, I still don't regret that marriage. I was really glad that Lady Amelia gave you leave to go home with me and tell Mammy and Daddy,' Polly added fervently. 'I think Mammy might have killed me stone dead that day if you hadn't been there.'

'In all honesty I was little use to you,' Marion admitted, 'because when Mammy started laying into you and screaming vile and obscene words I never thought I would hear her say, I was too shocked to move. It was Daddy coming in from work that really saved you that day, though he too was shaken to the core at what you had done.'

'He didn't lay a hand on me either,' Polly said. 'For all Mammy wanted him to, he said there had been enough of that already and he went straight round to the Reillys. Pat always said he was tickled pink, learning that he was going to be a father.'

Pity he didn't try harder to provide for him then. The words were on the tip of Marion's tongue, but she bit them back as she remembered the shabby wedding hastily arranged at their parish church, Sacred Heart Catholic Church, on nearby Witton Road. The only people there were Pat's loud and rumbustious family, who didn't seem to see any shame in what the young people had done at all. Polly had worn an ordinary dress of tent-like proportions to try to hide her swollen stomach.

Polly was remembering that wedding too. 'Remember Father McIntyre, with his nose stuck in the air like me and Pat smelled bad or summat?'

'I remember,' Marion said. 'I suppose he was showing his disapproval. After all, he has known you all your life.'

'He's known Pat all his life too,' Polly said, 'but it didn't give him any sort of right to behave like that. And then Mammy wouldn't have any sort of celebration.' She looked at Marion with a great smile on her face. 'Pat's family couldn't believe it. All the way home they were complaining about it and in the end they went to the Outdoor and got some carry-out and we had our own celebration.'

Marion knew that the Reillys had been astounded because she had heard more than one complain, 'Not even a drink? Mean buggers!'

However, Clara had thought there was nothing to celebrate. In her opinion, though marriage – any sort of marriage – brought partial respectability, the stupidest person in the world was able to count to nine when it mattered. Polly had behaved shamelessly and that would reflect on her, as Polly's mother, and no way did she feel like celebrating that fact.

Marion thought, though, that Polly had paid a heavy price for marrying Pat Reilly. That vision she had seen of Polly's life the day she admitted her pregnancy had come true with a vengeance, for the babies came thick and fast. Polly's first son, Chris, arrived when Marion had been married just two weeks and he was followed by Colm, Mary Ellen, Siobhan, Orla and Jack. When Jack was born something went wrong and Polly was told that she would be unlikely to conceive ever again. Marion comforted her sister, who was distressed at the news, but really she was glad that there were to be no more children as they couldn't afford to keep the ones they had and over the years she'd had to help her sister out financially many a time.

Later that night she told Bill the news about the boys' jobs and he too was glad that life might get a bit easier for them.

'I'm sure Pat could have done more, and sooner than this,' Marion said. 'Course, if I say anything to our Polly she defends him to the hilt and claims he is trying to get work.'

'Well, he may be,' Bill said. 'This is a major slump, you know. Jobs aren't that easy to come by. Pat Reilly isn't the only one unemployed today.'

'He's the only one married to my sister,' Marion snapped. 'Anyroad, when they haven't food to put on the table you will see the man in the pub. You told me that yourself.'

Bill had indeed told her that, as he'd also said that Pat would often make a half-pint last all evening, but she chose not to remember that. In her eyes he was the man that had taken her young sister down and Bill doubted that she would ever really forgive Pat for it.

In bed that night, after listening to a broadcast that said if war was declared there would undoubtedly be raids from the air, Marion hoped that war would somehow be averted. It had been German planes that had bombed the Spanish town of Guernica two years before, in support of the dictator Franco, and many seemed to think then that Germany was showing the world what they could do.

Marion, remembering the newspaper pictures of the devastation, the town nearly razed to the ground, and knowing the numbers killed and badly injured, knew full well that what had been done in Spain could be done in Birmingham and other towns and cities if Britain were to declare war. She knew she would be worried chiefly for her family, but she didn't want anything to happen to her home either. It wasn't just bricks and mortar, it was where Bill had taken her after their marriage and she had taken pleasure in raising her children. All her dearest memories were wrapped up in that house, and these memories now crowded into her brain, driving away sleep.

She recalled that she had been in a fever of impatience to see where they would be living and so Bill had brought her here a week before the wedding. She knew the house was on Albert Road and that ran from the entrance to Aston Park to

Witton Road, near to the vast array of shops on the Lichfield Road. It was wide enough for trams to run down the centre of it, and smallish factories and shops were mixed among the housing: a wholesale grocers, Marion noticed as she'd walked down the road arm in arm with Bill that first day, a clinic, a small factory and, across the road, a garage and repair shop and a sizeable office block.

The house itself was red brick, two-storeyed, with wide bay windows to the front, set back a little from the road behind a low grey stone wall. An entry ran down the side, which Bill told her was shared between their house and the one next door, and which led to the back gardens. Marion had loved it at first sight.

Bill had led her over the blue-brick yard to the white front door with an arch above it and a brass knocker and letterbox. She noticed the step needed a good scrubbing. Inside, the hall was decorated with black and white tiles. Stairs led off the right and there was a door to the left. When Bill told her that was the parlour she couldn't believe it. A parlour! And she opened the door to have a look and gave a sigh of contentment. Of course it would only be used on high days and holidays. But just to own a parlour raised a person's status.

A short corridor led to the back of the house. The room at the end was where Bill said they would spend most of their time, though Marion was surprised when Bill told her that she wouldn't be cooking on the range set into the fireplace, but on a brand-new gas cooker in the kitchen. Marion remembered how nervous she had been. She had never had a gas cooker before and wasn't at all sure that it was safe, but Bill assured her that it was, that it was the latest thing, and she had found it so easy to use after a very little while.

Bill had also opened the door to the cellar as they went towards the kitchen and Marion had thought that that would be where the coalman would tip his load because she had seen the grating just to the side of the bay window. But Bill had ordered a shed to be erected in the back garden for the coal: he didn't think it healthy to have all that coal dust swirling in the air inside the house. Marion thought he was being overcautious until she remembered both Bill's parents had died from lung disease. Then she could more understand his concern.

Marion enthused over the house to her parents: 'A sizeable kitchen and a scullery and a yard, and a lovely little garden at the back, and upstairs three large bedrooms and a bathroom, no less, and even hot water from this geyser on the wall you light when you want a bath or owt, and electric lights all over the house . . .'

She knew her parents would be glad at least one daughter was being looked after properly by her husband.

A week later Marion married Bill Whittaker, a man her parents approved of, who she had been courting for six months, and who was in full employment in a brass foundry. Her wedding day was a sharp contrast to her sister's. She had worn a white dress that she was entitled to wear, which finished daringly halfway down her calf, and a veil fastened to her hair with a halo of rosebuds. The reception was well attended with family, friends and neighbours to toast the bride and groom's health.

Polly hadn't been allowed to go because she was too near her time and, Clara said, not fit to be seen. She thought it scandalous that Polly would go about without a coat to cover herself up, but Marion knew that she probably hadn't the money to buy a coat that would fit her swollen body.

When Polly moved into Upper Thomas Street, just a few months later, the dissimilarity in the two sister's lives was even more obvious. Marion had indeed fallen on her feet and anyone but Polly might have been envious, but she had never shown that.

As Marion drifted to sleep she wondered if she'd have been so generous that if the positions had been reversed.

Despite the war talk around them, Magda and Missie were very excited as June approached. Their seventh birthdays were in the first week and then just two weeks later they were going to make their First Holy Communion. The whole class at school had been preparing for it for months.

One of the things they had to know was their catechism, and Magda and Missie had tried really hard to learn it because sometimes the classroom door would open suddenly and Father McIntyre would be there to test everyone.

The whole class would be on edge – even the teacher looked all tense and stern, Magda noticed – as Father McIntyre would point at the children at random and fire questions from the catechism at them. Magda would feel as if she was sitting on hot pins because she was pretty sure that if the priest pointed at her and barked out a question, her mind would go blank. So she avoided his eye at all costs and was mightily glad he never chose her. He seemed more interested in the boys, who often gave wrong answers and didn't seem to care. She knew, though, they would get it in the neck from the teacher later.

There was another trial to go through first before Communion and that was confession. The twins were familiar with the little wooden box in the church where the priest went in one side and they would have to go in the other and tell the priest all the bold things they had done.

'It won't be so bad when we're going every week or so,' Missie said as they made their way to school the morning that they were going to confession for the first time. 'I don't know that I can remember what I have done wrong over the past seven years.'

'Not a lot, I wouldn't have said,' Sarah told her. 'You never seem to get into trouble.'

'Not like me,' Magda said gloomily. 'Grandma Murray called me a limb of Satan last Sunday.'

Sarah laughed. 'Well,' she said, 'I wouldn't take that to heart, if I were you. But then,' she went on with a wry smile, 'she might be a help to you if you can't remember what you've done wrong over the years. If you call and see her she could probably supply you with a list.'

'And if you told the priest all that Grandma told you to say you would spend ages on your knees doing the penance he gave you,' Missie said, smiling at the vision that conjured up.

'I'm not going anywhere near Grandma Murray,' Magda said with a slight shudder. 'I will just tell the priest what I remember and that will be that.'

'Are you nervous?' Sarah asked.

'A bit,' Magda admitted.

'It's just strange, that's all,' Sarah said. 'You get used to it and, remember, he can't say anything you tell him to anyone else.'

'I know that, but he'll know, won't he?'

'Well, of course. But won't it be worth all this nervousness to wear that beautiful white dress and veil?'

'Ooh, yes,' Magda said, and Missie nodded emphatically. Just to think about her Communion dress sent tingles of excitement all though Magda, which began in her toes and spread all over her body. Marion had taken the girls to the Bull Ring to buy them both snow-white dresses decorated with beautiful sparkling seed pearls and lace and pretty pale blue rosebuds. The veils were fastened to their hair with white satin bands also decorated with the pale blue rosebuds, and they had new white socks and sandals. When they got home they tried their outfits on for their father to see and he'd said they looked like a couple of princesses. When he kissed them both Magda was very surprised to see tears in his eyes.

'I had a dress like that once,' Sarah said, remembering her First Communion day.

'I know,' Magda said. 'Mom told me. She said she gave it to Aunt Polly after.'

'Yes,' Sarah said. 'Poor Mary Ellen had to have a dress loaned from the school, but my dress came in for Siobhan and Orla.'

'I would have hated to have a First Communion dress loaned that way,' Missie said. 'Wouldn't you, Magda?'

Magda nodded and Sarah said, 'You thank your lucky stars that you didn't have to, but there are far worst things about being poor than a second-hand Communion dress.'

'I'd hate to be poor as well.'

'Be glad that you're not then,' Sarah said. 'There are a great many poor these days. We are luckier than a lot of families, and don't you ever forget that.'

The twins knew all about the poor. Uncle Pat and Auntie Polly were poor, and their children wore boots and clothes donated by the *Evening Mail* Christmas Tree Fund. They knew that despite the help their mother gave Polly, without the Christmas Tree Fund their cousins would probably have had to go barefoot to school a lot of the time, and been without warm, adequate clothing through the winter. Sarah was right, they were luckier than many families. But the twins didn't feel lucky when they filed into church that Friday afternoon for their confession.

When it was Magda's turn she slid from her pew, aware her legs were all of a dither, and went into the little box. It was quite dim with the door shut, and when she kneeled down beside the grille she could just about see the outline of Father McIntyre on the other side and she whispered the words they had been practising at school: 'Bless me, Father for I have sinned. This is my first confession.'

She stopped then, not sure what to say because whatever her grandmother said, Magda thought she hadn't sinned much. She was never cheeky or disobedient to her parents, grandparents or teachers or any other grown-up, because she would have had the legs smacked off her if she had been, and the same thing would happen if she was found to be telling lies. She'd never dream of taking something that didn't belong to her and had never even put half her collection money in her shoe as she had seen Tony do sometimes.

Then she remembered how lax she was about prayers and how she was often in bed before she thought of them, but she always told her mother that she had said them when she came to tuck the twins in, so that was adding lying to it as well and so she told the priest that. She didn't mention the fact that she sometimes hated Tony, and her grandmother too, and she supposed that was a sin, though not, she thought, the sort of thing she could admit to a priest. She had to say three Hail Marys and a Glory Be as a penance. Missie and most of their classmates had been given the same.

'We must make sure that we don't do something really dreadful tomorrow,' Missie warned as she and Magda walked home together afterwards. 'The teacher said that our souls must be as white as snow to receive Holy Communion.'

'We never get the chance to do something really dreadful,' Magda said, but she made a mental note that she would make sure she didn't forget her prayers that night, or Saturday either, to make sure she'd have no stain on her soul when she went to the rails.

That Sunday morning all the girls were to the left of the aisle and Magda sneaked a look at the boys on the other side. Many had smart new white shirts, and the richer amongst them also had black shiny shoes and new grey trousers, and socks that probably stayed up better than the ones many wore to school, which resided in concertina rolls around their ankles unless they were held up by garters. But all in all the boys' clothes were very commonplace when compared to the girls' finery. In fact, the only thing that marked this day as a special one for the boys was the satin sash they each had around their shoulders, which lay across the body and fastened at the hip.

The strains of the organ brought people to their feet. Marion watched all the children looking so angelic on this very special day. They were quieter than she had ever known them. The sense of occasion had got into even the most mischievous, and there was no fidgeting or whispering, and no one dropped their pennies for the collection. As they left their seats to go up to the rails a little later, she felt tears stinging her eyes as she wondered what was in store for these young children if their country went to war.

THREE

Everywhere that sultry summer there was evidence of things to come. Big trenches were dug in Aston Park, swathes of brown where once there had been green grass, and the following week all the railings were hacked down. By early August, strange windowless buildings appeared everywhere and the older children were drafted in to fill sacks with sand.

By mid-August they heard about the blackout that would come into force on 1 September. Every householder was told to black out the windows, streetlights would be turned off, no cars would be allowed lights, and even torches would be forbidden.

'So you are right as usual, Bill,' Marion said. 'They must expect attacks from the air or they wouldn't be going to so much trouble. And there's a fine of two hundred pounds if there is a chink of light showing. I'd better go down the Bull Ring Saturday and see what I can get.' She sighed as she went on, 'It will cost something, too, to recurtain the whole house. Thank God Polly's two lads are working now. She will probably have the money to buy the material. Mammy has an old treadle she won't mind us using, especially if we offer to make hers up as well.'

But before Marion got to go down to the Bull Ring, an education officer called round with the headmaster of the school to talk about evacuation of the children. Though Marion was worried about them, and how they would cope in the event of war, she thought it a monstrous plan to send her children to some strangers in what the Government deemed 'a place of safety'. She rejected the idea quite definitely, and Polly, she found, had done the same.

'Whatever we face, we face together. That's how I see it,' Polly said to Marion. 'I mean, they could end up going to anyone.'

'Couldn't agree more,' Marion said. 'The twins are just seven and Tony was only nine in April. They're far too young to be sent away from home, and Sarah said she wanted to go nowhere either. It would feel like running away, she said, and anyway, she's looking forward to leaving school and earning some money.'

'Can't blame them, though, can you?' Polly said. 'Can't do owt in this world without money, and that I know only too well.'

One Friday evening towards the end of August Marion turned on the wireless and caught the tail end of an announcement: 'As a precaution gas masks are being issued to every person in Britain. These will be available from 1 September. Please study your local papers to find out where your nearest collection point will be.'

'Gas masks, Bill, for God's sake,' Marion cried, and her face was as white as lint.

'It's just in case,' Bill said. 'You heard what he said.'

'Yes, but even so . . .'

'In the last war the Germans used gas to disable the troops,' Bill reminded her. 'You know that yourself. You've seen some poor sods down the Bull Ring with their lungs near ate away with mustard gas. Twenty years on they might have worked out how to drop it on the civilian population. I'm not saying they will,' he added, looking at Marion's terror-stricken face, 'but surely it's better to be safe than sorry?'

'I suppose it is,' Marion said. 'It's just that I don't want to think of it.'

Bill put his arms around her. 'None of us do, not really, and there is something else that I must tell you now that war seems inevitable.'

'What?'

'Well, it has been in my head for some time, but I haven't wanted to upset you by speaking of it sooner,' Bill said. 'But now you really need to know that when war is declared, I intend to enlist.'

'No, Bill!' Marion cried. 'No, Bill, you can't.'

Bill tightened his arms around her. 'Don't take

on, old girl,' he said. 'You must have known this was on the cards.'

But Marion hadn't known. Such thoughts had never crossed her mind. Bill had a family, responsibilities, and she had thought that would make him safe, or as safe as anyone can be in a war. She pulled herself out of his embrace and said, 'Just how did you expect me to react, Bill? Did you think that I would be jumping up and down with delight?'

'You know how I feel about Hitler and his bloody bunch of hoodlum Germans,' Bill protested. 'I'm doing this because I want to try and protect you.'

'Sorry, Bill, that doesn't make me feel any better.'

'Look,' said Bill, 'Hitler and his armies are marching all over Europe. He already has Austria and Czechoslovakia, and now he is casting his eye over Poland. Where will he look next? If he conquers the Low Countries he will make his way to France, and if France falls we are just a step across the Channel. Believe me, Marion, Britain will need every man they can get to take on the German Army and try and stop them in their tracks.'

'I can see they might need young men,' Marion conceded. 'But not men as old as you, and family men at that.'

'I'm thirty-nine and that's not old,' Bill said. 'Not according to the army, anyway.'

'But what of your job?' Marion cried. 'How will they manage at the foundry if all the men go off soldiering?'

'The foundry will manage well enough without me,' Bill said. 'And I imagine the families of men fighting for their King and Country are well enough provided for. After all, I am unlikely to be the only family man in the Forces. Pat's enlisting with me.'

'He may as well,' Marion said bitterly. 'He at least has no job to leave, nor ever has had.' Marion began to sob in earnest then for she knew that before making any big decision, Bill would always weigh up the pros and cons, and he would have done it this time because this was one of the biggest decisions he would ever make. Once he was resolved on a course of action, though, he was immovable. She saw the lift of his chin and the glint in his eyes, and though tears gushed from her eyes she knew her husband would leave her – leave them all – and go to a war from which he might never return.

When Tony, Magda and Missie were told about their father going to be a soldier they thought at first that it was the most exciting news in the world. They couldn't understand why their mother wasn't as delighted as they were.

'Well, I suppose that she doesn't want him going away,' Sarah said as they walked to school the following day.

It was news to Magda that her father would have to go and live elsewhere and she said, 'Won't he be able to be a soldier and stay at home then?'

Tony gave a hoot of laughter. 'Course he can't stay

here, stupid. He'll have to go away and kill Germans, won't he? He'll be shooting them with his rifle and sticking his bayonet in their innards and . . .'

'That's enough, Tony,' Sarah said sharply.

Tony gave a shrug. 'Well, Magda is such a baby.'

'No I ain't.'

'Yes you are,' Tony said. 'I bet you thought all he would do was march around all day in his smart uniform behind a big brass band. You did, dain't you? That's all you thought they did?'

Magda didn't know what soldiers did, but she wasn't going to admit that to Tony, so she stuck her tongue out at him, taking care that Sarah didn't see, before saying, 'No I dain't, see.'

'Yes you did,' Tony retorted. 'You really are stupid, Magda Whittaker. We're at war, ain't we?'

'I know that, don't I?' Magda cried. 'But what's war, anyroad?'

Tony wasn't absolutely sure either, but he said, 'War means that our dad has got to go and kill people before they kill him, don't it, Sarah?'

Both the twins' faces paled – they'd never thought of anyone killing their father – and Sarah was cross at Tony just blurting it out like that. But that's what *was* going to happen eventually and it would be doing the twins no favours to tell them lies, so her voice was gentle as she said, 'Tony's got it about right, because that's what soldiers have to do.'

Magda caught Missie's eyes and suddenly

45

thought maybe it wasn't such a good idea for her father to be a soldier after all. She knew that Missie felt the same.

Tony saw the look and said, 'The pair of you are plain stupid.'

'Tony, I won't tell you again,' Sarah said sharply. 'Magda and Missie are over two years younger than you. How are they to know these things? We have never been to war before. And don't worry,' she added to the twins as they went into the school yard, 'Dad won't be in danger for ages yet, because he will have to be trained to be a soldier.'

Magda sighed with relief. Tony was probably right, she thought. She didn't know much about going to war but she knew one thing: just talking about it made everyone bad-tempered.

The following Sunday the children's grandparents came to tea as usual. Bill had known that his mother-in-law would have something to say about his decision to enlist and he wasn't disappointed. As soon as he entered the house with the twins after their walk, she started on him, berating him roundly for his lack of concern and understanding, and was still going strong when they sat down to tea. Tony had sloped off as usual, so it was just the twins sitting on the horsehair sofa, being stabbed to death with its stuffing, while their grandmother continued to carp on in her thin, shrill voice, even more vitriolic than she usually was.

Magda, casting a glimpse her way, thought that it was just as if she had anger bubbling up inside her, so much so, that it was coming up in spittle and forming a white line along her thin bloodless lips. Her grandfather valiantly tried to deflect the conversation away from Bill until in the end she snapped, 'Be quiet, Eddie. What are you going on about? There is only one concern here and that's Bill and his stupidity.'

Bill looked up at Clara's face and sighed before saying mildly enough, 'Well, Clara, I know from experience you won't let a matter drop until you have worried it to death like a dog with a bone so you might as well have your say.'

Clara glared at him and wiped her mouth and fingers on a napkin before saying, 'What I really want to know is whatever possessed you to even think about enlisting like this? It's totally irresponsible.'

Bill shook his head. 'I don't see it that way.'

'There is no other way to see it,' Clara burst out, 'What's the matter with you?'

'I am prepared to fight, because I see the Germans gaining more and more power as each day passes,' Bill said. 'They won't stop until they have the whole of Europe under their dominance and we must all fight to prevent that. I'm going to war because I love my family and want to protect them, and I would feel less of a man if I didn't do it.'

Even Marion, who didn't want her husband to

join in any war, was impressed by the sincere and yet firm way Bill had answered her mother. The children were all awed, not so much by the words their father had used, but by the fact that he was the first person they knew to render their grandmother speechless.

Before Clara had time to think of some retort, Bill spoke directly to his father-in-law, for whom he had always had great respect. 'Do you see my point in any of this, Eddie?'

Eddie glanced first at his wife, but then he said, 'I do, Bill. You've put it very well and you're right. It is no good expecting the man either side of you to volunteer while you stay safe and dry. Britain is a much smaller country than Germany and so needs all the soldiers that it can get. This will not be just a young man's war. Sometimes, however painful, sacrifices have to be made.'

'Pat is enlisting along with me,' Bill said.

He heard the snort of disapproval from Clara because she had less time for Pat Reilly than Marion had. 'You can be as scornful as you like,' he snapped, 'but Pat Reilly at least has as much courage as the next man, for we all know that what we're going to be involved in will be no picnic.'

Marion knew it wasn't, and while she had exercised her right to say something to Bill on the subject, she hated her mother criticising him so, and in front of the children too. Anyway, she knew the die was cast. As she got to her feet, she said to her mother, 'There's no point in going on and on about it now, Mammy. The decision has been made and Bill has told you why he made it and that's an end to it as far as I'm concerned.'

Bill looked at Marion with astonishment.

She never stood up to her mother, but she had suddenly thought that if Bill wasn't going to be around, it was time she developed some backbone and she was far too old to allow herself to be browbeaten by her mother.

'And if we've all finished, shall we clear up here so that the children can eat?' she went on. 'I'm sure they think their throats have been cut.'

Still Clara said nothing, but the atmosphere could have been cut with a knife as, with a sniff of disapproval, she rose from the table. She left the room in silence, outrage and anger showing on every line of her body.

'Methinks it's a little frosty on the Western Front this evening,' Bill commented quietly, and both Richard and Sarah had to bite their lips to stop their laughter escaping.

'Why are you putting those horrible black curtains up at the windows?' Magda asked her mother a few days later.

'We have to, and that's all there is to it,' Marion said from her precarious stance on the dining chair. 'They have to go up at all the windows.'

'Even ours?' Magda said. 'Our bedrooms and that?'

49

''Fraid so.'

'But why?'

'So the enemy aircraft won't see us, that's why,' Tony said.

'How do you know that?' Marion asked sharply.

'Jack told me.'

'He would.'

'Well, he's right, ain't he?' Tony said.

Marion sighed. She knew that she couldn't protect her children with a load of lies – the time was past for that. They had a right to know what might happen if the country went to war. She said, 'Yes, Tony, Jack is right.'

And then Tony turned to his younger sisters and said, 'Jack told me that enemy aircraft will carry bombs that they'll drop on us and try and blow us all up.'

'They won't, will they, Mom?' Missie said, and Marion could hear the nervous wobble in her voice.

She knew Missie and Magda wanted an assurance that she couldn't give them and so she got off the chair and put her arms around each of them as she answered carefully. 'No one knows yet what the Germans will do when the war begins, but your dad is having someone come to look at our cellar in the next couple of days, and if necessary they will reinforce it and then Hitler and his planes can do his worst and we will be as safe as houses, especially if it is pitch black here, because then the German pilots wouldn't know where to drop their bombs, would they?'

'Won't they see by the streetlights?' Magda asked.

'No, because they won't be on either.'

'Ooh,' Missie said, 'it will be real scary to go out then.'

'It will take some getting used to,' Marion conceded. 'But if that's how it must be then that's how it must be.'

By the time they were ready for bed that night, all the horrid black curtains were hung at the windows, but not before Sarah had crisscrossed tape on the glass. She saw the twins' eyes upon her and explained, 'If the bombs do fall, then this prevents the glass from flying into the room.'

Magda imagined bombs exploding loud enough and near enough to blow out a person's windows. She shuddered in sudden fear as she said, 'So this is just in case as well?'

'That's it.'

'Some of the kids at school are going to the country the day after tomorrow, in case there's a war,' Magda said.

'Yeah, Mary Cox had to get her gas mask early 'cos her mom is sending her to the country,' Missie said. 'They told her the kids' masks look like Mickey Mouse, but she said they don't and they stink like mad. She said we've all got to get them.'

'That's another precaution,' Sarah said. 'In case the Germans drop gas.'

'I think war, even preparing for war, is all really frightening,' Missie said.

'Not half,' Magda agreed. 'Bloody terrifying, that's what it is.'

Sarah cuffed her sister lightly on the side of the head. 'War or no war, Magda Whittaker,' she said sternly, 'I will wash your mouth out with carbolic if I hear you using words like that.'

'Dad uses words like that, 'cos I've heard him,' Magda maintained.

'That's different, and you know it, and if you don't listen to me, I'll tell Mom. Then you'll be sorry.'

Magda knew she would be. Her mother had far harder hands than Sarah. So, though she still thought the world a bloody scary place, she kept those thoughts to herself.

On Friday morning the children to be evacuated were assembled in the school yard and Marion took Tony and the twins down to see their friends go off. The evacuees had labels with their names on pinned to their coats, and boxes, which Marion said held their gas masks, were hung around their necks. Some had their change of clothes and personal bits and pieces in carrier bags, while others held small cases, or had haversacks strapped to their back, like Mary, who was standing in the playground looking a little lost, but hanging on to her five-year-old brother, Raymond, for grim death.

She gave a half-hearted attempt at a smile when she saw the twins, but despite that, she seemed cloaked in misery. In fact most of the children looked the same, and the mothers were little better, for many of them were in tears, though some were trying to put a brave face on it.

The teachers going with them rallied the children into some sort of order and then the headmaster led them in a rendition of 'Run Rabbit Run' as they marched towards the gate and to Aston station.

'Where is the place of safety they're going, anyroad?' Magda asked as they walked home.

'No one knows,' Marion said. 'That's the terrible thing. Phyllis, Mary and Raymond's mother, said all they were told was that wherever it was there would be host families ready to take in the children and care for them. She has no idea where that place is or what sort of family her two will end up with.'

'Mary dain't want to go,' Magda said, "cos she was blarting her eyes out on the bus.'

'Her mother was as well,' Missie added.

'Ah, yes,' Marion said. 'Poor woman was in a right state about it. One of the problems is that she doesn't know whether she's doing the right thing or not. She was just thinking that if the raids do come, she has to see to the two other little ones at home, so the eldest two would be better out of it for a while. If there are no raids she will have them back quick as lightning, I think.'

No one made any response to this because as they turned into their road, right beside their front gate women had gathered, earnestly discussing something.

'What is it? What's up?' Marion said.

Marion's next-door neighbour, Deidre Whitehead, answered, 'News just came through on the wireless. Hitler's armies have invaded Poland and they are fighting for their lives.'

Marion felt quite faint, although it was news that she had been expecting.

Ada Shipley said, 'That's it then. The balloon has definitely gone up. We're going to have another war and if my lad's right it will be bloodier even than the Great War. God help him, wherever he is tonight.'

Hear, hear, thought Marion as she hurried the children indoors. God help all of us.

The gas masks that Marion brought home for them later that day were just as awful as Mary had said, and they didn't look a bit like any picture of Mickey Mouse that Magda had ever seen.

'I can't wear that,' she complained, frantically tugging off the mask that Marion fitted on her. 'I can't breathe with that flipping thing covering my face.'

'Of course you can,' Marion said unsympathetically. 'You will be glad enough to wear it if there are gas attacks. This is not the time to make a fuss about little things.'

'If you ask me, not being able to breathe is a pretty big thing,' Tony said. 'I can't breathe either, and I'll tell you summat else as well: they won't have to bother with sending no gas over here; the stink of rubber will do the job for them.'

Sarah felt sorry for the children. The gas masks were hideous, very smelly and uncomfortable to wear, and breathing once they were on was not easy. However, she felt she had to show the lead in this and so she said, 'All right, so they're not nice, but if we have to wear them then we have to, and that's all there is to it. I'm sure that it's just a case of getting used to it.'

'Huh!' said Tony contemptuously, but Marion threw Sarah a look of gratitude.

That night the talk around the tea table was all about the news that day. 'The bosses heard it announced and came and told us lot on the shop floor,' Bill said. 'We have no option now, so I told the gaffer I'm off to enlist on Monday morning. He was prepared for it because I told him a while ago what I intended, once war was official, like.'

Marion swallowed the lump that seemed lodged in her throat and said, 'Did he mind?'

'Ain't no good minding things like this in a war situation,' Bill said. 'Anyroad, he didn't. He actually said if he had been a younger man he would have done the same thing and I weren't the only one to go, by any means.'

'He ain't either, Mom,' Richard said. 'Remember them Jewish apprentices I told you about? Well, they're all enlisting too. One of them said that he's avenging the death of his parents because he thinks they must be dead or they would have got word to him by now. I can quite see how he feels. There were others as well. There was a right buzz in the canteen over dinner, wasn't there, Dad?'

'There was, son. And if all those who said they were enlisting actually do it, the foundry will be very short-handed. Although women can take on a lot of the men's work, like they're talking about, some of the foundry tasks will probably be too heavy for most of them.'

'So what will they do about that?'

Bill shrugged. 'Search me,' he said. 'But every man jack of us that can get out there and fight should, because we have to stop the Nazis while there's still time.'

Bill's words brought a chill to all of them.

'I can't help wishing you didn't feel this way, just as I wish that we were not at war with anyone,' Marion said, breaking the silence, 'but I know what you have to do and though I can't say truthfully that you go with my blessing, I'll support you the best way I can.'

'You can't say fairer than that,' Bill replied, and as he put his hand over hers on the table, Marion saw his eyes were very bright.

No one dawdled at Mass that Sunday for the Prime Minister was going to speak to the nation on the wireless just after eleven o'clock. Polly and Pat, and other neighbours without their own wireless sets, were crowded into the Whittakers' and at a quarter past eleven they learned 'this country is at war with Germany'. As the broadcast came to an end, some of the listeners had tears trickling down their cheeks, yet no one was surprised by the news.

Just then, a dreadful, ear-splitting sound rent the air. They all knew what it was – the siren signalling an attack – and they all looked at each other fearfully, not sure what to do. It proved to be a false alarm but it galvanised Marion into action. For days, both in the newspaper and on the wireless, the Government had been advising householders to get together a shelter bag and put into it anything of value, such as ration books, identity cards, saving and bank books, insurance policies, treasured photographs, and maybe a pack of cards or dominoes, or favourite books for the children.

Marion hadn't done it, as if not doing it was going to change what had been staring her in the face for weeks. Nor had she cleared out the cellar, though now that it had been reinforced it was where they might be spending a lot of their time. Their cellar was bigger than most, but this just meant that there was more room to house junk. As the all clear sounded, Marion said to Polly, 'I went down yesterday and I had quite forgotten the rubbish we put in there, like the rickety wooden chairs, and that battered sagging sofa that we bought when we were first married.'

'You might be glad of places to sit when the raids come.'

'I know,' Marion said. 'I shan't throw anything

away. But I will ask Bill to look at the chairs. He'll soon make them a bit sturdier; he's very handy that way.'

'Oh, I wish Pat was,' Polly said. 'He finds it hard to knock a nail in.'

Marion said nothing, because that was best whenever Pat's name came up. Instead she said, 'I wonder what Mammy will say about the recent turn of events.'

'Well, you'll know soon enough, won't you?' Polly said. 'I suppose they're coming to tea as usual?'

Marion nodded.

'You might not be so keen on having them over every week once Bill joins the army,' Polly went on. 'I doubt a soldier will get as much money as Bill picks up now, and you may find it a bit of a struggle. If you're strapped at all we can help you out. God knows, you've helped us out enough in the past.'

'Let's just see how we go for now,' Marion said. 'We'll likely know more when the men come back from the recruiting office tomorrow.'

FOUR

It was a fair step to Thorpe Street Barracks, the other side of town, near the Horse Fair in Edgbaston, not a place either Pat or Bill had been to before. They kept up a steady pace, though as they passed the White Lion pub Pat looked at it longingly because the day was warm one.

'I could murder a cold pint just now.'

'It would be welcome right enough,' Bill said, 'but the pubs won't be open yet awhile. Anyroad, it wouldn't look well, enlisting in the army stinking of beer.'

'Yeah, maybe not,' Pat conceded. 'And we're nearly there, I'd say. This bloke down our yard, who went last week, said the barracks is about halfway down the road.'

As they passed rows of back-to-back houses Bill asked Pat how Polly had taken the news that he was going to enlist. 'Well, she weren't over the moon or owt,' Pat said. 'She come round, like, in the end, 'cos it isn't as if I've got a job to leave, like you have. Anyroad, as I said to Poll, if we can kick them Jerries into shape soon, like, then our Chris might not be drawn into it. Tell you the truth, Bill, I'd give my right arm for my lads to stay out of this little lot. I mean, they haven't really had any sort of life yet, have they?'

'No, you're right, of course,' Bill agreed.

'How did Marion cope with it?'

'She kicked up a bit of a stink,' Bill said. 'Mind you, she doesn't hold a candle to her mother. Bloody old vixen, she is.'

'Did you tell Clara that we were enlisting together?'

'Yeah, I did.'

'Bet that didn't go down too well. That woman hates my guts. I've never managed to provide for Polly the way the old woman thought I should.'

'Yeah, but that wasn't your fault,' Bill said. 'Anyroad, I think she has a short memory. She came from very humble beginnings herself, Marion told me. For the first few years of her life she was brought up in a damp, smelly, rat-infested cellar because her parents couldn't afford anything better. Eddie wasn't at the rolling mills then; he was a porter down at New Street railway station and he had to go each day to see if he'd be set on. Marion said that sometimes he had no work and so no money for days. She was often hungry and bare-foot. D'you know, she began life as scullery maid in a large country house in Edgbaston when she was just ten years old?'

'Did she?' Pat said. 'Polly never told me that. Course, being younger, she'd hardly be aware of it. Anyroad, I thought there were laws about that kind of thing?'

Bill nodded. 'Marion should by rights have been at school until she was twelve, but apparently Clara said she could read, write and reckon up, and that was all the learning she would need, and a sight more than Clara herself had ever had, and it was time that she was working. She was so small when she began work she couldn't reach the sinks and had to stand on a board. It must have been hard for her for she said some of the pots were nearly as big as she was and there were a great many of them and the hours were long. And yet she claims she was happy because when she began there it was the first time she could ever remember being warm and properly dressed, even in the winter. She lived in the attic of the big house, which she shared with the kitchen maid and two housemaids. For the first time in her life she had a comfortable bed of her own and a cupboard beside it to put her clothes in. She said it was like luxury.

'She also had plenty to eat, because the master and mistress were generous, and Cook was a kindly soul who always maintained that the staff worked harder when their stomachs were full.'

'Polly told me that,' Pat said. 'She said they always looked forward to her coming home on a day off because the cook would pack up a big basket for them all. Apart from that, their lives were hard enough and she said nearly all her brothers and sisters died. Eddie must have been glad to get that job at the rolling mills.'

'Well, it meant at least they could move into that back-to-back in Yates Street,' Bill said. 'Marion thought that things might get better for them all at last.'

'Aye, and then old Clara was knocked for six when Michael died on one of those bleeding coffin ships,' Pat said. 'Polly remembers the unhappiness in the house then, although she was only young herself.'

'Yeah, but Clara never let herself get over it,' Bill said. 'I'm not saying that you wouldn't be upset – Christ, it would tear the heart out of me to lose just one of my kids – but in the end you have to face it and go on, and she's never done that. All I'm saying is, Eddie couldn't get a regular job for years and neither could his sons, which is why they made for the States in the first place, so I can't understand why Clara should take against you for finding things to be the same. That's just life, that is.'

'Huh, I don't worry myself about anything that old harridan says to me. It's like water off a duck's back.'

'Good job,' Bill said. 'Anyroad, here we are.'

The barracks were large and imposing, and decorated with posters urging men to enlist.

'Come on, let's get it over with,' Pat said, and they went in through the wide, square entrance with turrets on either side.

The entrance hall was packed, but those in

charge seemed to have it all in hand and the recruits were dealt with speedily. When all the formalities had been done and the forms filled in, they signed their names and were officially enlisted in the army, subject to their medicals.

When Bill learned that in the army he would be earning fourteen shillings a week of which one shilling and eleven pence would be deducted for his keep he was not unduly alarmed. In wartime he assumed he would have little to spend his money on, but he was interested in how much his family would be allocated while he was away fighting for King and Country.

'That will depend on how many children you have,' the official told him.

'I have five,' Bill said.

'Are any of those children working?'

'The eldest one.'

'There will be no allowance for that one then,' the official said. 'For the others a penny for each of them will be taken from your wages every week.'

'A penny?'

'Yes, and the Government will add tuppence for each child in addition to that, which brings it to another shilling a week.'

It was a pittance. A shilling a week to feed and clothe four growing children. With a sinking feeling in the pit of his stomach Bill asked, 'And my wife, – what allowance has she?'

'She has what is called a Separation Allowance, which amounts to one shilling and one penny a day, and there will also be another sixpence taken from your wages for her.'

Bill did the calculations. Marion would have the princely sum of nine shillings and a penny for all of them to live on.

'Is that all?' Bill cried. 'She won't be able to live on that. Almighty Christ, the rent alone is twelve shillings a week.'

'Everyone has the same, Mr Whittaker,' the official said coldly. 'We cannot make a special case for your wife.'

'No, but—'

'Mr Whittaker, those are the rates and that is that,' the official told him firmly. 'I have a lot of people to see besides yourself and however long you argue, your family's entitlement will remain the same.'

Bill had no alternative but to leave. Outside in the corridor he found Pat waiting for him.

'God,' Pat said ironically, 'at least they give the wife and kids plenty to live on. Keep them in the lap of luxury, that.'

Bill shook his head. 'I don't know how I am going to face Marion and tell her this. She'll never manage on it. Richard can't give her any more than he does because his wage as a junior apprentice is only nine and eleven pence. Sarah is fourteen next month and will be leaving school then, but even if she is able to get a job it won't pay very well. Christ, Pat, I've been bringing home three pounds ten shillings every week, more with overtime, which I did most weeks.'

His heart sank as he remembered how Marion would often say with pride that she had never visited a pawn shop, never had reason to, not like her sister, Polly, who never seemed to be out of the place. As he and Pat turned for home again he gave a heavy sigh.

'That's the sigh of a weary man,' Pat smiled.

'A guilty one, perhaps,' Bill said. 'How do they expect a woman to buy food, coal and pay the rent on the pittance they allow them? And that's taking no account of clothes and boots growing children need.'

'I know,' Pat said. 'It's a bugger, all right. Polly won't be so bad, see, because the boys get good enough money at Ansell's. And even in a war, people will still want beer, won't they? More rather than less, I would have said, and Mary Ellen has been working in Woolworths for over a year now and she tips up her share too.'

Bill saw that, for the first time, the Reillys would be better off than the Whittakers. Their rent, too, was less than half what the Whittakers paid. 'And don't forget the Christmas Tree Fund will help you with clothes and boots for the kids,' Pat went on.

Bill shook his head dumbly. Marion had often said she would die of shame if she couldn't provide for their own children and had to rely on handouts from the *Evening Mail* Christmas Tree Fund.

Pat saw the look on Bill's face. 'And don't look like that,' he snapped. 'Better take them and be grateful than let the kids suffer. Pride and fine principals are all very well when you have plenty of money coming in.'

Bill felt ashamed, for he knew that Pat was only trying to be helpful. 'I'm sorry,' he said, 'it's just that neither Marion nor me envisaged going cap in hand to anyone.'

'Well, we ain't never been at war before, have we, and so we have to do the best we can.'

'I know,' said Bill, 'but I don't think there are words written that will ease any of this for Marion.'

Pat watched his brother-in-law trudge away from him, his head lowered and his shoulders hunched, and he didn't envy him a bit. He and Polly had had a lot of knocks in their journey through life and he knew that she would view this as yet another challenge to overcome. After all, he reasoned, they wouldn't be the only wives and mothers in the same situation.

Marion was in the scullery where she was rinsing out the boiler that she had used for the Monday wash. She looked up when she heard Bill and was slightly alarmed by the wretched look on his face. For a split second she thought that the army had refused him. That news would delight her, but she knew that it would devastate him and so she said, 'Did everything go all right?'

Bill nodded. 'I am to report on Wednesday for my medical and, provided I pass that, I will be in.'

Marion knew he would pass. Bill had always been a fit man.

'Where are the children?' he asked. 'I need to talk to you.'

'Sarah and Siobhan have taken the lot of them down the park,' Marion said. 'Talk away if you must, but I will have to get on . . .'

'Marion, please.' Bill placed his hands over Marion's, which were reddened and still damp. 'I need us both to sit down and talk.'

She looked into his troubled eyes and realised that she didn't want to hear what he had to say. But that wouldn't help, she knew, and so she followed him into the living room, where they sat on the two easy chairs in front of the range.

Knowing that there was no way of softening the blow, Bill said immediately, 'When I decided to enlist, I knew that a soldier's wages wouldn't be near as much as I was earning, but I didn't believe it would be so little.'

'How little?' Marion said in a steely voice, and as Bill told her he saw her large eyes widen in horrified surprise.

She wondered why she wasn't shouting and screaming and throwing things about the room because it was what she really wanted to do. She also wanted to lash out at the husband she thought she knew and say it wasn't to be borne that he could leave them almost destitute. But she did none of these things, because overriding her white-hot anger was the panicky thought that once he left there was a real risk of the family starving, or, at the very least, being put

67

out of their house if she couldn't raise the rent money.

'So, I will have the princely sum of nine shillings and a penny to live on while you are away hunting down Germans?' she spat.

'I didn't know,' Bill said. 'I had no idea that the wages or Separation Allowance would be so low. I would have thought that they would value our contribution to the army higher than that.'

'Well, they don't,' Marion hissed. 'And it might have been better for us all if you had made sure of the facts before you signed the forms.'

'I know that,' Bill said miserably. 'I will send you what I can.'

'Out of fourteen shillings a week?' Marion said disparagingly. 'With one shilling and eleven pence already taken out of your wages, and the money for the children and me as well? We might get short shrift if we relied on money from you to put food on the table.'

'I know,' Bill said. 'And I'm sorry.'

'Oh, that's all right then, if you're sorry,' Marion said bitterly. 'That will make a lot of bloody difference.'

The very fact that she had used an expletive at all, showed Bill the level of her distress. He tried to put his arms around her but she fought him off, for she heard the children coming in.

The following day Bill walked to the foundry with Richard to tell his gaffer what had transpired and to collect his wages, for they operated a week-in-hand system, and also draw out any holiday money due to him. But he also wanted to snatch a private word with his son.

'You'll be the man of the house when I'm gone.'

'I know, Dad,' Richard said. 'Don't worry.'

'It's up to you to look after your mother,' Bill went on. 'Sarah will help you. She's a good girl that way. And for God's sake keep a weather eye on young Tony. There's no real harm in him, but I know he'd go to hell and back to get into Jack's good books.'

Richard knew that only too well. 'I'll do my best,' he said. 'But I'm at work all day.'

'I know. And if he was at school all day I wouldn't worry so much, but your mother says most of the teachers have gone with the evacuated children, so there will be no school until they have sorted something else for those left behind. And,' Bill added with a wry smile, 'idleness and therefore boredom can lead to all sorts of mischief.'

Richard nodded. 'I know. And like I told you before, I'll do my level best to help out.'

Bill felt much relieved because he knew that Richard could be trusted. They parted at the gates and Bill went to the wages office to get what was due to him, which amounted to nearly ten pounds. Which he gave straight to Marion.

'Go easy with this,' he warned her. 'I don't know how long it will take them to sort out your allowance. Once I've had the medical, providing that is all clear and everything, I'm not to report until Friday, and they might not put things in motion until it is sort of official.'

'And what if they do take weeks to sort it out?'

'They'd hardly do that,' Bill said. 'They'll know you've all got to live. God knows, they are giving you little enough as it is.'

Marion gave a sigh. 'Remember, I have tasted extreme poverty before and, I'd rather cut off my right arm than let my children suffer as I did throughout my childhood.'

Bill didn't want that either, but he was utterly helpless to ease the predicament that he had put them in by enlisting. Pat didn't seem to feel the gut-wrenching guilt Bill did, and Bill wished he could view life the same way, but he was made in a different mould entirely from Pat.

As Marion expected, Bill was passed as A1, fit to serve overseas. He was issued with a uniform and a kitbag, and had to report to Thorpe Street Barracks at seven o'clock on Friday morning.

She was surprised when he said that Pat had failed the medical. 'Why?' Marion said. 'He looks all right to me.'

Bill shrugged. 'I didn't get to see him after,' he said. 'Folk that did said he was gutted.'

'I wish it was you,' Marion said.

'God, don't say that,' Bill cried. 'The man could have anything wrong with him.'

'Huh, not Pat Reilly. The man is too pickled from alcohol for germs to live long on him. And now he's somehow managed to wriggle out of the army. Well, I'm away to our Polly's to find what that lying hypochondriac told them on the Medical Board so that they sent him home.'

The whole family got up to see Bill off that Friday. When he descended the stairs, dressed in his uniform, his wife and children assembled below thought they had never seen him look so smart. But, as Magda said to Missie later, 'It didn't look like our dad, though, did it?'

'No, dain't smell like him, either.'

'Yeah, it was like kissing a stranger,' Magda said.

For all that, they both cried bitterly when they did kiss Bill goodbye, though he kept assuring them that he'd be home again in a few weeks' time.

Eventually they were calmer and when Magda said, 'Are you calling for Uncle Pat?' they were all surprised when he told them that their uncle had failed the medical.

'Why?' Tony asked. 'Jack never said owt.'

'Maybe he didn't want to say,' Bill said. 'Maybe he didn't know himself.'

'But why did he fail, anyroad?' Magda asked.

'Ask no questions and you'll be told no lies,' Marion said.

Magda thought that just about headed a long list of annoying things mothers said. How were you to get to know anything if you didn't ask questions? She didn't bother asking again, though, because her mother could get right angry sometimes when she did that sort of thing. And that day she had two spots of colour on her cheeks, and her eyes looked very bright, which were two bad signs.

It was still very early, so when they had had their breakfast of bread and dripping and had a cat lick of a wash, they went out into the yard.

'I can't understand why our mom won't say what's wrong with Uncle Pat,' Magda said.

''Cos she's a grown-up, that's why,' Tony said darkly. 'And that's what they do.'

Magda knew that, but Sarah was a different kettle of fish. She was almost fourteen and not yet a real adult, so she collared her in the bedroom later and said, 'Why didn't Uncle Pat get into the army, Sarah?'

'Because he has flat feet.'

Missie and Tony were still in the yard, and when Magda went out and told them what Sarah had said they both looked at her in astonishment.

'Don't be daft!' Tony said,

'I'm not,' Magda said indignantly. 'That's what Sarah said.'

'It couldn't be just that, though.'

Magda shrugged. 'Well, that's all she said.' Then suddenly she sat down on the back step, where she unlaced her shoes and peeled off her socks.

'What you doing?' Missie cried.

'Looking at my feet.' Magda wriggled her toes. 'All feet are sort of flat, aren't they? I mean, you don't get round feet or square or owt.'

'Maybe Uncle Pat's feet are dead flat all over,'

Missie said. 'I mean, we wouldn't see that through his boots.'

'They ain't,' Tony put in. 'I've seen Uncle Pat's feet a few times and they looked the same as everyone else's feet to me.'

'Don't stop him walking, does it?' Magda said.

'Shouldn't stop him marching then, should it?' Tony said. 'Don't think his feet can have much to do with it. Our Sarah must have picked it up wrong.'

The two girls nodded solemnly. It was easily done to get the wrong end of the stick, especially when you shouldn't have overheard in the first place, as Magda knew to her cost.

'You'd better put your things back on,' Missie said, 'before Mom catches sight of you.'

Magda pulled her socks on and pushed her feet into her shoes, but the laces defeated her and she had to leave them dangling. Fortunately, it was Sarah who came to bring the children inside and she only grumbled good naturedly at Magda as she fastened up the shoes.

'And let me straighten your hair before Mom sees it,' she said. 'How you get it in such a tangle in minutes beats me.'

'I don't know how I do it either,' Magda said. 'It's a mystery.'

Sarah laughed at the crestfallen look on her young sister's face. 'Magda Whittaker, you are one on your own,' she said as she rebraided one of Magda's plaits. 'And thank God for it.'

FIVE

Now that the twins had made their First Holy Communion, all the Whittakers went to Communion every Sunday. As no one was allowed to eat or drink beforehand, when they returned from Mass they were usually more than ready for a big feed. However, the first Sunday after Bill had left for the training camp there was no big breakfast. Instead, Marion made a big saucepan full of porridge. It was thin because it was made with water, and there was no jug of creamy milk to pour over it and just one small teaspoon of sugar each.

'I'm still hungry,' Tony declared as he cleared his plate.

Magda was as well, but again she had seen the two bright red spots appear in her mother's cheeks. She was a great respecter of those spots because they would always appear before she got her legs smacked for something or other, so she waited to see what reaction Tony would get.

'Well then,' said Marion, 'you will have to stay hungry until dinner time.'

'Yeah, but—'

'If you have any more now you will have no appetite for dinner.'

'Yeah I will, Mom,' Tony cried. 'Honest. I'm starving.'

'Starving,' snorted Marion. 'You don't even know what that word means. Anyway, there is no help for it and you will just have to make do with the porridge. No one else is making such a fuss.'

Oh, but I could, Magda thought, for I bet that I'm just as hungry as Tony. There was little point in saying any of this, though, and anyroad, her twin sister, Richard and Sarah seemed satisfied, and Sarah had already started clearing up the bowls.

Sarah could have said that the porridge barely took the edge off her appetite, but she knew that that was the type of meal that they had to get used to when so little money was coming into the house.

Later, in the yard, Magda said to Missie, 'D'you suppose we're poor now, 'cos Mom only gave us two farthings for the collection instead of the two pennies we usually have?'

'I don't know if we're really poor,' Missie said, 'but Sarah did tell me that there will be less money about now that Dad has enlisted.'

'Oh.'

'She even said that some weeks we may get no collection money at all.'

'Well, I'm going round Aunt Polly's,' Tony

declared. 'She'll give me a jam piece or summat when I tell her that I'm still hungry.'

'You can't tell Aunt Polly that,' Missie said, clearly shocked.

'Why not?' Tony demanded. 'It's the truth.'

'Because Mom would be hurt if you did,' Missie explained.

'She wouldn't half,' Magda agreed. 'Hurt and angry, I'd say. Anyroad, Tony, why d'you think that you're the only one that's still hungry? I am as well, if you want to know, but I don't make as much fuss as you. It'll be dinner time soon.'

'Not for flipping hours it won't.'

'Oh, stop moaning. It'll do no good.'

'I wish Dad was here,' Tony said wistfully. 'If he took us down the park or summat I'd probably forget about being hungry.'

'We all wish Daddy was here,' Magda said. 'But it ain't no good going on about it.'

Tony sighed. Maybe there wasn't, but there was no way that he was going to stay cooped up in the garden with his kid sisters. 'Well, I ain't staying here, anyroad,' he said. 'I'm off.'

'Don't you dare go to Aunt Polly's.'

'I ain't,' Tony said, because he knew Magda was right, his mother would be very angry should she find out that he had gone to his aunt's house to be fed. He had no wish to cope with his mother's temper as well as starvation. 'I'm going to find our Jack and have a game of summat.'

When he had gone Magda said, 'What shall we do? Shall I get our skipping ropes out?'

Missie made a face. 'I'm bored of skipping.'

'Tell you what then, let's see if we can throw two balls at the wall like our Sarah can?'

'She can do three,' Missie corrected. 'I've seen her. I have trouble enough doing one.'

'And me, but Sarah says practice makes perfect.'

'If you like then,' Missie said. 'I don't care what we do really.'

Magda sighed as she looked at her twin sister. 'This is probably what being at war's like,' she said, 'and our Sarah says we have to put up with it like everyone else.'

'I know,' Missie replied heavily. 'It's just everything's so strange, and I do miss Daddy. But go and get the balls and we'll see what we can play.'

However, the whole flavour of the day was wrong. Eventually the girls were called in for dinner. Magda sniffed because she loved the smells that would waft through from the kitchen on Sundays: the succulent aroma of a large piece of meat roasting slowly in the oven, surrounded by golden brown potatoes, and there might be apple crumble or treacle sponge bubbling away on the shelf below.

That day, however, she was in for an unpleasant shock for there was no roasting meat and golden brown potatoes and no pudding at all.

Marion didn't know how long it would be before she had some more money coming in and she had been horrified at the price of meat, which had rocketed up since war had been declared, though no one could give a satisfactory reason as to why this was. So she made a casserole with a small piece of beef she had diced so that it would cook quicker and filled the pot with vegetables.

Usually, while the dinner was cooking Marion would be hard at it making pastries, pies and sponge cakes for Sunday tea, and by the time the dinner was ready there would normally be some of these cooling on wire trays. But Marion knew those teas would be a thing of the past. She had explained it all to her parents, though when she told them of the pittance that she was being given to feed the family they could understand that for themselves.

Everyone was too hungry to grumble about the casserole that day, though, and so they ate it without complaint.

Later Magda said to Missie, 'It's great that we haven't got Grandma Murray to put up with today, ain't it?' Missie agreed it was and Magda went on, 'Maybe Grandma and Granddad will never be able to come again. That would be even better.'

'Not half,' Missie agreed. 'I don't mind Granddad, though.'

'I don't either,' Magda conceded. 'He couldn't come on his own, though. But what's really smashing is the thought of never having to sit on that blooming horsehair sofa ever again.'

Bill Whittaker had been gone just over a week and they had just received the first letter from him, telling them how he'd settled down in the camp, when Polly came around with news of her own. Only the twins were in the house with their mother because Sarah was shopping and Tony playing out in the street.

'Oh, Marion, what do you think?' Aunt Polly said as she came in, her eyes aglow. 'Our Pat has been offered a fine job at the munitions works at Witton and the wage is six pounds a week.'

Magda, glancing at her mother, knew that she wasn't overpleased at Pat's good fortune because her mouth had gone all tight. She shooed the girls into the garden but they lingered in the scullery.

'I don't understand why Mom's so cross about Uncle Pat getting a job,' Magda said in a low voice. 'I mean, for years she has been moaning about the fact he doesn't have one.'

Missie gave a little sigh, 'I know. I think grown-ups are really confusing.'

'Six pounds a week?' they heard their mother exclaim. 'What in God's name does Pat know about making explosives?'

'Enough, seemingly,' Polly said. 'Oh God, Marion, what does anyone know about anything these days? When did you think that you would ever see woman drivers and conductors on the trams, or working alongside men in the factories? The world has been turned on its head and I suppose Pat will be trained like all the rest. Anyroad,' she added with a touch of pride, 'they must think he had something about him because he only went for

79

a job in the factory, like, and when he said as how he failed his medical to get in the army because of his flat feet they offered him the job as foreman.'

'Sarah was right,' Missie whispered. 'It was just flat feet after all.'

'Well, I hope it stays fine for you,' the twins heard their mother say in a sort of clipped voice. Then she added, 'Have you time to stay for a cup of tea?'

'I shouldn't,' Polly said. 'And I can't stay too long, but I will have a quick cup because we haven't had a good old natter for ages.'

'Out, quick,' Magda said, pushing Missie in front of her, and they escaped to the garden before their mother would catch them eavesdropping.

Later that night, when the house was still, Marion admitted to herself that she couldn't be really happy for her sister's good fortune, just incredibly envious. Polly had been poor all her married life and now she would have plenty of money, at least as long as the war lasted, while she, Marion, would have to scrimp and scrape. It was her husband who was putting his life on the line, not Polly's. She found it very hard not to feel resentful.

Clara quite understood how Marion felt when she next came round.

'It hardly seems fair that my Bill will soon be risking his life daily for a pittance,' Marion said to her mother, 'and because Pat Reilly is not fit for that, he's sitting pretty and earning a wage many would give their eyeteeth for.'

'I know,' Clara said. 'And all this came about because they said he had flat feet. I ask you! If they had refused him because he had chronic liver failure, I could have understood it more. Anyroad, Marion, just imagine how bad the others after jobs were for Pat Reilly to be the best of them.'

Marion gave a grim smile. 'I thought that too.'

'And, of course, Pat's fine wages will do them no good at all,' Clara said. 'It will just dribble through Polly's fingers.'

Marion thought that a little unfair, for Polly was always very good with money, but she didn't say anything because for once her mother seemed to understand how aggrieved she had felt at her sister's good fortune. 'And just think, with extra money at his disposal, Pat Reilly could easily drink himself into an early grave. Mind you, in his case that could be a blessing.'

'Oh, Mam!' Marion said, shocked.

'Don't tell me you haven't thought the same, for I'll not believe it.'

A crimson flush flooded Marion's face because her mother was right, though she felt so ashamed of it. 'Bill always said there wasn't that much wrong with Pat,' she ventured.

'There is a great deal wrong with a man who takes a young girl down and fills her belly every year without any idea how he is going to provide for any of his kids. They have lived like paupers.'

They had, as Marion knew only too well, so why then couldn't she take joy in the fact that life was going to be easier for them from now on? That she couldn't disturbed her because she realised she was not half as generous as her sister, who didn't seem to have a resentful bone in her body.

As one week followed another no bombs fell and the only sign that Britain was at war at all was the news of ships being sunk, and everyone trying to cope with the blackout. Those who could, stayed indoors when darkness fell because to venture out was risking life and limb in such inky blackness.

The Government advised people to paint white lines on the kerbs outside their houses, and around any trees, pillar boxes and lampposts to try to cut down on the number of accidents.

'It won't work, of course,' Polly said. 'The white paint won't show up in the pitch black any more than any other colour would.'

'I know,' Marion said. 'It's stupid, and so was sending the kids away when we've had no bombs. A lot of mothers like Phyllis Cox are bringing them back home.'

'Don't blame them.'

'Nor do I. But I wish they would organise something for the children left behind. It does no good for kids to be hanging about all the time. It only leads to mischief when they have too much time on their hands.'

'Oh, I'll say so,' Polly said. 'Gladys Kent complained about our Jack only the other day. She has a house that opens on to the street and the little bugger tied her knocker in such a way that he could operate it from a distance. Course, when she tried to open the door she couldn't. She said she knew it was him because she heard him killing himself laughing behind the wall.'

'Was Tony involved as well?'

'Think so.'

'Why didn't you come and tell me?'

'It was only a prank, Marion,' Polly said. 'Pat gave them both a good talking to and they won't do it again.'

'I miss Bill for that,' Marion said. 'He was always so good with Tony over something like that. Mind, I miss Bill for more than just that, and though he includes postal orders in his letters he hasn't much to spare either. I am so worried about money because it's five weeks now since Bill left, with no sign of any Separation Allowance from the Government. Each morning when I wake I feel as if I've a lump of lead in my stomach when I think of the day ahead and trying to feed hungry children on a pittance. I mean, Bill left me ten pounds but twelve shillings a week for the rent makes a big hole in that.'

'But there is no reason for you or the nippers to go without,' Polly said. 'I've told you many a time. We have the money now and, God knows, you've helped me and mine enough in the past. Why are you so pig-headed?'

'Polly, if I had money from you, I haven't the least idea when I would ever be able to pay you back.'

'Have I ever asked for you to pay me back?' Polly said, exasperated by her sister's stubbornness.

'I would *have* to pay you back,' Marion said. 'It's the way I am.'

'Have you managed to pay the rent?'

'Marion made a face. 'No, not for the last week I didn't, and I can't see it being any better this week, or next either.'

'You'll have to pay summat off soon,' Polly warned. 'Some of these landlords only give you three or four weeks, especially in posh houses like these.'

'Polly, don't you think that I'm not panic-stricken about just that?' Marion snapped. 'But I can't magic money out of the air.'

'Well,' said Polly, 'if you're adamant that you won't accept help from me, listen to this. I was talking to a woman down our yard and she said that her old man joined up in the spring because, like Pat, he hadn't ever really had what you'd call regular work, and she told me that they dain't get her Separation Allowance sorted out for over two months.'

'Oh God!' Marion cried. 'If that happens to me I will be out on my ear. It would be the workhouse for the lot of us.'

'Don't be so bloody soft,' Polly said. 'Me and Pat would never let that happen to you or the nippers. Anyroad, what I'm trying to tell you is there is somewhere you can go, some organisation that helps in situations like this. This woman was telling me all about it, 'cos she was on her beam ends, she said, and she had to go and see them.'

'Beam ends,' Marion said, 'I know how that feels all right. And did this place help her?'

'Yeah,' Polly said. 'You can't go every week or owt to top up your Separation Allowance, for all you might need it, but if they are taking their time sorting out what you are due, they'll help you. It's called the SSAFA, which stands for Soldiers, Sailors, Airmen and Families Association and they have a big office place on Colmore Row. I'll go with you tomorrow if you like.'

'Oh, Polly, would you really?'

'Course I would, you daft sod,' Polly said cheerfully. 'In things like this you are like a babe in arms, our Marion.'

Polly had advised her to take her marriage lines, the kids' birth certificates and her rent book with her. 'They don't know who you are, do they?' she said. 'I mean, you could be just someone come in off the street trying to get money they ain't entitled to.'

Marion knew that her sister was right. She took all the details of the Royal Warwickshires, the regiment in which Bill had enlisted, and even took the three letters that he had sent her from the training camp. A woman came out to see her where she waited on the wooden bench in the reception hall to which she had been directed, and Marion was a little unnerved by her smartness. She wore a pink, high-necked frilled blouse and navy skirt, proper silk seamed stockings and high-heeled navy shoes. She had also used cosmetics on her face and her light-coloured hair was gathered up in a very neat bun at the base of her neck. Marion followed her into a small office with some trepidation.

However, the woman's eyes were kind and she was very understanding when Marion explained the difficulties she was having. When she had filled in the claim form she was awarded an interim payment of fifteen shillings to tide her over to the next week.

'And then what?' Marion asked.

'If your Separation Allowance is not worked out by that time, you must come back,' the woman said. 'We will continue to help you till the Government steps in.'

'I am most grateful.'

'These are hard times for everyone,' the woman said. 'But the one thing many of our servicemen are worried about are the families they have left behind. We try to help to relieve some of that stress for you and your children, and also for your husband.'

'She's right as well, ain't she?' Polly said as they made their way home and Marion told her what the woman had said. 'I think that our soldiers and sailors and that have enough to worry about facing the enemy without worrying about how their families are faring.'

Marion nodded. 'And she was such a kind and sympathetic woman.'

'Yeah,' Polly said. 'The bit I saw of her she

seemed genuine enough, for all she was a bit posh, like. I think they're all volunteers – that's what the woman down the yard said, anyroad. Too rich to need paying for a job like normal folk.'

'I don't care who they are,' Marion said. 'They have saved my bacon for this week at least, and some of this is going to pay off my rent arrears.'

'Yeah, that's sensible,' Polly said. 'But keep some back.'

'Don't worry,' Marion said. 'I need to buy coal – we're nearly all out. I will give the rent man the least amount I can get away with.'

Despite the help Marion received from the SSAFA, the rent man pressed her for more money than she wanted to pay, and with the coal bought there was very little left.

'Go back,' Polly advised, when she popped around to see Marion. 'Tell them what you had to pay out.'

Marion shook her head. 'I couldn't. I would be that ashamed, but I am down to my last shilling.'

'Well,' said Polly, 'the only way to get quick cash is to pawn summat.'

Marion felt as if a lead weight had landed in the pit of her stomach and she remembered her boast that she had never crossed the doorstep of a pawnbroker's. She felt tears of shame and humiliation prickle the back of her eyes but she brushed them away impatiently. There was no allowing herself the luxury of tears.

'And what should I pawn?' she asked.

'Well, you can start with the old man's clothes,' Polly said. 'Most women in your position would have pawned his suit before he'd passed the end of the street.'

Marion was aghast. 'I can't do that.'

'Course you can,' Polly said dismissively. 'He'll not be wanting his stuff at the Front, will he? Anyroad, it's his fault that you're in this mess.'

Marion remembered the day that Bill had bought that suit. In the Bull Ring a two-piece suit cost two guineas; a three-piece, two pounds and ten shillings.

'He wanted the waistcoat so that he could wear his watch,' Marion told Polly, laying it out on the bed.

Polly extracted the watch from the waistcoat pocket. 'Good watch, that.'

'It's gold,' Marion said. 'It was Bill's father's and Bill is almighty fond of it.'

Polly shrugged. 'Might have to go despite that,' she said. 'But it would be better to take that in on its own, not mixed in with a pile of clothes. That way you'll probably get more for it. Now, what about his second-best suit that this one replaced?'

'No,' Marion said. 'I was going to cut it down for Richard – he's fast growing out of the one he has now – and any extra material I was going to save to patch Tony's trousers. He goes through the seat of those more often than I have hot dinners, and I'll not send him to school like some poor souls with their bottoms nearly exposed.'

'All right, we'll leave the second-best suit and the watch for now,' Polly said, pulling out more of Bill's clothes to lay on the bed. 'This is a sizeable bundle anyway.'

'I'm really nervous,' Marion said. 'I've never been in a pawnbroker's before.'

'You're luckier than most round these doors then.'

'Not these doors,' Marion corrected. 'You never see anyone here taking a bundle to be pawned on Monday morning.'

'Yeah, well, maybe none of their husbands thought it their duty to fight for King and Country to try and protect the rest of us,' Polly said. 'And while they're doing that the bloody Government think a few measly shillings a week is all a woman needs to feed and clothe her family and keep them warm.

'Now,' Polly said as the two women left the house, 'I usually go to Sarah Moore, but she can be a mean bugger, so we'll try Jones on the corners of Wheeler Street and Clifford Street. He's a bit stern-looking – is a retired JP, I heard – but he is fair.'

Marion had always had an assumption that pawn shops were dark and rather seedy places but she was pleasantly surprised because Jones looked quite respectable from the outside. She had a surreptitious look round to see if anyone she knew was watching her before she went in the door, feeling sick to her soul that she had to part with Bill's clothes in such a way in order for them all to survive.

Despite this, though, she thought the inside of the shop had an air of respectability about it and this was compounded by the very smart and erect white-haired gentleman who came to attend to them. As Polly had said, he was rather severe-looking, but his voice and manner were pleasant enough.

On the way down to the shop Polly had warned Marion what to expect, and Jones did just as she said and examined each article with a disparaging look on his face. Then he rubbed the material of the suit between his finger and thumb, and though he said nothing, by the look on his face Marion knew he didn't think much of it.

'I'll give you ten shillings for the lot,' he said eventually.

Polly gave a toss of her head. 'Don't make me laugh,' she said. 'That bundle is well worth a pound and you know it.'

'They will be left on my hands,' Jones complained.

'That's your business,' Polly said. 'I don't care whether they are left on your hands or not. You are not getting a bundle like that for ten shillings.'

'Well, I will not pay as much as a pound,' Jones said. 'Shall we split the difference and I will give you fifteen shillings? You can't say fairer than that.'

'Yes, I can,' Polly said. 'Seventeen shillings and sixpence and the bundle's yours. That's all I will settle for.'

Jones sighed heavily. 'You will have me robbed between you all,' he said, but he went to the till as he spoke and wrote out the pawn ticket.

'It's all a bit of a game to them,' Polly said to Marion, as they walked away from the shop. 'Their aim is to give you as little as they possibly can for what you are trying to pawn. Course, if you pawn your old man's suit every Monday, like lots of women do round here, then you know what you will be offered for it, but with something like your bundle today, when he said ten shillings, I know that it was worth more than twice that amount.'

'He still gave you only seventeen and six, though.'

'I know,' Polly said. 'And I knew as well that that was as high as he was prepared to go and we'd have likely got less at Sarah Moore's.'

Marion sighed. 'It seems a terrible way to have to go on.'

Polly, catching sight of her sister's face and hearing the despondency in her voice, knew just how bad she was feeling, and she said gently, 'What you did today, Marion, some women have been doing for years because it's the only way of surviving.'

'I know,' Marion cried. 'I really do understand that. It's just . . .'

Polly laid a hand on her arm. 'Let's see what bargains are going in the Bull Ring, shall we? At least you have money enough for now.'

Marion managed to buy two bowls of faggots

91

and peas to share between them all, which cost her a shilling, spent another sixpence on potatoes to go with them, nine pence on a loaf for the morning, and still had money left for the rest of the week. She'd also be able to pay more off the rent arrears and she felt light-hearted with relief as she and Polly made their way home.

Later, sitting in Marion's kitchen with a cup of tea, Polly said, 'When Pat got that job in the munitions I was that proud. When he couldn't even get into the army he took it bad. Now he's doing a job that is well paid and he feels he's doing his bit as well.'

'Is that important to him?'

'Oh, yes. Of course, it's a novelty to have money in my purse and I'd be lying if I said the money didn't matter, but for Pat it means more than that. He said to me that he feels proud to earn the wage that he picks up at the end of the week. It's what he has wanted to do for years.'

Marion remembered laughing with her mother about Pat getting the job in the first place and saying he would drink himself to death with the extra money he would have in his pocket, but there had been no evidence of that, and she felt guilty that she made fun of him over the years. If she was honest, even though she helped Polly out financially, in a way she did it as a kind of looking down on her and Pat, and that was why she balked at the suggestion of accepting money from them. Whatever reason she gave Polly, the real one was because the tables would be turned completely and she couldn't really have borne that.

'You never understood Pat,' Polly went on, adding sadly, 'and you never really gave him a chance. It was true that he couldn't provide for me, but then neither could many other men.'

'It was that he used to drink. Even when you had no money he would drink,' Marion said. 'I could never understand that.'

'When you think what some of the poor sods have to come home to, it's no wonder they linger in the pub,' Polly said. 'But then you see the other side of the coin – what some of the wives and children have to put up with . . . Don't glare at me like that, our Marion, because Pat was never like that. Yes, he would go to the pub, but only once a week, and all he had in his pocket was just enough money for one pint of ale.'

Marion felt a little chastened by Polly's words and she remembered that Bill had always said something similar about Pat. But however she felt about him, it would do no good running him down in front of her sister.

'Pat tried so hard to get work that he used to wear his boots down to the uppers. I had to insist that he took a couple of pennies for himself, and he never would have more than that. He gave up the cigarettes years ago. He ain't a bad man, Marion, though he may sometimes be foolish, but then, God knows, few of us can put up our hands and say we are always so wise and sensible.'

'I'm sorry, Polly, and you're right,' Marion said contritely. 'I didn't fully understand your situation and I have never really let myself get to know Pat. My view of him was coloured by that day that you came to seek me out to tell me you were expecting.'

Polly was never one to bear a grudge, and she said, 'In a way I can understand it. You were my big sister and you used to look out for me. A forced marriage to one of the infamous Reillys was not what you wanted for me.'

'No,' Marion admitted, 'but Bill once said to me that Pat made you happy and that is what I wanted for you so I should have been a lot more understanding.'

She knew that Pat Reilly and his lax attitudes might still irritate her at times but he had been kindness itself since Bill enlisted. She vowed she would try harder to be more tolerant and certainly not carry tales back to her mother.

'The point is,' said Polly, 'when the boot was on the other foot and you had the money, you were always very good with me – with all of us – but now you're too stiff-necked to let me help you.'

'You are helping me,' said Marion with a wry smile. 'On my own I would never have got seventeen and sixpence for that bundle of clothes,' and the two women burst out laughing.

SIX

As November loomed, Marion's Separation Allowance was eventually worked out, and though the back pay was an added bonus, she knew that the normal weekly allowance would buy little but food for them all, and it didn't even pay the rent. Buying coal, which became more necessary as the days grew colder, was a constant headache, not to mention footwear for them all.

The evacuated children began filtering back home and, to Marion's grateful relief and that of many more mothers, the schools reopened. Marion didn't bother sending Sarah, who would have been leaving at Christmas anyway. Mrs Jenkins at the corner shop was looking for a girl to train up, and though the wages were only eight shillings, Sarah was anxious to take it, knowing even the small amount that she would be able to tip up would be welcomed.

First, though, despite the fact that she would be wearing an overall in the shop, Marion felt

Sarah had to have at least a couple of dresses that fitted her because she had developed a bust as she passed her fourteenth birthday and some of her dresses now strained to fasten and were decidedly skimpy. Richard's boots, too, needed cobbling again as they were leaking. He had to travel to work each day on the tram and Marion knew it would help none of them if he was to take sick because of his inadequate clothing.

She went to the Rag Market in the Bull Ring for the things she needed for the children, but even paying Rag Market prices left a sizeable hole in the backdated allowance, and she had nothing left for the twins or Tony, not if she were to pay the rent, though the younger children had all been complaining that their feet hurt.

The children's shoes were so tight that when they got to school they removed them, like many others. When the man came round from the Christmas Tree Fund, when they had been back at school only a few days, he gave them a docket for new boots and socks to collect from Sheepcote Road Clinic. Marion was mortified by shame when the children came home from school and told her this. She tried to be grateful but she only felt degraded that she wasn't able to provide for her own children, and this feeling intensified when she was also given a jersey and trousers for Tony, and skirts and jerseys for the two girls.

This is what it is to be poor, she thought that night as she lay in bed. She remembered with remorse how she had looked down on Polly for years. Now she was in the same boat herself and she knew the children needed the things too much for her to refuse them.

Neither Marion nor her sister envied Sarah working for Mrs Jenkins, who was known as a mean and nasty old woman. Her character was apparent in her thin lips, though her face was plump. There were plenty of lines of discontent on it, and the powder she obviously applied in the morning lay in the folds of her skin by afternoon. Her hair was piled untidily on her head, but her glittering eyes were as cold as ice and so was her thin nasal voice.

'Wouldn't give you as much as the skin off a rice pudding,' Polly said one Saturday afternoon when Sarah arrived home after she had been working at the corner shop a fortnight. But Sarah knew one of the reasons Polly said that was because Mrs Jenkins wouldn't allow people to put things on the slate and pay at the end of the week. She had made it plain to Sarah when she arrived.

'Now I don't want you to stand any nonsense,' she'd said, looming closer so that Sarah's face was inches from her and she smelled the stale smell of her and saw rotting teeth in her mouth. 'If they don't have the money then they don't get the goods. Point out the notice to them if they object.' There was the notice, stuck on the wall behind the till: 'Don't ask for credit for refusal often offends.'

When Sarah told her aunt this, she snorted in contempt. 'Stingy old bugger,' she said. 'And your mom tells me that although Mrs Jenkins pays you only eight shillings she don't throw a few groceries in as well to make it up, like.'

Sarah laughed. 'Oh, Aunt Polly, you must be joking,' she said. 'I'm not even allowed to take home the odd cracked egg or stale buns at the end of the day.'

'I can't understand the woman at all,' Polly said, shaking her head. 'Do you serve in the shop all day?'

'No,' Sarah said. 'My first job when I go in is to bag things up in the storeroom upstairs and send them down the chute to the shop.'

'Like sugar and that?'

Sarah nodded. 'And flour, tea and mixed fruit, raisins and that, and anything else Mrs Jenkins wants me to weigh up. She says there's rationing coming in January so things might be different then, and it might not be so easy to have things under the counter for favoured customers.'

'I'd say not,' Marion said. 'Course, it all depends what's being rationed.'

'So do you like the job?' Polly persisted. 'Because I heard the last girl left in a tear.'

'Well, I won't,' Sarah said. 'We need the money too much.'

Neither Polly or Marion argued with that because they knew Sarah was right.

Sarah didn't moan much, but she did find Mrs Jenkins hard going, and her grating, complaining voice really got on Sarah's nerves. And Aunt Polly was right: Mrs Jenkins was incredibly mean. She'd give her a cup of weak tea mid-morning, usually when she had finished the bagging up, and another mid-afternoon, but she had to drink these on the shop floor because as soon as she was in the shop Mrs Jenkins made herself scarce. She even seemed to begrudge her the half an hour she gave her to eat the sandwiches Marion put up for her, and there was no cup of tea made then so Sarah usually washed them down with water. However, a job was a job and she thought this would do until something better turned up.

The only cheering thing was that the Government had relaxed the blackout restrictions a little because so many people had been injured or even killed in accidents on the road. Shielded lights on cars were now allowed, and so were shaded torches. It was immensely comforting to have that small pencil of light to guide a person's way in that dense inky blackness. That was, of course, if batteries could be obtained, for they disappeared from shops quicker than the speed of light.

But then none of this mattered because Bill was coming home on leave. Marion could hardly wait to see him. In a way it was a bittersweet pleasure, because she knew that it was without doubt embark-ation leave, and that when he returned he would more than likely be sent overseas to join in the war already claiming many, many lives.

When he arrived that cold, foggy Saturday he was shocked by the state of his family. He noted how thin and pasty-looking the children were, but when he drew Marion into his arms and he could feel her bones, he was shocked to the core.

Marion had a stew ready, made with cow's heel and vegetables, and because it was Bill's first night home they were all allowed bread to mop up the gravy, a luxury Marion couldn't usually allow.

Tony finished his helping, sat back in his chair and said with a sigh of contentment, 'Crikey, I'd forgotten what it was like to feel really full.'

Tony's words made Bill feel even worse, and that night in bed beside his wife he said, 'God, Marion, I am so sorry. I had no idea that you were suffering this way.'

Marion couldn't reassure Bill and tell him that everything was all right, and yet she felt that she couldn't berate him either. She wasn't stupid and she knew that when Bill left her he would be exposed to God alone knew what danger, and she couldn't let him do that with any angry words that she had thrown at him ringing in his ears. And so she said, 'We will likely manage well enough if the war doesn't go on too long.'

'I hope it doesn't,' Bill said. 'I imagine we'll be over in France soon and then we'll know what's what, and soon have Jerry on the run.'

Marion gave a sudden shiver at Bill's word and he put his arms around her and held her tight, glad that the bolster had been removed from the bed. Not that he would ever go further than a cuddle, however much he might want to. The doctor had warned him about the danger of another pregnancy after the twins had struggled to be born, and he loved his wife too much to put her at risk. He wasn't some sex-crazed beast, but to cuddle together was nice and comforting for both of them.

Bill wore his uniform to Mass the next morning as it was the only clothes he had left, but he soon saw that he wasn't the only one. He found that people respected the uniform and his hand was wrung many times, including by Father McIntyre.

Back home, he ate the thin porridge with everyone else and though he could have eaten three times that amount and still been peckish, he wouldn't let Marion offer him anything else. After it, to take their mind off how hungry they still were, he suggested taking Tony and the twins down to the canal.

'Don't be too long,' Marion told Bill. 'I want dinner fairly early because my parents are coming afterwards to see you and they won't want to go home in the dark.' She saw his eyes widen and said, 'They're not coming for a meal. It takes every penny I have to feed my own. Those fancy Sunday teas are a thing of the past, as I said in my letters to you.'

Bill had no desire to see Clara, but he nodded. 'We'll be back in plenty of time.'

The children thoroughly enjoyed having their father back. Tony in particular had really missed him, and in his company he forgot his growling stomach, and the cold of the day, which caused wispy white trails to escape from their mouths when they spoke.

They all knew they were having liver for dinner because Aunt Polly had brought it round the previous day. She'd said the butcher had some going cheap and so she'd bought extra for them.

'What we eat is sort of hit and miss,' Marion had told Bill when he'd asked how they were managing. 'You go to the Bull Ring on Saturday night and buy what is cheap because they are trying to get rid of it. But now Polly has brought liver that's what we'll eat.'

'But I thought Tony and the twins, Magda in particular, hate liver.'

'Huh,' said Marion grimly. 'It's amazing what you can develop a taste for if the alternative is starving. None of the children can afford to be fussy these days.'

And they weren't. Bill saw that every plate was soon cleaned.

They had barely washed up before Clara and Eddie Murray were at the door. Eddie was quick to shake Bill's hand, say he was glad to see him and remarked on how well he was looking. Clara, however, barely returned his greeting before launching into him.

'Your selfishness in enlisting has reduced your

family to penury. They scarcely have enough to live on. You must have noticed how skinny they all are.'

Bill didn't need it pointing out to him, but Marion was well aware of how he was feeling and she was annoyed with her mother.

'This really isn't the time to go into this, Mammy,' she said. 'Bill can do nothing now to ease the situation and he just has a couple of days at home. The time for any recriminations at all is well past.'

'Well said,' Eddie told his daughter approvingly, and to Bill he said, 'Shall we leave them to chat and I'll treat you to a pint? Then you can tell me all about life in the army.'

Bill was glad to get away from the malicious eyes of his mother-in-law. The children wished they could go too, but they had to stay and talk to their grandmother, though most of her conversation was criticising and finding fault with what they said and did.

In the convivial pub, where Bill was greeted by many, Eddie waited until their pints were in front of them before saying, 'Tell me how life is treating you?'

Bill told him all about the training camp and what he had to do, and Eddie listened with interest.

'And I suppose the training is over now and this is embarkation leave?' Eddie asked finally.

'I imagine so,' Bill said, 'though they tell us nothing definite. To be honest it's the family I worry about. What Clara said today, well, she was right, because I was shocked at the state of them when I came home. Marion made this stew for us all and afterwards young Tony said he had forgotten what it was like to feel full. And you know why that was? It was because, in honour of my coming home, Marion had allowed them bread to mop up the gravy. Usually she can't afford to do that.'

'Things have been hard for her,' Eddie said. 'Hard for all the wives of servicemen, especially if they're mothers too, like the vast majority are.'

'I feel so helpless,' Bill said. 'That's what's so hard.'

'Seems to me all that you can do is get over there and finish this war just as soon as you can so life can get back to normal again,' Eddie said.

Bill smiled wryly. 'I'll do my best. As for the family, I saved my cigarette money and had thought to take them to the music hall or cinema for a treat, but I know now a few good feeds is what they really want. Tomorrow early I'm going to the shop to buy extra sugar and full-cream milk for their porridge, and I'll treat them to a fish-and-chip dinner tomorrow evening. Anything I have got left over I'll give Marion before I leave.'

'I would say that they'll be grateful for that,' Eddie said.

And they were pleased with the extra sugar and milk on their porridge before they left for school and work the next day.

Bill was shocked to see the younger children

dressed in clothes and boots provided by the Christmas Tree Fund, this stamped on them so that they couldn't be pawned, and he felt shame steal all over him.

Marion saw his face and guessed his feelings. When the children had gone, she said, 'I felt the same way at the time, and wished that I could have refused them. But how could I have done that? You should see the state of some of their other things, and their warm clothes from last winter won't go near them now.'

'I just wish I could make things easier for you,' Bill said.

'There is no way you can,' Marion replied.

Bill nodded miserably. 'There is one thing I can do to put a smile on their faces.'

'What?'

'I intend to buy fish and chips for us all this evening.'

Marion felt her mouth watering at the thought. 'Oh, Bill, you couldn't buy anything that would please them more. They'll think they have died and gone to heaven, so they will. You just wait and see when you tell them that tonight.'

And Bill did see. The children were almost speechless with pleasure. And later he watched them devouring the meal with such relish it brought tears to his eyes.

A couple of days after Bill had left, Polly said to her sister, 'Look, Marion, if you won't take any money off me then at least let Tony and the twins come to our house dinner time for a bite to eat. You and all, if you want.'

Marion hesitated and Polly said, 'Go on, Marion. Don't be so stiff-necked.'

Marion knew Polly could afford to give the children something wholesome. Then bread and scrape for tea, and thin porridge for breakfast would matter less. On the other hand rationing was coming in soon and everyone would get only so much. 'It wouldn't be fair to take yours,' she said.

'We don't know what's going to be rationed yet,' Polly pointed out. 'We'll have to wait and see. But now Pat, the boys and Mary Ellen eat their dinners in their works' canteens and so I'll save on any rations they would eat.'

'All right,' Marion said. 'Thank you, Polly. We'll see how it goes. But you just see to the children. I'll get something for myself.'

Polly knew she probably wouldn't. She ate not nearly enough, in her sister's opinion, but at least Polly could ensure that the children were well fed once a day.

The children were delighted when Marion told them they would be having dinner at their Auntie Polly's. They all loved her crowded and untidy house. Aunt Polly wasn't one to be always on about people washing their hands either, and as there were barely enough chairs to sit down at the table, which was mostly cluttered anyway, they usually stood around with food in their hands, which the Whittaker children thought wonderful.

'The only downside to all this,' Marion said to Sarah one evening when the younger ones were in bed, 'is that Tony sees even more of Jack.'

'Jack isn't that bad,' Sarah protested.

Marion shook her head. 'I'm worried about Tony and the power Jack seems to have over him. I'm very much afraid our Tony needs a father's hand to stop him going to the bad altogether.'

In a way she was right, because Tony missed his father so much it was like an ache inside him. Richard, sitting in Bill's chair when he came in from work and rustling the paper he often bought on the way home, as his father had, just annoyed Tony more and he tended to gravitate more to his uncle Pat and envied Jack that his father came home each night.

In fact, he envied Jack for many things, not least because he could think up such exciting things to do. When Tony was with him and up to some mischief or other, he didn't miss his father half as much.

At some point, most boys tried to hitch a ride on a horse-drawn dray, and Jack and Tony had done so many times. The journeys never lasted long because the driver was either aware they were there or a passer-by would alert him. 'Oi, put yer whip be'ind,' they would shout, and any clinging boy would drop swiftly from the cart before the driver's curling whip could bite into his skin.

However, when Jack suggested doing the same to a clattering swaying tram Tony thought it the most exciting thing he had ever done. Neither the conductor nor the driver noticed them, but they were thrown off into the road when the tram took a corner at speed and they narrowly missed being crushed to death by a delivery van, whose driver swerved just in time to avoid them.

Marion was told this by the policeman who delivered the shamefaced and tearful Tony home, but his contriteness was wasted on her when the policeman told her that the delivery driver might never be the same again. After hauling her son inside, she paddled his bottom with a hairbrush and wished she could administer the same punishment to her nephew.

All the other children were shocked at what Tony had done and both Richard and Sarah told him so.

'Haven't you got a brain in that bonehead of yours?' Sarah railed at him. 'Didn't you think for one minute what a stupid idea it was?'

Tony was silent. He was feeling incredibly miserable. His bottom felt as if it was on fire and his stomach yawned emptily, for he had been sent to bed without anything to eat. It hadn't seemed stupid when Jack suggested it. It had seemed daring, and that's what he tried to tell his sister. Sarah looked at his brick-red face and his eyes still so full of tears that his voice was broken and husky but she felt no sympathy for him.

'Well, that one daring act might have cost you your life,' she cried, and added witheringly, 'Oh, you must be very proud of yourself.'

'I ain't,' Tony sniffed. 'I never said I was proud of it. I just thought it would be a bit of fun.'

'Fun!' Sarah repeated as if she couldn't believe she had heard right. 'Well, do you realise that you have probably cost that van driver his job? He more than likely has a wife and children dependent on him and, according to what the policeman told Mom, he might never be able to drive again. So you think on that, Tony Whittaker.'

Tony did think about it, though he couldn't help wondering what Jack felt about it all now. He knew that his family would probably not be half as harsh with him. Uncle Pat might even laugh at his antics. He often did. That was always a great puzzle to Tony.

The thin porridge the next morning didn't even go part way to assuaging his appetite but he did feel ashamed when he noticed lines of strain on his mother's face that he had never seen before.

'I have enough to worry about as it is, with your dad away and us barely having enough to live on,' Marion said to him as she cleared away his bowl. 'You can at least try to be good and listen more to me and less to Jack Reilly.'

'I'm sorry, Mom,' Tony said sincerely. 'It was just a lark but I won't do it again.'

'See you don't then,' Marion said grimly. 'You could have been killed.'

'I know. I really am sorry.'

'All right then,' Marian said, mollified a little. 'We'll say no more about it.'

Jack and Tony gave trams a wide berth after that little episode. It had given them quite a scare, not that either of them ever admitted that.

Marion opened the door the following Saturday morning to see the priest, Father McIntyre, on the doorstep. She was a little flustered because she hadn't been expecting him, but she smiled and said, 'This is a surprise, Father. Come away in and I'll put the kettle on.'

'No, Marion,' the priest said stiffly. 'This isn't a social call.'

'Oh?' Marion felt her stomach sink as she looked at the priest's disgruntled face and suddenly she knew that her younger son had something to do with Father McIntyre's ill humour. Jack and Tony, like most Catholic boys of their age, had been trained to serve at Mass, and they should both have been serving at early Mass that morning. 'Did the boys not turn up, Father?' Marion asked anxiously.

'Oh, they were there, all right,' the priest said. 'And afterwards showed total disrespect for the Church and the sacrament they had just taken part in.'

'What did they do, Father?' Marion asked fearfully.

'They each had a water pistol and I caught them filling them up from the holy water font.'

'Oh, Father!' cried Marion, shocked. 'I'm so sorry.'

'It's not your place to be sorry,' the priest said. 'It's up to your son to be sorry and mend his ways. Jack Reilly admitted that both pistols were his and that he had given one to Tony.'

'Somehow Tony seems to lose all sense of right and wrong when he's with that boy,' Marion said. 'I will deal with him, Father never fear. Where is he?'

'Knowing that your husband is away, I have taken them both to Pat Reilly's house to let him deal with the pair of them.'

'Thank you, Father,' Marion said. 'I will be away now to fetch Tony home.'

And she did fetch him and berated him every step of the way. That night she wrote to tell Bill all about his recalcitrant son.

Not surprisingly, Pat didn't take it at all seriously. Do you know, he even asked the boys if they had chosen holy water because it improved their aim . . .

Bill smiled when he read that because he could well imagine Pat saying it, and knew he himself would have taken the same line and viewed it for what it was, a boyhood prank. He also knew that Marion would never see it like that. She was really upset over it.

How is Jack to grow up with any sort of moral fibre with a father like that one as an example? And whatever mischief he is at, Tony is right behind him. I cannot seem to keep any sort of check on him and never know what he might be up to next.

A week after the last upset with Tony, Marion pawned the silver locket Bill had bought her the year after they were married and the delicate chiming carriage clock that had been Lady Amelia's present to her when she'd left service to marry Bill. It had pride of place on the mantelpiece in the parlour for it was easily the most beautiful thing the family owned. Marion shed bitter tears when she was alone for she hated having to part with such treasured items.

Sarah missed the clock almost straight away, but she said nothing because she could see from her mother's sad face and woebegone eyes that she was heart sore that she'd had to take it to the pawnbroker. When her grandparents had been coming to tea every Sunday, one of the jobs that Sarah did on a Saturday was to dust the parlour. She used to dust that clock with very great care indeed, always afraid that she might drop it or damage it in some other way. Now she thought the mantelpiece looked terribly bare without it.

And so it did, but Marion needed the money. She was a week behind with the rent again, badly needed coal, and she would liked to have her leaky boots resoled. Also she wanted to pick up a trinket for the children for Christmas, which was only two weeks away. She knew that it would be a poor one for the family this year, with no presents and nothing in the way of festive food either. She made a bit of an effort, though, and brought the little Christmas tree down from the loft, and hung around the garlands the children had made over the years.

Sarah knew the twins still firmly believed in Santa Claus, though she wasn't sure about Tony, and she thought she had better warn them about the lack of presents. 'Santa won't be visiting us this year,' she told them one evening.

They all looked at her in amazement. Tony wasn't sure that he believed in Santa any more. Jack said it was eyewash and it was just your parents filled your stockings and that, but though he usually accepted everything Jack said as gospel truth, Tony had held on to the belief that this time he was wrong and that his bulging stockings of the past had been filled by a genial man in a red suit and sporting a long white beard.

At Sarah's words he saw at once that that wasn't so. Jack had been right all along and that the hunting knife that he had coveted for so long would not be in his possession by Boxing Day, this year anyway.

'Why ever not?' asked Magda.

'It's because of the war,' Sarah said.

Magda and Missie looked at one another. They

knew all about the war, but that surely had nothing to do with Santa. 'What about the war?'

'Well, if he set off with a sleigh full of toys the Germans could capture him,' Sarah said.

The twins' mouths dropped agape at that terribly shocking news. They knew how horrid the Germans were because the adults were always talking about it and what they got up to, and the girls often saw the headlines of newspapers on their way to school. So Santa in German hands didn't bear thinking about. What if they hurt him, killed him, even? Magda thought she wouldn't put it past them. They were as bad as it was possible to be.

So when Sarah said, 'He thought this year he is safer staying where he is at the North Pole,' the twins nodded solemnly. They were disappointed, but keeping Santa safe was paramount in their minds.

SEVEN

Marion had in the end taken the five shillings that Polly had pressed upon her so that the children could eat well on Christmas Day. To give the twins at least something to open Christmas morning she also got the two girls a couple of wind-up toys from a man in the Bull Ring selling them from a tray round his neck, but she could find nothing for Tony, and neither could Sarah and Richard. They all felt bad about that.

Then after breakfast on Christmas Day, Richard dropped a cloth bag into his young brother's hands. 'Happy Christmas, Tony.'

Tony's mouth dropped open with astonishment. 'Your marble collection,' he said with awe, his voice choked with emotion, because it was the one thing that he had coveted for ages, which Richard would never let him touch.

Richard knew better than to comment on Tony's reaction and instead he said almost nonchalantly,

'You may as well have them. I never play with them any more.'

Tony tipped them out onto the table and examined them. He knew he'd be the envy of his friends when he hit the streets with those. Not even Jack had so many, or such fine ones.

'Thanks, Richard,' he said. 'I'll take real good care of them.'

Marion was glad that for Tony and the twins, a little magic of the day was retained.

After dinner Polly came around with a bundle of clothes for them all. She had a warm coat for Tony that she said was an old one of Jack's, but Marion had never seen Jack wearing anything like it and it was rather big for Tony. However, before she was able to say anything at all, Tony exclaimed in delight and put it on, very glad to have it because the only coat that fitted him was very thin and did nothing to keep the cold out.

'This is great,' he said, and Marion saw his eyes were shining so, though her eyes met her sister's over Tony's head, she said nothing.

There were also scarves, gloves and smart berets for the twins, and a smart cap with ear flaps, the same brown as the coat, for Tony. Polly even had a couple of dresses and a cardigan for Marion she said she had no use for. Marion was moved to tears by her sister's kindness and generosity. When she tried to say this, however, Polly waved her thanks away almost impatiently.

'Think nothing of it. How many times did you help me out?'

'That was nothing,' Marion said. 'It was just a bit and, anyway, I didn't do it so you would feel you had to pay it back.'

'And I didn't do it for that, like a kind of duty,' Polly said. 'You made life much more comfortable for me and mine for years and years.' She put her hand over Marion's. 'Now, through no fault of yours or mine, the positions have reversed a bit. It pleases me to be able to help you. Let me do it while I have the means to do so.'

Marion couldn't speak, the lump in her throat was too large, and tears trickled down her cheeks.

Polly stood up, jerked Marion to her feet and put her arms around her. 'Come here, you silly sod,' she said. 'You shouldn't be crying on Christmas Day.'

Marion made a valiant effort and wiped her eyes on the sleeve of her cardigan. 'I know I shouldn't, but it's made me feel . . . I don't really know . . . Anyway, Happy Christmas, Polly.'

'And to you,' Polly said, and her smile seemed to light up her whole face.

Marion thought that although that Christmas was one of the poorest she had ever spent, because of Polly and her kindness she felt suddenly filled with warmth and happiness.

The year turned, though Marion had no great hope that 1940 would be any better than 1939. All they had to look forward to was rationing starting on 8 January.

'We'll have to register with a grocer and a butcher,' Marion told Polly. 'Everyone gets a ration book, even the nippers.'

'Well, that's not that surprising, is it?' Polly said. 'I mean, the smallest has to eat.'

'Well, they won't get much on the ration,' Marion said. 'It's only bacon, butter and sugar that are rationed so far, but they reckon there'll soon be plenty more.'

'Yeah, I think every damned thing will be rationed in the end,' Polly said. 'They're just breaking us in gently. Shall we go down this afternoon and get ourselves sorted?'

'If you like, but I've got to do something first.'

'What?'

'I've got to pawn Bill's watch,' Marion said. 'I hung on to that till the last minute, but I've fallen behind with the rent and need more coal.'

'Do you want me to come?'

Marion shook her head. 'I must do this on my own,' she said. 'I can't keep relying on you holding my hand all the time.'

'Well, don't let yourself get fleeced,' Polly cautioned. 'Don't accept the first offer.'

Marion, though, was too saddened at having to pawn all the things she had treasured so much to argue overly about the value of the watch. She knew the money raised would buy food and coal and pay off her rent, but she was very much aware that she had pawned the last item of value that she possessed apart from her wedding ring. She knew that would be the next thing to disappear and she was filled with depression at the thought of losing that golden band that she had never taken from her finger since Bill had put it there in 1922.

Just a day or so after this, Tony and Jack were once more serving at early morning Mass. Tony felt very miserable because the previous evening meal hadn't really filled him up and he had gone to bed with his stomach grumbling. And then he had to get up early in the coal black of a winter's day and go out into the frost-rimed streets with nothing to eat or drink at all because he would be taking Communion. By the time he got to the church, despite his good thick coat, he was cold all through and feeling very sorry for himself.

Jack was already in the vestry when he got there and he took one look at Tony's glum face and said, 'What's up with you?'

'Nothing,' Tony growled out. 'I'm all right.'

'God, are you really?' Jack said ironically. His dark eyes sparkled with humour. 'Hate to see you when you're not all right, that's all I can say. You have a face on you that would turn the milk sour.'

'Oh, shurrup, can't you?' Tony cried.

'Now, boys,' the priest said, coming in at that moment, 'what's all this? I hope you're not arguing in God's house.'

'No, Father,' the boys said in unison, and the

priest, not believing them for an instant, said, 'Good. Now I have to go out for a while. One of my parishioners is very ill and asking for me and I want you to wait here until my return.'

'What about school, Father?'

'You'll be away in plenty of time to go to school, Jack, never fear.'

But shall we be in time to eat some breakfast, such as it is, before school? Tony thought, but didn't say anything. Father McIntyre had been a bit sharp with both of them since the business with the holy water font. So the boys waited as the minutes ticked by.

Eventually Jack said, 'I reckon he's not coming back. Shall we just go home?'

'We can't do that,' Tony answered. 'If he comes back and we're not here, I will get in one heap of trouble.'

'We'll get the strap if we're late for school.'

'And if I don't have something to eat soon I'll fall into a dead heap on the floor,' Tony said. 'I'm starving.'

'I could eat something too,' Jack said as he began to prowl around the room.

He opened a long cupboard and saw the priest's vestments hanging there. They were very beautiful, in vibrant colours or stark white, according to the Church calendar, in satin or shiny silk and heavily embossed and decorated with intricate embroidery in gold or silver.

'My dad said these cost a packet to make,' Jack

said, flicking his finger through them. 'He said before the war, when people were starving 'cos there weren't no jobs or owt, it seemed all wrong to him to see the priests dressed up in these when they came to Mass on Sunday morning. Price of them, he reckoned, would feed ten families for a year.'

Tony didn't doubt it. 'Don't you think you'd better shut the door now, Jack? If Father McIntyre comes back—'

'Aren't you one scaredy-cat, Tony Whittaker?' Jack said jeeringly. He shut the door, though, but opened the door on the other side. There was the bottle of Communion wine. The bottle had been opened ready to mix with water in the chalice at the Mass. 'D'you suppose it's real wine?' he said, withdrawing it from the cupboard.

'I don't know, but put the flipping thing back, Jack, before the pair of us are killed.'

'Like I said, you're a scaredy-cat.'

That jibe, issued for the second time in so many minutes, cut Tony to the quick. 'I ain't,' he said, 'but I just get punished much more than you if we do owt.'

'Prove you ain't scared then.'

'How?'

'Let's try some.'

'You're barmy.'

'And you're scared,' Jack said. 'I dare you. I'll do it first, if you like. He won't miss a few sips of wine, will he? He has a whole bottle.'

Tony thought that he would show Jack what

he was made of and he grabbed the bottle from Jack, put it to his mouth, took a couple of hefty swigs and began spluttering and gasping.

'Don't think you're supposed to neck it like that,' Jack said. 'And you have taken an awful lot. He's sure to notice.'

'Now who's scared,' Tony said, wiping his eyes with his sleeve.

'I ain't scared,' Jack declared, taking a hefty swig himself.

'God, Jack, there ain't that much left. What we going to do?'

''S all right, we'll fill it up with water,' Jack said. 'He mixes it with water, anyroad, so he won't even notice.'

'Come on then.'

'Not yet. We can have a bit more if we're going to fill the bottle up anyway. Let's have some more. It's good stuff, this, ain't it?'

Tony had actually never tasted anything so foul, but no way was he going to admit that, and he nodded his head vigorously and put his hand out for the bottle.

When Father McIntyre returned a little later he found two highly intoxicated altar boys in his vestry, and the bottle of Communion wine only a quarter full.

That evening, Marion wrote to Bill.

I told you about the incident with the water pistols, and Pat's reaction to it. Well, early this morning the boys did something far worse. While they were supposed to be serving at Mass, the priest was called out of the sacristy to deal with something and what did those two rips do but help themselves to the Communion wine. They drank so much that they were unable to serve at the Mass, or do anything else either. The pair were once again marched to our Polly's. Pat hadn't left for work and Father McIntyre told him that if he didn't thrash his son and Tony too, as you are away, then he would do the job himself. So he had to thrash them, for once. Honest to God, Bill, if we're not careful that son of ours will end up in Winson Green Prison. When you come home I want you to have a stern word with him.

Bill knew the boys had to be punished, but he was very glad that Pat had done the thrashing and not the priest. Father McIntyre would have seen it as his bounden duty to scourge the wickedness out of them. And yet he felt sorry that Marion had to deal with all this on her own. She did have her hands full and he could do little to ease it, but he did write a censorious letter to Tony, telling him that he was letting the family down and he had to behave himself. He only hoped that it might make a difference.

It did make a difference. Bill had never written to Tony in that way before, and Tony valued his good opinion, so he was determined to try to be good.

Marion was glad that he was behaving because she had so much more to worry about. She was forced to part with her wedding ring and Mary Ellen brought her one in Woolworths to replace it.

Now Marion was really worried because she had nothing else left to pawn. Soon she would need coal again and she didn't know how she was going to scrape the money together.

When she mentioned this to Polly she said, 'You must get your Tony doing what Chris and Colm had to do many a time.'

'What was that?' Marion asked.

'He'll have to go down the Saltley Gas Works real early in the morning . . .' Polly said.

'The carts the horses are pulling are laden down with coal,' Marion told Tony later. 'And when they come out the gate and speed up over the cobbles some of it falls off. You must go down with a bucket to collect it up and you must be there before seven in the morning.'

'Ah, Mom!' Tony cried. 'That's miles away.'

'Not at all,' Marion said briskly, though she felt for her younger son. 'If you go down Rocky Lane and along the canal it will take you no time at all.' Then seeing his disbelieving expression she said sharply, 'And you can take that look off your face because that is what you must do and that's all there is to it.'

When Tony related this to Jack at school that

morning he knew all about it. 'My brothers did that,' he said, 'but I never had to. Our Chris used to say that some kids took two buckets, one for the coal and one to collect the horse shit to use on their garden or allotment.'

'Ugh! That's disgusting!'

'Well, you ain't got to do that, anyway,' Jack said. 'D'you want me to come with you?'

'Would you?' Tony would be glad of his cousin's company in those inky black and dismal mornings.

'Course,' Jack said airily. 'Anyroad, two's better than one.'

'Won't your mom mind?' Tony asked.

'Course not,' Jack said confidently. 'Why would she mind?'

Tony could think of a hundred and one objections his mother might have made to such a plan, but Jack's parents were a different kettle of fish altogether. Tony didn't tell his mother of Jack's involvement, though.

From the first day Tony was glad that Jack was beside him. Jack was much bigger than Tony, for a start, and not so easily pushed around. That was important because there were loads of other boys at the same thing. By the time they set off home Jack always had more in his bucket than Tony did. Not far from the Whittaker house, Jack would tip the contents of his bucket into Tony's and he would take it home and tip it into the coal shed. Even with the two of them scavenging, he only had a meagre amount of coal, but he knew that every penny counted to his mother, and buying coal was an expensive business.

One morning, when Tony had been collecting the coal for a fortnight, he was full of misery when he met Jack.

Catching sight of his glowering face in the beam of the shielded torch he had thought to bring, Jack said, 'What's up with you? You have a face on you like a smacked bum.'

'There ain't nothing wrong,' Tony muttered.

'Don't give me that.'

'Well, what's the use of telling you owt anyway?' Tony said. 'It ain't as if you can do owt about it.'

'Well, I can't if you don't tell me.'

'All right then,' Tony burst out. 'Every day we stand here to collect a piddling bit of coal that does no good at all. When I come home from school, the house is always sort of cold and damp, and there's usually just a glow in the range, nearly buried under a heap of slack.'

'Well,' said Jack, 'we know where the coal's kept, so why don't we wait until it's dark, crawl under the fence and get ourselves a couple of bucketfuls?'

Tony was doubtful. 'Ain't that stealing?'

Jack considered the matter. 'It ain't any more stealing than picking up the lumps that fall off the carts when they clatter up the road. They fill them up too full on purpose so that some will fall off and we get to pick them up. This way we are sort of saving them the bother.'

The way Jack explained, it sounded fine to Tony. After all, there was so much coal in the gas works mound; he had seen it through the gate. Surely they wouldn't miss a little bit. Then Jack said, 'Let's see what we can get this morning anyway, and then tonight when everyone has gone to sleep we'll go for plan B. What time in your house does everyone go to bed, 'cos it would be best to keep this to ourselves?'

'About ten or so,' Tony said. 'I'm not really that sure because I'm usually asleep myself by then.'

'Better make it eleven, then, to be on the safe side,' Jack suggested. 'Meet me at the end of your road at eleven.'

'Yeah, all right.' Tony was hardly able to believe that he had agreed to sneak out of his home that night when everyone was asleep. It wasn't something that he had ever considered doing, in the whole of his life. He was scared stiff, but he couldn't bear to see the disdain in Jack's eyes if he said he couldn't do such a thing, so he knew he would be there with his bucket at eleven o'clock.

Two or three times that night Tony nearly nodded off. The early mornings were beginning to tell on him and he had to get out of bed and walk around the room. When Richard came to bed, however, he couldn't do that, and he curled in a ball and pretended to be asleep. He dared not shut his eyes, however, but kept them wide open and forced himself to lie still until Richard's even breathing told Tony he was asleep.

Still he lay there until he heard his mother's tread on the stairs. He was glad he did because she opened the door but, seeing everything was quiet, didn't go into the room. Tony counted to five hundred slowly, and then slid stealthily out of bed. He knew that he would be dressing in the dark and so he had left his clothes out on the chair by his side of the bed in a particular way and was dressing himself as quietly as possible when Richard turned over and said, 'Where you going?'

'Ssh,' Tony said frantically. 'You'll have Mom awake.'

'Oh, don't worry about that,' Richard said. 'I'll wake her all right if you don't tell what you're up to.'

Tony bit his lip. Jack said to tell no one. That was all right to say in his house, where no one seemed to give a tuppenny damn what anyone else was doing, but in his house it was a different matter and he knew if he refused to tell Richard he would fetch their mother, and the plan he and Jack had cooked up would be scuppered before it had even been tried.

So Tony said, 'I'm going to get some coal from the gas yard.'

'Tony, that's stealing.'

'No it ain't,' Tony cried. 'No more than standing there every bloody morning and fighting with every other bugger for any tiny bits that fall off the carts.'

'Shurrup,' Richard said. 'You told me quick enough. It's you that will have our mom awake, and she'll be armed with a cake of soap to wash out your mouth.'

'It's all right for you.' Tony went on, lowering his voice to a hissing whisper and ignoring the reference to the soap. 'You don't know what it's like, and even though Jack comes with me all we get is a piddling bit in the bottom of the perishing bucket.'

It was news to Richard that Jack had been going to the gas works gates every morning with his young brother, and now he had told him what he intended to do Richard didn't know what action to take. He knew really that he ought to go across the landing and tell his mother. What would they all do if he did that? Freeze to bloody death, that's what, and so he said to Tony, 'Are you doing this on your own?'

'No,' Tony said. 'Our Jack's going with us.'

Richard groaned silently. He might have known that it was one of Jack's harebrained notions. Tony hardly ever thought up things like this – he left that to Jack – but he was not averse to taking part in any mischief going. However, this was more than mere mischief, and yet with Jack involved the scheme might well work.

'All right,' Richard said at last. 'Try not to get caught, and if you are, remember I know nothing about any of it.'

Jack had done his work well. He had gone down

to the gas works as soon as he was out from school. It was becoming dark then and he'd been able to examine the perimeter fence and check where it was weakest and where they could not only wriggle underneath, but pull their buckets after them. He had still been there when the night watchman came and he had timed him for an hour until he knew his routine.

When he met his cousin Tony saw he had entered into the spirit of the enterprise and had coated his ruddy cheeks with coal dust. Even his tousled curls, which no barber had been able to tame, were jet black.

However, when under the light of a wavering torch he administered the same treatment to Tony with a nugget of coal he had brought with him, Tony's sandy hair showed up like a beacon.

'I should cover your hair with a hat or summat tomorrow night,' Jack said.

'Yeah, I can pinch one of the twins' berets,' Tony hissed.

'Good,' Jack said. 'Doesn't do to take chances. We don't want to be spotted by a wandering bobby.'

No, thought Tony, indeed we don't. He felt the dread that they might be caught trickling through his veins as he and Jack stole through the inky blackness, the cold seeping into them as they dared not go fast. They dared not go down the canal either, because there was nowhere to hide if they met anyone. They had to keep to the back roads where there were lots of entries they could duck into if they saw or heard anyone coming, though the courting couples were probably too interested in each other to notice two skulking boys.

The men returning from the pub were a different matter, especially if they decided to stand on a corner and talk. Tony willed them to go home as he felt his feet turn into blocks of ice and his hands tingle with the cold. Worse by far, though, were the bobbies on the beat. The boys could only be glad of their big boots ringing on the cobbles, which gave them valuable time to hide away.

Despite the hair-raising hike to the gas works, everything ran like clockwork that first night, and the next, and the next. Each time they had two near-full buckets of coal to tip into the shed, and Jack had to go all the way to the Whittakers' house because Tony could never have managed the load on his own.

On the fourth night sleety rain was falling as Tony slipped outside. It soon saturated his coat and soaked him to the skin, and his teeth began to chatter; Jack was little better. Although there were few people about, there were still policemen so Jack wouldn't allow them to hurry. If they got careless he said, that's when they would be caught.

Once home, Tony wouldn't allow himself to sleep properly because he knew he had to be up and out before his mother got up the next morning so that she wouldn't see the state of his clothes. It was the hardest thing in the world to get up in the dark of a winter morning and dress in sodden clothes and then go out into the cold. It was still raining, but that scarcely mattered.

When he got in that morning, though, Marion felt so guilty at the state of him. She had hot water for him to wash in and dry clothes laid out ready, and a big bowl of porridge, which he was allowed two spoons of sugar on, and some milk. Tony watched all the fuss his mother made of him and felt as guilty as hell.

He was also incredibly tired, for the late nights and early mornings were beginning to take their toll. Over the next few days he fell foul of his mother as he was so hard to rouse in the morning.

Every morning the boys made their own bed so Marion hadn't seen the state of the sheets until she went into the boys' bedroom to change them when Tony had been making his nocturnal journeys for ten days or so. She was appalled to see how dirty they were on Tony's side and couldn't remember him going to bed in that state. As she whipped the sheets off she vowed to make her son have a strip wash before he went up that night.

Just a few days after that in the Bull Ring she picked up a scrag end of lamb that could be the basis of a good, nourishing stew for the children. However, in those cold days, as she had to have the range on anyway for warmth, Marion had taken to cooking in the range oven to save on the gas. So that afternoon she went out to the coal shed to check if she had enough coal to feed the range sufficiently so the food would cook through. She hadn't been in the coal house for some days, for Tony or Richard were always only too willing to fetch her in a bucket of coal, but she knew there would be very little because Tony would only be able to collect a few nuggets each day.

She stood at the door and surveyed the level of coal in the shed with alarm. She knew that there was no way Tony could have collected that amount of coal if he had stood outside the gas works for a year or more. A feeling of dread began in her stomach and began to seep all over her because she knew there was only one way that he could have got so much.

When he came in from school she was waiting for him like an avenging angel.

Tony was no match for her. He was too tired, for he never allowed himself the slightest doze before he was out of bed and off to meet Jack. Then there was the fear of crawling under the wire, once they had established the watchman was nowhere to be seen, and then trying soundlessly to pull their buckets through behind them. Filling those buckets was painfully slow. It had to be done nugget by nugget, and then there was the hard slog back with the laden buckets. Tony would be nearly dropping with tiredness by then, and did little more than rub a rag over his hands and face before falling into bed and going straight into an exhausted sleep.

Marion could see the weariness in his black

smudged eyes standing out in his pale face, but she hardened her heart. 'Go round to your Auntie Polly's,' she told the chattering twins, who had come in with Tony. They stood and stared at her and she snapped, 'Go on, you heard what I said. I need to speak to your brother. Tell Polly that.'

There were so many questions the girls wanted to ask but they dared not, not when their mother spoke in that clipped sort of way. With a sympathetic glance at Tony, they did as they were told, and not totally unwillingly because they knew their Aunt Polly would likely give them both a jam piece or summat, and there was something very satisfying about a jam piece.

Tony wasn't thinking about jam pieces. He knew that somehow his mother had found out about the coal and he wondered if she was going to kill him stone dead because of it. He didn't deny anything, knowing that there was no point, though he did try to explain why he had done it.

This time Marion didn't beat her son. She was afraid rather than angry. She knew that this was how the slide into thieving began: justifying pinching coal because they were poor and needed it more than the Gas Board. She wondered how she could make her young son understand that what he had done was stealing plain and simple, and not only a sin to confess and repent of but against the law too. She felt as if a tight band was encircling her, and her face blanched in sudden fear that she was not up to the task of teaching her incorrigible son right from wrong. Tears seeped from beneath her eyelids and trickled down her face.

Tony felt absolutely dreadful that he had made his mother cry. It achieved what no beating had done, for it made him feel bitterly ashamed. He felt a sharp pain in his heart and tears welled in his own eyes as he put his arms around his mother and the two of them sobbed together.

At last Tony wiped the tears from his eyes with his sleeve and gave a sniff before crying brokenly, 'I'm sorry, Mom, really sorry. I will never do anything like this again, ever.'

Marion heard the sincerity in her young son's voice and she held him tight. 'Promise me, Tony?' she said.

Tony nodded vigorously. 'I promise, Mom.' Though he knew that it would be hard not to listen to and follow Jack, he wanted to make his mother proud of him and definitely didn't want her to be reduced to tears again because of anything he had done.

Marion went round to see her sister straight away when Tony told her Jack had been involved too, and though the twins were very curious as to why they had been sent to their aunt's house and were now to go home again, Marion refused to tell them.

Once the girls had gone, she lost no time in telling her sister what the boys had been up to. Polly called Jack in from the street and he freely admitted it and without an ounce of shame.

'You might think that there is nothing worrying in the fact that your son doesn't seem to know right from wrong,' Marion told her sister sharply. 'That's your concern and Pat's. My son has broken his heart in shame over it. I'll leave you to punish Jack as you see fit.'

Marion never laid a hand on Tony, but she did send him to bed without his tea. The others thought this punishment justified when they heard what Tony had been doing, though Richard was rather shamefaced about it. His father had asked him to keep an eye on Tony and he had failed to do that. He was impressed, however, that Tony had said nothing about him knowing all along.

Tony hadn't thought of it. He wasn't a sneak and it wouldn't have helped his case any. As it was, he lay on the bed, his stomach yawning in emptiness and his mouth watering at the smells floating up the stairs. He heard the family sitting down to a meal that he would have given his eyeteeth for and bitterly regretted what he had done.

EIGHT

Tony was back to collecting the coal that fell off the carts leaving the gas works, and on his own, so there was even less collected, but he didn't say a word about it. He had been so ashamed at making his mother cry that he would do all in his power to make sure it never happened again.

That thought was in his mind one dusky evening in early March when Jack suggested climbing up on one of the smallish factories near Aston Cross because he had heard the roof was made of glass and he wanted to look inside.

'Don't you want to see in?' he demanded, surprised by Tony's reticence.

'Yeah,' Tony said, 'course I do, but I'll really catch it if I don't go home soon.'

'Won't take you a minute.'

Tony shook his head firmly. 'Mom's warned me against climbing on the factory roofs. Yours has as well.'

Jack shrugged. 'So?'

'Our mom wouldn't like it if I did. She might get upset and that.'

Even in the dusky half-light Tony could see the derision on Jack's face. 'Oh, you mommy's boy,' he chortled. '"My mom wouldn't like it,"' he mimicked as he began to climb the walls. 'You stay there then, scaredy-cat.'

Tony felt humiliated and dreadfully hurt by his cousin's words as he watched him scale the walls.

'Hey,' Jack shouted from the roof minutes later. 'It's great up here and it is glass. Crikey, Tony, you don't know what you're missing.'

Tony jumped from one foot to the other. He so wanted to follow Jack and see the glass roof for himself that he wondered whether he should follow him after all. He'd never know if he would have done because at that moment there was a loud crack, the sound of glass breaking, then a blood-curling scream and then silence.

'Jack!' Tony cried desperately. 'Jack! Are you all right?'

There was no answer, no sound at all, and Tony felt fear for his cousin trail all down his back as he yelled again, 'Jack! Talk to me! Jack!'

When there was still nothing, Tony set off to get help, the sobs he hadn't even been aware of almost stopping his throat. He wanted his mother, but before he reached home, he ran almost full tilt into a policeman.

'Hold it, young man,' he said, holding Tony by the shoulders. 'What's your hurry?'

Tony was usually wary of policemen, but he was too worried about Jack to care about that now, and the words spilled one over the other as he tried to explain.

Then events moved fast. The policeman found someone who could force the factory door open and before he had quite done that ambulance bells could be heard. Someone had alerted Tony's mother and Auntie Polly and Uncle Pat, and they were all there to see the unconscious Jack carried out of the factory.

In the end he was lucky, for though he had been knocked unconscious he had missed the big machines, from which he might have sustained more serious injuries. He had only mild concussion, a couple of broken ribs and an arm broken in two places, and was considered a lucky boy.

'I'm glad,' Marion said to Tony later that night, 'that you were sensible enough not to follow Jack onto that roof.'

Tony was silent, and Marion asked, 'You didn't go, did you?'

'No, course I didn't,' Tony said. 'Jack asked me to, and took the mickey when I said no, but I didn't care. Anyroad, now I ain't the one with the sore head and busted arm.'

Marion was glad that Tony had defied Jack at last. She couldn't see the attraction that made Tony think Jack quite wonderful. In fact everyone liked Jack, except perhaps the girls who had the misfortune to sit in front of him in the classroom because he was a dab hand at undoing the bows on their dresses and tying them to the chairs. And if they wore their hair in long plaits, like the Whittaker twins, he took great delight in dipping the ends of their plaits into his inkwell.

Jack was fascinated by the ink that was made up each day with powder and water. It wasn't much good for writing with, but Jack would soak little bits of blotting paper in it and use a bendy ruler to propel it across the room to slap into some other child's unsuspecting cheek. He exasperated teachers, who broke rulers over his hand in an attempt to tame his rebellious spirit.

And that was something else. Jack was punished often and yet he never made a sound, nor did he flinch as the ruler would come down again and again, though the watching children, girls in particular, would wince for him and a shuddering sympathetic 'Ooh' would ripple through the class.

And when it was over, he would return to his chair without waving his hands about in an effort to cool them, nor did he tuck them under his arms for a measure of comfort. That earned him the respect of many of the lads, even the hard lads, and Tony would watch his fearless cousin with envy and wish he could be like him.

Jack returned to school after a few days with his ribs bound up and his arm in a plaster cast. Tony wondered how he was able to turn every situation to his advantage. He regaled the boys with tales of how he received his injury and the girls ran around him doing things for him. The worst of these girls was his own sister Magda.

Magda had always loved Jack. As the youngest in his family he had taken more of an interest in Magda and Missie than ever Tony had, amazed that they looked so alike. He was kinder than Tony too, in the main, and he teased them less. Sarah had always said he was a handsome boy and Magda supposed he probably was. She had certainly never seen a person with such dark eyes and hair. His skin was darkish too, except for his red cheeks, and his wide mouth had an upward lift to it as if he was constantly amused about something. He was seldom down about anything for long. Nothing would have pleased Magda more than to be allowed to trail after Jack and Tony, but she knew she would never have been allowed to do that.

One Saturday about a fortnight or so after Jack's accident, that longing got the better of her. Missie was in the house and Magda was bored to tears. Knowing Tony was off to meet Jack, she climbed over the wall after him, even though she was expressly forbidden to do that.

The two boys met at Aston Cross and she followed behind them stealthily as they made their way down Rocky Lane to the Cut. The sky was grey and miserable. It had been raining and there was still dampness in the air. Magda felt her boots slithering over the mud as she splashed her way through the puddles. The boys stopped suddenly on the towpath and she slipped behind a bush so they wouldn't spot her and send her home. She disturbed the raindrops caught in the leaves, and she felt a thorny twig rip the thick stockings her mother made her and Missie wear in the winter, and she gave a sigh of resignation. As she turned round to examine it, however, a straggly overhanging branch snatched the beret from her head, scattering Kirbigrips with gay abandon.

However, she had no time to worry about this because Jack was telling Tony something about her parents and she leaned forward to hear better.

'I tell you, our dad would never stand it,' she heard Jack say. 'I've heard him tell our mom.'

Tony, she could see, was mystified. 'What's wrong with having a bolster in the bed? It's only to put your head on, ain't it?'

'Course it ain't,' Jack said scornfully. 'Not where your mom puts it, anyroad. She has it down the middle of the bed, between them like.'

Tony shrugged, 'So what?'

'It's to stop them doing stuff.'

'What sort of stuff?'

'God blimey, Tony, don't you know nothing?' Jack exploded. 'It's to stop them doing IT. You know? Making babies and that.'

Tony had no idea where babies came from and nor had the avidly listening Magda. Magda thought babies were a gift from God, like the priest said, and although Tony knew there was more to it than that, he knew only that it was some secretive thing that happened in the bedroom that he would probably understand better when he was older.

'Do you really not know?' Jack asked incredulously, and when Tony shook his head he told him in a whisper that was quite loud enough for Magda to hear. Suddenly she ceased to mind about the blood seeping from the scratch on her leg and the hair wild about her face. What Jack was saying drove such concerns from her mind. Her eyes stood out in her head and her mouth dropped open and she wished she could stop herself listening because she was disgusted by the words coming from his mouth. She knew it was true – Jack never told lies – and she thought fiercely that there would be no need for a bolster in her bed once she was grown up. She would make sure that no man would get within a mile of her, just in case he should have such a crazy notion in his head.

'How d'you know all this?' Tony cried, leaping away from Jack.

Jack shrugged. 'Just do, that's all. And the bolster keeps them apart, see? Keeps them from touching. Your mom told my mom to do it after Mary Ellen was born. Dad let it slip one night when he was bottled. Mom never liked the idea and Dad said if she had tried that caper he would have thrown the sodding thing out the bleeding window, and her after it.'

Tony looked around nervously in case anyone was close enough to hear the swear words slipping so effortlessly from his cousin's lips and in the murky gloom he caught sight of Magda's eyes peering out from behind the bush. She tried to run but she was hampered by the bush and Tony was able to grab her easily.

'What are you doing spying on people?'

'I wasn't,' Magda replied with spirit. 'I have as much right to be here as you have, and you touch me, Tony Whittaker, and I'll tell our mom what you have been talking about.'

Jack laughed. 'You do that, Magda, and you'll be in far bigger trouble than we will.'

Magda knew that was true. They would be excused as the sort of thing boys talked about or some such thing so that they would escape any sort of censure, she guessed, but she would be in trouble for listening and not making her presence known sooner. Anyway, how could she tell her mother things like Jack had been saying, which made her feel a bit sick? She knew she would be in enough trouble as it was for leaving the garden alone and without permission. If her mother thought she had trailed after the boys it wouldn't help her case at all.

Jack saw her biting her lip in agitation and he said disdainfully, 'Go home, little girl, where you belong, and don't meddle with things you don't understand.'

Jack's scorn seared into Magda's very soul and made her flush crimson. With a baleful look at both of them she turned and ran.

*   *   *

While Magda had been trailing after the boys, Polly had been around to see Marion. In and around Aston there were lots of firms making things for the war effort, and with more and more men joining the services, the need for more women in the workforce was growing. Recruits had had to come from further afield, and young women had begun arriving in the city to take up some of the jobs.

Accommodation had not been found for these female workers and people were now taking them in as lodgers. The back-to-back houses hadn't usually enough space for the families that lived in them, but as soon as Polly heard about all these girls being drafted into the area she had gone round to tell her sister. As she said, Marion had a fine big house that could put up a few girls with ease.

Marion had listened to Polly's enthusiasm but she herself was not at all sure that she wanted lodgers. But when she said this, Polly said, 'All right then, what's the alternative if you want you and the kids to survive through the winter?'

Marion bit her lip because she knew that really there was no alternative. 'But how do I know that anyone would come?'

'Are you kidding?' Polly cried. 'They've got to live somewhere. Pat said most employers have lists of places offering accommodation. He feels sorry for the young girls who have never left home before, and these days that seems to mean the majority of them. Pat can take your details into the munitions works, and Jack and Tony can run your address round all the other places.'

'But where would these girls sleep?' Marion asked.

'Well, I'd put them in your lads' room and they could bed down in the parlour. They would only need somewhere to put their things.'

'But, Polly, I haven't got money for extra beds or bedding or anything else – you know that. It takes me all my time to make ends meet, and even they don't always meet very well because I haven't been able to pay the rent for two weeks now.'

'Listen to me,' Polly said. 'These girls will be getting good money, because all war-related work is well paid, so you can charge a decent amount in rent for staying in a place like this. You'll be doing them a favour and they'll be doing you one. But to get started you'll need to borrow some money from me, and don't bloody well shake your head before I've finished.'

'You know how I feel about—'

'It's a loan, I said,' Polly insisted. 'And a loan I meant. God Almighty, Marion,' she added with a ghost of a smile, 'I'll even charge you bleeding interest if it makes you feel better.'

'What if I can't pay it back?'

'Why are you such a bloody pessimist?' Polly said. 'Look, we can go down the Bull Ring tonight. We'll likely get the stuff cheaper there, anyroad, and set this in action straight away.'

'All right,' Marion said at last. 'God, I wonder what the kids will say.'

'Where are they?'

'God knows where Tony is,' Marion said. 'Richard has got hold of some orange boxes and he's breaking them up in the yard. Missie is helping him. Magda was supposed to stay in the garden with Missie, but she slipped out when Missie came inside for something.' Marion frowned heavily. 'I'll have something to say to her when she does come in. I'll not have her running the streets.'

'She'll come to no harm.'

'That's not the point,' Marion said, tight-lipped. 'I understand that it's hard for the pair of them with Bill not here to take them out and about, but they have to put up with it. Magda said the other day she was bored. God, I sometimes wish I had the time to be bored.'

Polly felt sorry for her nieces penned in the garden. No wonder Magda wanted to be out on the streets playing with the other children. Missie probably wanted to go too, but Magda was more rebellious than her sister. But Polly said nothing about it because she didn't want to start an argument with Marion. Instead she said, 'And where's Sarah?'

'Sarah's in the kitchen having the meal I left for her. She isn't in from work long,' Marion said.

'She's late, isn't she? It's going on for three now.'

'She's often late coming home on Saturdays,' Marion said. 'She's only supposed to work till lunchtime, and that's all she gets paid for, but as soon as she's ready to go, that Jenkins woman finds her lots of other jobs to do. She gets right cheesed off and . . .'

But whatever else she was going to say was forgotten because just at that moment Magda made her untimely entrance and both women stared at her as if they couldn't believe their eyes.

Marion was filled with fury. She leaped to her feet and took Magda by the shoulders. 'Look at the state of you,' she cried, shaking her violently. 'You're like a child a tinker would be ashamed to own. What in God's name have you been doing running the streets like some little hoyden?'

Magda didn't know what a hoyden was but it didn't sound a very nice thing to be.

Still holding her by the shoulders, Marion held her away from her. 'You have a rip in your skirt and yet another hole in your stockings,' she said angrily. 'Clothes don't grow on trees, you know. You're covered in mud and your hair is one unholy mess. God, Magda, as if I haven't enough to worry about. And where the hell is your beret?'

Magda knew that it was probably still hanging on the overhanging bush down by the canal. She had forgotten all about it as she listened to Jack telling Tony things so shocking she could scarcely believe her very straight and respectable mother agreeing to any of it. Suddenly the events of that day, the disturbing things she had heard, Jack's scorn, her mother's anger and the fact that the scratch on her leg had begun to throb and sting, were all too much for her to bear and she burst into tears.

'Marion, give the kid a break, for God's sake?' Polly said. 'Mine have come home in that state or worse many a time.'

Marion released her daughter, almost pushing her away, and Sarah, who came in at that moment, looked from her still raging mother to her distressed sister and said, 'What's up?'

'Oh, I'll tell you all later,' Marion said. 'Just for now, can you do something with this little tramp?' She pushed Magda in Sarah's direction. 'Keep her out of my sight for now or I'll not be responsible for my actions.'

Sarah put out her hand. 'Come on,' she said to Magda. 'I'll see what I can do about cleaning you up.'

Magda was glad to get away from her mother. Sarah lifted her up beside the sink, washed her and tended the deep scratch on her leg. 'You really are in the wars,' she said. 'Where did you get that?'

'Don't tell Mom?'

'What d'you take me for?'

'I went up the Cut and scratched myself on a thorn bush.'

'On your own?'

Magda nodded slowly. She wasn't going to mention either of the boys and she knew they wouldn't say anything either.

'Oh, Magda,' Sarah said, 'you do ask for it, you know. That alone would put Mom in a tear, and then to come home in this state. Oh, don't start crying again,' she said as she saw tears seeping under Magda's lashes. 'I'll have you as right as rain in no time . . .'

In the room, as soon as the door closed behind Magda and Sarah, Marion said, 'Magda is always such a mess and she doesn't seem to care.'

'She's just a child.'

'She's a girl,' Marion corrected, 'not some hooligan boy. And then to run through the streets like that. I mean, I wonder what the neighbours made of it. I would hate them to think I'd let her out looking like that.'

Polly laughed. 'You care too much what the neighbours think. Who the bloody hell cares in the end? And your Magda will grow up and become respectable soon enough. Anyroad, ain't we got more important things to discuss if you're going to take in lodgers?'

'Lodgers?' Tony exclaimed later that day as the family sat eating a meagre meal. 'Where the blooming heck are we going to put lodgers?'

'In the room you share with Richard now,' Marion said.

'So where're we going to sleep?' Tony asked. 'In the yard outside?'

'You well might if I have any more of your lip,' Marion commented grimly. 'But my intention was that you and Richard will sleep in the parlour. There's plenty of room if we move things around a bit.'

'Are you moving the bed down or are we

sleeping on a mattress on the floor?' Richard asked.

'Oh, I think for any long-term solution you will need the bed down,' Marion said. 'Polly is loaning me the money to get the things I'll need. I'll clear out one of the sideboard cupboards for you to put your clothes in, and anything else – like your suit, Richard – you'll have to hang in my wardrobe.'

Richard nodded. 'That'll be all right. One room is much the same as another to me, but where will we get the lodgers from?'

'Oh, that's easy,' Marion said. 'Women and girls are being drafted in from all over to work in the industries and factories round here, according to Polly. As soon as I have the room ready I will start advertising.'

Richard knew his mother was right about the female workforce. In the brass foundry, as soon as one man was called up, there was a woman to take his place. It had always been a male-dominated industry, but it couldn't be that any longer. He had doubted before the war that women could do the some of the jobs. The heat from the white-hot furnaces was tremendous, and he'd been so exhausted when he begun the work that he could barely put one foot in front of the other in the evening as he and his father made their way home. And though his innards might be growling with hunger, first he had to wash and change his shirt, which was always damp with sweat. He always appreciated the fact that his mother had hot water ready for him and a dry shirt to hand.

Richard's idealised vision of women being wives and mothers was being turned completely on its head, for the women in the brass foundry had donned the overalls, bundled their hair under a scarf worn turban-style, and got on with the job. He had to admit they did it very well.

It was odd now to see a male conductor on the tram or bus. He had even seen women driving them, and also delivery vans and lorries. He remembered his mother telling him that the last lot of coal they'd bought had been delivered by the wife of the coalman after her husband had been called up. It seemed there was nothing a woman couldn't do any more.

Later that night, as they lay in bed, Magda said, 'I don't know whether I will like lodgers in the house.'

'You like to eat, don't you?' Sarah said.

'Course I do,' Magda said. 'I would often like to eat more than Mom gives me.'

'Well,' said Sarah. 'The way I can see it, we won't even get the little we're having now without lodgers.'

'Is it sort of like it or lump it?' Missie said. 'Seems like there's a lot of that in this war.'

Sarah laughed. 'That seems the way of it all right,' she said. 'I would say that you have hit the nail on the head there, Missie.'

NINE

The following afternoon Marion and Polly were moving the things around in the parlour to make room for the boys' bed when Clara and Eddie made a surprise visit. Marion, knowing that her mother would hardly approve of her decision, had not mentioned a word about taking in lodgers that morning when she had seen her at Mass, and so her heart sank when she caught sight of Clara's discontented face.

'Hello, Mammy, Daddy,' she said nervously. 'This is a surprise.'

'Shock, more like,' Clara snapped peevishly. 'I had to see for myself. I could hardly believe my ears when Beattie Roberts, her next door, told me about you thinking about taking lodgers in. You out of your tiny mind, or what?'

'No,' Marion answered mildly. 'I don't think so.'

'You're having perfect strangers living in your house that you know nowt about, and you a mother as well,' Clara went on. 'You have responsibilities to your kids. And where the hell you going to put lodgers anyroad?'

'In the room Richard and Tony share now,' Marion explained. 'The boys will sleep in the parlour. We're rearranging everything now so that we can get the beds in.'

'And how do they feel about that?' Clara demanded.

'They said that they didn't mind where they sleep,' Marion said. 'Though they do mind being hungry and cold all the time. None of us is keen on that.' She faced her mother and, though her knees were quaking, her voice was resolute enough as she said, 'You reminded me that I'm a mother, that I have responsibilities to my children and that means that I must care for them the best I can. At the moment taking in lodgers seems the way to do that, and we all understand this.'

'I bet that this was all your idea?' Clara snapped at Polly.

But before Polly could speak, Marion said, 'Polly didn't have to tell me. Many are doing the same thing as me at the moment. These girls arriving in Birmingham to work have got to live somewhere.'

'And what does Bill say about it?'

'I haven't had a chance to tell Bill anything yet,' Marion admitted.

'One of the bosses told Pat that he heard there is a law coming in,' Polly said. 'Every woman will have to do summat whether they like it or not.'

'They can't force women to work,' Clara said. 'I've never heard of such nonsense.'

'Course they can,' Polly said to her mother. 'We're at war, in case it's escaped your notice. With the men called up the women will have to set to and do the jobs the men did, as well as make uniforms, guns and ammunition and so on.'

'Polly's right,' Marion said to her parents. 'Anyroad, all Polly did was offer to help me.'

'I see that,' Clara snapped. 'Does a day of rest mean nothing to you?'

Marion laughed. 'Sunday, a day of rest! I worked harder on that day than any other before the war. There used to be a big breakfast after Mass and then a bigger dinner, and both before dinner and after it I would be cooking cakes and pastries and tarts, and all for the Sunday teas you used to enjoy. I didn't magic them out of the air, and yet you never seemed to mind me doing that.'

'Marion has a point,' Eddie said. 'I often remarked on how hard she must have worked, for there was always plenty on the table.'

'That was different.'

'I don't see it,' Marion said. 'But I really haven't time to argue with you. The room the lads had will need a good clean before I could put anyone else in it, so I need to get the parlour sorted so they can sleep in there. Me and Polly went down the Bull Ring last night and ordered new beds, and they're coming tomorrow.'

'And where, pray, did you get the money for all that?'

Marion wished she could tell her mother that it was none of her business. It had surprised her that her mother had never offered her a penny piece, however hard up she had been, and yet her father was still in employment. She knew she hadn't lifted a finger to help Polly over the years either.

'Polly loaned me the money, and I'll pay her back as soon as I can,' she said, looking her mother in the eye.

'And what if you've gone to all this trouble and expense and no lodgers come?'

'That's looking on the black side of things, Mammy,' Marion replied. 'I think they will.'

'We're not waiting on the money, anyway,' Polly said. 'We have plenty now and set to have more because Mary Ellen is going to work in the munitions with Pat after Easter. She'll be sixteen then.'

Marion gasped and stared at Polly as if she couldn't believe what she had heard, and even Clara was stunned into silence. In the end Marion said, 'Oh, Polly, isn't that very dangerous work?'

'Maybe,' Polly said. 'Probably that's why it's so well paid.'

'But won't you worry about her?'

'Course I will,' Polly said. 'But that will be nothing new. Don't we worry about them all every minute of the day anyway? Part and parcel of being a mother, that is, ain't it?'

'I think the whole thing is a monstrous idea,' Clara burst out. 'What kind of mother are you anyroad to allow your daughter to work in such a dangerous industry?'

'The kind of mother with a daughter who wants to do this,' Polly said heatedly. 'She's not a fool and she knows the dangers, but she also knows that later this year her eldest brother will get his call-up papers, and Colm the year after. They'll both be putting their lives on the line, as Bill is now. How safe will they be then? In fact, if we get raids from the air, like everyone says we will, how safe will any of us be? After all, Pat's been there this good while now, and nothing has happened to him, and he'll see Mary Ellen is all right as well.'

'So it seems that it's all signed and sealed then?' Clara said, her eyes glittering with malice as they caught Polly's.

Polly her mother's gaze defiantly. 'Yeah, near enough.'

Marion thought the antagonism between them could almost be felt. She sighed inwardly and then, placatory as always, she said, 'Look, I really am busy, as I said, but we both have time for a quick cup of tea. Shall I put the kettle on?'

Eddie looked as if he was about to accept, but Clara forestalled him. 'We haven't come to drink tea,' she said, getting to her feet. 'I came to try and dissuade you from this stupid idea, but I see that it's too late for that because you seem to have already decided it between you. So I'll leave you to get on with it, Sunday or not. Come along, Eddie.'

'Daddy shouldn't let her get away with talking to him like that,' Polly said as the door slammed behind her parents. 'Pat said that he doesn't know how he has put up with it all these years. And she's crackers as well. She was all for you giving up this lodgers idea, but she hadn't a plan of action to put in its place.'

'Oh, let's stop talking about them,' Marion said. 'It just depresses me. Let's finish off that parlour and make the boys' old room like a little palace for all these potential lodgers.'

Less than a week later, Marion opened the door to two girls who said they were looking for a room. They introduced themselves as Peggy Wagstaffe and Violet Clooney. Marion thought Violet looked about twelve, with her chubby face, blonde hair and blue eyes, despite the fact that her hair was caught up in a bun at the nape of her neck. Peggy wore her dark brown hair the same way, but she was older and far more self-assured. Her brown eyes were open and clear, and Marion felt herself relax. She wouldn't mind either girl living in her house.

Marion and Polly had worked hard on the bedroom and Marion was pleased that even the lino didn't look that bad after a good clean. Polly had brought along a blue rug she said she was fed up of and had set it down between the two brand-new beds made up with the sheets and blankets from the Bull Ring. She saw by the girls' eyes that they were impressed. But she left them to talk it over while she waited downstairs.

'So what do you think?' Violet asked Peggy, a smile playing around her lips and her eyes shining.

'I think we've fell right on our feet, that's what I think,' Peggy said. 'Even the road this house is on is a pleasant one.' She crossed to the window and looked through the net curtains. 'And there's a lovely little garden out the back.'

'Oh, yes,' Violet said, joining her. She spun round as she exclaimed, 'I think the whole place is lovely and we have a bed each! In that other place they expected us to share.'

'Yeah, and the sheets were decidedly grey,' Peggy said. Turning from the window she folded back the sheets on the two beds and nodded approvingly. 'These are spotlessly clean.'

'Yeah, and there wasn't much storage for our clothes either, and it was the same price as this place,' Violet said. 'While here we have a large chest of drawers, a wardrobe to share, and I love that rug. I cannot abide putting my feet on cold lino first thing in the morning.'

'And best of all is the inside toilet and proper bathroom,' Peggy said. 'Height of luxury, that is.'

'So we'll take it then?'

'Think we'd be mad not to,' Peggy said. 'I don't think we'll get better. Let's go and tell the woman and then we can go back to the Buckinghams and give our notice.'

Marion was delighted when the girls said that they would take the room and felt the knot of worry in her stomach ease a little, for she knew with the fifteen shillings they would each give her every week she would be able to manage much better. However, though she had an initial good first impression of the girls, she wanted to know something about them.

They understood that perfectly and told her of their families in a little village called Rugeley, which was some way from Aston. 'It's a pretty isolated place,' Peggy said. 'To get there from here you would need to get a train from Aston station as far as Lichfield, and then a bus out to the village. Our place is at the end of a lane.'

'And the bus runs only three times a day,' Violet put in.

'Yes, and so virtually the only chance of a job there was at the one of the big houses in the area. We worked at Birchenfield House, owned by Lord and Lady Buckingham. Still do, of course, until we go back and give our notice. We've been set on at Tube Investments. Marion looked at the two young women before her, little more than girls. 'But why did you choose work in Tube Investments? That's a drop forge. Did you know that?'

'Oh, yes,' Peggy said. 'The man who came around recruiting people told us that, and he also said they needed more people there. There was munitions work as well, but I'd given my word to my mother that I wouldn't do that.' And then, at Marion's raised eyebrows, she went on, 'My mother's younger sister, Dolly, did it in the last war. Mom said that she was tempted herself but my elder brother, Sam, was a handful and I was only a baby, and we were too much for our grandmother to handle and so Mom had to stay behind and look after us. She told us that after only a little time, Dolly's skin went all yellow and her hair went all coarse and turned a sort of red colour, and she had a permanent cough. After the war she married, but never had any children and died before she was thirty, poisoned, Mom always said, by the sulphur. I said it was probably different now, but she wouldn't hear of me working somewhere like that.'

Marion thought of her niece Mary Ellen, who would be involved in that dangerous work very soon and she gave an involuntary shiver. 'I do understand that, but neither of you will have done any work in a drop forge before, I'm sure.'

'No, of course not,' Peggy said. 'But these days lots of people are doing things that they have no experience of.'

Marion couldn't disagree with that.

'I suppose we can learn as well as the next person,' Peggy continued. 'And neither of us is a stranger to hard work.'

Marion saw the determination in the two girls' faces and acknowledged that they certainly looked robust enough. Even Violet, despite her diminutive stature, didn't cut a frail, delicate figure. But Marion did hope that they hadn't bitten off more than they could chew, not least because she liked the girls and she also thought they would fit in well to her household.

'So when do you intend moving in?' Marion asked.

'Well, the man we saw at Tube Investments was keen for us to start as soon as possible,' Peggy said. 'It all hinged really on whether we were able to find somewhere nearby to stay. We said that we would call back and tell him as soon as we found somewhere suitable. Then we have to give notice, of course. It should be a month, but for war work these things are waived, and it's a particularly early Easter this year.'

'Yes,' Marion agreed, 'a week today is Good Friday.'

'Right, so what if we leave the Buckinghams at Easter, move in here Easter Monday and start at the drop forge on the Tuesday?' Peggy said. 'How does that suit?'

'That suits just perfectly,' Marion said.

Marion had loved her time in service and so she said, 'Will you miss your old lives?'

'Not likely we won't,' Peggy said fiercely. 'I've had my fill of bobbing my knee and kowtowing to people who think they're better than me because they have money.'

'And me,' Violet said. 'One of my jobs was to

162

light the fires in the rooms, and I would always fill up the coal scuttles before I left. Yet when the fires burned low the family would ring the bell for me to go and see to it. Not one of them seemingly was capable of putting coal on the fire, and yet the tongs were there for them to use.'

'Oh, aye,' Peggy said. 'That's what they were like.'

'Do they know that you're after war work?'

Peggy nodded. 'We told them, but they knew anyroad because a man came round trying to recruit people, and my brother, Sam, and most young men his age in the village are already in the army.'

'My husband is in the thick of it as well,' Marion said.

'That why you're taking lodgers in?'

'Yes,' Marion said. Though she seldom discussed her finances outside of the family she found herself saying, 'Before the war my Bill worked in the brass industry. Birmingham is famous for its brass and he earned a good wage. It was a shock to me to manage on the little amount the army pays.' She gave a smile. 'I always find that there's too much week at the end of the money.'

Peggy and Violet laughed. 'My mother finds the same, I think,' Peggy said. 'My dad was crippled in the last war, see. He nearly lost his foot but though they saved it, he has to have his shoe built up and still walks with a pronounced limp, so we knew he wouldn't be called up.'

'Have you a farm?'

Peggy shook her head. 'A farm is too grand a name for it,' she said. 'I'd call it a smallholding. We have a few hens, two big fat sows and a host of piglets, and a few cows. Dad missed Sam when he enlisted because his leg is often painful.'

'Yes,' said Marion. 'I'm sure your brother was a great help to him.'

'He was,' Peggy said. 'Though my younger brother, Peter, is no slouch, but he is only twelve yet and so has another two years at school. Sam will be virtually running the place, I should imagine, when the war is over.' She paused and added softly, 'That's, of course, if he survives.'

'Ooh, don't say that,' said Violet.

'Got to be faced,' Peggy said, and gave a rueful smile. 'But I know it will break my heart if anything does happen to him.'

She gave a sudden shiver and Marion knew just how she felt. She tried to lighten the mood a little. 'Violet's right,' she said. 'Dwelling on things that may not happen does no good at all, so let's not even think of it.' Turning to Violet she said. 'Do you have a similar setup to Peggy's?'

'Yes,' Violet said. 'But ours isn't so big. My dad also fought in the last war, and he was gassed. His breathing sounds like a steam engine sometimes and a lot of the work falls to my mother or my brothers when Dad has a bad spell. That's why it was so hard for them when Mom was ill with pleurisy last year. She does most of the digging, see.'

'So you are able to grow your own vegetables as well?'

'Yes, but there's other free food about in the country,' Violet said. 'Like rabbits. Your dad traps them, don't he, Peggy? He's brought a few to us. Dad was sure it was the good food that pulled Mom round.'

'But a lot of bartering goes on,' Peggy said. 'You swap anything for what you haven't got and sell any surplus at the market, and the butchers are always glad of the rabbits. We have an orchard too, so we can also swap or sell apples, pears and plums. Of course, when a pig is slaughtered by any farmer, the meat is shared around our neighbours.'

'Oh, Peggy, you're making my mouth water,' Marion cried. 'What I wouldn't give for a bacon sandwich right now.'

Both girls laughed and Marion said, 'I'm really surprised, as you're both country girls, you didn't opt for the Land Army.'

'Our mothers would have preferred us to do that,' Violet admitted. 'They thought it meant that we'd be nearer home, but there's no guarantee of that. They could send you anywhere.'

'And you didn't fancy it anyway?'

The girls shook their heads emphatically. 'We wouldn't be any better off and might have been worse,' Peggy said. 'The village is surrounded by farmland and so we know many of the big farmers – those with farms big enough to need to hire staff, at any rate. Some of the wealthier ones were sometimes asked to dinner at the Buckinghams' and we would wait on them and hear them talking. Most of them seemed to have little time for the Land Girls they claimed were being forced on them, and no intention of having the girls sleep in the house, but thought a draughty barn quite adequate.'

'We thought them in the same mould as the Buckinghams,' Violet put in. 'All posh and stuck up, and we knew they would treat us like dirt – and the wages were rubbish as well.'

'Yeah, they were,' Peggy agreed. 'Anyroad, we wanted to see somewhere other than our village, and try a different kind of work.'

'But won't your parents worry about you living so far away from home?' Marion said.

'Not really,' Peggy said. 'In service we had to live away from home anyway. I mean, our houses were close and all that, but we still had only the same time off as anyone else.'

'Yes, but that's different somehow,' Marion said. 'You are looked after, in a way, by the housekeeper, or perhaps the cook if you worked in the kitchen.'

'Watched over, more like,' Peggy muttered resentfully, 'to see if we were enjoying ourselves too much or, Heaven forbid, if any of us met a boy we liked because we weren't allowed followers.'

'Yeah, like they wanted to control all of our lives,' Violet said. 'How were we ever to make a lives of our own, living in a place like that? My parents are used to me not being there now because I haven't lived at home since I was fourteen.'

'I don't wish to be rude,' Marion said tentatively, 'but to me you don't look much older than that now.'

Violet sighed. 'I know. I can't help how I look, and I know that I'm not very big, but I am turned seventeen.'

'Even so . . .'

'Her mom made me promise to look out for her,' Peggy said. 'And I am twenty, and sensible enough,' she added with a twinkle in her eye, 'when I need to be.'

Her comment brought a wry laugh from Violet and Marion, but still Marion wondered if the girls realised exactly what they were taking on. One of Polly's neighbours, being declared unfit for the army, had taken a job at the forge and he told Polly when the ovens were opened it was like Dante's inferno, whatever the hell that was, and the noise was indescribable. Marion could only imagine it, but she did know that when the huge hammers dropped anyone standing in Lichfield Road would feel the vibration under their feet.

The children were agog with questions about the new lodgers they would soon have living in the house. 'If we're having lodgers will I still have to go and get coal every morning?' Tony asked.

'No you won't, Tony,' Marion told him, and saw the relieved smile steal over his face. 'And I will no longer be beholden to the Christmas Tree Fund and will be able to buy you clothes myself. So it's good news all round.'

Polly, who popped in later, also wanted to know all about Marion's lodgers, what they looked like, where they came from. She couldn't understand either why they had chosen to work in a drop forge.

'These girls' families have small farms out in the country and it seems a completely different world from ours,' Marion told her.

'Then God help them, that's all I can say,' Polly said. 'They'll likely not stick it.'

'I hope they do, Poll,' Marion said. 'I badly need the money.'

'I know you do. But don't worry. If it don't work out for them there, I'll have Pat put in a word for them at the munitions.'

'That won't do no good,' Marion said. 'Peggy promised her mom she wouldn't work in a munitions factory.' She recounted the tale that Peggy had told her about her aunt. 'Doesn't that worry you, Poll?' she asked as she finished.

'No,' Polly said, and then added more truthfully, 'Well, I suppose a bit, but Pat said things are different now from the conditions in the Great War. He said then there were explosions, and people say that it sometimes stopped women conceiving, although facts like that weren't made public, like. Imagine the outcry if they had been?'

'Well, how do you know that things are much better now?'

'Marion, it was over twenty years ago,' Polly said. 'Name me one thing that has stayed the same for twenty years?'

'Yes, but . . .'

'They will have learned summat from making them munitions in that first lot,' Polly said. 'And this time around they have factory inspectors and everything, to make sure all the rules are obeyed. It's safe as houses now compared to what it was, and I know that our Mary Ellen would prefer it to work in a drop forge any day of the week.'

'I can't say I blame her one bit,' Marion said. 'Even the sound of those drop hammers sends chills running down my spine. Let's hope that Peggy Wagstaffe and Violet Clooney are tougher than me.'

TEN

Peggy and Violet found the work in the forge harder than anything they had ever done in their lives, but they made a pact not to complain about it at the Whittakers'. They had made the choice to go into the forge of their own free will and therefore they thought they had no right to moan. But Marion guessed they were finding it hard because she had seen the exhaustion on their faces.

But it wasn't just the work that was so unnerving, it was everything. In their sleepy little village they had never seen so many people, nor so much traffic nor such a vast array of shops, and that took a bit of getting used to.

'Didn't you notice the crowds that day you came to look at the room?' Marion asked.

'Yeah, we did,' Peggy said, 'but we just thought it looked exciting then. I mean, we chose somewhere that was as unlike home as possible, but it's different when you live in a place.'

'Yeah,' Violet added. 'It's the smell of the place too, and that's all mixed together with the things made in the factories, particularly around here, where so much is made.'

'Beer, sauce and custard, to name just three,' Peggy agreed. 'That's what makes it such a vibrant place, of course.'

'The country is all well and good, but not much is happening,' Violet explained. 'We love it here now, but crikey, the first time I went on a tram I was sure that it was going to jump off the rails and we would all be killed.'

Marion laughed. 'Yes, I can see exactly what you mean.'

'Now we never give getting on a tram a second's thought, and as for the work in the forge, well, I'm sure we will get into the swing of that too eventually.'

'It's happening already,' Violet said. 'We're not half as tired as we used to be when we come home in the evening.'

Marion had to agree with that. She had immense respect for both girls, and it was just amazing how well they had settled into the family, considering they had been there not quite three weeks.

Just a couple of days later Sarah, meeting her grandmother outside the church one Sunday morning, let slip about the lodgers working at the drop forge. Marion hadn't told any of them to keep what work the lodgers did a secret, though she had not told her mother for she knew that

Clara would think it a totally unsuitable place for two young girls to work.

Sarah quickly realised her mistake as she watched her grandmother go puce in the face and begin exclaiming so loudly about the couple of guttersnipes her daughter had taken to live in her house that many stopped and stared, including the priest, who was in the porch. Sarah, mortified with shame, left her grandfather remonstrating with his wife and slipped into the pew beside her mother. She told her what had happened.

'Sorry,' she whispered. 'I just didn't think.'

'Don't worry,' Marion whispered back. 'I had thought that with the girls at work all week and Sunday teas being a thing of the past, they might never need to meet my mother, or at least not very often. I did explain to Peggy and Violet just the other day that my mother was very old-fashioned and didn't really approve of women taking over many traditionally male occupations, but really this had to come out sooner or later. After all, Peggy and Violet are doing nothing they have to be ashamed of. That being said, I don't want a scene outside church so we will all slip away in the last hymn.'

She knew, though, that her mother never let things drop and was heartily glad she had said something to the girls when she saw Clara come in the back gate, just as the family were finishing their bowls of porridge. Marion and Sarah exchanged looks across the table and Marion gave an inward sigh. She guessed Clara was here to finish the tirade begun before Mass and, because she had come alone, that her father had not approved of what she was doing.

However, the two girls stood up as Clara came in and Peggy turned to face her with a smile on her face and her hand outstretched as Marion said, 'Mammy, these are the two girls I told you about, Peggy and Violet.'

Clara ignored her daughter's words and Peggy's hand. She glared at them both with a face that Peggy maintained later would have soured cream, and almost hissed, 'I'll have you know that this was once a respectable home.'

Peggy dropped her hand and said mildly, 'Yes, I know that. That's one of the reasons we chose to stay here.'

Clara was outraged. 'You have the effrontery to . . . Don't you realise that your presence here has tainted that respectability?' she almost snarled.

'Just how do you work that out?' Peggy asked in a reasonable tone.

'Because you are two sluts, for only sluts would work in a drop forge, of all places,' Clara said. 'You are not wanted here so the sooner you go back where you came from, the better it will be for everybody.'

Sarah wanted to floor to open up and swallow her, and Marion gasped at her mother's insults. But she was angry too and she burst out, 'Just a minute. In case it escapes your notice, this is my house and I say who stays here and who doesn't. And just now, and for as long as it takes, Peggy and Violet are more than welcome. I will thank you to keep your nose out of my affairs.'

'I'm telling you they will corrupt your children.'

'Don't be ridiculous!' Marion snapped. 'They will do no such thing. And now if you have said your piece and thoroughly upset and insulted everyone, it would be better if you left.'

'I'll go when I am good and ready.'

Richard knew it was up to him. It was what his father would have done and so he stepped forward and said, 'No you won't, Grandma. As Mom said, this is her house and just now she doesn't want you in it.'

Marion was astounded and yet very grateful to her son, but her mother, she saw, was even more amazed. Her malicious eyes raked round them all, from the nervous younger children to Sarah, her face red with shame, and Richard, with the steely glint in his eyes that she had never noticed before, and finally rested on her daughter. 'On your own head be it then,' she snapped. 'I think I will write to Bill and tell him what's going on under his roof.' And with this parting shot she swept from the room.

'Phew!' Tony said with feeling, and Marion hadn't the heart to chide him because she felt much the same.

'Will she do that?' Peggy said to Marion. 'Write to your husband, I mean.'

'I've given up trying to work out what she might do next,' Marion said. 'She may write to Bill, but she'll be wasting her time because I've already written and told him all about you and Violet, and where you're working. In contrast to my mother he has nothing but praise for the two of you because he knows the hard, though essential, work you will be doing working in a drop forge. But after that little upset it wouldn't surprise me if you intend to look for other lodgings straight away.'

'Oh, don't be daft,' Peggy said. 'As if we would let ourselves be pushed out by one sad and embittered old woman. Anyroad, that's how I feel. How about you, Vi?'

'I agree with you,' Violet said. 'But, Marion, as you said, it is your house and if you would like us to go—'

'Oh, no!' Marion cried. 'No I don't, not at all, but at the very least, you deserve some sort of explanation as to why my mother behaves the way she does . . .'

Marion explained about Clara's life and how many of her siblings had died, and then about the death of Michael on one of the coffin ships en route to America.

'His death, more than any of the others, seemed to break my mother up completely,' she said. 'To tell you the truth I often felt the lack of a mother because mine has always been so linked to the past and those she had lost.'

175

'I never knew you felt that way, Mom,' Sarah said. 'You never said.'

'There wasn't any point to saying anything, was there?' Marion said. 'It would have changed nothing.'

'I know exactly how you felt,' Peggy said. 'Our family had something similar. My mother had a little boy stillborn when I was not quite two years old and my elder brother, Sam, was four. My mother said the doctor warned her not to try for a baby too soon, to give her body time to recover, but she had a little girl the following year that she called Therese. She was a frail little thing, always ailing, so everyone has told me since, but I can't remember that. What I can remember is seeing her lying in her little coffin as if she was fast asleep and would wake up any minute.'

'How old was she?' Marion asked gently.

'Three,' Peggy said. 'And she had died from whooping cough. I was six and I remember her funeral and everyone crying, and my mother's white face. Afterwards it was like my mother was behind a pane of glass. It was as though I could see her and hear her and yet seemed unable to touch her and there was no light in her eyes. I just felt so lonely and so did Sam. We sort of looked after one another. My father seemed at a loss too.'

'That describes it very well,' Marion said. 'I was lonely too and my mother stayed behind that pane of glass.'

'I thought mine would,' Peggy said. 'In the end, Mom said the vicar went to see her and, while he commiserated with her and acknowledged the deep sorrow she was feeling, he told her that a mother with other children couldn't allow herself the luxury of wallowing in grief for ever, and she should be thankful for the two healthy children she did have.'

'I so wish that someone had had the courage to say that to my mother,' Marion said.

'It might have helped you all if someone had,' Peggy said, 'because from that moment, it was as if our mother returned to us. Then my brother Peter was born when I was eight years old and Daisy three years later.'

'We dealt with it by giving our mother incredible licence,' Marion said, 'always making allowances, and you see the result. Now I wouldn't know what to do to correct it.'

'I don't think you can,' Peggy said. 'Not now. What you can change is the way you respond to it. Stand up to her like you did today.'

'I'll try,' Marion said. 'I do see that you're right but it's incredibly hard to face up to her when I've spent a lifetime appeasing her.'

A couple of days after this, there were more important things to worry about because German troops marched into Denmark and Norway, and both countries surrendered without really putting up any sort of fight. Everyone assumed that Hitler would turn his attention to the Low Countries next. However, the news broadcasts claimed he wouldn't conquer them so easily. Belgium and Holland were protected by a heavily manned impregnable fortress, which guarded three strategic bridges to prevent the German army just marching through their countries. The French had the Maginot Line, which they also claimed was impregnable, a strong line of heavily manned forts that ran from the Swiss border to the Ardennes.

'With Hitler and his armies getting closer,' Violet said that night as Marion switched off the wireless, 'I'm really glad me and Peggy didn't throw the towel in at that drop forge.'

'Did you think of it?'

'I'll say. It was pride kept us going for the second week – and money, of course. Three pounds a week is not to be sneezed at.'

'I wouldn't have blamed you if you had given it up,' Marion said. 'I'd say you earn every penny. I remember the exhaustion and strain was written all over your faces that first week, and you were as grateful as Richard for a bowl of water in the scullery to wash when you got in.'

'Yeah, and we used to go to bed not long after the evening meal as I remember,' Peggy said. 'God, we were not prepared for such intense heat. I mean, sweat broke out on our foreheads as soon as we entered the shop floor, and within minutes we would feel the bead of sweats trickling between our breasts and down our spines.'

'It must have been awful,' Sarah said, and Marion agreed.

'And we wear these horrible green overalls,' Violet said. 'But most of the men wear flannelette shirts as well, to soak up the sweat, and they have scarves around their necks that they use to protect their faces from the heat when they have to open the furnaces.'

'Do you have to do that as well?'

'No, only men do that, thank God,' said Peggy. 'At first when the doors were opened the searing heat was so powerful we both found it difficult to breathe. And the furnaces have to be attended all the time, turning the load to make sure it's the right consistency to be able to roll it.'

'What happens then?' Sarah asked.

'Well, it goes through other rollers, getting finer and finer,' Violet said. 'Then it's cut into lengths, loaded on to a bogey with tongs and weighed. That's my job, manning the weighing machine, because they didn't think I was strong enough to wheel the bogeys away to the other shop where they are turned into railway lines.'

'Sounds like my idea of hell,' Marion said.

'And mine,' Sarah replied.

'It helps that I feel I'm doing something useful,' Peggy said. 'I suppose we could have chosen something else, but then I think of Sam – all the men, really. I mean, they had little choice, did they?'

'I suppose not,' Marion said. 'And I think the hardest thing is not knowing where they are,

179

especially when Europe is such a scary place to be with country after country falling into German hands.'

'Well, then,' said Peggy. 'Let's hope that that fort holds up like it's supposed to and protects Holland and Belgium.'

'Oh, hear, hear to that,' said Marion.

In early May Hitler's Luftwaffe attacked Holland's airfields. They called it blitzkrieg – lightning war – and the savagery of it left the Dutch Air Force with just twelve planes. At the same time, paratroopers were landed on the impregnable fort and it was in German hands in less than twenty-four hours, opening up the way for tanks and armies to cross unopposed into Belgium. No one was surprised when Holland finally surrendered after the Luftwaffe blitzed Rotterdam so badly that almost a thousand people were killed.

Then on the evening of Tuesday 14 May, Anthony Eden, Secretary of State for War, gave a broadcast on the BBC Home Service. '. . . we are going to ask you to help us in a manner which I know will be welcome to thousands of you. Since the war began we have received countless enquiries from all over the kingdom from men of all ages who are for one reason or another not at present engaged in military service and who wish to do something for the defence of their country. Well, now is your opportunity.

'We want large numbers of such men in Great

Britain, who are British subjects, between the ages of seventeen and sixty-five . . . to come forward and offer their services . . . the name of the new Force which is now to be raised will be "the Local Defence Volunteers". . . . a part-time job, so there will be no need for any volunteer to abandon his present occupation. You will not be paid but you will be armed . . . In order to volunteer what you have to do is give in your name at the local police station . . .'

Richard was cross that he wasn't yet even sixteen and could do nothing to help protect his country. He had a horror of jackbooted Nazis parading the streets of Birmingham and he knew it could easily happen for it really did seem as if the Germans were unstoppable.

Marion was also desperately worried about Bill because letters from him, which had previously come on a fairly regular basis, had stopped. Everyone was well aware of this except the younger children.

Sarah, worried herself, tried to assure her mother. 'If Dad is actively engaged in something then he wouldn't be able to write letters or get them to you, would he?'

'No,' Marion said sadly. 'But it might be far worse than that, and you know it as well as I do. He might have been killed. Some of the fighting has been ferocious.'

'Yes, I know,' Sarah said. 'I'm not stupid. But,' she added almost fiercely, 'I shan't think of it or believe it until I'm told otherwise, and neither should you, if only for the sake of the twins and Tony.'

Marion knew that Sarah's attitude was the right one and yet it was hard to accept for every day the news worsened. Then a directive was broadcast that all owners of boats of 30 foot long or more and capable of crossing the Channel, and living on the south coast had to register them with the Admiralty. This applied to yachts and pleasure boats of all sorts, barges, and fishing boats.

'What's that all about?' Marion said.

Nobody knew then, but a few days later, when news reached them that the Allied army was in retreat, Richard could see from his map that the Germans were trying to drive the Allies onto the beaches.

'If they manage to do that then the big naval ships won't be able to go in very far to take them off, will they?'

'Oh, you mean when they asked for the small boats capable of crossing the Channel it was all about rescuing our soldiers?' Peggy cried.

'I think so.'

'You're probably right,' Marion said. 'But I don't see that little boats will get many off.'

'No,' Richard said morosely, well aware that one of those soldiers trapped on the beaches could be his father, and when his eyes met Sarah's he knew that she thought exactly the same.

Marion was nearly out of her mind with worry

over Bill, but trying to keep a lid on it for the sake of the children. Her anxiety was, however, shared with Peggy, who'd had a letter from her mother to ask her if she'd heard from Sam for they'd heard nothing from him for some time. Neither had Peggy, and all they could do was wait.

By the time the owners of the registered boats had been asked to assemble at Sheerness on 27 May, they revealed that Operation Dynamo, which was the code name for evacuation of the Allies from the beaches of Dunkirk, had already been going on for five days. Now the veil of secrecy was lifted and as well as private boats, the lifeboats were lifted from liners and the tugs sailed down from the Thames. Even some of the owners of unregistered boats, hearing of the plight of the stranded soldiers, set sail on their own.

The boats were used to ferry the men to Royal Naval ships lying at anchor in deeper water. When the ships were filled to capacity they would head back to Ramsgate to unload the soldiers and return to start again. All the time, bombs would be falling round them and the Stukas dive-bombing the soldiers and rescuers alike.

By the time the operation was disbanded on 4 June it was estimated that over 192,000 British, and 140,000 French soldiers had been rescued. It had been an amazing achievement, but lots of equipment and artillery had been lost.

The night the evacuation was stopped, Winston

Churchill gave a speech in the House of Parliament, which was broadcast on the wireless.

'We shall go on to the end . . . we shall fight on the seas and oceans, we shall fight with growing confidence and growing strength in the air, we shall defend our island, whatever the cost may be, we shall fight on the beaches, we shall fight on the landing grounds, we shall fight in the fields and in the streets, we shall fight in hills; we shall never surrender . . .'

It was stirring stuff and just what the British people needed, for nearly all were at least apprehensive and some plain scared: a very small stretch of water separated Britain from France, which was fighting for its very survival.

There was still no news of Bill, though. Then, a week later, a letter dropped through the letterbox. Marion snatched it up from the mat. She knew Bill's writing well, and if he could write her a letter he couldn't be dead. Then she was running down the corridor to the kitchen, ripping the envelope open as she did so.

The lodgers and Richard had left for work but the children and Sarah were eating their breakfasts at the table and saw their mother's face wreathed in a smile the like of which they hadn't seen for some time.

Sarah looked at her quizzically and Marion, after scanning the letter, burst out breathlessly, 'Your father is alive and well. He's hurt his leg and is in hospital in Ramsgate, but he will be all right.'

'Oh, Mom.' Tears of relief ran down Sarah's face as she hugged her mother. 'Didn't I tell you not to worry till you had cause?'

Magda looked at Missie and knew she thought the same, about grown-ups crying when they should be happy. Tony took advantage of her mother's preoccupation to put an extra spoon of sugar on his porridge and Magda opened her mouth to protest, but shut it again, knowing instinctively her mother was in no mood to deal with it, and contented herself with kicking Tony on the shin.

ELEVEN

When Paris fell and France formally surrendered on 22 June, everyone in Britain knew that they were staring the threat of invasion in the face. The frantic government advised people to hide maps, and disable cars and bicycles not in use. Signposts were removed and the names of stations blacked out to confuse any invader.

Peggy and Violet worked till seven o'clock most nights, and so did Richard. Much valuable equipment had been left in France and on the borders of Belgium, and replacements had to be made as quickly as possible. Overtime was not seen as merely an option any more. Then the anticipated bombing from the air began as the Luftwaffe pounded the southern coastal towns night after night. People looked at the newspaper pictures of the destruction wreaked on innocent civilians and their homes with dismay and fear.

'Well,' Polly said to Marion one day not long after the bombing began, 'the gloves are well and truly off now. Five nights running those poor souls have had to suffer it. We know what them German buggers are capable of. The poor little kids evacuated to the South Coast out of the cities because they decided that they were safer there have changed their tune now. They'll have to find some other place for them. Some of the mothers are taking them back, anyroad. I mean, I know they did that anyway in the beginning when no bombs fell or owt, but more have taken them back now. All them posters are going up everywhere to dissuade them. You know, the one showing kids in the country having a great time, with the sun shining and the sky blue, and "Don't Do It Mother" written across the top.'

'Yeah, but it isn't always like that,' Marion said. 'It's been in the paper that some evacuated kids have had a dreadful time.'

'They have,' Polly said. 'Gladys Kendrick down our yard sent her two lads. We said she was mad to even consider it but anyroad they went. One was nine and one eleven, and when she went to this farm in Wales to see them she was shocked. The farmer was using them in place of his farm hands that had been called up, and had them up at the crack of dawn and hard at work before and after school and all weekend. Gladys said their hands was all cracked and the only place they had to sleep was in a little cubbyhole off the landing. She said they was skin and bone because they weren't given enough to eat.'

187

'That's dreadful!'

'I agree,' Polly said. 'As you can imagine, Gladys had them out of there straight away. She went to the evacuation centre in the Council House and wiped the floor with them. She said she didn't want any other child sent there. When she got them home the kids also told her that unless the farmer or his wife was telling them to do summat, they spoke Welsh all the time. They was real unhappy. Anyroad, whatever happens, she's not sending them away again and she's promised them that.'

'I never considered it,' Marion said. 'Anyway, there won't be any place of safety if we are invaded.'

'You're right,' Polly said with an emphatic nod. 'If invasion does come, I'd want us all to face it together.'

'I'll say,' Marion agreed. 'And yet it must be awful as well for the people going through these raids. How do they cope with their houses being destroyed like that? I would be heartbroken.'

Polly shrugged. 'God knows. Good job they moved Bill out, though. Poor sods – to be rescued from Dunkirk only to be bloody bombed to bits once they reached Blighty.'

'It must have been awful, but at least now he's here it will be easier for me to get to see him,' Marion said.

'Fancy him being moved to the General, just a short tram ride away.'

Marion nodded happily. 'He said that as the military hospitals are bursting at the seams, ordinary hospitals are reserving so many wards for servicemen.'

'And how is he in himself like?' Polly asked. 'Did he tell you in the letter?'

'He's doing well. The doctors are pleased with him, anyroad, though the move was a bit uncomfortable for him, but whichever way you look at it he was lucky. He's alive and doing well, and I'm off to see him this weekend. I can't wait, I can't take the twins or Tony, though, because they don't allow children under twelve onto the wards, but in his last letter Bill did say that when the Hospital are finished with him he'll be having some time at home to convalesce. It cheered the kids up a bit when I told them that. Ooh, Polly,' Marion said, wrapping her arms around her sister with delight, 'it will be just smashing to have him home for a few days.'

'Yeah, I should think so,' Polly said, smiling. She knew she would have felt the same as Marion if the circumstances had been reversed and Marion knew that the bolster would stay at the back of the wardrobe, where she had put when Bill came home on embarkation leave the last time.

She saw her sister looking at her quizzically and felt her face flush, and to stop Polly asking embarrassing questions she said, 'Good news about Peggy's brother Sam too, isn't it?'

Polly hid her smile because she knew what

189

Marion was doing, and why. She said, 'Yes, shot up with shrapnel, wasn't he?'

'Yeah,' Marion said. 'He was transferred to a military hospital in Sutton Coldfield while they dig it all out.'

'Oh, Sutton Coldfield, where the posh nobs live?'

'That's the place Bill should have gone to. They have a barracks up there so I suppose it is a good place to site a military hospital,' Marion explained. 'Anyway, Peggy has been to see him and says he's bearing up well, considering he was peppered with the stuff. Apparently, they thought at one point that he wouldn't make it, but he's proved to be a fighter and he reckons he will be out in a week or two. Peggy asked if he could come down to see her then, and of course I said he'd be welcome. If he wants he can stay over and bunk in with the boys. Still first things first, and that is me going to see Bill and trying to keep my excitement in check until then. Magda told me once that when she is excited about something, she fizzes inside like a bottle of pop. I laughed at the time, but now I know just what she means.'

'Get away with you,' Polly said with a chuckle, giving her sister a push. 'It's two full days more before you can get to see your precious Bill.'

When Marion did eventually get to see Bill the following Sunday afternoon, she was shocked by his appearance. His face was etched with lines that hasn't been there before and his skin was the colour of putty. His hair, which had been streaked with grey when he had marched off to war, was now steel grey all over.

His eyes were the same, though, and they brightened when he saw Marion. 'Ain't you got kiss for me then?'

'I don't want to hurt you.'

'How could a kiss hurt me?'

'Oh, I don't know,' Marion said. 'What's the bulge in the bed?'

'Oh, that's a cage thing protecting my leg, that's all,' Bill said. 'Come on, you've got to welcome a returning hero properly. Let's have a big smacker.'

Marion leaned over gingerly, but when their lips touched she was staggered by the shaft of desire that shot through her.

Bill was surprised and very pleased by the kiss. He smelled again the lily of the valley perfume Marion had always worn and when they eventually broke away, he sighed in contentment as he said, 'Oh, Marion, you're a sight for sore eyes. I can't tell you how good it is to see you.'

'I feel the same,' Marion told him, and her eyes were shining. 'It looks like you haven't been looked after properly. You never carried much weight, but now you are positively skinny and you have big bags under your eyes.'

'I'm all right,' Bill protested. 'I have little appetite because I'm not doing much, and the bags are probably because I'm not sleeping that well.'

Marion was immediately solicitous. 'Ah, Bill! Is your leg giving you much pain?'

Bill didn't tell Marion that it wasn't his leg keeping him awake as much as the memories stored in his head. He just said that it was getting better so the pain was easing.

'How's the kids?' he asked, changing the subject.

'Fine.'

'Tony behaving himself?'

'Yeah, I suppose,' Marion said. 'He seems either a bit more responsible or better at not getting caught. He hasn't been brought home by a policeman or the priest this long time, anyroad.'

Bill grinned. 'And Richard?'

'Can't wait to join up,' Marion said. 'He's your son, Bill, and like you, once he has decided a thing then that is that. He knows what we are up against as well as anyone, and if those pleasure cruisers and the like could cross the Channel, so could Hitler's invasion force, which people say are massed on the other side.'

'I heard that the Germans have got to smash the RAF before an invasion takes place.'

'Well, they're having a good go at that,' Marion said. 'I watched a dogfight myself the other day. We all stood in the street and cheered the pilot on like mad and when the German plane turned for home, the Spitfire pursued him and, so we heard, shot him down over the allotments. Tony and Jack went to see but the wardens wouldn't let them near and then the police came and shooed them away. I heard the German pilot was killed, and I suppose they didn't want young boys seeing a sight like that.'

'No,' Bill agreed. 'They will see death and destruction soon enough as it is.'

'You think there will be bombing here?'

'Almost certain to be. Birmingham makes so much for the war effort.' He looked at Marion steadily and went on, 'I think that we have got to brace ourselves for the worst. Thank God you've all got the cellar to shelter in.'

'Yes . . .' Marion said. And then because she didn't want to talk about the threat of bombing any more she said, 'Do you want to speak to Richard and Sarah?'

'Are they here?'

'Yes. They are desperate to see you but I left them in the visitors' room because only two are allowed around the bed at a time.'

'Then send them in,' Bill said.

Unlike Marion, Sarah and Richard wanted to know all about the rescue from the beaches of Dunkirk. Bill missed out the gory bits, but he did say that the Stukas and bombers were overhead all the time. The soldiers had hastily erected field guns and were trying to shoot them down, and the RAF planes were fighting the German ones, and the noise was incredible.

'Were you manning the guns, Dad?' Richard asked.

'No, I was helping construct makeshift piers,'

Bill told his son, 'using anything we could find littering the beaches so it was easier for the smaller boats to come alongside and not be stuck on the sand, see?'

'That's what it said in the papers,' Richard said. 'And it showed pictures of them boats taking the soldiers to the warships.'

'Yeah they did,' Bill said.

'What did you come on?' Sarah asked.

'A fishing smack,' Bill said, and added with a smile, 'I stunk to high heaven. See, I was on the pier waiting and the Stukas came in from nowhere. I tried to hide but it wasn't easy, and they got my leg and I fell in the water. This fishing smack was just setting off going back and he hauled me out of the drink and brought me along too.'

'God, Dad, was it exciting?' Richard asked.

Bill looked at his face full of eagerness and zeal, and knew that if he was to be involved in that war, as he so longed to be, he had to be truthful with him. 'Sorry to disappoint you, son, but it wasn't exciting. It was bloody exhausting and terrifying most of the time, if you want the truth, like trying to make your way across a beach with bombs hurtling down and the wheeling Stukas trying to rip you to pieces with machine-gun fire.

'It sounds awful, Dad,' Sarah said.

'All war is awful, pet,' Bill said. 'And yet however bad it is no one can run away from it.'

'Yeah,' Richard said. 'And that's exactly why I will enlist just as soon as I can.'

Bill heard the fervour in his son's voice and knew that Marion was right, his mind was made up.

Marion and the older children visited Bill every Sunday afternoon, delighted with his progress although Marion's joy was tempered with apprehension for she knew when Bill was pronounced fully fit he would be off again. In one way she hoped that he would never be fully fit, but despite the fact that he had had many painful operations to rebuild his leg, and had pins inserted in places, he continued to improve.

Peggy's brother had improved faster than Bill, though, and two weeks after Marion's first visit to Bill, one shrapnel-free Sam Wagstaffe was released from hospital. He had five days' convalescence before rejoining his battalion and, as planned, he came to the Whittakers' for a couple of days to see his sister.

He arrived by train on Friday afternoon to spend the weekend with them and Peggy got permission to leave work a little earlier to meet him off the train at Aston station. She was so pleased to see him, and he looked so smart in his uniform, that tears seeped from her eyes and ran down her cheeks as she hugged him tight, feeling the rough khaki against her cheek. She tried to hide her distress from Sam lest he tease her about being soppy. However, he would never have done that, because he knew just how close he had come to death and that sort of experience can change a person's outlook a great deal. His own eyes glistened with tears at seeing his sister again.

Peggy had been writing to him fairly regularly so he felt he knew the Whittakers fairly well. She filled him in on Bill's injuries as they walked arm in arm to the house. 'He should have been in the same hospital as you, but there was no space,' she said.

'That doesn't surprise me,' Sam said. 'The injury list must have been colossal, because when they ran out of ward space they had men lying on stretchers in corridors.'

'It sounds horrendous.'

'Well, let's say it was nothing like a vicar's tea party.'

Peggy knew that was Sam's way of saying he didn't want to talk about it and so she said, 'I can't wait for you to meet all the family.'

'And me,' Sam said. 'It will be nice to put faces to the names.'

Peggy nodded. 'They're all lovely, particularly Marion, and her sister, Polly, is such a card . . .'

'But?'

'But what?'

Sam shrugged. 'I don't know what, but there has to be some fly in the ointment because I heard it in your voice.'

'Oh, that's just Clara, the mother of Marion and Polly. I told you about her in the letters.'

'You said she was a bit of a tartar.'

'That's putting it mildly,' Peggy said. 'I mean,

she's had a hard life, there's no denying it, but she plays on it and is full of resentment and spite.'

'Well, forewarned is forearmed, they say, so at least when I meet the old harridan I will know what to expect.' Sam flashed Peggy the mischievous grin she was so familiar with. 'Don't worry, if I should meet this woman I will be the soul of tact and discretion.'

Peggy laughed. 'Sam Wagstaffe, you wouldn't know tact and discretion if it leaped up and socked you between the eyes.' She gave his arm a playful punch. 'Anyroad, you're here to rest and recuperate, not bandy angry words with the embittered old woman.'

Fortunately Marion had no intention of giving her mother the opportunity to spoil the few precious days that Sam had with his sister and so she never told her about Sam's visit, but Marion and the children were in the house when they arrived, all wanting to welcome Peggy's brother.

He was a very presentable young man, Marion thought, and she could see the resemblance between the siblings: he had the same dark hair, open face and wide mouth that Peggy had. However, he hadn't got her slightly snub nose and his eyes were much darker brown, so dark they were almost black. He also had the longest lashes she had ever seen, which Marion considered wasted on a man. But she was more than pleased with his good manners as he thanked her for looking after his sister and Violet so well.

He got on well with the younger children too because he was used to his young brother and sister and their friends. 'Shall I show you a few card tricks?' he asked and was almost deafened by the response. He sat at one side of the table, the children opposite him, and Peggy, with a smile on her face, went into the kitchen to help Marion prepare the meal for them all.

'Is Sam all right out there?' Marion asked.

'He's fine,' Peggy replied. 'He likes kids and he's good at card tricks. He really used to baffle Pete and Daisy.'

A few moments later they heard Tony exclaim, 'How did you do that?' and Magda say, 'How did you know that it was the ace of spades he took?'

'Magic,' Sam claimed.

'Ah, Sam, tell us how you did it?'

'Can't do that,' Sam said. 'Trade secret. But I'll do it again and you watch carefully.'

They did, but were none the wiser. Nor did they know how he could make a card disappear and turn up in the box it had come out of. Nor did they understand why the top card of four random piles should turn out to be an ace. But the best trick of all was when he counted the cards and found one was missing and he withdrew the missing card from behind Tony's ear. That flabbergasted them all.

When Sam began to tidy away the cards, though, the children clamoured for more, but he shook his head. 'No, your mother will probably be needing the table soon.'

'So what shall we do now?' Tony asked.

'Well, let's see,' Sam said, stroking his chin. 'How clever are you on solving riddles?'

'I'm great at them,' said Tony.

The twins looked unsure. 'Don't think we're that good really,' Magda said.

'Never mind,' Sam assured her. 'Give it a go anyway. Now what can go up the chimney down but not down the chimney up?'

The children thought hard, especially Tony after his boast, but in the end they had to admit defeat.

'An umbrella,' Sam said.

'Give us another one,' Tony said. 'Bet I get this.'

'All right then. What gets wetter the more it dries?'

Again the children were flummoxed.

'A towel,' Sam said in the end, and there was a groan of exasperation.

'Just one more?' Tony pleaded.

Sam laughed. 'Just one then. What month has twenty-eight days?'

'That ain't a real riddle, is it?' Tony said. 'And the answer is February of course.'

'No it isn't,' Magda cried. 'The answer is all of them. They all have twenty-eight days.'

'Well done, Magda,' Sam said. 'All of them is the right answer.'

Before any one could say anything further, Marion came out with knives and forks. 'Hope the meal is all right for you, Sam,' she said as she began to lay the table.

'Oh, I'm an easy man to please,' Sam said. 'And I know rationing must make life very difficult.'

'It is,' Marion said. 'Me and my sister, Polly, have started listening to *The Kitchen Front* on the wireless after the eight o'clock news in the morning because it suggests recipes to try out.'

'So what are we trying out tonight?'

'Poor Man's Goose,' Marion said with a smile. 'Only it's never been near a goose. It's made with liver.'

'With a name like that it's got to be delicious.'

'Not necessarily,' Marion said. 'But it's all there is, so it's that or nothing.'

It was almost ready when Violet and Richard came in together. With Sam arriving that day, neither had elected to do overtime. 'Sarah not with you?' Marion asked as Richard, after shaking hands with Sam, went to have his wash.

'No,' Richard said. 'Shouldn't think she'll be long, though there were still people in the shop when we passed.'

Marion clicked her tongue in disapproval. 'Sarah's always complaining about that,' she said to Sam. 'She said the shop might be quiet as a tomb all afternoon and just before closing time droves of people come in. She said she could understand it if they were working, but not that many are. Some have all day to collect their groceries.'

'That's human nature for you,' Sam said. 'All told, we are an inconsiderate lot.'

Marion gave a sigh. 'You're right there, Sam. Anyway,' she said to Violet, 'by the time you've had your wash Sarah will likely be in, and I hope she is because I'm starving.'

And so when Sarah arrived home a little later, Violet and Richard were in the scullery, Peggy helping Marion dish up in the kitchen, and the children listening to the wireless. Sarah looked across the room to Sam Wagstaff and thought he was the most handsome man she had ever seen in her life, and she was struck dumb.

Sam noticed her awkwardness and though he was a little flattered because she was a pretty girl, she was very young, little more than a child, and he said, 'You must be Sarah?'

He extended his hand, and though Sarah took it she seemed incapable of speech. He went on, 'I bet you're hungry. I always was when I came home from work, but I think the meal is about ready.'

He smiled at her and she felt sudden heat flood her face. When Marion came in with the plates she looked from one to the other and saw her young daughter just gazing at Sam Wagstaffe.

Everyone was taking his or her place at the table as the meal was shared out and all were talking fifteen to the dozen. Sam entertained them royally, answering the children's many questions without a hint of impatience, and Sarah listened to the timbre of his voice and watched his expressive eyes as he spoke.

He was a natural storyteller and had a knack

of making the commonplace seem interesting and amusing, so that even Tony would listen. Richard was really keen on learning as much as he could about the regular army, and Sam told him all about life at the barracks when he was in training, the endless parades and route marches, and inspection, when his bed had to be made with hospital corners, and everything – his boots, certainly, but even the buttons on his uniform and the buckle on his belt – had to shine like a new pin.

'And God help you if they find your gun is dirty,' he added. 'You're really for the high jump then. Fortunately I was warned about that and I always worked on my gun first, so I've never been hauled over the coals over the state of it.'

'I'm pleased about that, at any rate,' Marion said.

'Do you enjoy the army?' Richard asked.

'Yes and no,' Sam said. 'They're a great bunch of lads I'm with, and they've become almost closer than brothers because you know your life might depend on them – and vice versa, of course – but though I'm not that keen on being shot at, I know that I'm where I should be, so I suppose, yes, I do enjoy the life mostly. I couldn't be a conscientious objector, for instance.'

'I'm glad you feel that way,' Marion said. 'I'm grateful to all the men out there fighting for us. I think all of you are extremely brave.'

'And I do,' Sarah said, but her mouth was so dry that her voice came out in a croak.

Magda looked at her across the table and said, 'Are you getting a cold? My voice goes like that when I am getting a cold.'

Sarah, embarrassed beyond measure, cleared her throat and said, 'No, I'm not getting a cold.'

'Well, why was your voice all funny then?'

'It just was.'

'Yeah, but . . ,'

'That's enough, Magda,' Marion said.

'Yeah, but I was only saying—'

'No one wants to hear what you're saying, Magda,' Marion said. 'What I want is for you to eat your dinner quickly. Polly is coming around later and I want to get everything cleared away before she gets here.'

TWELVE

The next morning Marion took the twins around to Polly's. Polly's three daughters descended on the two young girls and they went into the street to play, leaving Marion and Polly chance to talk. Marion was glad about this because she wanted her sister's advice on a matter that was troubling her.

Polly knew Marion had something on her mind and so she made a cup of tea and when it was before them both said, 'Come then. What's nagging you?'

'You'll probably think me silly . . .' Marion said.

Polly smiled. 'Possibly. But we'll never know until you tell me what you're so agitated about.'

'Last night,' Marion said. 'Did you notice the way our Sarah was looking at Peggy's brother?'

Polly gave a chuckle. 'I noticed all right. It was clear as the nose on your face, and all I can say is the girl has good taste for the man is a charmer and as dishy as they come.'

'She's far too young for that sort of thing.'

'Oh, you can't put an age on matters of the heart,' Polly said, and then, seeing the horrified look on her sister's face: 'I'm joking, Marion. Sarah is in the throes of her first great passion and there will probably be many more before she meets the one she's going to marry.'

'She makes it so obvious, though,' Marion said. 'I mean, you and I both noticed; what if Sam is aware of it too?'

'That won't be the end of the world,' Polly said. 'He knows how old Sarah is and he will take this for what it is, a childish infatuation.'

'I hope you're right.'

'Course I am,' Polly said confidently. 'Anyway, what difference will it make? Sam Wagstaffe will be back in the army in a day or two.'

'D'you think I should say anything to Peggy?'

'Wouldn't do any harm to mention it,' Polly said. 'But do stop worrying. We're staring the threat of invasion in the face and that is far more important than your Sarah having a childish fancy for Peggy's brother.'

'You're right,' Marion agreed morosely. 'The thought of this country under Nazi dominance makes me feel sick.'

'Ah, but there is one thing about the British people,' Polly said a little fiercely. 'When their backs are to the wall, they don't give up, but fight that little bit harder. I think we mustn't forget that.'

*   *   *

Marion left her daughters behind when she went home later, having decided to have a quiet word with Peggy if she had the opportunity. When she got in, Violet and Peggy were there on their own because Sarah was at work and the boys had all gone to the park with Richard's football.

'We're taking Sam down the Bull Ring later,' Peggy said. 'He said it sounded interesting and he'd like to look around the place.'

'He also suggested treating us to the pictures later,' Violet said.

'That's nice of him. You and Peggy, do you mean?'

'Yeah, and Richard and Sarah if they want to come,' Peggy told Marion.

'Oh, I'm sure they will. They'll be thrilled,' Marion said. 'It will be such a treat for them. What's on?'

'Well, according to the paper the Globe is showing *Pinocchio* and the Orient has Charlie Chaplin in *The Great Dictator*,' Peggy said.

Marion made a face. 'Too close to home to be funny, judging by that title, *The Great Dictator*,' she said. 'I'm sick of hearing about dictators, to tell you the truth.'

'I think it's meant to be a comedy,' Peggy said. 'Or, I should say, bound to be a comedy if it has Chaplin in it.'

'Even so, I shouldn't fancy it,' Marion said. 'But then I'm not the one going. And isn't the other one a cartoon made by that American Walt Disney?'

'That's the one,' Peggy said. 'It's supposed to be ever so good.'

'More one for the children, I'd have thought,' Marion said. 'You might need to go into town for a better choice.'

'People say *Pinocchio* is very cleverly done,' Peggy said. 'Some of the girls at work have seen it and I wouldn't mind giving it a go.'

'Nor me,' said Violet. 'But I bet Richard and Sam would kick up if we suggested it. It's going to be Sam's treat so I suppose he's got to have first choice.'

'I don't see that,' said Peggy. 'No point in giving someone a treat if you are going to choose what they see. I bet Sarah would like to see *Pinocchio*.'

'She might,' Violet said, and her amused eyes met those of Peggy's as she went on, 'but she will go with whatever Sam wants, as you well know.'

'Speaking of Sarah . . .' Marion began.

But she got no further because Peggy jumped in with, 'She thinks herself in love with Sam, doesn't she? I wasn't sure that you'd noticed.'

'I did,' Marion said. 'In fact, I am a little concerned.'

'No need to be,' Peggy said. 'I remember having similar feelings for a farm hand on a neighbouring farm when I was just a little younger than Sarah. I used to go mooning after him any chance I got. Course, he never really knew I existed and after a while I grew out of it. Sam is aware of how Sarah feels and fully understands. He knows how old she is. And from early Monday morning she'll have to worship him from afar, anyroad, for he's leaving to spend a couple of days at home before his medical, which I know will pass him perfectly fit to rejoin his unit.' Peggy's sombre eyes met those of Marion as she added, 'And then God knows when any of us will see him again.'

Richard was really pleased when Sam told him of the proposed trip to the cinema as they walked home from the park, but not that he was prepared to let the girls choose the film because he knew they would choose *Pinocchio*, which they'd been talking about for days.

However, Sam told the girls they could go where they pleased and so that evening they made their way to the Globe. Richard couldn't help feeling a little short-changed because he never went to the pictures, and the last thing he wanted to see on this rare visit was a tale about a puppet, especially when *The Thief of Bagdad*, *The Grapes of Wrath* and *Broadway Melody* were on in the town.

Sarah was ecstatic with pleasure, though she positioned herself as far away from Sam as she could get. She wanted to enjoy the film, and Sam disturbed her so much – she had no idea why – that if he spoke to her at all she was certain that she wouldn't be able to answer him, so it was best to keep well away.

Even Richard was quite amazed by the cartoon, which was the first one any of them had ever seen, and they talked about it enthusiastically as they made their way home.

Sam brushed their thanks aside. 'It was my pleasure,' he said. 'It's lovely to give a treat to people who really appreciate it.'

'Nothing to stop us doing this more often now,' Peggy said. 'Before we came here me and Violet had never even seen a picture house – villages don't have them – so how about us all trying them out once a week?'

Sarah felt excitement course through her. It would be wonderful to go to the pictures every week, and they could now money wasn't such an issue.

'Why don't you?' Sam said. 'It would do you all good and there's no harm in it.'

He turned and smiled at Sarah as he spoke, and she felt her heart flip in a most alarming way.

Then suddenly Richard cried, 'There's a queue outside the chip shop. They must have some fish in.'

'Let's join it and find out, shall we?' Sam said. 'That smell alone is guaranteed to make anyone hungry.'

It took nearly half an hour, but at last their wait was rewarded and they came away with a portion each and one for Marion. She was more than glad to see the young people's eyes dancing in excitement, and as they ate the fish and chips and drank the tea she had made they regaled her with tales of Pinocchio.

Later, Sarah, curled in bed, thought it was the perfect end to an almost perfect day.

The following day after dinner, Marion, Richard and Sarah set off to see Bill as usual, leaving Peggy and Violet, together with Sam, to look after Tony and the twins. Marion was delighted to find Bill out of bed and sitting beside it in a wheelchair. His injured leg was still stretched out in front of him, but it was an improvement. 'Oh, Bill,' she cried, 'wait till the children see this.'

'Yeah,' Bill said. 'I think they'll be chucking me out before long. The doctor said I'll have to come back for physio, but I can do that through Outpatients.'

'It will be marvellous to have you home.'

'It will be marvellous to be home,' Bill said. 'Whoever it was said that a person often doesn't appreciate a thing till it is taken away from him knew what he was talking about.'

'I think we're all the same in that respect,' Marion said. 'But talking about appreciating things, Sam treated Sarah and Richard to the pictures last night. They saw a cartoon, which I thought they might find babyish, but they were full of it when they came in. Anyroad, they've now decided to go every week, and even Richard was all for it. I think it will be good for them.'

'Yeah,' Bill said. 'It will. The war news is depressing enough at the moment, but no one can think of doom or gloom all the time. You'd best send the kids in and let them tell me all about this film.'

They did tell him, and they extolled the generosity and kindness of Sam, yet Bill saw something lurking behind Richard's eyes.

Eventually Bill said to him, 'All right then, son, what is it?'

Richard took a deep breath and said, 'I want to join the Local Defence Volunteers next week when I'm sixteen. I have looked into it because one of my mates from work does it. They meet at Sacred Heart school hall.'

'Anthony Eden said in that broadcast in May that you had to be seventeen,' Sarah reminded him.

'I'm going to tell them I'm seventeen,' Richard said.

'And what about your mother?'

'Mom won't have to know,' Richard said. 'She didn't listen to the broadcast, so I'll tell her that I can join at sixteen. I've being thinking about it. Everyone knows invasion is very likely. I want to be there ready and waiting if that time comes.'

'Oh, I wish I could do something too,' Sarah cried. She too ached to be helping the war effort, but it would be fifteen months before she turned sixteen.

'When you're a little older, I'm sure that there will be some opening for you,' Bill said consolingly.

'Yeah,' said Sarah morosely. 'The only trouble is, Dad, growing up seems to take one hell of a long time.' She couldn't understand why her father laughed so loudly that Marion heard him in the visitors' room.

Sam left the following morning. He was ready early so he could say goodbye to his sister before she left for work. Peggy kissed him with tears in her eyes, and so did Violet, and even Richard's voice was gruff as he shook hands with him.

'Goodbye, Sam,' he said. 'And for God's sake look after yourself.'

'I'll do my level best,' Sam promised.

The children were sad to see him leave as well. He kissed the girls on the cheek, and punched Tony lightly on the arm and told him he was a mean little footballer. Tony positively glowed with pride. He turned to shake Marion by the hand and as she faced him she glimpsed the bleak look in Sarah's eyes and she felt so sorry for her, and also rather silly for her anxiety over the infatuation Sarah had for Sam. And that's what it was, a childish infatuation. She was as aware as everyone else that once Sam left she might never see him again. So Marion said, 'Goodbye, Sam. We have loved having you to stay. Please feel free to come again any time.'

'Thank you,' said Sam. 'But the army might have some say in that. Maybe I should get myself shot at more often.'

'Don't you dare,' Marion said.

And Sarah added, 'Don't even joke of such a thing.'

Sam heard the disconsolate tone in Sarah's voice and he took her two hands in his own. Sarah felt as if she was drowning in those dark eyes as he said, 'That was a silly thing to say. You're right, it's no joking matter. But don't worry, I'll keep my head well down.'

'See you do as well.' Marion's words broke the spell between them and Sam dropped Sarah's hands.

'Goodbye, Sam,' Sarah said, and her voice was little more than a whisper.

It was nearly lunchtime on Friday 19 July when the ambulance bringing Bill home arrived outside the front door. Marion opened it to see Bill being helped down the steps of the vehicle and onto the pavement. 'Here y'are, missus,' said one of the ambulance men with a cheery grin. 'One conquering hero home again.'

'Yes. Thank you.'

'Do you want a hand into the house, sir?' the same man said to Bill as he handed him the crutch that he would need for now to help him walk.

'No, thank you,' Bill said firmly enough, though through tightened lips. 'I think I can manage.'

'Right you are, then, sir,' the man said, and to Marion: 'They're giving Mr Whittaker a chance to rest over the weekend, but an ambulance will be sent for him on Monday morning at about eight o'clock.'

'That was explained to me,' Marion confirmed.

Bill's leg was not completely mended and the doctor had told her he would need daily physio if he were ever to recover totally. Still, she was delighted to have him home to fuss over for a while.

She stood back as Bill began his slow progress into the house with the ambulance man hovering behind him. Marion glanced up and down the street before following him. She knew many neighbours would be watching. Some knew Bill was returning home that day and others would be alerted by the unusual sight of an ambulance parked in the road. She knew that in Polly's street everyone would have been out there in a public display of support, probably shouting encouraging words to them both, but in Albert Road most would be content to peer through their net curtains, though Deidre from next door would likely pop in later to see if she could do anything.

The ambulance men took their leave when Bill reached the door at the end of the corridor. Leaning heavily on his crutch he walked through to the living room before turning to Marion and asking 'Well? Will I do?'

Marion's eyes filled with tears and her throat was blocked as she said huskily, 'Ah, Bill . . .'

Bill lifted up his hand before she reached him and said, 'If you want to hug me, and I am all in favour of that, let me sit down first? My balance is as yet quite precarious.'

He lowered himself onto the settee and Marion

sat beside him. As his arms went around her he sighed contentedly as he said, 'I have dreamed of doing this for weeks – months, even. As I stood on that bloody pier head at Dunkirk, waiting for rescue, it was the thought of you at home waiting for me that made me determined not to give up, to get back to you if I possibly could.'

Marion swallowed the lump in her throat and said gently, 'I'm so glad you did, but you look so tired.'

'I am,' Bill admitted. 'Getting up and washed early this morning absolutely exhausted me. I was done and dusted by eight o'clock, had my breakfast and everything, but then I had to wait until an available ambulance was ready to take me home, and waiting around is always tiring.'

'Yes,' Marion agreed. 'But you must remember as well that you have been quite ill, Bill. Your body is going to take time to recover. I think that you are going to need plenty of rest and feeding up, and though the rest part will be simple, the food part will not be so easy, with rationing the way it is and general shortages on goods not on ration. But I'll do my best to get you some decent food.'

'I know how difficult things are,' Bill said. 'Some of the meals served up in hospital were very strange indeed.'

'Well, you'll have a casserole this evening when everyone is home,' Marion said. 'And the meat is rabbit, which is not on ration, though it sometimes isn't available. They sell it on the stalls down the Bull Ring and I went yesterday to see what I could find. Thought I was out of luck too, and then I found a stall near the back of the meat market that still had some in. I bought such a lot the butcher threw me in a pot of pork dripping as well.'

'Isn't that on ration either?'

'Well, fats are – butter, margarine, lard and stuff like that,' Marion said, 'but he said he renders his own dripping and what the authorities don't know they won't worry about.'

'I could murder a piece of dripping toast now,' Bill said. 'My mouth is watering at the thought of it. And a big mug of tea. That would be just perfect.'

'Then you shall have it,' Marion said, getting to her feet. 'And after that I should go to bed for an hour or so, if I were you. Today the schools break up for the long summer break. The children will be excited about that, and having you home as well is like the icing on the cake for them. They might kill you with their exuberance. And I shouldn't try to manage the stairs just yet either. I have the boys' bed made up in the parlour, which you can use for now.'

Bill knew what Marion said made sense and so after he had eaten, he heaved himself to his feet, and using his crutch to balance on waved away her offer of help. 'You're not to treat me as an invalid,' he warned. 'Mollycoddling me is no way to help me get better.'

Bill knew that Marion worried about him so he was heartily glad she hadn't come down to see him in Ramsgate as she'd threatened to do before he'd been moved, because for a lot of the time there he had been raving. He did wonder at times if he was losing his mind, though the doctors had assured him that it was one of the effects of trauma or shock. And he had calmed down in the end and was able to keep his feelings in check through the day, though they continued to invade his mind at night and he would wake with a shriek or a yell and find the bedclothes tangled around him.

He wasn't the only serviceman to be afflicted this way, but the nurses were always there to reassure and soothe. He hadn't had one of these terrifying nightmares for over a week, though, and was fairly certain that in the confines of his own house, and with his family around him, he would soon be back to his old self.

The younger children were just as excited as Marion had said they would be when they came home from school and virtually launched themselves at Bill as he sat on the settee, with Marion warning them to mind his leg. The twins settled on either side of him, while Tony and Jack, who had come to see his uncle, were very impressed with Bill's crutch. They took turns trying to use it, though it was far too big for them.

'It's not to play with, you two,' Marion chided

when she saw them. 'It isn't a toy, and your father would rather not have to use it.'

'That's right enough,' Bill said. 'Nothing will give me greater pleasure than handing it back to the hospital when I no longer need it.'

'Hope it's not all that soon,' Tony said quietly, lying the crutch down beside his father, "cos then you'll have to go back, won't you?'

"Fraid so,' Bill said. 'So isn't it a great thing that I'm home for now and in time to help you enjoy your holidays. I might even be able to keep you and Jack out of mischief.'

'I'm not going to get into mischief, Uncle Bill,' Jack said. 'I won't have time. I'm going to be a messenger when the bombs come. A kid at school was telling me his brother is training for it and they've given him a bike.'

'They won't have people of your age, Jack,' Marion said. 'You're far too young.'

'I'm eleven next month.'

'That's what I mean,' Marion said. 'And you can get that look off your face, Tony,' she said, concerned with the awestruck way Tony was gazing at his cousin. 'If the bombs fall you're going to go down the cellar with the rest of us and there will be no argument about it. Anyway, why are we discussing something that hasn't happened yet?'

'Yes,' Bill said. 'Let's just be glad that Hitler has left us alone so far. I was in Ramsgate when they started the bombardment there and it was terrifying for the ordinary people. The devastation

I glimpsed from the ambulance on the way to Brum was dreadful. You have no idea. Bombs hurtling down is not exciting, believe me.'

Marion believed him totally. She felt a *frisson* of apprehension trickle down her spine, and she fought to get a grip on herself. No one had any control over the future.

When Bill was introduced to Peggy and Violet that evening he saw straight away from their firm handshakes, open faces and clear eyes that they were respectable girls, as Marion had told him they were. And they were also firm favourites with the children, if the banter between them was anything to go by, and he had felt his tense shoulders relax.

The rabbit casserole was delicious and everyone tucked into it with obvious enjoyment as they discussed the events of the day. Then, towards the end of the meal, Marion's composure was shaken a little when Richard announced his intention to join the Local Defence Volunteers now that he was sixteen.

'Anthony Eden asked for volunteers over the wireless,' he told his mother. 'It was a few months ago. Remember I told you about it at the time?'

Marion nodded. 'I do remember something about it, yes.'

'Well, I sort of decided then, but talking to Sam and hearing what he had to go through sort of put the tin hat on it, as it were.'

Marion looked across the table at her elder son. He was tall for his age and, though fairly thin, he was well muscled due to his work in the brass foundry. There was nothing of the child left in either Richard's body or his face, and his voice resembled Bill's. Marion knew that soon he would tip right over into adulthood. Part of her felt proud that he wanted to join this force to try to protect civilians who might find themselves caught up in this awful war, and part of her was frightened for him.

However, she knew this had to be Richard's decision and Bill, she could see, was all for it as he clapped his son on his back. 'I'm proud of you,' he said. 'It's important that we have people trained here at home as well.'

'Will you have a gun and that?' Tony asked.

'I should say so. They'll hardly issue us with cata-pults now, will they?' Richard said sarcastically.

'Golly,' Tony said, ignoring his brother's sarcasm. 'A real live gun. I'd love to see one of them.'

'It's not the kind of thing I'm ever likely to bring home,' Richard said. 'One of the first things they will have to teach me is how to fire it.'

'You'll soon pick it up,' Peggy said. 'Where Violet and I came from, every farmer's son over the age of twelve or so could shoot, and well, to be able to kill rabbits for the pot.'

'If that rabbit casserole was anything to go by, I should say that you lived very well,' said Bill.

'We didn't do bad,' Peggy said.

'Yeah,' Violet said. 'People in the country probably do much better than them in the cities now that rationing is beginning to bite, but I think we've all got to agree that Marion makes the best of anything she can get hold off. She's a wonderful cook.'

'Hear, hear,' the others said.

Marion flushed with embarrassment at the unaccustomed praise. 'Don't say that until you've tasted the cake,' she laughed.

Marion had made the cake to celebrate both Bill's homecoming and Richard's sixteenth birthday, which had been the previous day. She had been saving her sugar and fat rations for weeks. Pat had got some eggs from an old man who kept hens on his strip of allotment down by the munitions factory, Polly had loaned out her biggest cake tin, and Marion had made a large jam sponge. She had even made mock cream, using dried milk, margarine and sugar blended together, which had been a tip from *The Kitchen Front* recipe programme. She used it to cover the top of the cake and she'd even found one of the candles she used to put on birthday cakes when the children had been small, for Richard to blow out.

When she carried it out to the table that evening there were roars of approval. Bill declared it a culinary masterpiece and there wasn't a crumb of it left by the time everyone rose from the table.

That night, Bill climbed awkwardly up the stairs

and got into bed beside Marion, delighted that the bed was bolster free, as it had been when he was home on embarkation leave. He remembered his rage when Marion had first installed it on the advice of her mother after the birth of the twins. In his opinion, putting a bolster in the bed was like saying he had no control over his carnal desires, but he had swallowed his anger lest he upset Marion further. In fact, he had asked the doctor if there was something he could use to prevent pregnancy, and had been told there was and that he could buy them in any barber shop. He really needed to discuss what the doctor had recommended, and bugger the Catholic Church in its stance on contraception, but Marion was always too embarrassed to discuss sexual matters.

That night, though, after climbing the stairs, his leg was throbbing. Going any further than cuddling together was beyond his capabilities, but just to enjoy each other's closeness was wonderful.

He was unaware of the dream he had a few hours later, which woke Marion. She saw her husband writhing on the bed, his lips moving as if he was speaking to someone, though there was no sound, and her heart contracted in pity for what Bill had gone through.

Even the visit from her parents the following day went better than Marion could have envisaged. They both shook hands with Bill and even Clara was civil. Eddie said sincerely that he was really pleased to seeing Bill looking so well. For a change he had news of his own: he had taken on an allotment.

'Daddy, you dark horse,' Marion said in surprise. 'You never said a word.'

'Well, I only decided yesterday after I heard this bloke on the wireless talking about saving our ships, and I thought about how nice it would be to have home-grown vegetables and that. I went to enquire about putting my name down for one, but the upshot was they had one going and so I took it on.'

'Good for you,' Bill said. 'What's it like?'

'Overgrown,' Eddie said. 'Fellow that had it died last year and his family didn't tell the allotment people until his subscription came up for renewal. Forgot, I suppose. Anyroad, it looks as if he wasn't able to do much before that either. Be all right, though, when I've licked it into shape.'

'I told him that it's madness,' Clara snapped. Turning to her husband she continued, 'You work full time, for God's sake, and you'll do your back in with all that heavy digging, not to mention what you might be doing to your heart. Who d'you think you are? Superman? You ain't no spring chicken.'

'Don't mean I have to be put out to grass,' Eddie said, bristling in annoyance.

For once, though, Marion thought her mother had a point. 'Come on, Daddy,' she said. 'There ain't no need for you to kill yourself either. The

223

kids finished school yesterday for seven weeks. Jack and Tony can give you a hand to do the digging through the week and any really heavy stuff the bigger ones can do next weekend.'

'Sure they'll not mind doing that?'

'Course they won't,' Marion said confidently. 'None of them will mind. Anyroad, as far as Jack and Tony go, you would be doing me a favour. Both of them have too much energy than is good for them and that, together with too much time on their hands, is a recipe for disaster.'

'Yeah,' Bill said. 'You keep them hard at it, Eddie, and it might turn Jack off his latest hare-brained idea of putting himself forward as a messenger if the bombs come.'

'A messenger!' Clara exclaimed. 'But he's only . . .'

'Eleven next month, as he pointed out to me,' Bill said with a grin. 'He said it like it was some great age, you know.'

'But what put such an idea in his head?'

'I would guess the bike that he said messengers are given is the real lure.'

Clara gave a snort of disapproval.

'Of course, he won't be let do it; he's too young,' Bill said, 'but knowing Jack, he would lie about his age. He is half a head taller than our Tony, and if they weren't that bothered about checking . . . Well, let's say I would feel happier if he had something else to do instead.'

'Yes,' agreed Marion, 'because where he goes

our Tony usually follows. If they think that working on the allotment is helping the war effort in some way, then they'll be even keener.'

'And of course it is,' Eddie said. '"Dig for Victory" is what everyone is saying now.'

'Ah, said Marion wistfully, 'if only victory was that easily won.'

Jack was stunned when even his father forbade him to think of being a messenger. Polly and Pat were such easy-going parents that until now Jack had got away with most things he'd wanted to do. It was a shock to him that on this issue his parents stood firm. He saw the dream he had of cycling around the roads in the teeth of a gale would have to stay a dream.

'I can't believe that you're so unpatriotic,' he said to his father.

'You can level many things at this family but not that,' Pat said, angered at Jack's words.

'If you want to do something for the war effort,' Polly put in, before Jack had time to answer his father, 'do what Auntie Marion suggested and help your granddad on the allotment.'

'How can growing a few potatoes help the war effort?' Jack said disparagingly.

'I'll tell you how, my lad,' Pat said unusually firmly. 'Merchant ships are being sunk every day. You know that as well as me. These unarmed ships are doing the dangerous job of bringing food into Britain, and when ships are sunk that food, which the merchant sailors have lost their lives for, is lying at the bottom of the ocean. So it's important, if we are not to be starved to death altogether, that we grow as much food as possible. Be in no doubt about it, Jack, helping your granddad is definitely also helping the war effort.'

Jack understood every word his father had said and, being Jack, threw himself wholeheartedly in growing as much as he possibly could. Tony, being Tony, tried to match his cousin in the effort he put in.

THIRTEEN

It was Bill's greatest desire to get better as soon as he could and so he worked hard at his daily physio sessions. The doctors were delighted with him, so much so that on Wednesday of that same week he came home from his session with a stick rather than a crutch. His mental state, however, was a different matter. The images he had seen at Dunkirk continued to haunt him and he had many disturbing nightmares. He had no recollection of these in the morning and when Marion tried to talk to him about them he was less than enthusiastic.

'Look, Marion,' he said at last. 'I did go through it, and there's no good me telling you anything else, and I suppose the memories do disturb my sleep, but there's nothing you or anyone else can do to help me cope with that.'

'Maybe if you told me it could help relieve the burden. It'd be better than bottling it up.'

Bill knew he could never share the horrors of Dunkirk with Marion, especially when she knew that, once fit, he might be returning to similar horrors. 'This is something I need to cope with on my own,' he insisted. 'I'm sure that the dreams will calm down in a day or two.'

Marion had to be content with that. She didn't feel she should press Bill to say any more than he wanted to, though she often saw shadows flit across his eyes.

However, the memories festering in Bill's brain were increasingly disturbing. He had been home just over a week when he woke in the early hours with a primeval scream and shot up in the bed.

Marion, struggling from sleep, was alarmed. She got out of bed and turned on the light to see Bill still in the midst of some inner torment. He was still threshing his arms about and the eyes he turned to her were wild. She had the feeling he was not seeing her but something very sinister.

'Bill, oh my darling, what is it?' she cried leaping back into bed and holding his shuddering body tight.

The sobs came then, controlled weeping but gut-wrenching sobs that shook Bill's whole body. His torment was so immeasurably sad that Marion wept too while she rocked him gently in an effort to bring him some comfort.

When he was eventually calmer and he lay back down, Marion wiped her eyes and went to see the children, knowing the girls at least would have heard the scream and be worried. The twins were lying either side of their big sister, their eyes were full of fear.

'It's all right,' Marion told them. 'Your daddy had a nightmare but he's better now and almost asleep again.'

They all sighed with relief. They understood nightmares; they had all had those at one time or another.

'So you settle down now too,' Marion said, tucking them in solicitously, 'or we will all be like chewed rags in the morning.'

The girls lay down easily enough, for they were still tired, and Marion went down to the boys, but they were still fast asleep and obviously had heard nothing. She was hesitant to visit the lodgers and so she returned to bed.

'Telling me might help banish the fears,' she said to Bill. 'That's what I've always told the children if they've had nightmares.'

'There's nothing to say,' Bill answered brusquely. 'I just had a bad dream, that's all.' It had shaken him, though, for it was reminiscent of the ones he used to have when he was recovering at Ramsgate and he dreaded going back to those again.

'All right,' Marion said. 'Just thought something might be bothering you, that's all.'

'No, I'm fine now,' Bill told her.

She lay wide-eyed long after Bill's even breathing told her he had fallen asleep and she noted that even in slumber his face was contorted and drawn and there was tension in every line of his body. Her heart ached for him, but if he wouldn't share his troubles then she couldn't force him, and she eventually turned off the light and snuggled in beside him.

The next day Bill slept in late, so when Peggy and Violet asked about the disturbed night Marion was able to discuss it with them.

'It isn't to be wondered at,' Peggy said. 'Those Dunkirk survivors would have seen some sights. Sam had nightmares like that to start with.'

'Bill insisted it was *just* a nightmare, but I know it was much more than that,' Marion confided.

'What about Pat?' Peggy said. 'Would he be someone Bill could share his fears with?'

Marion made a face, because Pat's lackadaisical attitude still irritated her at times. Pat saw the funny side of most situations too, and she didn't know whether he was the right person for Bill to confide in. On the other hand, he had come every evening to see Bill, who looked forward to his company.

Anyway, there was nobody else, and Marion was sure that if Bill didn't unburden himself to someone he would never fully recover. 'He has always got on with Pat,' she said to the two girls, 'but the man is such a fool at times.'

'Only when it doesn't matter,' Peggy pointed out.

'Yeah, he just tries to lighten the load a bit,' Violet said. 'I'm pretty certain he can be serious when he needs to be. I'm sure he would be able to help.'

'I agree with Violet,' Peggy said, 'but if Bill doesn't want you to hear about his experiences, then he's not going to say anything to Pat when you or one of the children might overhear.'

'You're right, of course,' Marion said. 'I think he's walking well enough to go out for a pint with Pat now. It will do him good to get out of the house, anyway. I think I'll pop round to Polly's in a minute and she can have a word with Pat when he comes in.'

Pat wasn't at all surprised with what Marion had told his Polly about Bill. Pat had sometimes glimpsed desolation in Bill's eyes and seen the strain inside him like a coiled spring.

'So Marion actually wants me to take Bill for a pint,' he laughed that evening. 'God, that's a turn up for the book, that is.'

'Give over, Pat,' Polly said, though she was laughing too. 'Our Marion has been a lot better with you these last months. Bill won't share his troubles with her, and she thinks he may well talk to you.'

'I hope he does,' Pat said. 'He can't deal with all that bad stuff on his own. Anyone with half an eye can see how the man is suffering.'

Pat decided to take Bill to the Victoria Inn, which was only at the end of Albert Road. Bill said nothing when Pat suggested it, but he seemed happy to be out. The pub was a fairly noisy place, which smelled of beer, and the smoke from cigarettes and pipes hung in the air like a blue fug. Pat was well known at the pub, and he was greeted by many of the men grouped around the bar. Pat had told them all about his brother-in-law injured at Dunkirk, and more than a few pumped Bill's hand and remarked on how well he was doing.

Pat ordered two pints from the buxom barmaid and then, as he handed one to Bill, he said to the others, 'Must excuse us. Spot of business to discuss.' He led the way to the very back of the pub where he found a table.

Bill sat down heavily and took a sip of his pint, and then he began to tell Pat of the nightmare he had had the previous night.

'Woke up screaming and threshing out like a mad man,' he said. 'Scared the living daylights out of Marion, of course, and the kids, 'cos the twins asked me about it this morning.'

Pat nodded. 'Marion came and told Polly about that this morning. She said she'd not only been scared, she'd felt helpless as well.'

'I know,' Bill said. 'In my mind I was grappling with the German who'd appeared from nowhere as we were trying to reach the Dunkirk beaches. He'd just sliced my mate Charley clean in half with a bayonet he had fixed to his rifle. I was a little bit behind him and semi-hidden in the undergrowth, so he probably thought that Charley was on his own. I didn't want to load that on Marion. She was upset enough at the state I was in.'

232

'No,' Pat agreed. 'Some aspects of war are not for women's ears, especially when they know that their men are going out to face the same again. What happened to the scout?'

'I killed him,' Bill said, and he gave a sad little grimace. 'At least he died quick. As for Charley . . . Oh Christ, Pat, he just lay there, his guts spilled out beside him, and he was covered in blood. There was a massive gash in his head, but he wasn't dead. He was screaming in agony. If he had been a horse or a dog I would have put my gun to his head and put him out of his misery. I wanted to do the same for him, but I just couldn't pull the trigger, though he was begging me to. His tortured screams will live with me always as I ploughed my way forward and hoped and prayed he would die soon.'

He turned anguished eyes to Pat. 'There were so many dead, or nearly dead, in that débâcle, friends and comrades. There was so much blood the stink of it lodges in my brain still, and the acrid smells of cordite and fear that clothed every one of us. The whole Dunkirk thing was a mess, and a gigantic defeat, whichever way you look at it.'

Pat didn't speak for he guessed Bill hadn't finished. Suddenly the words were tumbling from his lips as he tried to convey the bloodbath the road to Dunkirk became and the total carnage enacted on the beaches. Pat, watching his eyes as he spoke, realised Bill wasn't just telling him the way it was, he was reliving it all again. Christ, he thought as he signed for more drinks, no wonder the poor sod has nightmares.

Bill was now telling Pat of the armada of little boats that appeared from nowhere to ferry the men to the naval ships anchored in deeper water, and the helpless wretchedness he had felt when he saw a fair few of those ships, filled with rescued soldiers, bombed out of the water.

'The Government called Operation Dynamo a triumph,' Bill said. 'It was anything but. Many of us were in despair, for we all knew, with the best will in the world, not everyone could be rescued in time. The rumour was that the Germans were taking few prisoners. Many would never leave those beaches and a great number of those soldiers there were not long out of boyhood.

'I had befriended one of them; I suppose he reminded me of our Richard. John Barlow was his name and he was such a joker, always with a smile on his face. He'd lied about his age to enlist and was just eighteen before we set off on that ill-fated jaunt across the Channel. I could see he was scared when he realised what we were up against when we were given orders to retreat, though he didn't speak of his fear. None of us did that. But he did ask me if I thought we would make it. I had no idea, of course, but he was little more than a lad and so I said that of course we would and that the Allies would have some plan to rescue us.'

He gave a sudden bitter smile. 'I even said when we were back in Blighty I would stand him a pint now that he was legally old enough to have one.' Bill stopped and his eyes filled with tears.

Pat waited while he fought for composure and then said gently, 'And what happened to him?'

'I passed him in a hollow in the sands as I was making my way to the pier head we'd erected.' Bill said. 'He had both his legs blown off and he lay in a puddle of blood that was draining from him and seeping into the sand. He wasn't dead either, and he turned to look at me as I passed. Ah, dear Christ, when I saw who it was I was completely devastated. I had to turn away from the look in his pain-glazed eyes. Ah, Pat you have no idea . . .'

'No,' Pat agreed. 'I haven't, and I can't share any of the things you experienced, but I am more than prepared to listen. In fact I consider it a privilege that you have confided in me.'

Bill sighed. 'No, I must thank you,' he said. 'I've had to keep so much in so as not to upset those at home. I told Richard and Sarah a little at the hospital when Richard was seeing only the glory of war. I didn't want him to approach it like that – I've seen too many recruits thinking that way – but even then I didn't go into the gory details. Marion knows nothing. I haven't even told her I would have been one of the wounded left behind in Dunkirk if Churchill had got his way.'

'How come?'

Bill gave a shrug. 'He gave orders to leave the wounded behind and take only the able-bodied. I heard two officers talking about it and they sounded quite scandalised. Anyway, they chose to ignore those orders.'

'Glad they did,' Pat said heatedly. 'Why did he say that?'

'Something about the injured taking up too much space in the smaller boats,' Bill said. 'Some undoubtedly did, but how can a civilised country have a policy of leaving injured soldiers to the mercy of the enemy?'

It was beyond Pat's understanding, and he went to get more drinks in with his head reeling.

He was surprised at how tipsy Bill was when he tried to stand at closing time, for he hadn't drunk that much, but then he was probably not used to it any more. Anyway, he couldn't really feel sorry about it either, because the drink had likely loosened his tongue and he'd said things that had to be said.

And so Pat helped Bill home, expecting a tirade from Marion, but he didn't get one.

'Shall I get him up the stairs for you?' he said when she opened the door.

'If you would,' she said.

When the two of them had dealt with Bill, Pat said, 'Don't go for him, will you? He hasn't drunk that much really. It's just that he's not used to it.'

'Well, he wouldn't be, would he?' Marion said.

'I won't go for him, never fear, but did it do any good? Did he open up for you?'

'Oh, yes,' said Pat, 'and I think that it's probably helped him.'

'Then thank you, Pat,' Marion said. 'And what odds if he has taken a drop too much?'

'None at all.' Pat added with a grin, 'Though I would not like to have his head in the morning.'

Marion answered his smile as she agreed, 'No, nor me.'

The next morning a hundred hammers were banging in Bill's head and his mouth was as dry as dust. However, despite that, he felt as if a load had been lifted from between his shoulders making him lighter somehow. He got to his feet gingerly and dressed, ready to face the music.

Marion was in the kitchen and she glanced round as he came to stand beside her. 'I didn't think you would be up so early.'

Bill didn't comment on that. Instead he said, 'I'm sorry, Marion.'

But Marion wasn't sorry because his eyes looked less haunted and she couldn't be anything but pleased about that, and grateful to Pat. So she just kissed Bill lightly on the cheek and said, 'Nothing to be sorry about, Bill.'

'Yes, but . . .'

'Not another word about it,' Marion said firmly. 'Now sit up to the table and I'll have some porridge ready directly.'

Bill was surprised and pleased at Marion's understanding. Glancing round, he said, 'Where is everybody?'

'Well, Sarah is at the shop as she is every Saturday morning, and Richard, Violet and Peggy are at work too. Remember I told you overtime is almost compulsory? The twins have gone round to Polly's because I didn't know what state you would be in this morning.'

Bill had the grace to look sheepish. 'What about Tony?' he asked.

'He and Jack have gone down the allotment,' Marion said. 'In fact, if you are up to it maybe you could take some sandwiches and drinks down for them later?'

'I don't mind at all,' Bill said. 'It's good for my leg to walk it, and anyway, I'd like to see what those two rips have been up to.'

Bill was impressed by what they had achieved when he wandered down later that morning. Eddie too gave credit to his two grandsons and said that he could never have managed so much without them.

Bill told Marion all this when he got home. 'I can understood why your father likes it so much down there,' he said, 'because although there is obviously a lot of work goes on, it's a strangely restful place. The shed is very comfortable and even has an armchair where your dad can sit and smoke his pipe in peace. It's a lovely bolt hole, and well away from your mother. Eddie says she's never set foot in the place and he doesn't think she ever will.'

'Well, I bet he didn't look upset when he told you that.'

'No,' Bill said with a smile. 'No, he didn't at all and, God knows, if I was married to a woman like your mother I would have had to have a bolt hole long ago.'

Two more weeks passed with Bill improving daily. Since the night he unburdened himself to Pat he'd had fewer nightmares, and those he did have he had been able to deal with without raising the house. He was soon able to take the twins to the park again, and Tony and Jack too, if they weren't needed on the allotment. He had even managed a kick-about with the boys a time or two. He was always ready for a game of cards or Ludo, or Snakes and Ladders, and he tucked Magda and Missie in each night and read them a story.

Marion was delighted that Bill seemed so much better in every way, though she knew that meant he wouldn't be with them much longer, and she did worry about that.

Peggy and Violet had met two chaps, Ralph and Terry, from the RAF at the pictures one day, and they'd taken the girls for a drink afterwards. Marion had been a bit concerned that something might have happened to them when they were late home and she waited up for them. Bill thought she was being silly because they were grown young women, but he agreed to stay up with her. They were having a cup of cocoa before bed when Peggy and Violet arrived.

'Had a nice time?' Marion asked.

'Smashing, thanks,' Peggy said.

'What did you see?'

'*The Lady Vanishes*,' Violet said. 'It was ever so good. We met these two RAF chaps and they took us for a drink afterwards.'

'Yes,' Peggy said. 'And when we were in the pub they were saying that Hitler has only got till September to invade us because then the tides will be against him or something.'

'I never heard that before,' Bill said.

'But you were right about one thing,' Violet said. 'Remember when you said that Hitler had to knock the air force out before he could invade?'

'Yeah, but I was only quoting what I read in the paper.'

'Well, it's right, according to these fellows, anyway, and they're doing their level best to stop them.'

'Isn't it scary that seemingly our whole survival lies solely on the slim shoulders of those young pilots in the RAF.'

'I'll say,' Peggy said. 'They let you know it, mind. They're real cocky, ain't they, Vi?'

'Oh, yes,' said Violet. 'And think that they're God's gift. But for all that they were good fun and we've agreed to see them again next week.'

'I think they've got to be really brave to go up in an aeroplane in the first place,' Marion said. 'You'd never get me up in one of those things.'

'Yeah, and they told us that they have only a few weeks' training.'

'Small wonder so many of them are shot down, then,' said Marion.

'I know,' Bill said. 'It's like some deadly football match score: we lose five to their twenty-five.'

Marion nodded slowly. 'When I go to Mass now I don't know what to pray for,' she said. 'Peace, but what peace? Peace at any cost, peace where we can let Hitler do what he wants, let him take any land he wants, excuse his brutality against innocent people.'

'That wouldn't be peace, that would be anarchy or worse,' Bill said. 'Just pray for us all to get through this in one piece. That's all most people want.'

Richard, now a member of the Local Defence Volunteers, was very frustrated. 'I seem to spend all my time marching up and down my old school playground with a broomstick on my shoulder,' he complained to his father. 'They say they're short on rifles but they're making us a laughing stock.'

'They're short on uniforms too,' Marion said. 'I mean, all you have got to identify what organisation you belong to is that khaki armband I stitched to the sleeve of your jumper.'

'I suppose I can fight without uniforms or

241

armbands,' Richard said, 'but they will have to get a move on finding us some rifles soon. I've never even learned to fire one yet, never mind tried to hit a target. If Hitler does invade I can hardly frighten him off with a broom handle.'

Bill did see his son's point. It didn't exactly inspire confidence that if invasion actually happened, there was only this body of ill-equipped men to defend them. Much as he valued the time with his family, he was anxious to get well enough to rejoin his unit as quickly as possible.

Bill didn't sleep for some time that night, and when he did he was woken up by a blast. Marion had also been jerked awake, but she wasn't aware what had woken her. She didn't know what a bomb blast sounded like and she opened her eyes to see Bill sitting on the side of the bed, pulling on his trousers.

'What was that?' she said as another blast rent the air, and then another.

Bill was at the window now, lifting the blackout curtain aside and peering in to the night. 'Bombs,' he said.

'Bombs!' Marion exclaimed. 'Where's the sirens?'

'God knows,' Bill said. 'But there's only one plane that I can see, so it might have slipped through.'

Marion joined him at the window and saw that skies were clear and, though the moon was no longer completely full, in its golden light they could see the glow of a fire in the distance and the plane, flying away now it had delivered its lethal cargo.

'D'you think there will be more?' Marion whispered.

'I don't know,' Bill said, 'but I'll keep watch. You lie down and rest while you can.'

'You should be the one resting.'

'Not any more,' Bill said. 'I am nearly fully fit again now, and trained as a soldier. I can keep awake for days if I have to. Now I'm awake there's no point in my coming back to bed; I'll not be able to rest again tonight.'

In the end, Marion was prevailed upon to lie down, but she barely slept and in the end was glad when the alarm heralded the sound of another day.

Everyone was talking about the bombs over breakfast. The lodgers and Richard had heard them; so had Sarah, it but she'd been only semi awake and thought it had been thunder. Tony was annoyed that he had slept right through it.

Later that day Marion found out the bombs had fallen in Erdington and a young soldier had been killed. 'The paper says the bomber was probably looking for Fort Dunlop,' Bill said that evening after scrutinising the *Evening Mail*. 'Course, he would find that hard to do now that the canals are boarded every night.'

Marion nodded, yet when it had first been proposed she hadn't seen the sense of it. Bill had pointed out that many smallish factories now making things for the war effort, like those on the Lichfield Road, backed on to canals. 'They were built like that years ago because the canal was a handy place to tip the factory waste,' he said. 'Then that canal meets with others at Salford Bridge and from there one runs up the Tyburn Road, which is full of smallish factories and workshops, also backing on to the canal. It goes on to run alongside Fort Dunlop and then the Vickers factory where they're making the Spitfires. Think of the killing the Luftwaffe could make if their bombers caught sight of the gleam of water. They would just have to follow it and could annihilate everything in no time at all. Anyroad, last night is evidence that boarding the canal works, though I'm sorry about the young soldier killed.'

People of Birmingham braced themselves that night for a further, more widespread, attack, feeling sure that the German planes would be back to have another go. However, nothing happened that night or the next, though an uneasy feel hung in the air all that weekend. The attack galvanised the Whittakers into getting the cellar prepared in case they had to stay in it for any length of time. That Sunday, after Mass, Marion and Sarah scrubbed and cleaned with great enthusiasm and then Bill and Richard whitewashed the walls.

Bill also fitted a blackout shutter across the grating. 'If I didn't, you couldn't turn the light on down here, could you?' he told Marion.

She looked round the dim room. For all their efforts it was a cold and uninviting place, with some wooden chairs that Bill had done his best to repair and the sagging old sofa. No one would linger there by choice, but Marion was well aware that they might have to stay down there for some time, and to do that in the pitch black would be unthinkable.

Bill caught sight of her face. 'I know it ain't a palace, old girl, but it will be a sight safer for you down here. It's got to be, really.'

'I know,' Marion said. 'It's just that . . . well, I don't want to have to use it much.'

'I can understand that,' Bill said. 'I hope you don't, either. But in the meantime, when I go back I can rest in the knowledge that whatever Hitler throws at Brum you and the kids will be safe. Even your old ma has come up trumps with the mattress because of this flaming war, though personally I think it's your father's influence, because the boys are doing such good work on that allotment. But whatever the reason, a mattress is a mattress and somewhere for the kids to lie, and you too if the raids go on for hours. Now Richard and me are going round to fetch it.'

'Why don't you take Pat with you?'

'Because I don't need to take Pat with me,' Bill said, 'I'm almost as fit now as ever I was, and that's what the Medical Board will say next week. You know that as well as I do.'

Marion felt her heart sink at the thought that soon her Bill would be in danger again, and yet she could almost feel his itchiness to be gone. She followed him up into the living room where she set about preparing her shelter bag. She had been shocked into doing it when war had been declared and the sirens blared out, but now she realised she was totally unprepared. The bank books and insurance policies were still there, but some of the photos were missing and the children had taken out the cards, books and dominoes. So she collected everything together again and added a packet of biscuits she was lucky enough to have got. Whatever happened now she would take that shelter bag with her at all times, she decided.

FOURTEEN

Bill was proclaimed a hundred per cent fit, but he tried to swallow his pleasure as he entered the house because he knew that Marion wouldn't consider that good news at all. She tried to be pleased for him and said all the right words and yet she was fooling no one. Peggy knew a little of what she was going through because she confessed to Sarah that she had felt the same when Sam was declared fit to go back.

The younger children were openly upset for they had got used to having their father around.

'I haven't got to go back till the seventeenth and that's a few days away yet,' Bill told them.

They were still despondent and in the end, Bill with a glance across the table to Marion, said, 'How about if tomorrow is fine we all take off to Sutton Park for the day?'

'Where's Sutton Park?' Tony asked.

'A really big place a bit of a distance from here,' Bill said. 'I've not been there very often myself, to tell you the truth.'

'I remember it,' Sarah said. 'You and Mom took me and Richard before Tony was born. It's got big lakes in it, and it's so huge that rich people used to drive round it in their cars. You'll have to go on the train, or at least that's how we went.'

The twins were speechless with excitement and their eyes danced as Tony cried, 'A train? Oh boy! We're going on a train.'

Bill smiled at Tony's awestruck tones. 'I take it that meets with your approval?'

'You bet,' Tony said, and Magda and Missie nodded vigorously.

'We could take a picnic. What d'you say, Marion?'

Marion hated disappointing the children but taking off for the day like that was such an alien thing for her to do that she found herself saying, 'Don't be silly, Bill. I can't do that.'

'Course you can,' Bill said. 'What's stopping you?'

'Well, I have things to do and—'

'Please don't worry about us, Marion,' Violet said. 'We are all big enough to look after ourselves. I would go while you have the chance.'

'Oh, go on, Mum,' Sarah said. 'It will do you good. Don't you think so, Richard?'

'I'll say,' Richard said. 'You'll have a great time. I remember I loved that park. I only wish I could come too.'

'We can ask your Poll along,' Bill said, seeing that Marion was wavering, 'and she can bring Orla and Jack.'

'Oh, yippee!' Tony said, punching the air with his fists. Magda cast her eyes to the ceiling and everyone burst out laughing. Through the laughter, though, Marion saw Bill's eyes and she guessed he wanted this day to hold as a memory to take with him when he left them again. How could she deny him that?

The magic of that day was helped by the weather. The sun shone on them from a bright blue sky as they walked to the station. The children were so excited because none of them had ever been on a train before and the amazement on their faces when that little train puffed into the station with a hiss of steam brought smiles to the three adults' faces.

They loved the journey, especially when it reached the open countryside, and they crowded against the long window pointing things out one to another. They had seen plenty of things growing since the war began, though, in addition to their granddad's allotment, because parts of parks and ornamental gardens had been given over to growing food. However, the children had never seen cows placidly chewing the cud, horses gazing at the passing train over a five-barred gate or galloping in the fields, and sheep relentlessly tugging at the grass, and they were enchanted by it all.

'Oh, I wish it was a longer journey,' Orla said when Bill told them the next stop was theirs.

'Me too in a way,' Magda agreed. 'But I want to see this park as well.'

'Why haven't we ever come before?' Tony said, as train pulled into the little station.

Before Bill or Marion had a chance to answer, Jack said, 'Why worry? We're going now, ain't we? And we've got the train journey back to look forward to as well.'

At the bottom of a little hill that led down from the station, was a shop selling an assortment of goods. Bill went in and bought each child a net on a rod.

'What's it for?' Tony asked.

'What does it look like it's for?' Bill said, leading the way towards the Park gates. 'It's for catching tiddlers, and anything else you may find in the river. We've brought a couple of jam jars with us.'

'Are tiddlers fish?' Magda asked. 'Proper fish.'

Bill smiled, 'If you find any real fish in the streams of Sutton Park then I'm a Dutchman, Magda, and anyway, you'd never catch them with nets like these. But you might catch other things and when you've had a good look at them in the jam jar we'll let them go again.'

'Good,' said Missie. 'I don't like killing things.'

'Well, there's no need to do that.'

'Let's not talk about killing,' Polly said. 'There's enough talk about that all around us as it is. Let's have one day when we can try and forget the blooming war and everything about it.'

'Hear, hear,' Marion said heartily. 'Let's just concentrate on enjoying ourselves.'

They were surprised that they had to pay to go into a park.

'Sutton Coldfield is a separate town from Birmingham, but if we lived here we wouldn't have to pay anything,' Bill explained.

'Oh, look at the playground,' Magda cried, as they went through the gate. 'Come on, Missie. Let's see if we can grab a swing.'

Marion, Bill and Polly watched the twins pounding across the grass with Tony, Jack and even Orla in hot pursuit. 'They'll be lucky,' Marion said. 'They'll have to stand in a queue with everyone else.' Many people had taken advantage of the good weather and the park was packed.

When the children had finished in the playground there were the streams to paddle in and fish with their nets. They were exhilarated when they managed to catch a wriggling tiddler to tip into one of the jam jars. In the woods, the girls explored the many paths and collected leaves and pine cones while Tony and Jack found numerous trees to climb before they sat down to devour the picnic that Polly and Marion had spread on table-cloths laid on the grass.

After they had all eaten their fill, Polly and Marion tidied up and lay down for a little snooze while Bill took the children around to see the lakes, though a fair bit of the park was out of bounds: some of it cultivated, and a large area given over to the army. When they returned to the woods Bills organised the children in a game of hide-and-seek.

They returned home tired, grubby, sun-kissed and very happy. Marion knew it was a day she would always remember. To put the icing on the cake, the chippy they passed on their way home from the train station had fish in, though the queue was out of the door, but they joined it anyway and they were all able to enjoy a fish and chip supper when they got in.

However, barely had the last chip been eaten than the first explosions were heard in the distance. There was a collective groan and Marion exclaimed, 'Bloody hell! We have this to contend with now. We've had such a wonderful day and this seems to taint it.'

'No,' Bill said, 'nothing could do that. Anyway, this might just be a skirmish, but we'd better not take chances. Come on down the cellar.'

Everyone was reluctant but no one refused.

As they were descending the steps Peggy said, 'I'd like to know where those blooming sirens are.'

'So would I,' Marion said. 'Our Polly said that when she came up the entry the other day to go to the public shelters in Aston Park, she spotted a policeman riding up the Lichfield Road on a bike and ringing a bell.'

'Doesn't hit you with the same sense of urgency somehow, does it?' Violet said, and Marion had to agree.

It was three and a half hours later before they heard the all clear. Again, none of the explosions had come that close. The children were so tired by then that they could barely keep their eyes open. Marion and Bill were also feeling the effects of that long day and they went to bed not long after the children.

Marion lay cuddled against Bill and wished that she could stop time. She also wished she could love Bill as she longed to do, but she knew he wouldn't allow himself to do anything that might be potentially harmful to her. She gave an almost involuntary sob, and Bill leaned over and kissed the salt tears from her cheeks.

'Marion,' he said, 'I love you with all my heart and soul, and I would really like to show you how much, but , . .'

'Hush,' Marion said. 'It isn't that, not totally that, anyroad. It's just that when you're gone and in the thick of it again, I'll worry about you so much. I know that you're a brave man, Bill, but don't be too brave, will you? I want a live husband to come back to me, not a dead hero.'

'Don't fret yourself,' Bill said, and he gave Marion a reassuring squeeze. 'I intend to come back in one piece. I have too much to lose to want to throw my life away.'

Everyone got up to see Bill off the day he had to report back to Thorpe Street Barracks, even the lodgers. Marion had promised herself she wouldn't cry because it only made it more difficult for Bill. It was hard to remain stoical, though, with the children so upset. Magda and Missie were crying in earnest and Tony was pretending he wasn't, while unshed tears also glittered in Sarah and Richard's eyes. Even Peggy and Violet were a bit sniffy.

Bill wrapped his arms around his two younger daughters and told them how much he loved them and would miss them, but that only made them cry the louder. Then he hugged Tony and Richard, saying to his eldest son, 'Right, son. You're man of the house now and from what I have seen while I have been at home, I couldn't leave the family in better hands.'

Marion saw two tears seep out of Richard's eyes and trickle down his cheeks at his father's words.

'Bye, Dad,' he said huskily. 'Look after yourself.'

Then it was Sarah's turn, and as Bill took her in his arms he noticed how much she had come to resemble her mother as she was growing up. He held his daughter tight and kissed her cheek as she said, 'Bye, Dad, I ain't half going to miss you.'

'I'll miss you too. All of you. Look after your mother.'

'Ah, Dad, you don't have to ask me that,' Sarah said as she kissed his smooth cheek.

Bill nodded and turned to Peggy and Violet,

intending to shake them by the hand. However, he felt he had got to know them well in the time he had been home, and liked them both very much, and so he hugged them too.

And then Sarah saw the look pass between her parents, and so did the others, and the lodgers, followed by Richard and more reluctantly Tony, made their way to the kitchen to give them a bit of privacy.

At the door Magda protested strongly, 'I want to say goodbye to Dad.'

'You've said goodbye,' Sarah said, firmly. 'Now it's Mom's turn and she wants to say goodbye to Dad on her own.'

Magda knew that when Sarah spoke in a certain way it was better to obey her and so allowed herself to be led into the kitchen, though she continued to grumble.

The woebegone, hard-done-by look on her face made Marion and Bill smile. 'There goes one very disgruntled lady,' whispered Bill as the door closed and they were alone in the hall. 'But how right they were to leave us alone because I want to do this,' and he pulled Marion into his arms with a sigh. 'I love you with everything in me,' he said. 'And I want you to promise me something?'

'Anything?'

'I want you to go to the cellar any time there is a raid, however far away it seems to be.'

'I will, of course.'

'Ah, that's easy to say here and now,' Bill said.

'But what if the raid was to come in the middle of the night and you are warm and cozy and the children fast asleep in bed? You must get up and take shelter, even if you would rather turn over and forget it was happening. You are all very dear to me, and you most of all. Promise me?' he demanded, looking deep in her eyes.

'I promise,' Marion said. 'I've as much desire to keep us all safe as you have.'

'That makes my heart easier,' Bill said, and he drew Marion close once more. As they drew apart he lifted his kitbag onto his shoulder as he said, 'Be there waiting when I come home again.'

Marion couldn't make any sort of reply, her throat was too tight, but she nodded as she opened the door and stood watching as Bill marched away, his back straight and resolute, she noticed, his strides firm and his boots ringing out against the cobbles. She felt proud of him, but was afraid for him too. He turned to wave at the corner and she drank in the last sight she would have of her beloved husband for a long long time. She went back in the house with a sigh, shut the door behind her and, leaning back against it, eventually gave way to the tears that she had bravely kept in check. But even those she scrubbed away before going in to face the family.

Polly, knowing how Marion would be feeling, popped round to see her later that morning. 'On your own?' she said.

'Except for Magda and Missie,' Marion said, going into the kitchen to put the kettle on. 'They're in the garden. Tony set off to call for your Jack to go down the allotment. I thank God for that place, you know. It's kept them both mischief free all summer and now it's something for Tony to focus his mind on because he was very sad saying goodbye to his father this morning. The others are all at work so they have had no time to dwell on it either. I suppose you won't say no to a cup of tea?'

'I'd love a cup, if it won't leave you short.'

'No, I'm all right,' Marion said as she set out the cups. 'With the big ones out most days, the ration stretches quite well.'

With the tea made the women sat either side of the kitchen table, their normal place for a good old gossip.

'Everyone seems to be working their socks off at the moment,' Polly remarked. 'As Mary Ellen said, they don't say you've got to do overtime but if you don't half feel guilty if you say no.'

'Richard, Peggy and Violet are the same,' Marion said. 'And they all like the extra money. In fact, Sarah is quite envious.'

'Well, that Mrs Jenkins is known as a stingy cow.'

'She is,' Marion agreed. 'And because of the way she is, when rationing was introduced I had no intention of registering her as my grocer. I wouldn't give her that satisfaction.'

'You want to get your Sarah shifted from there.'

'I think she might shift herself when she's sixteen,' Marion said. 'She keeps threatening to, anyroad, 'cos it ain't only the money. She feels she ain't doing nothing for the war effort like everyone else in the house, especially Richard in this volunteer force. And talking of Richard,' she said as she got to her feet, 'I must hurry and get a bite ready for him at least. He don't have long at home because there's training this afternoon.'

'That's tough when he's at work in the morning.'

'Yeah,' Marion agreed. 'But he says that he isn't the only one. He trains on Wednesday evening and Sunday morning, as well. Course, he's missed Mass to do this and Father McIntyre came here on Tuesday to see the reason why. He didn't seem to care when I said that he'd been training with the Home Guard. I didn't dare tell Bill and I was very glad that he'd gone down to the allotment when Father McIntyre called because I think he would have given him short shrift, priest or not. Anyway Father McIntyre said that nothing should come before Richard's immortal soul and he still had to go to Mass every Sunday regardless. The only one he can go to and still make the training is the half six Mass, and I will hate waking him that early, but I shall have to.'

'Huh,' said Polly. 'You'd think that there would be some dispensation. You know, McIntyre might be one of the few people in Great Britain who might need to be reminded that there is a war on. Surely normal rules don't apply?'

'They do from where he's standing.'

'Bloody priests, they're all the same.'

'Polly!' Marion said in mock horror. 'Fancy cursing the clergy!'

'They need cursing the way they prate on,' Polly said. 'God, it's enough to make a saint swear.'

Marion, with a laugh, gave her a sister a push. 'And you are nothing like a saint.'

'Too bloody right I'm not,' Polly said with a definite nod. 'All that holier-than thou business would get you down. Not comfortable people to have around at all, I wouldn't have thought.' Heaving herself to her feet she said, 'Just for now, though, I'd best get back to my lot, before they come looking for me. Shall I see if the twins want to come back up to our house for an hour or two? You know how we love having them.'

'It would probably do them good,' Marion said. 'They went out with their skipping ropes, but when I looked out they was just sitting on the steps looking as miserable as sin.'

It was the very best thing Polly could have done for the twins, for they were almost consumed with sadness. But they loved their aunt dearly, and also liked the fact that Aunt Polly didn't have a garden so all of the kids from the yard and streets around would play together. They were never stopped from playing with anybody, not the girls who seemed to have a terribly itchy heads, or even the one with purple around her mouth because she had impetigo.

Much later, as they walked home, Missie said, 'I feel a bit guilty that after we got to Auntie Polly's I didn't think about Daddy, not once.'

Magda knew exactly how her sister felt but she said, 'I know, but I bet Daddy wouldn't want us to be sad all the time. Remember if we were miserable or owt he used to always ask us what our long faces were about?'

'Yeah . . .'

'And he's being really brave going off to war again when he was hurt the once already,' Magda went on. 'So I think that we have got to be just as brave and not keep on about missing him and that.'

'Like Mommy says, "What can't be cured must be endured",' Missie said.

The indiscriminate raids and skirmishes went on, though none came very close to Aston. As soon as the crumps and crashes were heard Richard reported to the ARP headquarters, as the Home Guard commander had advised his men to do in the event of a raid to see if they could be of use. Everyone was soon complaining about the lack of warning sirens and the *Evening Mail* eventually printed details of how the system was supposed to work.

Sarah read it out to the others. 'Apparently the lookouts for the planes are volunteers from the Royal Observer Corps and they are based in 1,400 bases nationwide,' she said. 'Then they relay information to Fighter Command and ARP Headquarters and that information is then sent to schools and factories where the sirens are placed.'

'Well, it isn't terrible efficient, is it?' Marion said. 'After all, it's governments start wars, not ordinary people, but we have to live with the decisions they make. The very least they can do, I would have thought, is devise a system that gives people enough warning so that they can take cover!'

'Hear, hear,' Peggy and Violet said.

But it was 23 August before the sirens were sounded in time. The eerie wail was enough to strike fear into the stoutest heart. It began just as Marion was thinking of following the children to bed and she roused them quickly. The younger children were sleepy and uncooperative. Marion soon had them bedding down on the mattress and they went to sleep again regardless of what was going on around them.

'I wish I could drop off like that,' Sarah said, enviously regarding her sleeping brother and sisters. 'I'm tired enough. My eyes are gritty with tiredness.'

'And mine,' Peggy said. 'But I'm afraid to close them.'

They were immensely glad to hear the reassuring sound of the all clear belting out after only two and a half hours, rousing even the children from their slumber. The twins still rubbed their eyes sleepily.

'Thank God,' Peggy said fervently, as they made

their way upstairs. 'We might be able to grab a bit of shuteye, if we're lucky.'

Tony complained as he often did. 'I'm not tired any more after that kip I had in the cellar.'

Marion, though, was totally unsympathetic. 'Stop moaning and get upstairs while you can,' she said with such asperity that he and the twins knew that any further opposition was useless.

Despite her tiredness Marion waited up for Richard, knowing that he might be hungry when he came in, but even when he had eaten and gone to bed and the house grew still and quiet, Marion found it difficult to sleep. She tossed from side to side in the bed and only fell into a fitful doze as dawn was painting the sky with a rosy hue.

FIFTEEN

Although it was still summer, the cellar felt really clammy and Marion had decided to buy an oil stove to warm the place up a bit. But the morning after the raid she felt like death warmed up and had no enthusiasm at all for going down the Bull Ring to look for one. She knew that she should also check on her parents but she had even less enthusiasm for that. Instead, she went round to see Polly, taking the twins with her. Tony had already set off for the allotment.

Tiredness was also etched on Polly's white face and her eyes had blue smudges beneath them.

Marion said, 'You look as tired as I feel.'

'Well, them shelters under the tennis courts in Aston Park ain't built for comfort,' Polly said. 'And then when we came home again, after it was all over, the night air roused me and I couldn't seem to get off again. Do you want me to come down the Bull Ring with you today?'

'Oh, I wasn't going to bother.'

'Why, just 'cos you lost a bit of beauty sleep?' Polly said. 'Come on, Marion. Do you want an oil stove or don't you?'

'Yes, but . . .'

'This ain't the time for buts,' Polly said firmly. 'One thing I do know is that somehow normal life has to go on, despite these raids, or Hitler will have won. And think of the good bargains we might find at the same time.' Then she turned to the girls. 'Bet you two would like a gander down the Bull Ring, wouldn't you?'

'Not half!' Magda exclaimed, while her sister more politely said, 'Oh, yes please.'

'Oh, all right then,' Marion said. 'You've convinced me that it is far more beneficial traipsing into town to buy an oil stove than it is to go back home and have forty winks, though that's more appealing to me at the moment.'

'Stop moaning,' Polly said as she shrugged herself into her cardigan. 'Get a move on. The sooner we get there the sooner we'll be back, and then you might still have time for forty winks.'

With the twins between them they scurried off to catch one of the trams running down the Lichfield Road.

Marion bought an oil stove at a very reasonable price from a man in the Rag Market. Many people had had the same idea, the man told her, and he'd had a run on them since the raids began. When Marion said she lived in Aston he readily agreed to deliver it to her house that night after he had finished on his stall.

'What time will that be?' Marion asked. 'Before the war the Saturday market could go on till quite late.'

'The blackout effectively put paid to that,' the man told her. 'We're far more controlled by the hours of daylight, and now the nights are really starting to draw in. Anyroad, Aston ain't that far away. Give us your address and I can have it over to your place by about seven this evening. That do you?'

Marion thought that would do very well.

After they left the Rag Market, Polly said, 'There, that was easy enough. Now we can have a dekko round the stalls.'

The Bull Ring was a sad place in wartime. Many of the stalls were gone and those selling produce had little of it as so much was either on ration or unavailable. Marion would have loved to get hold of sausages. All the family loved them, but they hadn't tasted one since the start of the war. Sausages were not rationed, but the merest rumour that one of the butchers had anything like that would result in queues that snaked around other stalls. The couple of times Marion had joined such a queue the sausages had run out long before she'd reached the counter.

There was no hint of sausages that day, though, and looking around, Polly felt strangely dispirited. 'The buzz and clamour of the place ain't the same, is it?' she said.

Marion shook her head sadly. 'The flower sellers are gone as well. I used to love to see them grouped round Nelson's Statue or in front of St Martin's. Do you remember them, girls?'

Magda and Missie nodded eagerly and Magda said, 'I loved all the colours of the flowers in their baskets.'

'And the smells when you passed them,' Missie said. 'Why aren't they here no more?'

'I suppose because people can't eat flowers,' Marion said. 'Likely the gardens where they used to grow flowers have had to start growing vegetables.'

Magda gave a sudden sigh and burst out, 'Oh, isn't war horrible? It spoils just about everything.'

'Nowt stops her, though,' Polly said, jerking her head in the direction of Woolworths. And there in front of the store was the blind old lady selling carrier bags. They had never been to the Bull Ring and not seen her there. Her thin slightly nasal voice rang out over everything, adding to the general cacophony as she chanted continuously, 'Carriers. Handy Carriers.'

'Yes,' Marion agreed in admiration. 'She's here every day regardless.'

'Maybe we should all try to be the same,' Polly said. 'Let's take a leaf out of her book, shall we, and cheer up a bit? Come on, I know what will put a smile on your faces, anyroad, girls. Let's go into the Market Hall and look at the animals.'

'Oh, yes,' said Missie, who would have loved a pet of her own.

'Can we wait till the clock chimes as well?' Magda asked.

'Well,' said Polly, glancing at her watch, 'if we put our skates on we should be in time to hear it now because it's very nearly ten o'clock.'

The girls glanced at one another. They needed no further bidding and they were off speeding across the cobblestones, dodging the barrow boys and the busy shoppers and galloping up the steps of the Market Hall. They gave only a cursory glance to the old lags lining them, who their father had told them were flotsam from the Great War. They held trays around their necks that sold razor blades, shoelaces and the like, and Magda had always felt so sorry for them, but there was no time to spare that morning, and the two of them burst through the doors of the old Market Hall side by side. When they skidded to a stop beneath the magnificent clock they saw that they just had one minute to spare.

It seemed like everyone, even the adults, had stopped what they were doing and were waiting and a hush seemed to fall over the whole place. The twins looked up at the massive and elaborate construction, which was carved out of solid oak, the chimes sounded by the figures of three knights and a dame striking three brass bells. Suddenly the clock ticked forward and the tunes heralding the hour began, just as Marion and Polly caught up with the girls and smiled to one another at the rapt attention on their faces as the ten chimes began.

When it was finished and the babble of voices rose again in the Market Hall, Polly said, 'Come on then, let's be away to Pimm's pet stall,' and Magda and Missie followed her eagerly.

They left the girls there playing with the pretty kittens, boisterous puppies and cuddly rabbits, and trying to teach the budgies to talk, while they searched for bargains. There was horse meat for sale and they both bought some, though Marion complained to Polly that it was daylight robbery at two and six a pound. It was off ration, however, and so was offal, and so she added liver and a few kidneys to her purchases, because with them all working so hard she liked to give the older children and the lodgers something nourishing in the evening. She bought a variety of vegetables and some fruit as well, all at bargain prices.

It was as they set off for home that they spotted a tout opening his suitcase in a side road, out of the gaze of any passing policeman, though a scout was posted at the entry to keep a weather eye out. The touts sold black market stuff, and though it was against the law and you had to watch what you bought from them, they always had a crowd around them, listening to their patter and the banter they exchanged with the watching women.

'Shall we see what they're flogging today?' Marion asked.

'May as well now we're here,' Polly said.

The two women were very pleased they did, because in the suitcase were flasks of various sizes and hot-water bottles, things that were never now seen in the shops. Marion thought how comforting it would be to have a warm cup of tea to drink in that dingy cellar, and Polly felt the same, so they bought a large flask each. Marion also bought two hot-water bottles to warm the mattress and blankets up for the children if the raids should continue into the winter.

All in all she was very pleased with her purchases, and as they made for the tram home she thought Polly had been right to persuade her to make the effort to go down to the Bull Ring that day.

Marion cooked the meal early that night so that everyone would be all finished by the time the man came with the oil stove. When he arrived they all trooped down to the cellar to have a look at it.

'Might stink a bit,' Peggy said. 'Well, bound to really, but it will keep the place warmer if these raids go on into the autumn.'

'Let's hope there isn't one tonight,' Marion said. 'I could do with a good sleep in my own bed.'

Everyone agreed with that.

The night was so still and quiet, and Marion was beginning to feel quite hopeful as she got the children ready for bed. However, because they'd eaten earlier than usual they all claimed that they were too hungry to sleep. Marion was unsure if was just a delaying tactic. It was already nearly an hour past their normal bedtime when they were at school.

But she wasn't up to dealing with the grumbles and complaints and so she went into the kitchen to make them some bread and dripping. When the siren blasted out Marion dropped the knife she'd been holding and then, with fingers that shook, made up drinks for the children, made tea in the new flask and threw into the bag some of the apples she had bought in the Bull Ring that morning.

Richard slipped out of the door as the first explosions could be heard in the distance and the children, even Sarah, were urging her to hurry.

At first, they played cards to pass the time, but Marion could see that though Magda, Missie and even Tony were dropping with tiredness, they were also very scared as the blasts and explosions were louder and closer than they had been in previous raids.

'Why don't you lie down?' Marion suggested. 'If you do manage to drop off you won't hear the bangs.'

'I don't think I'll sleep much,' Magda said. 'And it ain't only the bangs either. I'll be too hungry.'

'I'm too hungry too.' Tony said. 'My belly's grumbling like mad.'

'Well, I have nothing for you to eat but apples,' Marion said. 'But you're welcome to one of them, if you like.'

Magda didn't want apples. If the sirens hadn't gone off when they did, she would have had a piece of bread spread with delicious dripping, liberally sprinkled with salt. She felt the saliva fill her mouth at the thought of it. What was one mangy apple to that? But it was no good saying anything because that was all there was, and so she took the apple her mother was offering her without complaint.

The children did fall asleep in the end and the others had a very welcome cup of tea from the flask before Sarah and Violet got in the other end of the mattress. Peggy refused to leave Marion, who wouldn't allow herself to sleep while a raid was going on.

'I know it's silly,' she said to Peggy, 'But I just feel that someone should be at least semi alert in case anything should happen, though if it goes on very long then I think I will have to prop up my eyelids with matchsticks. But there's no need for you to stop up as well. I'll wake you if necessary.'

Peggy shook her head. 'I won't leave you on your own,' she said. 'There's nothing worse. It can't be much longer now.'

But the raid went on hour upon hour, some explosions so loud they made Marion and Peggy jump as they sat stoically on the old rickety kitchen chairs. However, when the all clear sounded Marion woke with a jerk to find she and Peggy had fallen asleep leaning against one another.

'So much for staying awake while the raid was going on,' Marion remarked ruefully. 'And it serves me right, I know, but I've got a terrific crick in my neck.'

'Me too.' Peggy got to her feet with difficulty. 'And it's not surprising that we fell asleep in the end because it's almost five o'clock,' she said, astounded, looking blearily at her watch.

Violet groaned as she pulled herself from under the blankets. 'I feel as if I've hardly been to bed at all,' she said. 'Thank God it's Sunday tomorrow.'

'Today, you mean,' Peggy corrected.

'Yeah,' Violet said. 'Well, in my opinion there shouldn't be a five o'clock on a Sunday morning, and if it is all the same to you, I'm going back to bed when we get in.'

'I don't mind in the least,' Marion said. 'It's the most sensible thing to do, but do you want a bite to eat first?'

Violet shook her head. 'I must be in a bad way,' she said, 'because I'm far more tired than I am hungry.'

'I ain't,' Tony burst out. 'I'm starving, I am, and I bet that Missie and Magda are as well.'

Magda nodded vigorously. 'You bet I am,' she said. 'I was hungry even before I came down the cellar.'

'All right,' Marion said decisively 'After a night like that no one has to go to Communion this morning, so help me fold up these blankets, and then what do you say to dripping toast all round?'

The roar of approval was answer enough and just a little later, when Richard came in the door grey-faced with exhaustion, she insisted that he sit and eat with them. 'Then you're going to bed,' she said. 'Have you training today?'

'No,' Richard said. 'After yesterday it was cancelled. But what about Mass?'

'You leave Mass and Father McIntyre to me,' Marion said emphatically. 'God will understand that you need all the rest that you can get at the moment because I don't think that Hitler has finished with us yet.'

And that was what she told the priest that same morning when she stayed behind after the eleven o'clock Mass, after sending the others home with Sarah. The priest looked at her almost coldly and said, 'You don't seem to realise that it is a mortal sin to miss Mass.'

'Oh, I realise that all right,' Marion snapped. 'What you don't seem to realise is that there is a war on, only I don't for the life of me see how that has escaped your notice.'

Father McIntyre ignored the sarcasm. 'War or no war—' he began.

But he got no further for Marion leaped in, 'Now look here, Father, I haven't come to bandy words with you, or ask permission or any rubbish like that. I am telling you how it is going to be and that's that. My son is not a machine and from now on he will come to Mass as often as he is able to and that is all. And as for mortal sin? Well, we'll both take our chances with the Almighty.'

Father McIntyre was astounded. He could

maybe understand Polly talking to him in this way, but he would never thought it of Marion, and he snapped out, 'You are being blasphemous, Marion.'

'No, I'm not,' Marion retorted. 'How can what I said be blasphemous? I mean it. God knows what we are going through, and I imagine that He will be far more sympathetic than you. Anyway,' she went on with a toss of her head, 'there is little more to be said.'

'I advise you to think about what you're doing.'

'I have thought about it, Father,' Marion said firmly. 'And now I'll bid you good day.'

All the way home, Marion went over and over the things she had said to the priest, a little embarrassed and yet amazed at her temerity. Before the war she couldn't have envisaged any occasion when she would have done such a thing, and yet the more she thought of it the more glad she was that she had stood up to the priest at long last.

Many bombs had landed in Aston so that afternoon Marion went round to see if her parents were all right.

'And why shouldn't we be all right?' Clara asked.

'Well, Mammy, there were houses damaged in Aston last night,' Marion said. 'I just think that under the stairs is not very secure. If this house was hit—'

'No Hitler will make me leave my house and go scurrying through the night,' Clara snapped, and Marion suppressed a sigh.

She knew part of her mother's problem was that she was very envious of her having a cellar that was deemed safe enough to shelter them all, so when Clara spat out, 'And what if your house was hit and the whole thing was to collapse in on top of you all?' she answered mildly, 'It won't. Bill had the cellar checked and reinforced.'

'Hmmph,' Clara snorted. 'Well, there's one thing that you've never considered.'

'What's that?'

'Gas,' said Clara, almost triumphantly. 'You have gas pipes in that cellar. What if one of them was shattered? The whole lot of you would be choked to death.'

'That will do, Clara,' said Eddie, who had watched the colour suddenly drain from Marion's face.

'I'm only saying what could easily happen.'

'I don't think it needed to be said,' Eddie chided.

'No it didn't,' Marion said angrily. She remembered her tussle with the priest that morning and she felt her backbone stiffen as she faced her mother. 'And particularly as it was said for no purpose other than to frighten me. You can sit out the raids wherever you like, Mammy, because I don't want you in our cellar like some sort of prophet of doom and gloom scaring the children rigid.'

'Well, I like that, I must say,' Clara said, affronted. 'If I were you, I would ask the doctor about a bottle of something for those nerves of yours.'

'There was nothing wrong with my nerves until I came here,' Marion said through gritted teeth.

And she snatched up her handbag as she said, 'And if I stay much longer, I will say things I may regret and so I'd better leave.'

'Wait,' Eddie said, as Marion wrenched open the door. 'I'll walk a little way with you.'

'You will not,' Clara said.

'Oh, but I will, Clara,' Eddie said. 'I didn't think that I needed permission to do that, and anyway, I have to call in at the allotment later.'

Marion was surprised at her father's response. For years he had taken the line of least resistance and that usually meant giving in to his wife all the time, so as they walked side by side she said, 'Daddy what has come over you?'

'Maybe common sense at long last,' Eddie said ruefully. 'Clara has wallowed in self-pity long enough. Other people have suffered as much and get over it. In this war all of us are at risk and Birmingham will not be spared, with all the war-related factories in this area.'

'Do the Germans know that, though?'

'They will have ways of finding out,' Eddie said. 'Believe me.'

'I feel almost as if we are sort of balanced on a knife edge and all we can do is wait,' Marion said.

'That's all,' her father agreed. 'Because we cannot let that madman win.'

That night the bombers returned as Marion was getting ready for bed. The younger children were already asleep and Sarah roused the twins and

Richard, his younger brother, and they helped them get ready and sort out blankets. Marion made drinks for them all and, mindful of the twins' hunger the previous night, also added a loaf, a knife and pot of dripping. By then they were all ready, Richard had already gone, and the noise of many planes was in the air.

Marion sat and listened to the drone of the Luftwaffe, realising there were more than ever before. Suddenly she knew that this was no short skirmish. The first blasts were so close to them, she felt icy fingers of fear run down her spine. Her mother's words came back to haunt her. For the sake of the others, especially the children, she fought the panic threatening to engulf her as the raid gained in intensity all around them.

She saw the twins' eyes widen in fear as the hours passed, with no let-up, and in the end she lay on the mattress so that she could put her arms around them both, with Tony right beside them. Even underground they heard the scream of the descending bombs and the terrifying crump and crash as they hit the buildings around. She felt the children shuddering as one explosion followed another, and no one begrudged them the odd yelp of fear because they were all scared.

Sarah quite envied her sisters and brother. She would have liked her mother's arms comforting her too and her thoughts were also with Richard, out there somewhere in the thick of it.

The twins and Tony, filled up with bread and

dripping, eventually slept cuddled against their mother, though they were constantly being jerked semi awake by the explosions. Marion prayed for God to keep them all safe. She even dozed off a time or two, despite the noise, but it wasn't any sort of deep refreshing sleep, more the odd snatches of the totally exhausted.

Eventually, the nightmare was over and they looked around at one another, hardly able to believe the all clear was blasting out through the early morning. 'God, I can't ever remember being so tired,' Violet said, slowly, getting up from the mattress.

'Nor me,' said Peggy. 'But we might be able to grab a couple of hours' sleep before the alarm if we're quick.'

'Have the morning off,' Marion said. 'You look so tired, both of you.'

Peggy said, 'But every worker at the factory will be feeling like us, or worse, and production of vital stuff to win this damned war can't be halted because we're all a bit tired.'

'I agree with Peggy,' Violet said. 'I wish I didn't, but I do. Just now, though, I am almost too weary to think straight.'

Sarah felt the same way and Richard too was determined to go into work, though it was an hour after the all clear when he came in, white-faced with exhaustion, and his eyes wide with horror. Sarah guessed that he had seen things that night that would stay burned in his mind for ever, but she didn't quiz him.

Richard was glad of that. The devastation and human tragedy that he'd witnessed that night had shocked him to the core and he wanted to close his eyes and try to forget it. But when he eventually sank down in the bed beside his slumbering brother, he found that he was only able to doze fitfully as the memories kept leaping back into his consciousness.

Much later that day Polly popped in to see Marion to discuss the raid.

'The point is,' Polly said, 'though bombs did fall here last night, it was the city centre that took a real pounding. Pat and the lads were drafted there to fight the fires. They said the Bull Ring caught it bad. The Market Hall's gone.'

'Gone?'

'Well, the walls are just about standing but the roof's gone, and that clock that Magda and Missie set such store by was burned to a crisp.'

'Ah, that's a shame.'

'I'll say. Part of St Martin's was damaged too, and all them shops down the slope from High Street are mainly reduced to rubble now.'

'Good job it was Sunday,' Marion said. 'There would be few people about at that time.'

'Yeah,' Polly agreed. 'There was the night watchman. Name of Levington, Pat said. He was speaking to him afterwards and he told him that when it was obvious the planes were heading his way, he released all the animals from their cages in the Market Hall before taking cover himself.'

'The animals, of course!' Marion cried. 'I never gave them a thought.'

'Good job someone did,' Polly said. 'They may not survive, of course. The puppies and kittens might, but the rabbits will probably end up as someone's dinner, and I shouldn't think our garden birds will take kindly to an influx of budgies and canaries.'

'Maybe not,' said Marion, 'but anything surely is better than being burned alive. He must be a brave man.'

'Must be,' Polly agreed. 'Tell you what gets me, though: twenty-five people were killed, countless more injured, fires started all over the place and buildings destroyed. All this was said on the wireless this morning only they didn't even mention Birmingham by name, but just said it was a Midlands town.'

'Why was that?'

Polly shrugged. 'I don't know. Can't understand it. But even if they don't say it was Birmingham that was attacked, us lot that live here know full well that it was.'

'Oh, yes,' Marion said. 'We don't half.'

SIXTEEN

Everyone was cheered when the RAF routed the Luftwaffe in a decisive battle on 15 September. That caused Hitler to abandon Operation Sealion, the code name for his plans to invade Britain. The invasion threat might be over, but the raids went on. The Whittakers eventually got used to disturbed nights though Marion couldn't ever remember feeling so tired, and Richard was sometimes like a walking zombie. So when the Germans began their daylight raids it seemed like the last straw, especially as the bombers were often followed by Stukas, which strafed civilians indiscriminately.

The girls gave up their weekly trip to the cinema because they didn't feel confident walking the streets any more. Marion, concerned for their safety was glad of that. 'D'you know where you'll go if the planes come when you're at school?' she asked the children one night when a couple of daylight raids had been reported.

'Yes, we have to go in the crypt in the church,'

Tony told her reassuringly. 'They took us down to show us.'

Marion was relieved. 'At least that will be underground.'

'I think it's creepy,' Magda said. 'I hope we never have to go down there.'

'We all have to do things we don't want to do these days, my girl,' Marion said sharply.

'Yes,' Peggy added with a smile, 'don't you know there's a war on?'

'Is there?' said Sarah sarcastically. 'What gave you that idea?'

'It's all right joking about it,' Marion said, 'but some of it is no joking matter. It's obvious the Germans are a monstrous race.'

No one contradicted this.

A few days later there was quite an extensive daylight raid and the children were full of it when they came home.

Later, when they sat around the table for the evening meal Magda said, 'It was just as creepy down in that flipping crypt as I thought it would be.'

'Yeah, and it smelled horrid,' Missie agreed.

'What did it smell of?' Violet asked.

'Dead bodies,' Magda said ominously.

She was annoyed when everyone burst out laughing, and Tony said scornfully, 'No it dain't, Magda. You're stupid, you are. And how d'you know what a dead body smells like, anyroad?' Without giving Magda time to think up a reply, he went on, 'It's all right, and better than arithmetic any day of the week. We can't hear much down there, and it's a bit of a laugh – or it would be, anyroad only we have to wear our flipping gas masks all the time.'

'Well,' Marion said unsympathetically, 'they are taking no chances, and rightly, I'd say.'

'Yeah, but there weren't no gas,' Tony protested, 'cos there weren't no policeman on a bike rattling that thing they give them to warn us.'

'How would you know?' Richard commented. 'You just said you couldn't hear much down there.'

'Anyway, none of this matters,' Marion said. 'I'm just glad that the teachers are taking this seriously and have everything organised so that you all had somewhere to take shelter, and underground as well, which is much better than anything on the surface, I'd have thought.'

In the middle of October, Churchill's wife, Clementine, visited the neighbourhoods and factories that had been affected by enemy bombing, and there were pictures of her in the newspaper, talking to the homeless and dispossessed people. Some of the women had placed Union flags in the piles of rubble that had once been their homes, and one was reputed to have told Clementine Churchill, 'Our house might be down, but our spirits are still up.' The reporter went on the praise the courage of these feisty people, whom he said showed unflinching courage.

That night that courage was tested again as

enemy bombers attacked the city once more. The raid was reminiscent of those on 25 and 26 August in its intensity. Subsequently there was an article in the newspaper detailing the bravery of a Home Guard officer. He had been called to a bombed-out house near the city centre where there were people trapped in a gas-filled cellar, and without any hesitation he had gone in to rescue them. Though he'd pulled two people clear, on his third attempt he had collapsed and died from the effects of the gas, leaving behind a widow and seven-year-old son, and all the people still in the cellar had died as well.

Marion felt slightly sick as she folded the paper up. She remembered her mother's words but she knew it would help no one if she were to share her fear with the others, so she kept the news article to herself.

The nightly raids were back in earnest, causing widespread damage and deaths across the city. When they emerged from the cellar, if they pulled back the blackout curtain the Whittakers would see the fires started by the incendiaries, with orange and yellow flames licking the midnight-blue sky.

Then one morning in October, while they were eating breakfast, Richard spoke about the previous night's raid.

'God, the flames were roaring,' he said. 'The firemen's hoses didn't seem to touch them and the air was full of cordite and steam and smoke and stank of heat – scorching, you know – and one whole corner of New Street has been wiped out. All that's left is this gigantic mound of rubble and mangled iron girders. There're these dirty great craters in the middle of the road and tramlines all over the place, and the road and pavements are full of splintered glass. And a bomb hit the Carlton Cinema and there were nineteen people killed in there and they didn't have a mark on them.'

'Nineteen people dead and not a mark on them?' Marion repeated incredulously. 'You're having us on.'

'No,' Richard said, 'honest, but it is hard to believe it. I dain't at first. And I wouldn't normally have heard owt about it.'

'So how come you did?'

'Well, we pulled this bloke out of some rubble. He'd cut his arm real bad and the doctor asked me to go with him in the ambulance so that I could hold his arm up and that. Selly Oak was the only hospital that had any space, and one of the ARP blokes that pulled the people out the picture house was in there. He was having treatment for burns and that, but he was really shook up. He said there were nineteen people sat in their seats as if they were waiting for the main film, like, and their lungs had been burned away by a bomb blast as they sat there.'

'Crikey!' Violet cried. 'What a way to die.'

'They probably felt nothing,' Marion said soothingly.

'Some of them did,' Richard said. 'That's what really upset this chap. They was all taken to Selly Oak and he was waiting beside a young lad lying on a stretcher, and the hospital managed to located his father and when his father came in he heard the boy speak to him and then he closed his eyes and just pegged it.'

'Oh God!'

'That's enough!' Marion said firmly because she had seen the shock and repugnance on the children's faces. They had just gone through a terrible raid and then woken for school after only a few hours' sleep and this she thought was too much for them to have to cope with. So she spoke briskly. 'All war's awful. I think that we're all agreed on that, but now isn't the time to discuss it any more or you will all be late.'

The others saw the look in Marion's eyes and knew what she was saying and why, and Richard felt a bit ashamed that he had told them about the people in the cinema when the children were there, particularly his younger bloodthirsty brother. He vowed that he would wait until they were out of the earshot before he recounted anything like that again.

For the next three weeks Birmingham was battered, causing death and injury to many Brummies and destruction and chaos to all as factories and houses crumpled in the wake of so many bombs.

At Mass on Sunday 10 November prayers were

said for the repose of the soul of Neville Chamberlain, who had died the previous day.

In the Whittaker household opinion was divided about the role he had played in leading the country into war.

'D'you think he really did believe in appeasement?' Violet asked.

'Maybe he did,' Richard conceded, 'but what was the alternative if he hadn't tried, at least?'

'I think whatever that man did would have been wrong. He was between a rock and a hard place,' Peggy put in. 'Hitler wanted power and world dominance at any price, and if that included war, then he was ready for it.'

'And we weren't,' Richard said. 'And Chamberlain at least did give us almost a year to prepare ourselves.' He glanced at his mother and said, 'I suppose the funeral is in London?'

'Yes,' Marion said, 'despite the fact that he was MP for Edgbaston for years, but there's to be a memorial service at St Martin's down the Bull Ring on the fifteenth.'

'Will you go?' Peggy asked.

Marion shook her head. 'I can't even if I wanted to,' she said. 'Catholics aren't allowed to attend, or take part in a service in any other Church.'

'Why?'

'To tell you the truth, Peggy, I haven't a clue,' Marion said. 'I asked the priest once and his answer was that a Catholic shouldn't question the Mother Church.'

So no one in the Whittaker household went to the memorial service, but that morning they listened to the news as they ate their breakfasts and heard of the massive air raid on Coventry the previous night.

The newscaster's voice shook as he announced that the city had been annihilated. Using the benefit of a clear night and a full moon Coventry had been pounded ceaselessly. Firemen were drafted in from all over to help fight the fires, and yet within a square mile eighty per cent of buildings were destroyed and 568 people were killed. Coventry had experienced raids before, but never on that scale. From that night, the voice on the wireless told them, a new word had entered the German language: *Coventrieren*, or Coventration, which meant the razing of a place to the ground.

When the news report was over, the adults looked at each other in sudden fear. They knew that what had been done in Coventry could be done just as easily in Birmingham.

The following Tuesday, at just after a quarter past seven, the sirens sent up their unearthly wail and everyone sprung into action. While the kettle boiled, drinks for the children and the makings for sandwiches were thrown into the shelter bag along with a packet of biscuits Marion had put on one side for emergencies. Peggy and Violet went down to light the paraffin stove, Sarah helped the twins get ready and Richard and Tony carried down the blankets from their bed. Marion could hear the first sticks of incendiaries falling before the kettle was completely boiled and she made tea and filled hot-water bottles with hands that trembled.

When all was done, she went down to the cellar as Richard slipped out of the door. 'No bombs yet,' Violet said.

'Plenty of incendiaries, though,' Marion said. 'I didn't need to see them, I heard them well enough.'

'Yeah, and they will light the way for the bloody bombers like daylight,' Peggy said. 'Little point in the blackout then.'

The words were hardly out of Peggy's mouth when the faint whistle of the first bomb was heard, then another, and then a succession of them clumped so close together it was hard to distinguish between them and even in the cellar the drone of planes was so loud that it seemed all around them as if they were under attack from all sides.

As the hours dragged by, Marion's fear increased and the tension in the cellar rose. She had been frightened before, but after reading about the gas-filled cellar the previous month, and what had been done to Coventry just a few nights before, her stomach was in knots and she felt as if she had ice running through her veins. She saw the twins were as terrified as she was, almost frozen with terror, and Tony's eyes looked large and frightened in his white face.

Marion sat on the saggy old settee, held the

twins tight and tried to keep the lid on her own panic as she saw Tony, kneeling on the mattress with Sarah, leaning against her while her arms went round him. Peggy, at the other end of the settee, had her arms around Violet, who had begun to weep quietly. Marion knew with a sort of dread certainty that this was Birmingham's own Coventration.

A sudden explosion, very close, rocked the walls of the cellar and the twins both emitted primeval shrieks of terror and burrowed closer into their mother, who held their shuddering bodies even closer as they sobbed. Sarah was more frightened than she ever remembered being in her life. She saw that though Tony was trying to be brave and manly, his eyes were standing out in terror and he was shaking from head to foot. She tightened her arms around him as a bomb came hurtling down so close they bent their heads against the onslaught.

But the explosion didn't happen, and they looked up surprised that they were all still alive, while the raid continued as fiercely as ever.

The cellar door was suddenly wrenched open and Richard was standing on the threshold. 'Thank God you're all right,' he said.

'Richard, what are you doing here?' Marion gasped.

'I've come to tell you that you have to get out,' Richard said. 'And quickly too.'

'What are you saying?'

'There's an unexploded bomb in the road. 'It's a big one so the whole area is being evacuated.'

'But where are we to go?'

'Atkinson's Brewery have opened their cellar,' Richard said. 'Come on! Take only what you can carry and let's get out of here.'

Marion was the last one out of the cellar and was strangely reluctant to leave.

'Come on, Mom! What are you waiting for?' Richard's voice came from the top of the cellar steps.

'Nothing,' Marion said. 'I'm coming.'

How could she expect Richard to understand how much she resented being forced from her home? She gazed all around her before following the others into the street and her heart was heavy because she felt as if she had just said goodbye to the house she loved.

None of them ever forgot that night. Immediately they stepped into the street they were aware of the arc lights raking the sky, pinpointing the droning German planes that the barking ack-ack guns were trying to bring down. The screams of the descending bombs and the crashing of explosions were much louder and more frightening outside, and the air stunk from the brick dust, mixed with cordite and gas. Smoke from the many fires and the smouldering incendiaries swirled about them and caught in the backs of their throats.

They all saw the bomb in a massive crater only yards from their home and though no one said anything they all knew they would have been killed if the bomb had gone off. ARP wardens and members of the Home Guard were urging all the residents of Albert Road to hurry. Mothers tried to catch hold of small children and soothe restless crying babies, and all around, disoriented people were scurrying along, carrying what they could.

As they neared the brewery they could see fires burning all over the city. Magda looked up to see even more German planes thronging the sky, flying in formation like gigantic menacing black beetles. So intrigued was she, she had unwittingly come to a stop on the pavement, flabbergasted when she actually saw the bomb doors open and the bombs tumble out and head downward with piercing whistles.

'For God's sake, child, what are you doing?' Marion cried, giving Magda's arm a yank just as the bombs found their mark with horrifying blasts and booms. These were followed by the unmistakable sound of falling masonry. Suddenly Magda wanted to be anywhere underground where this death and destruction could be muffled a little.

Inside the cellar the noise at first was horrendous. Many babies and toddlers continued to keen and grizzle, and they weren't the only ones. Children and adults were doing the same, while others were praying. There were shouts from some and even laughter, and the Whittakers were pushed further forward as more and more came into that brewery cellar that night.

When Marion spotted Polly with her daughters and Jack she was so pleased. The two sisters hugged one another, Sarah and the twins hugged their cousins, while Jack, with a wide smile on his face, punched Tony on the arm and said, 'What ho, Tone,' and Tony grinned back at him.

'Right bugger this, ain't it?' Polly said. 'They took us all out the shelter in the park, said it weren't safe with that big bomb.'

'Where's Pat?'

'Out helping,' Polly said. 'Him and Colm, and I'm that worried about them.'

'I feel the same about Richard,' Marion said. 'Part of me wants him to come into the cellar and be relatively safe, like the rest of us, and part of me is proud that he won't even consider that. And maybe I should look out for Mammy and Daddy and see if they have been brought here too.'

'No need,' Polly said. 'Orla and Siobhan spotted them. I thought they might be shook up and that, you know, so I went over.'

'And they weren't?'

'Daddy was a bit,' Polly said. 'But Mammy wasn't upset in the slightest. She was just bloody angry and letting everyone know about it as well. Daddy said she didn't want to leave the house and they had to carry her out.'

'I didn't want to leave my house,' Marion said. 'Most people would feel the same, but you have to be sensible about these things.'

'Yeah,' Polly said, 'and I suppose even Mammy

will settle down eventually. Till then I should leave her well alone.'

'Yeah,' Marion wearily. 'I'm not up to Mammy's temper at the moment. I'm fair jiggered, to tell you the truth, and the children must be worse, and there ain't even anywhere to sit down.'

'Well, it's a brewery cellar, ain't it?' Polly pointed out reasonably. 'They're not geared up for people. But we can use the blanket.' She spread out the one that she had carried from the shelter as she spoke. 'We can sit on that.'

'And we'll do the same,' Marion said, 'and do our best to cheer ourselves up.'

After that they made the most of their time in Atkinson's Brewery cellar, pooling their food and drink. Then when someone began a singsong they sang any song they knew.

When the all clear sounded Marion wakened from a doze, though she couldn't remember falling asleep, to find Sarah gently tapping her arm.

'The bomb has been detonated safely, Mom,' she said. 'We can go back home.' Marion gave a brief nod before stumbling stiff-legged to her feet.

There was a gaping hole in the middle of the road just in front of the Whittakers' house. Inside, the whole place was covered in fine grey dust. Marion knew that they had been more than lucky to have a house to come back to. Some of her neighbours hadn't fared so well and houses either side of the street just a little further on were just smouldering piles of rubbish.

'Where will those poor sods sleep tonight?' Peggy said, indicating the desolate people looking askance at what had once been their homes.

'Who knows?' Marion said with a sigh. 'Maybe they'll go back to the cellar.'

'Not that much of the night left, anyway,' Violet said. 'And I'm away to my bed to sleep till the alarm goes off.'

Marion, though, waited for Richard, knowing she wouldn't settle till she knew he was in and safe.

SEVENTEEN

The next day on the early news on the wireless, the Whittakers learned of the three hundred and fifty bombers that had attacked a 'Midlands town' the previous night causing widespread devastation. Many people were dead or badly injured.

'I'm not surprised at the damage,' Peggy said decidedly. 'We've never had a raid so fierce.'

'They didn't get the clock at Aston Cross, though,' Richard said. 'It was still there, sort of surrounded by a sea of rubble, and this bloke said to me it was like a beacon of defiance to Hitler.'

'Would have been a shame if they had destroyed it,' Marion said. 'It's been there as long as I remember.'

'Yeah,' Richard agreed. 'But even worse is the sad and helpless look on people's faces when they come out the shelters and find their houses gone. Some of them were crying, and not just kids but grown-ups as well, and others just stand there, like they can't really believe it, or start searching the rubble of where their houses had once stood for anything they can salvage. And often the numbers of people dead or injured brings tears to my eyes.'

'I'm not surprised,' Marion said. 'But aren't you ever frightened for yourself?'

Richard shook his head. 'Not at the time. There are so many needing help that I'm too busy to be scared. Afterwards it sometimes comes back to haunt me. Anyroad,' he went on, getting to his feet, 'I shall have to be off soon. They'll be no trams running along Albert Road today because as well as the great pit left by the unexploded bomb, the heat was so fierce it melted the tar and that, of course, buggered up the tramlines.

'I wonder when they will get them fixed.'

'Ages, I should say. Shouldn't think they'll see Albert Road as high priority. I think it's shanks's pony for me for a bit.'

'Maybe they'll be some trams running along the Lichfield Road?' Marion said.

Richard shook his head. 'I doubt it. Aston generally took one hell of a pasting after you went into Atkinson's cellar, and Lichfield Road didn't get away scot-free either.'

'We heard it,' Sarah said. 'Only it wasn't as scary because it was muffled.'

'Yeah, and there was a lot of noise in the cellar as well,' Peggy put in. 'But when we did come out there were so many fires it was like daylight and there was a bright orange glow all over the sky.'

'Yes,' said Richard quietly. 'That was Birmingham burning.'

There was a small silence as this fact was digested. Marion felt suddenly very depressed and she sighed as she said, 'I sometimes wonder if Birmingham will ever be the same again.'

'We'll get a paper on the way home, if you like,' Peggy said, 'and just see what damage has been done.' She added to Richard, 'We may as well walk along with you as far as Rocky Lane, anyroad.'

'Come on then, or I'll be late,' Richard said. 'At least you'll not need your torches today. You'll be able to save your batteries.'

Richard was right, for the red and orange glow in the sky lit their way. Peggy and Violet took time to wrap their scarves around their faces before they set out because there was still sour stinking smoke billowing in the air.

They came home with the *Evening Mail* and the *Despatch*.

'We thought we'd buy two papers and maybe get more detail than we heard on the wireless this morning,' Peggy said.

'I'm as anxious as you are to read about that,' Marion said, 'but have your wash first and I'll get the meal on the table as quickly as possible in case Jerry is going to pay us another visit tonight.'

They passed the papers over to Sarah and Richard. They both read of the destruction of many homes and businesses, factories and shops, and the estimated six hundred and fifteen dead and many hundreds more seriously injured. The dispossessed and the homeless had bedded down any place they could get. Those not lucky enough to have friends or relatives able to take them in slept in the cellars they had just emerged from, or halls belonging to churches or schools, and the WVS were doing a sterling job keeping them all fed and trying to find clothes and blankets.

'That news report only gave us the tip of the iceberg this morning,' Sarah said to her mother. 'But reading about it is heartbreaking.'

'New Street was hit again,' Richard said. 'I heard about that last night. New Street station copped it as well, and it says here just one naval mine destroyed the Prudential Insurance building in Colmore Row and badly damaged Boots, the Great Western Arcade, the Bank of England in Temple Row and Grey's in Bull Street.'

'What's a naval mine?' Magda asked.

Richard knew full well what a naval mine was: a powerful bomb that was carried by parachute and programmed to explode near the ground to maximise damage, but he didn't think he should share that with an eight-year-old and so he said, 'It's just another name for that type of bomb.'

'Anyroad,' Sarah said, 'it don't matter what they call them, does it? They all do the same job.'

'Yeah,' Richard said. 'Sorry as I am for the people, it's the loss of the factories and equipment that's a worry because it's all war-related stuff and all needed.'

'Like Kinloch's and the BSA.'

Richard nodded. 'The biggest factory attacked last night was the BSA. We should never underestimate the Germans; they are intelligent, and the bombing at the BSA just proved that. It was an odious thing to do and appallingly cruel, but still clever.'

Sarah had little time for saying anything positive about a race she considered barbaric and so she snapped out, 'What did they do that was so clever?'

'Well,' said Richard, 'it says in the paper that though the BSA had been bombed before, work was able to continue elsewhere almost immediately. That must have really annoyed the Germans 'cos apparently, yesterday early on, a German plane dropped a ring of smoke over the BSA and our planes couldn't get rid of it and all that damage was done by one bomber who came in low and dropped three highly explosive bombs through that ring.'

'God,' Marion said, 'they must have known just where to drop them to do the most damage.'

'Look at it now,' said Richard, opening the paper up so that they all could see the mangled mess of bricks and masonry still burning fiercely, with twisted, buckled girders sticking up out of it.

'The fires must have been terrible,' Sarah said. 'In the paper I read it said that they drained the canals and still didn't have enough water to put out the fires.'

'From what I heard you would have had to drain the sea to douse them,' Richard said.

'Was any of the workers hurt?' Violet said, coming into the room. 'I gather they had a big strong cellar underneath the factory.'

'Not strong enough, I think,' Marion said, and she picked up the paper and read the account aloud.

'The southern block disintegrated in a roaring landslide of concrete, machinery and twisted girders with dust and black smoke. Soon the whole building was ablaze and had started to collapse into the basement where a lot of the workers were taking shelter and many were trapped under mangled wreckage. The firemen worked ceaselessly to douse the fires, though the bombs were still falling steadfastly and then a nearby ammunition dump went up, spraying the fleeing people with shrapnel.'

Marion thought of the panic and terror and pain that those poor trapped people would go through as they burned to death in the cellar meant to protect them, and she felt sick. 'It must have been terrible, truly terrible. Those poor, poor people.'

The words were barely out of her mouth when the sirens went again. There was a collective groan and Marion turned to Richard, 'I suppose it's no

301

good asking you to have a night off duty? You look all in.'

'I'd love to say yes because I've never felt so tired in my life,' Richard confessed. 'Every man who worked with me yesterday will feel the same way, and yet they'll be there tonight as well, and that's where I must be too.'

Marion didn't bother arguing with Richard, knowing he was right. So with a sigh she turned off the gas under the meal she had been cooking and threw the makings for sandwiches in the shelter bag, which she began to prepare with a dread that seemed to touch her very soul.

In the cellar, as the screams of the siren died down, the first crashes were heard and the drone of the planes grew louder, she fed the children. Magda and Missie thought that if you could forget the noise of the raid, which so far was not as terrifying as the previous night, and ignore the smell of the paraffin stove, it was quite cozy wrapped up in the blankets on the mattress with a jam piece to eat and a mug of milk to drink.

It didn't really help the tiredness, though, and when Marion suggested they all lie down on the mattress even Tony was willing. They soon dropped off to sleep against the backdrop of the descending bombs, and when the planes drew nearer the children barely stirred, though the women in the cellar were well aware of it.

Suddenly, from among the isolated crashes, there was one concentrated and very loud boom that caused the cellar walls to shake. It threw the women into a state of alarm and eventually roused the children.

What's up?' Tony asked as he struggled to sit up, rubbing his eyes in confusion. 'I was asleep.'

'Sounds like the explosion was to the side of the park,' Violet said.

'Yeah,' Peggy said. 'Let's hope the people were taking shelter.'

'What if they drop one of them bombs on our house?' Missie asked in a frightened little voice.

'They tried that last night,' Tony said, with a fit of bravado he was far from feeling. 'Only it never went off.'

'You're daft, you are, Tony Whittaker,' Magda said. 'That don't mean that they won't try again, does it, Mom?'

'No,' Marion had to admit. 'But listen, the planes are much further away now. I bet soon the all clear will go and we'll be able to get back up to the house.'

But it wasn't soon – it was ages – though none of the children could sleep again, and they all sighed with relief when it was all over. When Richard came home he told his mother that the large explosion had been a naval mine that had landed on nearby Queens Road and destroyed the entire street.

There was no raid the following night, yet it did the family little good for all evening they listened for the sound of the sirens. When nothing happened Marion made for bed, but despite her weariness sleep was a long time coming and then she slept lightly, expecting any moment to hear the sirens blare out.

When Richard came in from work that night he said to his mother as she sorted out the water for his wash, 'I think that we are due for a repeat of Tuesday's raid tonight. It may even be worse than Tuesday.'

Marion face blanched and she felt her insides turn over. 'How on earth do you know?'

'This chap at work was listening to Lord Haw-Haw last night, "Germany Calling", you know?'

'Yes I know, and I never listen to it. I think it's unpatriotic,' Marion said. 'Nor would I give any credence to anything he said. That man's a traitor.'

'I know that, but listen, this chap Haw-Haw said owing to favourable weather conditions, all sorts of raids could be carried out in Birmingham tonight,' Richard told her. 'And he also said that though they will be concentrating their efforts on armaments targets not yet hit by German bombs, they expected smaller factories and whole streets to be destroyed.' He caught sight of his mother's appalled face and went on, 'Really, Mom, I know it's hateful, but it is best to be prepared.'

'All right, but it's not necessarily helpful for the others to know, especially the children,' Marion said. 'Lord Haw-Haw might be spouting rubbish and I don't want to frighten them to death. I know, and that's good enough for now.'

However, in case Richard was right about Haw-Haw's accuracy, by the time the siren sounded just after seven o'clock Marion was ready. She had already lit the oil stove, filled the hot-water bottles and wrapped them in blankets she had taken down from the boys' bedroom, and she'd filled the shelter bag with care.

The raid was as ferocious as the previous one, and any minute Marion expected their house to be hit. At the forefront of her mind was the thought that her son was out in the thick of another horrendous raid.

Five hours after the raid began more bombers could be heard approaching, and more still at three o'clock. No one could sleep. Even the tired children were held in a grip of terror, and Marion fought the desire to sink down on the cellar floor and howl out her distress as an injured animal might.

When the all clear went at six o'clock the next morning, Marion looked around at everybody as if she could hardly believe that they all had survived. They lumbered, still sluggish, to their feet and found the house still intact, though covered with the usual film of dust and the night sky as bright as day from the ongoing fires.

It looked as if once more they had got away scot-free. Then Marion went to fill the kettle to find there was no water coming out of the tap.

They tried the tap in the bathroom with the same result and Marion looked to the others in perplexity.

Richard came in as they were discussing this. 'So, it's true then?' he said.

'What is?'

'There was a rumour that three trunk water mains on the Bristol Road were fractured by bombs last night,' Richard said. 'Means the city, or most of it, at any rate, will be without water.'

'Without water?' Marion repeated. 'For how long?'

'Who knows?' said Richard with a shrug. 'I mean, they'll probably sort something out for people like us as soon as they can. It's just if there's no water coming into the city they won't be able to do owt about the fires and that if there's a raid tonight.'

Marion gave a gasp. 'I see what you mean,' she said, appalled. 'Birmingham could burn to the ground.'

'Yes, it well might.'

Even the children had picked up the gravity of the situation and the twins' eyes were like saucers in their heads.

'Come on,' Marion said decisively. 'You're asleep on your feet, and you can get into bed and thank your lucky stars that tomorrow is Saturday and you haven't to get up for school.'

The fracturing of the pipes wasn't mentioned on the eight o'clock news, but when there's no water coming out of your taps or your neighbours', it's pretty obvious that something very serious is wrong, and most Brummies guessed what had happened. Later that day, tankers of water were dispersed and members of the Labour Party went around in a van with a loudspeaker fitted on top, telling people where the tankers were.

Their immediate needs were met, yet they waited with more dread than usual for the sirens to sound that night. When they didn't everyone was relieved, though Richard said that he imagined it could take many days for the water mains to be repaired.

It was five days before water was running through the taps again, but there hadn't been a raid during those five days in Birmingham, and Brummies had been able to lie in their beds at night undisturbed. It took a few nights though, for Marion to relax enough to take advantage of this.

There was a lull in the bombing for the rest of that month and many homeless and dispossessed people, supported by the trade unions and the Co-operative Society, complained to the Lord Mayor about the predicament they were in.

'I don't blame them either, not one bit,' Marion said with spirit to Polly as they scrutinised the *Evening Mail*. 'More should have been done for them from the start. The Government knew there would be raids – that's what the blackout was all about – and people who have lost everything need more than just a place to lay their heads.'

'You're right there,' Polly said. 'It's a bloody disgrace. And did you read that people bombed out of their houses in Garrison Road didn't even get any food for twenty-four hours, and then that Canon Guy whatshisname said a large group of people had to shelter for a week in the bloody car park at New Street Market. Right comfy, they must have been. And without the WVS they would have fared even worse.'

'I'll say,' Marion agreed. 'They're demanding mobile canteens, clothes and blankets, and specific organisations to deal with the homeless and give them advice, and I don't think any of them are unreasonable demands.'

'No, nor do I see that it was down to the people to have to point it out either.'

'Yeah,' Marion said. 'It's dreadful. Still, something will probably be done for them now that it has got into the papers.'

'Maybe,' Polly said. 'And let's hope they are sorted before the bombs start falling again.'

However, the following night, 3 December, the sirens wailed out again as Marion was dishing up the evening meal. Unwilling to waste the food, she took the pans down to the cellar and continued dishing up there, while Sarah, Peggy and Violet collected the blankets and filled the flask and the hot-water bottles.

Everyone was very glad of the warm stew and tucked in hungrily before settling down to wait for the raid to ease. It did come perilously close to them at times, yet it was not as intense or as protracted as the raids of 19 or 22 November.

The siren shrilled out the following night as well, and this raid caused extensive damage to small factories standing cheek by jowl with terraces of houses. A week later the sirens went off at six o'clock, when everyone had just got in from work and the dinner was barely started. Marion hurriedly threw any food she had into the shelter bag and followed the others down to the cellar. A few bombs were heard and then the all clear sounded, but they had been in the house barely half an hour when the siren shrilled out once more. Again, there was the sound of a few exploding bombs, and then the all clear again.

When the sirens went a scant fifteen minutes later, Marion said, 'That's it! He's playing cat and mouse with us and I ain't playing his game and so we're all going to stay in this cellar until we know it's finally over.'

Everyone was in agreement with this, but they had no idea that when the raid began in earnest it would be similar to the heavy raids of the month before, nor that it would go on until seven o'clock the next morning. When they eventually returned to the house they did so tentatively, not sure whether the raid was over or not.

'I don't give a jot whether it is or it isn't,' Violet declared. 'Because if I don't get something to eat and drink soon, I will die anyway.'

Marion laughed. 'I'm not surprised. Never fear,

I'll soon have a big bowl of porridge on the table for all of you. I'm passing out with hunger myself, and everyone will feel the same I'm sure.'

'I am, anyroad,' Tony said. 'That raid went on for thirteen hours, you know.'

'Yes,' Marion said, 'and your brother has been out in it all that time. I do hope he's all right.'

'He don't half pong when he comes in as well,' Tony went on.

Richard was often covered with white brick dust, and the stink of that and cordite clung to his clothes and sometimes mixed with the acrid smell of blood. Marion never asked questions, knowing that while he would tell her about buildings and houses bombed to bits, he would usually only speak about the people in the most general terms, and she never pressured him to say any more.

'Talking about stinking,' Peggy said, breaking in on Marion's thoughts, 'Vi and me never got chance for a wash last night and I feel real grimy this morning. Can we have some of the water out the kettle and have at least a bit of a lick and promise before we go in to work this morning?'

'Help yourself,' Marion said. 'And by the time you're done I'll have the porridge ready to eat.'

It was as they were finishing that they heard Richard come in the door and Marion knew just how tired he was by his dragging heavy tread as he approached. She didn't have to see his grey haggard face and his black smudged eyes. She was on her feet immediately.

'Richard, we've finished the porridge, but I'll soon make some fresh.'

'No need,' Richard said in a voice dry and husky from the fires he had attended that night. 'I could murder a cup of tea, but the WVS cooked me up a right royal breakfast.'

'Huh, all right for some then,' Sarah said in mock annoyance. 'We just got porridge like usual.'

'And grateful for it,' Peggy said. 'That was some raid last night, and I bet many without a home this morning would give their eyeteeth for a comforting bowl of porridge. But I've had mine and it's time me and Violet got ready for work.' She nodded across at Richard. 'Glad to see you back safe and sound, though.'

Richard gave a wave to the girls as they left the room and then took a large gulp of the tea his mother pushed across the table to him, for all it was scalding. 'Thanks,' he said as he set the cup down again. 'God, I needed that.'

'Bad night?'

'Bad enough,' Richard said. 'I was sent into town sometime during the night because St Thomas's Church in Bath Row took a direct hit. You should have seen the mess: great slabs of masonry all over the churchyard, giant oak trees snapped like they was matchsticks, and tombstones torn up and spread about the place like pebbles. There was this organ as well, just mixed up in the

311

rubble, like, and I saw the pipes twisted into all sort of weird shapes. All that was left of that church was the bell tower over the main entrance in Granville Street. Course, the church wasn't the only thing they damaged and destroyed.'

'I know,' Marion said. 'But it upsets me when I hear of old buildings destroyed because it's like getting rid of our history, isn't it?'

'Yeah, I suppose it is. It upsets me too. And now,' Richard said as he drained his cup and got to his feet, 'if there's any water in that kettle I'll give myself a quick wash before I make for my bed.'

'You're not going in today?' Marion said, delighted but surprised.

'No I'm not,' Richard replied. 'The commander is going to clear it with my boss. Point is,' he lowered his voice, though he and his mother were the only ones in the room, 'I don't know how they get to know these things – it's supposed to be hush hush – but the King is visiting Birmingham today.'

'The King visiting here?' Marion exclaimed in surprise, and Sarah, coming into the room at that moment, said, 'Crikey! When's this happening?'

Richard smiled ruefully. 'I suppose that's how the news was spread. It's supposed to be top secret.'

'Well, it isn't now, is it?' said Tony, coming in after Sarah. 'So you might as well tell us the rest.'

'I don't know much,' Richard said. 'Just that he's probably visiting Aston in the afternoon and will quite likely want to see the Home Guard and ARP wardens and that, and so our commander told a few of us to take the morning off and that he would square it with our employers and we're to report to HQ at one o'clock.'

'Oh, how exciting,' Sarah said. 'But I bet I won't get to see hide nor hair of him.'

'Nor me,' Tony said and, glancing at his mother, he added, 'we could, though, if you gave us the day off.'

'Ah, but I'm not likely to do that, am I?'

'Don't see why not,' Magda said. 'I think it would be a very patriotic thing to do.'

Richard laughed. 'Well, you must fight it out amongst yourselves because I'm going to have a wash and a kip while I have the chance.'

EIGHTEEN

In the end only Marion and Polly waited on Lichfield Road to see if they could catch a glimpse of the King as he passed. It seemed that news of the royal visit had seeped through the neighbourhood, though, because the streets were thronged with people. Marion and Polly thought of going round to tell their mother but, as Polly said, they would get no thanks if they did.

'Anyway,' she went on, 'Mammy has little time for royalty. And it might disturb Mammy greatly to learn that Pat feels the same way. He said this morning that King George's visit won't make any bloody difference to us.'

'Bill would probably say the same,' Marion said. 'But I would like to see our King in real life and I think it's nice of him to be bothered to come and see how battered we have been.'

'Even more battered today,' Polly said. 'Did you read in the *Mail* last night that two hundred and

314

sixty-three people were killed in the raid last night, and nearly as many seriously injured?'

'I did,' Marion said. 'News like that knocks me sick. And maybe it's nice for the King to come and see for himself and sort of sympathise, like Winnie's wife did in October.'

'Yeah,' Polly said. 'But give me the King any day over bloody Winston Churchill, though his wife seemed quite nice.'

'Well, Bill never had any time for Churchill,' Marion said. 'Said he turned the guns on the miners, his own people.'

'All he's good for is delivering a stirring speech,' Polly said.

'Yes,' said Marion. 'The King at least is a man of honour. Look how he stepped up to do his duty to when Edward abdicated.'

'Well, we couldn't have Wallis Simpson, a divorced Yank, Queen of England, could we?' Polly said.

'I'll say not,' Marion agreed heartily. 'Bill always maintained that she was too friendly with the Germans, anyroad.'

'And he was, and all,' Polly said. 'Fancy the King even being on shaking hands terms with the leader of a country that is killing our men and trying to bomb the rest of us to kingdom come? I'd take Geroge over his brother any time.'

Marion was about to answer when a rustle ran through the crowd: the King's car had been spotted. Then, to everyone's delight and a spontaneous cheer, the car stopped by Atkinson's Brewery and the King emerged. He was bare-headed, despite the biting wind, and he turned up the collar of his grey woollen coat, and began to walk alongside the waiting crowds.

They surged forward but the police held them back though the King seemed unconcerned by it all. As he walked along he pulled off his leather gloves to gently touch the cheeks of infants held up for him to see, and shake people's hands while he expressed his sadness that they had suffered so much, and commended the bravery and endurance they had shown.

Suddenly, obviously overcome by it all, one old woman from the crowd dodged the police and planted a kiss on the King's cheeks, and a cheer went up. But the King only smiled and turned to ask the women if she lived in the area. She said she did, had always lived there, but she'd been bombed out and was camping in a church hall. Then she went on to say sadly that she had just had word that she had lost one of her three sons. Marion saw the King's eyes darken in sympathy as he placed a hand on the woman's shoulder and she felt herself warm to him. Later, when she shook his hand, she was able to see just how kindly those deep brown eyes were.

As they sat eating the evening meal that night, Marion said she was surprised how much more positive the King's visit had made her feel. 'I mean, he didn't do anything but walk around and smile and say a few words to this one and that, but it mattered somehow that he saw first-hand how it has been for us.'

'He was shocked and devastated by the damage,' Richard said. 'He told our commander that.'

'So he did go to see the Home Guard?'

'Oh, yes,' Richard said. 'He spoke to me and asked what I thought of the Volunteer Force and I told him truthfully that they do a wonderful job, but as soon as I was eighteen I would be enlisting. He shook me by the hand then and wished me good luck.'

'Lucky you,' Sarah said. 'I thought he was lovely, though I only had a quick peep.'

'I'm surprised that you even got that,' Marion said.

'Oh, I shouldn't have done,' Sarah said with a grin. 'Mrs Jenkins went, of course, as I knew she would. But no one came into the shop and the streets were empty 'cos they were all waiting to see the King. So I took off my overall, shut up shop and went along myself. I had to hide behind people because I couldn't risk Mrs Jenkins catching sight of me, and of course I couldn't stay very long, but I did see him.'

'Which is more than we did,' Peggy said ruefully. 'We didn't even know he was going to be in the area. I suppose he went into some factories connected with war work, but not ours.'

'He didn't go into schools either,' Magda said, slightly aggrieved. 'Or at least not ours, he dain't.'

'The man couldn't visit everywhere,' Marion said. 'He was only here a day, and I don't suppose that his time is his own either. I mean, he would have advisors and that to work out his itinerary.'

'Would he?' Tony said surprised. 'I thought you could do what you wanted when you was King, otherwise what's the point of being one?'

'Well, royalty usually don't choose, Tony. They're born into it,' Marion said. 'And you will find, as I did, that there are very few people in this world who can do as they please. Most people are responsible to someone.'

Tony frowned. He had thought that once he was finished with school he would be as free as a bird. Now his mother said that was not going to be the case. Suddenly the future looked very bleak to him.

Marion hid her smile at the dismal look on her young son's face for she knew what he was thinking. She thought she would be a happy person if she had as few worries as he had.

Peggy arrived home the following night struggling with a large box.

'What have you there?' Marion asked, intrigued.

'Well, I was going to keep it till Christmas,' Peggy said, 'but what's the odds? We'll have it now as an early Christmas present. It's a gramophone that I bought off a bloke at work for three pounds. See, a lot of the girls in our place go to dances and that, and they've asked us along. I said me and Vi wouldn't be able to do it, not properly. I mean, before we came here we'd only been to a couple of village hops, and we didn't want to look stupid.'

'Anyroad, one of the girls said she'd gone to dancing lessons,' Violet put in. 'She said there's dancing schools everywhere, and when you learn the steps the best way to get good at it quickly is to buy a gramophone and records and practise at home.'

'Anyroad, this bloke heard I was looking for a gramophone,' Peggy put in. 'And he had one to sell, so Bob's your uncle. You don't mind, do you, Marion?'

'How could I mind?' Marion said. 'It will give us all a bit of cheer of a night.'

'And we can take it down the cellar if there's a raid,' Peggy said. 'Maybe it will help drown out the sound of the planes and the explosions.'

'Oh, that's got to be a good idea,' Marion said. 'Then after Christmas I suppose you will be sorting out a dancing school?'

'That's the idea, yeah.'

'Let's hope the raids have eased by then.' Marion turned to Sarah. 'Do you want to go to dancing lessons too?'

'Oh, can I, Mom?' Sarah cried. 'I'd love to learn to dance properly.'

'It will do you good,' Marion said.

'You could come along too, Richard,' Violet said.

'One thing the other girls did say was that there was a shortage of boys and men at these places.'

'However short they were, they wouldn't want me,' Richard said assuredly. 'I have two left feet. It's a well-known fact. All I would be good for would be turning the handle of the gramophone.'

'Nonsense,' Peggy said. 'Your feet are as good as anyone else's. You would be no good in the army with two left feet.'

'All the army cares about is that you can put one before the other,' Richard said.

'Are you sure that you're not making excuses because you're scared?'

'You could be right at that,' Richard conceded. 'I've never considered myself a coward but I think I would rather face the German Army than a roomful of giggling girls.'

'Shame on you, Richard Whittaker!' Peggy cried as she caught hold of his hand and spun him around the room, and Marion smiled as she turned back to the stove.

'Can we have a look at the gramophone?' Tony asked. Peggy nodded. 'You can.' She placed it on the table and removed the brown paper it had been wrapped in. 'But it will be even better when we can actually play it.'

The gramophone was black and quite neat with 'His Master's Voice' written on the lid. 'I thought it would have a horn on, where the sound comes out,' Richard said. 'Any picture I have ever seen of a gramophone has been like that.'

'They all used to be like that one time,' Peggy said. 'This is a more modern one, though you still have to turn the handle to make it work.'

'And how does the sound come off the record?' Tony asked.

'Golly, I don't know,' Peggy exclaimed. 'It just does, that's all. Come Saturday Vi and I will go into the Bull Ring and buy a couple of records – they're only a tanner each in Woolies – and you'll hear it for yourself. There's a steel needle in here,' she said, raising up the arm to show him. 'You have to be real careful putting that on the record or you'll scratch it, but we will have a go Saturday and see what it sounds like.'

Marion was glad that the children had something to cheer them up. She had to admit she would like some lively music too. Again it was the lodgers who had brought lightness to the house and she blessed the day they had come knocking on her door. In her head she composed the letter that she would write to Bill later to explain about the gramophone and the proposed dancing lessons and Richard's left feet, and maybe make him smile too.

As Christmas 1940 approached the only thing that Marion could feel positive about was the fact that had been no air raids since 11 December. She could find little in the way of festive food, though, and even less to put in the stockings for the children, and she felt bad about that because in many ways the war had robbed them of a carefree childhood.

She was determined to buy them some new clothes, and though there was little choice in colour or style Marion thought it a satisfying feeling buying clothes for her own children and not being reliant on handouts from the Christmas Tree Fund. She knew that keeping the children respectably clad would probably be more difficult when the rationing of clothes began in the summer.

Tony didn't really care what he had to put on, even if it was a cast-off from his brother or his cousin Jack, but still she bought him a new pullover, navy corduroy trousers and new grey socks and laid them out on the chair by his bed. She thought Missie and Magda would love the dark red jumpers and blue woollen pinafores she'd bought for them. They even had new black boots to see them through the winter.

Getting things for their stockings was harder, though, but she did manage to find Tony a model of a sailing ship for him to make up, and a tin whistle she found on a junk stall in the Market Hall. Richard gave a grimace when he saw the whistle as they packed the stockings on Christmas Eve. 'If he plays one note on that in the early hours of the morning I'll brain him, whether it's Christmas Day or not.'

'You and me both,' said Sarah. 'Though I suppose the twins will be up with the lark.'

'Maybe they will,' Richard said. 'But a silver-backed dressing table set each and lengths of pretty hair ribbon will not make as much noise as a tin whistle.'

'Oh, aren't you the grump?' Marion chided her son. 'Christmas is for children, everyone knows that, and these will be grown up soon enough. Now, put the oranges that you queued nearly half a day to get in the toe of each of the stockings, and I'll add the thrupenny bit and bar of chocolate and we're done.'

'I got something else for the kids too,' Richard said, regaining his good humour. 'When I was down the Bull Ring for the oranges there was a tout there selling kids' books and I bought three: *Robinson Crusoe* for Tony because you bought me that book when I was about his age and it fell apart through overuse. I thought he might like it.'

'Ah, that was nice of you, Richard,' Marion said. 'I'm sure he'll love it.'

'How did you know what to buy the twins?' Sarah asked.

'A lady who had daughters the same age advised me,' Richard said. 'And so I bought *The Railway Children* for Magda and *Black Beauty* for Missie.

'Oh, they are sure to love those,' Sarah said. 'Despite the restrictions and everything, I think they will have a wonderful day.'

'I hope we all do,' Marion said. 'Though it will a different Christmas with Peggy and Violet staying with us.' She smiled over at both girls. 'We don't mind you being here in the least but I'm sure your families will miss you.'

'Well, yes,' Peggy said with a smile, 'but to quote a well-worn phrase, there's war on. I mean, we intended to go home until we heard that the forge was shutting only for Christmas Day. They have urgent new orders for train tracks, due to the bombing.'

'Are you sad about that?' Sarah asked.

'A bit,' Violet said. 'But it helps to know how important the work we do is.'

'And if we were in the Forces we wouldn't get time off, would we?' Peggy said. 'I mean, Sam would never make it home for Christmas and he never moans.'

'Yes, but Sam never moaned about anything,' Sarah said, and then could have bitten her tongue out because everyone was looking at her. She found herself colouring as she said, 'I mean, I don't know . . . It's just when he was here that time I never heard him moan much.'

Marion felt sorry for her daughter and she broke in with, 'Sarah's right, Sam didn't seem the moaning type. In fact, I thought him a fine young man. Now, anyone for a cup of cocoa before bed?'

Marion got up the next morning to a warm room as Sarah had lit the range. She had also done the girls' hair. Marion said they looked a treat dressed in their new things, with their hair gleaming and tied back with some of the Christmas ribbons.

Peggy and Violet endorsed that, and Magda smiled at the lodgers, whom she liked so much. 'I'm really glad you're here for Christmas,' she said, '''cos if you hadn't been our grandma and granddad would have wanted to come for Christmas dinner. With you here there just isn't the room, is there, Mom?'

'No, there isn't,' Marion said. 'But that, Magda, is one of the most uncharitable things I have ever heard you say. And on Christmas Day, as well. You should be thoroughly ashamed of yourself.'

Magda did bow her head, but not before she had caught the sympathetic glance from Peggy, who could quite understand her point of view.

'Anyway,' said Marion, 'you will see your grandparents later because Peggy and Violet are going to a workmate's for tea and your grandparents will be coming here then.'

Magda's head shot up at that news for she hadn't known that.

'And you can that look off your face, young lady, or I will take it off for you, Christmas or not,' Marion snapped. She relented a little when she saw the look pass between Magda and her sister and she said more gently, 'Now come on and let's get ourselves away to Mass and maybe that will put us all in a better frame of mind and remind us that Christmas is all about the birth of baby Jesus.'

Magda knew the safest thing for her to do then was to say nothing at all and get ready quickly, and just a few minutes later she was hurrying up the road with her family. The day was crisp and so cold that whispery vapour escaped from mouths, but Marion thought it quite pleasant if a body was well wrapped up.

She loved Christmas Day. People seemed so friendly calling out 'Happy Christmas' to them as they passed. Pat and Polly and their family were waiting for them in the porch of the church, and they all hugged one another as they wished each other Happy Christmas.

Then Marion saw her parents approach, and she sighed as she saw her mother had a face on her like she'd sucked a lemon. 'Happy Christmas, Mammy,' she said, but when she tried to hug her it was like hugging a board. She knew her mother was still cross that they hadn't been asked to Christmas dinner, though she had done her best to explain. The children all gave her a dutiful kiss on her cheek and wished her Happy Christmas, but she never said anything back. Her father made up for it as he enveloped Marion in a bear hug, then did the same to the twins and Sarah. He shook hands with Tony and Richard, and, warmed by his good wishes, they went into Mass together.

Back home, Peggy had porridge cooked and keeping warm in the double pan, knowing the family would be hungry when they returned. She waited until they had finished eating before she said to the twins and Tony, 'Me and Violet couldn't find anything for you in the shops so we are both giving you money instead,' and she dropped a two-bob piece into each of their hands and Violet did the same. The three children had never held so much money before – not money that was their very own, anyway – and they were overawed by it all.

After breakfast Christmas music was playing on the wireless and everyone dispersed: Sarah to help her mother, Peggy and Violet to tidy their room and make their beds, and Tony and Richard working on the sailing ship in their bedroom in the parlour. Missie and Magda sat either side of the crackling range reading the books from Richard, which they had been so pleased with, and it was all very pleasant and cozy.

Magda suddenly sat up straighter and said, 'Sniff.'

Missie looked up from her book. 'Sniff what?'

'The air.'

Missie obediently sniffed.

'Well, what can you smell?'

'Nothing.'

'You've got to be able to smell summat.'

'Well, nothing unusual, I mean. Just the meat cooking and that.'

'That's what I mean!' Magda cried. 'It's like the smells on Sundays before the war, the gorgeous smell of the roasting meat mixed with the sweet smells from the kitchen where Mom was making all the fancies and cakes and that when the grandparents always came to tea, remember?'

'I remember all right,' Missie said. 'I suppose it is like it used to be. It don't half make you hungry smelling it cooking, though.'

Tony came through from his bedroom at that point and he too sniffed the air appreciatively. 'Cor, summat smells good,' he said. 'When will it be ready?'

Magda shrugged. 'How should we know?'

Tony began to prowl around restlessly and Magda frowned. 'Give over, Tony.'

'Give over what?'

'Walking up and down like that. You're putting me off my book.'

Before Tony could answer this Missie said, 'Why don't you go back to your model, or have you already finished it?'

Tony shook his head. 'We've got to a bit where Richard says we have to let the glue dry. Should be fine after dinner, and he won't let me play my whistle, and anyroad, I'm starving.'

'You're always starving,' Magda said disparagingly.

Before Tony could think of a reply to this, Marion put her head round the kitchen door and when she shouted, 'I could do with a hand now. Who would like to lay the table?' Magda and Missie threw down their books and were in the kitchen in seconds.

The dinner was magnificent. Marion hadn't been

able to get any sort of fowl, but she had been able to buy a rabbit from a butcher down the Bull Ring so that's what was laid in their roasting tin, surrounded by masses of roast potatoes. There was also a large pan of creamed carrots, another of cabbage, and one more pan of boiled potatoes. All the vegetables had been grown on the allotment, and the whole family tucked in with relish.

Marion looked at her children all grouped around the table, chatting together and laughing and joking with Peggy and Violet, so much part of the family now, and felt a thrill of pride. She suddenly wished, God forgive her, that her mother wasn't coming to tea that day for she knew she would do her best to ruin everything and she definitely didn't want the harmony of the day broken. She realised she had spoken so sharply to Magda before Mass because the child had put into words what she herself was feeling and that made her feel guilty.

Just as if she could read her mother's mind Magda said, 'We won't have to sit on the horsehair sofa when Grandma and Granddad come, will we, because they can't eat in the parlour any more 'cos it's Richard and Tony's bedroom?'

'No,' Marion said, 'you won't have to sit anywhere except up at the table like everyone else.'

'Oh, good!'

It was said so fervently that it made Marion smile. 'Did you dislike the horsehair sofa so much?' she asked.

Magda nodded vehemently. 'I hated just sitting there,' she said. 'but the worst part was that the horsehair used to come through the stuff it was covered with and stick in our bottoms and our legs.'

Marion looked from Magda to Missie, who was nodding.

'It's true, Mom,' she said. 'They felt like thousands of needles pricking you.'

'Surely not?'

'They're right, Mom,' Sarah said. 'I suffered it too.'

'But why didn't any of you say?'

'You probably wouldn't have believed us,' Magda said. 'I mean, I've never seen an adult sitting on that sofa. 'Cos it was prickly I used to wag my legs about and that used to make Grandma really wild with me.'

'Well, I'm sorry I wasn't more observant,' Marion said. 'But rest assured there will be no more sitting on any horsehair sofa ever again. Now if everyone has finished their dinner do you all want pudding? It's apricot upside-down?'

She was almost deafened by the response. But after the meal was over and everyone replete, Marion was made to sit down with a cup of tea while the girls cleared away the remains of the dinner and washed everything up.

Marion was grateful but she was watching the clock anxiously, knowing that peace would soon be at an end, especially after Peggy and Violet left for their friend's house. She crept upstairs and peered out of the bay window in her bedroom and her heart sank when she saw the uncompromising strides of her mother as she turned into the road, arm in arm with her father. As she got nearer Marion could see that she was wearing the same expression as she'd on at Mass, and she went down the stairs dejectedly.

'But that's just what I am saying,' Clara whined. 'Because you agreed to house those girls over Christmas you were unable to accommodate me or your father. Your own flesh and blood. It's just not right.'

Marion suppressed a sigh. 'Mammy, I have explained how it was. The girls have only today off.'

'She has told us all this before, Clara,' Eddie said.

'Families should come first.'

'Come on, Mammy, let's not argue,' Marion said in a conciliatory manner. 'It's Christmas Day, after all, and soon we'll have a lovely tea with honey cakes and apple tart. I followed a recipe for a one-egg wonder cake too because I was light on eggs. Course, there so many of us I doubled up the quantities so ours is a two-egg wonder cake. I hope it's not too heavy.'

'I'm sure it will be fine,' Eddie said loyally. 'You're a grand cook and always have been.'

'Yeah, but with rations the way they are, I am

often paddling in uncharted waters,' Marion said. 'But before we start on the tea let me give you your presents.'

'You shouldn't have bothered,' Clara snapped. 'I have no time for fripperies.'

Keeping her temper with difficulty, Marion replied, 'Then it's a good thing I didn't buy you fripperies, but a nice soft woollen shawl to put around your shoulders on cold nights.'

It was a beautiful shawl in different shades of blue, which a woman Polly knew had knitted specially. It would be hard not to like it, but though Clara accepted it, and even allowed Marion to drape it around her shoulders, she uttered no word of thanks.

But when Marion presented her father with a new pipe she had gone into the town to buy from a proper tobacconist, he said, 'It's wonderful, pet,' turning it round in his hands. 'I've never had such a fine pipe.'

'Oh, Daddy . . .'

'You shouldn't spend so much on an old man like me. I know what pipes like this cost. The children—'

'The children had plenty and were pleased with everything they got,' Marion said. 'They know the score as well as the rest of us.'

'Well, I have some sweets for them all in my coat pocket,' Eddie said.

'You didn't tell me that you were bringing sweets,' Clara snapped.

'I didn't need to,' Eddie said. 'It was my own money I saved. I couldn't visit my grandchildren on Christmas Day empty-handed.'

'Thank you, Daddy,' Marion said before her mother could speak again. 'The children generally get little enough sweets. They'll be very grateful. Shall we go through for tea now? I'll get Sarah to give me a hand.'

'Where is she?' Clara demanded. 'In fact, where are any of the children?'

Marion knew the children had found pressing things to do elsewhere in the house as soon as they had seen their grandparents approaching, but she said vaguely, 'Oh, they're around somewhere.'

'They should be here, to greet guests,' Clara said.

They might if you showed the slightest pleasure in seeing them. For a moment Marion thought she had spoken the words aloud, but her mother's expression hadn't changed, and when she said, 'Your children, Marion, have appalling manners,' she had the desire to laugh at her mother and her hypocrisy. She restrained herself, but with difficulty, and needing to put some space between them, left in search of Sarah. Marion dreaded the meal, knowing that it would be a catalogue of complaints, and she knew she would be counting the hours until they would leave.

NINETEEN

The girls that worked with Peggy and Violet advised them to go to Madame Amie's Dancing Academy in Chain Walk, which was just the other side of Birchfield Road at the very end of Albert Road. 'She does the waltzes and quick steps, and that,' one of their workmates said. 'But they teaches you fun things as well like the swing, kangaroo hop and the jitterbug.'

'And what on earth are those, when they're at home?' Marion asked that evening when they told her this.

'They've come from America,' Violet said. 'This girl was telling us the jitterbug is banned in some dance halls, and that some places seem almost afraid of it.'

'I am not sure that I like the sound of this jitterbug,' Marion said with a wry smile. 'Maybe I should come with you as a chaperone.'

'Mom! Sarah cried. 'Mary Ellen and Siobhan want to go too, and Aunt Polly don't mind.' She made a face and then went on, 'Orla played it up to come too, but Aunt Polly said no. I mean, she ain't fourteen yet.'

Marion hid her smile at her daughter's indignation, speaking as she was from the lofty age of fifteen herself, with Mary Ellen and Siobhan seventeen and fifteen, but she made no mention of that. What she did say was, 'I was joking, Sarah. The time is past when I would be afraid of a dance. It's probably just a bit too lively for a lot of us old ones. I think you get little enough enjoyment in your lives at the moment and you're only young the once.'

And so every Wednesday evening, just before seven, the girls would be seen scurrying up Albert Road to their dancing class. Often at the weekend they would practise what they'd learned that week. They even got Richard up a time or two to partner one of them and didn't seem to care a jot about his two left feet.

This was the part that Richard liked best because he was very attracted to Violet, and had been almost as soon as she had come to live with them. He knew she thought of him as a young boy, but as he grew older his feelings for her grew stronger and he inveigled his way to sit by her as often as possible and was always asking her opinion on things. In fact, one of the reasons he had been so upset about not having a uniform for the Home Guard straight away was his need to impress Violet. One of his workmates, far more skilled than Richard about the opposite sex and matters of the heart, had assured him that women went a bundle for any man in uniform.

However, he had a uniform now and he had to admit that it had made little difference. Not that Violet was unkind or anything; it was more that she was disinterested. In fact, Violet was well aware of Richard's preoccupation with her and his love-sick eyes following her everywhere, and so was Peggy, and they had laughed about it, though gently.

'The point is,' Violet said to Peggy one day, 'he is sweet and I do like him, but not in the way he wants me to like him.'

'I think it could become quite awkward, anyway,' Peggy said. 'What if you did become emotionally entangled and then had a fallout or something. It could make living with the family really difficult.'

'I know, but as I said, I don't feel that way about him anyway.'

'I think it's best not to get involved anyway till the war is over,' Peggy said. 'Look at those pilots we met and were quite keen on. Both of them died in the Battle of Britain.'

'Yeah, and we might never have known if one of their friends hadn't seen us waiting for them outside the Globe and told us,' Violet said. 'Bloody shame it was as well. They were really nice, and so young.'

'All the pilots were young,' Peggy said. 'Good job we didn't get really attached. I'm not letting myself get tangled up with anyone again till this blessed war comes to an end.'

'I think I'll tell Richard that,' Violet said. 'It will let him down gently.'

So when Richard plucked up the courage to ask Violet if she wanted to go to the pictures, she said, 'I'd love to Richard. We all would.'

That wasn't at all what Richard had in mind. 'I meant you and me on our own,' he said. 'Or do you think I'm too young?'

'It isn't that, Richard,' Violet said. 'It's nothing to do with you at all. I do like you very much, but I just don't want to get serious with anyone at the moment. I have seen the heartache some of the girls at work have suffered. Anyway, your mother might not like us to go out together as we live in the same house and everything.' Then she caught sight of Richard's crestfallen face and added, 'I'm sorry.'

Richard was bitterly disappointed, but he knew that Violet's reasons for refusing him had been valid ones and so when she said, 'We can still go to the pictures, though. *Rebecca* is showing at the Globe. It's Alfred Hitchcock so we girls might need a big strapping man with us in case we get scared,' even he had to smile.

'You lot don't scare easy,' he said. 'But I might as well, I suppose.'

The film was good and they all enjoyed it, though it was not the date Richard had envisaged. Often at weekends Mary Ellen and Siobhan would come down to practise dancing, and they would all get Richard up to partner them, so he sometimes got to hold Violet tight in his arms. There was always a lot of fun and laughter at these sessions and Marion found the dancing quite entertaining to watch, though she marvelled at the energy they all had. The jitterbug in particular was very invigorating and fun, and she could quite see why the young girls would enjoy it so much.

There were air raids over the next few months but they were light and weeks apart, and none came near Aston. Marion became more hopeful that the raids were petering out, especially as the days passed and the grey low clouds and the icy blasts of winter were being replaced by clearer skies and spring sunshine. Everyone was looking forward to Easter and, after that, Tony's eleventh birthday, and so when the sirens rang out again on Wednesday 9 April, in Holy Week, everyone thought it would be another short, sharp skirmish.

It was half-past nine, but the children hadn't been in bed long because it was the Easter holidays, and Marion was tempted not to rouse them. The last few raids had been so slight and sporadic there had been little point in going to the cellar.

When she suggested staying where they were, though, Richard frowned. 'I don't know, Mom,' he said. 'Listen to the drone in the sky.'

Marion listened to the rumble getting louder every minute and she shivered as Richard said,

'I don't think it's worth taking a chance. Anyroad, didn't you say you promised Dad?'

Marion had. She looked at Sarah, Peggy and Violet. 'What do you think?'

'Well,' Peggy said, 'I've no desire to go down to the cellar, but as Richard said, maybe it's best not to take chances.'

'Yeah, I feel the same,' Violet said. 'Anyroad, if it is a short sharp one like the last few we will be back here in no time.'

'And a promise is a promise,' Sarah said.

Marion gave a groan and got to her feet. 'All right,' she said. 'You've convinced me. Sarah, will you see to the twins, and, Richard, can you see that Tony is up and carry the blankets down for me?'

'Yes,'Richard said. 'That's no problem, but get a move on. There certainly seem more planes than there have been in the last few raids.'

The children grumbled initially, but when they heard the first crashes the twins at least were anxious to get underground where the frightening sounds would be somewhat muffled. Tony was trying very hard to be brave, especially as Richard said before he left, 'All right, Tony it's up to you now. Remember you'll be man of the house once I enlist so you take care of everyone down here.'

Tony felt puffed up with pride. Richard had told him that before, and it had made Tony feel a bit scared but also excited. After all, he was very shortly going to be eleven and not a baby any more, so when Richard said, 'Think you can do that?' he said with all the assurance he could muster, 'Course I can.'

Tony took the other blankets from Richard as he spoke and then with a cheeky grin said, 'Best get yourself away if you're going.'

Richard smiled as he cuffed his young brother lightly around the head. 'I am going, so you all look after yourselves.'

'Who is he talking to, anyroad?' Marion said as the door closed behind her elder son. 'He's the one going out in the teeth of the raid, not us. We at least have a cellar to shelter in, and at least it's not as cold down here as it has been.'

'No,' Violet agreed. 'But there's a sort of dampness in the air just the same.'

'There is,' Marion agreed as the first bomb blasts were heard. 'I think I will light the paraffin stove anyway.'

Everyone was all right at first. The planes seemed far enough away not to trouble them, and they played dominoes or chatted together. Then, as the droning rumble got nearer, Peggy opened her gramophone and wound it up, and soon the stirring music of Glenn Miller filled the cellar.

The sounds of the raid almost overhead could still be plainly heard, though, and when there was one terrific explosion very close, Missie gave a yelp.

'We are really safe in here, aren't we?' she asked her mother.

Tony felt sorry for his young sister because he

saw she was really scared and so before his mother could find an answer, he said, 'Course we are. Have been so far, ain't we? Anyroad, Dad always said we'd be as safe as houses in the cellar, dain't he, Mom?'

'He did,' Marion said as confidently as she could. She realised now that this was no quick skirmish but another full-blown attack. She listened to the scream of the ever-descending bombs and the ack-ack guns barking into the sky, and she felt fear clutching at her as some bombs fell extremely close and shook the cellar walls.

She tried to hide her fear from the others and instead delved into her shelter bag. She had a packet of biscuits she gave to the children to share and she poured tea for the adults with hands that shook.

'I really did think we were over all this,' Violet said.

'And me,' Sarah agreed. 'It's awful isn't it? Just as you start to relax it starts all over again.'

'Oh God, I hope you're wrong about that,' Peggy said. 'I'd hate to think that this is the fore-runner of another blitz.'

'So would I,' Marion said. 'And there's no way of knowing. We'll just have to wait and see, though it's nerve-racking waiting for the sirens to wail out night after night.'

'Richard said some of the lads he works with listen to someone called Lord Haw-Haw,' Tony said. 'And he says what's going to happen some-times. He don't do it in a nice way or anything, though. Richard said he's horrible.'

'He is, Tony, and a traitor. He takes pleasure in terrorising people, prophesying what the Luftwaffe have planned next. I would never listen to him on principle.'

'Quite right too,' Peggy said. 'People aren't supposed to listen to him, anyroad.'

'I don't see why anyone does,' Sarah said. 'I don't think it will do morale any good. I mean, through all these raids and everything we've got to keep thinking that we're going to win this war, and from what Richard told me this Lord Haw-Haw doesn't help.'

There was a sudden shattering explosion right beside them. The cellar walls shook and Marion saw mortar dribble out from a few of the bricks. The adults looked at other in sudden fear and the children's eyes looked as if they were on stalks.

'God, that was close,' Peggy said.

'Yes,' Marion said, and to Tony and the twins: 'You must be worn out. It would be better if you could sleep for a wee while.'

'I don't think I could sleep,' Magda said. 'It's too scary and noisy.'

'I couldn't either,' Tony said. 'Them planes are all round us, and above us and everything.' Peggy packed the gramophone away as she said, 'I wonder if them ack-ack guns ever shoot any of them planes down. It doesn't seem to make any impression on them.'

'Maybe it's just done to make us feel better,' Tony said. 'Like fighting back, you know.'

'It doesn't make me feel any better,' Missie said.

'Come on,' Marion urged. 'Let's sit on the settee together and I'll read you a story.'

Marion had a big book of bedtime stories that Bill had bought when he had been home, and with the twins either side of her and Tony sitting cross-legged on the mattress, Marion began to read. Snuggling against their mother, with the lateness of the hour and her soothing voice, the twins soon grew very drowsy. Three loud bombs dropped in quick succession and very close jerked them awake.

Then Magda sat upright and said, 'What's that pong?'

Marion sniffed too and she knew what it was straight away. 'Gas!' she cried. 'Get out, quick.' She knew it was better to take their chance outside, even in the raid, because gas was a certain killer.

They all knew speed was essential and were soon pounding up the cellar steps, Marion behind them all. She was almost at the top when she remembered the lit paraffin stove. She knew when the cellar filled up with enough gas it would cause a massive explosion. She would be all right for a few minutes, as long as she could hold her breath, she told herself as she turned without a word to the others and began to go back down the steps.

Tony had been directly in front of his mother and the only one to be aware of what she had done. He opened his mouth to tell Sarah or one of the others but then he shut it again. He knew Richard wouldn't have let his mother return to a gas-filled cellar all alone and he had charged him that night to look after them all and so he followed her. By the time he had reached the bottom of the steps Marion had sprung across the room and turned off the tap of the stove. Her lungs felt as if they were bursting and she knew she had to get up the steps quickly, but as she turned she saw Tony and she felt fear grip her as he opened his mouth and said, 'What're you doing?'

Marion let out the breath she had been holding and cried in alarm, 'Get out of here, quick. Run! Go on!'

She saw Tony put his hand to his head and begin to cough and retch as poisonous fumes filled his lungs. He swayed on the steps and she fought to reach him through cloying blackness as she too began to cough and splutter, stinging water streaming from her eyes.

'Tony, run,' she pleaded huskily, but he was doubled over, choking as he fought for air and seemed incapable of doing anything. Desperately she groped for his hand, intending to drag them both up the steps. But it was too late. She felt a burning in her lungs and then blackness suddenly surrounded her and she fell into a heap on the floor of the cellar.

Outside, Sarah, though desperately worried about her mother and brother, and frightened by the bombs still cascading around them, had her hands full trying to prevent her sisters from going back into the house. They were shouting and screaming at her, and trying to push her restraining hands away. She didn't know what to do; none of them did.

She was incredibly relieved to see an ARP warden walking towards them, alerted by the noise the twins were making.

'What's up?'

'My mother and brother are inside,' Sarah cried in panic. 'We smelled gas.'

Events moved swiftly after that, and when the stretchers with the unconscious forms of Marion and Tony were brought out of the cellar there was an agonising wait for an ambulance. It was probably five minutes or less but it seemed longer as the family stood in the street in the middle of the air raid.

The bell of the ambulance had never been such a welcoming sound, and when the stretchers had been gently placed inside, the driver said, 'One of you had better come with us. We'll make for the General Hospital as it's closest, but we could be directed anywhere.'

Sarah wasn't sure where her duty lay – to go with her mother and brother or care for her sisters – and Peggy, seeing her dilemma, said, 'You go with Marion and Tony, Sarah. We'll take care of the girls, don't worry. I think our first priority is taking shelter somewhere.'

Sarah nodded dumbly and watched them all being shepherded away by a warden while she climbed into the ambulance and the doors shut behind her.

Many fires made it nearly as bright as day, and as the ambulance moved through the streets, Sarah could plainly see the black arrows of death shrieking down from the droning planes. The never ending rattle of the guns seemed to make no impression on them. She heard shouts and screams and cries, heard the ringing bells of the emergency services, saw buildings exploding in clouds of dust, or crumple with a shuddering thud, and the ambulance driver trying to negotiate potholes, buckled tramlines and piles of masonry and debris spilled into the roads.

When they reached the General Hospital, it was to find that it had been bombed too and parts of it were extensively damaged. Doctors and nurses, as well as patients, had been killed or badly injured, and some were still trapped. The ambulance was directed to Lewis's, a big department store close by, where the cellar had been offered for the injured. An acrid smell hit Sarah's nose and lodged in the back of her throat as soon as she entered the building. As she watched the ambulance men carry the stretchers down the wide staircase, she noted each side of it was crammed with blood-stained clothing.

She had been told to remain where she was, but she leaned forward to look down and saw the stretchers almost covering the floor. Many of the faces were a reddy brown colour from the brick dust, and most patients were obviously badly injured. She noted the doctors and nurses moving amongst the stretchers, stopping now and then to minister to a patient. There were so few of them, though, to deal with so many people, and they had so few facilities that any medical attention would have to be minimal. Sarah trembled in fear; her mother and Tony had both been incredibly still since they had been lifted out of the cellar.

She wasn't aware how long she had been there when her Aunt Polly joined her. 'Peggy and Violet took the twins to Atkinson's Brewery, knowing they'd find me there,' she said in explanation. 'They were trying to find Richard and alert Mammy and Daddy when I left. I came here to support you.'

'Oh, I'm so glad you did,' Sarah said earnestly. 'I'm so frightened, Aunt Polly.'

'I know, pet,' Polly said. 'It would be hard for you to feel any other way. I suppose there is no news?'

Sarah shook her head.

'So what actually happened?' Polly asked.

'We smelled gas and Mom told us to get out quick,' Sarah said. 'And we did. Least, I thought Mom was behind us. I don't know what made her go back down to the cellar. Tony must have followed her because she was lying on the cellar floor and Tony was at the bottom of the steps. That's what the ambulance men said, anyroad.'

'But they got them out real quick?'

'Yeah,' said Sarah. 'But was it quick enough? That stuff is terribly poisonous.'

There was no answer to that, and the words hung in the air.

Richard had arrived before they saw a white

coated doctor coming up the steps towards them. Sarah noted his grave eyes and the black bags beneath them.

'Whittaker?' he said questioningly and Richard stepped forward.

'I am Richard Whittaker.'

'I am very much afraid that we have been unable to save your brother,' the doctor said. 'He had inhaled too much gas.'

Richard's stomach gave a lurch and behind him he heard his aunt gasp and begin to cry. 'Dead?' Sarah burst out. 'Tony is dead?'

'It was too late. I am so very sorry,' the doctor said.

Richard's head was reeling, his mind shouting a denial. 'And my mother?'

'She is holding her own at the moment.'

'Can we see her?'

'There would be no point. She's still unconscious,' the doctor said. 'Come back later today. We will likely know more then anyway. You can see how we are placed at the moment.'

They could, of course, and numb with shock they made their way outside. It was full daylight now and though the all clear had sounded they were hardly aware of it and as they made their way up Corporation Street they saw devastation all around them. They smelled the smoke still swirling in the air from the many fires that were raging all around the city and saw the mangled and crushed remains of what had once been shops and offices.

They were almost too shocked to talk. They each had their own memory of Tony, and Richard in particular felt ashamed of the number of times he had lost patience with his young brother. He was so young to lose his life, and Richard felt as if he had a sharp ache in his heart.

'I can only imagine Marion's pain when she knows of this,' Polly said brokenly.

If she survives. Sarah didn't say the words but they hammered inside her head and she knew that though she was heartbroken over Tony's death, she would be lost altogether without her mother.

From Victoria Road they looked over a sea of rubble. Here and there piles were still smouldering, sending curls of grey smoke into the air. Many others had people scrambling over them, moving bricks and charred and fractured roof beams to see if there was anything worth salvaging from the mounds that had once been their homes. Richard, Sarah and Polly clambered over fallen masonry, often hearing glass splinter under their feet, and tried to avoid curling hoses still dribbling into the gutters, and sodden burst sandbags bleeding onto the pavements. Yet their feet dragged for they didn't want to take such bad news to those at home.

Marion's life hung in the balance for some days. She didn't regain consciousness until Easter Sunday morning. The doctor had worried that there might be brain damage, so as soon as the hovering nurse noticed movement she went over to her. 'Mrs Whittaker,' she said with a wide smile wreathing her face, 'I'm so glad you are back with us.'

Marion had a terrific pain in her chest and her throat was so swollen it hurt her to swallow. She had no earthly idea where she was. She opened her mouth to ask the nurse but all that came out was a croak and the nurse brought her a glass of water, lifting her and supporting her while she drank it. 'Now,' she said. 'I expect you want to know where you are. You're in Lewis's basement. The General Hospital was bombed and you had to be brought here. What can you remember?'

Marion cast her mind back and, in a voice still husky from the effects of the gas, she said, 'There was a raid, and Magda smelled gas, and I had to go back to the cellar to turn off the paraffin stove. Tony, my son, followed me. How is he?'

The nurse had thought she would become inured to death, as she had been a nurse since 1938, but she'd never been able to come to terms with the death of a child and so she felt extremely sorry for Marion. She bent her head and busied herself tucking Marion in as she said, 'Doctor will explain everything to you.'

'So when can I see him?'

'I'll see if he's free now, if you like?'

'Please. I would be most grateful.'

'Your parents are here too.'

'My parents?'

'Well, your father has been here hours and now your mother has joined him,' the nurse said. 'In fact, someone has been here all the time you were unconscious. You seem to have a very loving and supportive family.'

'I have,' Marion said simply. 'And I know it.'

The nurse was glad that Marion had that support because her grief when the doctor told of the death of her son was so profound and deep it was painful to witness. Marion was filled with anguish and despair. Tears streamed from her eyes in a torrent and sobs shook her body as she remembered with shame every occasion she had shouted at Tony, or sent him to bed without his tea, or even beat him with the hairbrush.

And then she felt strong arms around her and her father was saying, 'Oh, my darling girl . . .'

'Daddy, oh, Daddy,' Marion cried, clutching at him, glad of the solid bulk of him. 'I can't bear it, Daddy.'

'You can, Marion,' her father said firmly. 'The others need you and you will not be on your own. Aren't we all heartsore about the poor boy's death?'

'I didn't know it would hurt this much,' Marion cried. 'I never thought anything could hurt this much.'

'No, and maybe you will have a better understanding of the agony I have suffered over the years,' Clara said, appearing on Marion's other side. 'But in your case your son's death could have

351

been prevented, if you had heeded my warning about those gas pipes.'

'Clara!' Eddie gasped, shocked to the core. 'How can you say such a thing?'

'Because it's true,' Clara said, and added almost gleefully, 'and if Marion examines her conscience she will know I'm right.'

'You are going home,' Eddie said unusually firmly to his wife, 'where you can cause no further mischief and upset.' He took his daughter's hand and looked into her eyes, which were like pools of sadness in her head. 'You take no heed of this. Tony's death is not your fault.'

Marion, though, was racked with guilt. She'd known what Tony was like. Why hadn't she made sure that he was safe on the pavement before going to turn off the stove? Whichever way she looked at it, she had led that young boy, her own son, to his death, and she wondered if she was ever going to forgive herself.

Polly, who came to see her with Pat later, would have none of it when Marion told them of her parent's visit.

'I was afraid of an explosion,' Marion said. 'I'm disgusted with myself. I was putting the love of my house over the safety of my son.'

'But, Marion, it wouldn't just have been the house, would it?' Pat said. 'If it had exploded it would have killed, or at least badly injured, the kids outside. What you did saved the rest of them. Yours wasn't the only gas pipe fractured that night, you know. The whole area has been evacuated until they can repair the pipes and they must make sure any build up of gas has dispersed before they'll allow you back. The others are camping out in a school hall on the Lozell's Road for now. No, Marion, Tony's death was an accident. It was tragic, and there'll probably not be a day when we won't miss him and wish he was still here, but if anyone was responsible it was the German bombers.'

'Do you really think that?'

'I know that,' Pat said firmly. He thought for a fleeting moment of Bill, out in God alone knew where, unaware of the grievous blow his family had been dealt. He remembered the day they had enlisted, when he said it would tear the heart out of him to lose just one son, and Pat's heart burned for him. 'Bill needs to know,' he said to Marion. 'I could write to him, if you would like me to.'

'Would you, Pat?' Marion said gratefully and her eyes filled with tears again. 'He will be so upset and there'll be no one near him to give him any support.'

Pat knew no support in the world would lessen this blow for Bill, but he didn't share that with Marion; he just told her to get well and strong again, for all the family was pining for her.

Marion saw that herself when her older children came to see her, their eyes red-rimmed in their ravaged white faces. They seemed shrouded in misery. Peggy and Violet, who also came, were little better, and yet the hospital wouldn't think about discharging Marion until she could go back in her own house, which didn't happen until Thursday.

She arrived in the afternoon to a house cleaned from top to bottom by Polly and Sarah, who had taken time off from work.

Later that day Marion said, 'You know what tortures me, Polly?'

'What?'

'D'you think Tony knew I loved him?'

'Of course he did.'

'He might not have done,' Marion said, and her eyes were sombre. 'I mean, I never said I did.'

'Well, it ain't summat you have to say, is it?' Polly said. 'They just know, don't they?'

'I don't know,' Marion said helplessly. 'Our mam didn't love us, did she?'

'Our mam was one on her own.'

'Yeah, but was she, though?' Marion said. 'When I think back all I ever seemed to do was tell Tony off. It was just that I was worried that he'd go to the bad. I mean, he got up to some pranks.'

'Yeah, him and Jack together.'

'Thick as thieves, they were, and that's what I thought they were turning into when they stole that coal. I was frightened to death then and yet I never laid a hand on him that time. He reduced me to tears and it shocked him to bits to see me so upset. I knew he'd never do anything like that again.'

'Yes, because he cared about your good opinion

of him,' Polly said confidently, 'because he loved you and knew that you loved him. Believe me, Marion, you never told Tony off unless he deserved it, and he would know that too.'

'I did love him, you see,' Marion said. 'I loved him desperately, like I do all of them. I wish I could have told him just the once. It's awful if you don't feel loved by your mother.'

'You're thinking of our mam again and how she behaved,' Polly said. 'And you can never compare yourself with her. Her love shrivelled up when she lost Michael, and she had none left for anyone else. Your love was freely given to all your children and they're all a credit to you – and I include Tony in that, God rest his soul.'

'D'you know, I have been wondering why he followed me down that cellar,' Marion said. 'And I think it was because Richard had told him that he'd be man of the house when he enlisted.' She smiled ruefully. 'Tony was very impressed by that and that night I think he was sort of looking out for me.'

'See, what did I tell you?'

'Oh, Polly, you are good for me.'

'We'll always have each other, you know that,' Polly said, her voice thick with emotion, 'and I'll be right beside you at the funeral tomorrow.'

TWENTY

The following morning Polly and her daughters carried armloads of food from their house to Marion's, for the funeral guests. 'People were good when they knew it was for Tony's funeral, and gave up some of their rations. And it's amazing what could be found under many a grocer or butcher's counter when they knew what it was for,' Polly said, when Marion asked where all the food had come from.

'But you and the girls must have worked your fingers to the bone to do all this, and Pat has arranged the funeral and everything. I feel quite useless,' Marion said.

'Marion, you are not long out of hospital and you were injured yourself, don't forget,' Polly said. 'The funeral itself will be enough of an ordeal, believe me.'

It was an ordeal for them all. Marion looked at all the white faces and knew they were suffering in their own way as they walked together in a sombre group to church. Richard took his mother's arm and Sarah, Peggy and Violet took charge of the twins. Marion was surprised, though pleased, by the numbers that came. Neighbours and friends, Catholic and non-Catholic, nearly filled the church, along with Tony's classmates and his teacher and the headmaster.

It was the first time that Marion had seen Jack since the tragedy and she was shocked at his appearance. It was as if the lifeblood had been squeezed from him and his dark eyes, usually alight with devilment of one kind or another, looked huge in his gaunt face. At the Requiem Mass Father McIntyre described Tony as full of life with a highly developed sense of fun, and Marion was very glad he didn't go into details and recount the tale of him and Jack snaffling the Communion wine. But the priest's words stirred memories for the twins, and they wept for their brother. Jack, who had never been known to cry about anything, also sobbed for the cousin he would never see again.

Richard, fearing his mother might give way herself with such an open show of distress from the children, squeezed her arm in a gesture of support. She smiled at him sadly but she was able to swallow the lump threatening to choke her and blink away the tears prickling in her eyes, because she knew that if she began to cry now she would be unable to stop.

At the cemetery, after Jack had dropped the

clod of earth on top of Tony's coffin, he sidled up to Marion and said, 'I'm real sorry about Tony, Aunt Marion.'

Marion looked down at the woebegone child and wondered why she had ever had such an active dislike of him. 'I know you are, Jack,' she said gently.

'He was my best friend, Aunt Marion,' Jack said. 'I will miss him so much, and I'll never forget him, not even if I live to be a hundred.'

'I'll miss him too, Jack,' Marion said. 'Every day of my life I will miss him, and yet I know that we must learn to live our lives without him, however hard that is, because that's what Tony would want us to do.'

Despite Marion's words to Jack, it was hard for her to live without Tony, hard even to believe she would never see him again. The whole family missed him, each in their own way. Sarah had been four when he was born and she remembered looking at him for ages as he lay in his cot or in his mother's arms, and thought him so incredibly sweet. Marion remembered this and though she knew Tony would annoy Richard greatly sometimes, and tease the twins, there was no nastiness or malice in it; he was just mischievous. He had such a cheeky grin and infectious laugh no one was cross with him for long, even Magda, though sometimes they'd go at it hammer and tongs. What their mother would give to hear them quarrelling now.

Tony's death made a large hole in Bill's life too, and his hurt and pain could almost be lifted from the pages of the letter he sent Marion. He also felt a measure of guilt that he had exacted a promise from her that she would use the cellar whenever there was a raid, and hadn't given a thought to the gas taps. If it hadn't been for her mother, she wouldn't have thought of them either.

No one would agree to use the cellar any more and Marion could hardly blame them. She was just glad that since that fateful raid there was only light and sporadic bombing. The children found it very hard to speak about Tony and, as if by tacit consent, avoided his name, fearful of upsetting their mother further.

Then one evening, recounting some tale, Magda let Tony's name slip out and immediately clapped her hand over her mouth.

'I don't mind you talking about Tony,' Marion said. 'I won't promise not to get upset, but that isn't always a bad thing. Not to talk about him means that he might as well not have existed, and yet he was an important part of our lives for almost eleven years – all your lifetime, Magda, and yours too, Missie. We will all have our memories of him and if you want to share them, in the end it might help us all cope better.'

How Richard and Sarah admired their mother for that. They both knew that while Tony's death had affected them, it had knocked their mother for six. At first their attempts to talk about their brother were tentative and cautious. However, Tony had been full of life and mischief, and was often very funny, so that remembering the things he said and the escapades he had got up to meant the tears were frequently replaced by smiles. Marion found this strangely cathartic and it helped to fill the black hole.

By the last Saturday in July she felt strong enough to sort Tony's clothes out.

'Are you sure, Mom?' said Richard. 'It's early days yet.'

'There's too much of a shortage of clothes to hang on to any of Tony's that someone might make better use of,' she said. 'You can help, if you like.'

Richard did help, and so did Sarah. Marion found it more upsetting than she'd anticipated, making parcels of Tony's clothes, including the coat from Polly that he was just beginning to grow into. But in searching through Tony's other things, Richard came upon the bag of marbles he had given him for Christmas. He weighed it in his hand and his eyes filled with tears as he remembered how touched Tony had been when he had given him the bag, and the awe on his face when he had tipped them out onto the table.

'What have you there?' Marion asked.

'Tony's marbles, or marleys, as he insisted on calling them.'

'What are you going to do with them?' Sarah asked.

'I thought to give them to Jack.'

'Oh, Richard,' said Marion, 'you couldn't do a better thing. Polly is that worried about Jack because he doesn't seem to be coming to terms with Tony's death at all.'

'It's hard, Mom, hard for all of us,' Sarah said.

'God, don't I know that,' Marion said. 'But we have to battle through it because it's the only way. And being given something of Tony's that he placed such value on might make a difference to him, that's all I'm saying. If you want to see Jack now, you'll probably find him down the allotment. Polly's said he virtually lives there just now.'

'Well, if you don't need me at the moment,' Richard said, 'I'll go and see if I can bring a smile to his face.'

Richard had been surprised and pleased that his brother and cousin had started to help their grandfather on the allotment, but he had imagined it would be a passing fancy that they'd soon grow tired of, though he always been amazed what they had achieved whenever he'd gone down at weekends to give a hand. But they hadn't grown tired of it at all, and now the allotment was furrowed in perfectly straight rows. Richard saw potatoes, carrots and onions were ready to be dug up, and crisp cabbages just needed to be lifted from the ground, and the sweet succulent garden peas were climbing the trellis he remembered Colm making from scrap wood.

Jack was walking up and down each row

watering the plants. His grandfather came out of the shed wiping his hands on a rag as he saw Richard approach.

'What brings you here?' he asked.

'I've come to see Jack.'

At the sound of his name Jack raised his head.

'Come here,' Richard said. 'I have something for you.'

Jack approached slowly, almost reluctantly, and Richard was shocked by his grey pallor and the bleak bereft look in his deep dark eyes. 'You all right, Jack?'

Jack shrugged, and Richard saw the tremble of his bottom lip. He said gently, 'We all miss him, Jack.' Jack nodded, but didn't speak, and with a sigh, Richard withdrew the bag from his pocket and placed it in Jack's hands. 'I think Tony would have liked you to have these.'

Jack gave a gasp. He didn't need to open the bag to see what was in it; he had seen it often enough when it had belonged to Tony, and he remembered how proud he was when Richard gave him that wonderful marble collection. He could scarcely believe that now it would belong to him. Somehow it brought Tony closer, and when he looked at Richard his face was full of gratitude. But as he opened his mouth to thank him, the loss of his cousin hit him afresh and what came out of his mouth was a howl of deep distress. The tears that followed came from Jack's mouth and nose as well as his eyes, and he sank down into the earth.

Richard had never seen such a paroxysm of grief and he was shocked. 'I didn't mean to upset him,' he said, looking from Jack to his granddad, who was rushing towards them. 'I thought that he'd be pleased.'

'He is pleased,' Eddie said. 'Can you bring him into the shed?'

Richard lifted Jack as if he was half the age he was, carried his limp and weeping form into the shed and placed him in his grandfather's arms as he sat in the armchair.

Eddie's held his grandson tight as he said huskily, 'He needed those tears for he has not cried since the funeral. They have been tight inside, like a spring, and you've opened up the floodgates.'

'Oh,' said Richard. He felt a little at a loss because Jack's reaction was the last thing he had expected and he hovered uncertainly in the doorway. 'Can I help? Is there anything I can do?'

Eddie shook his head. 'You have already done a wonderful thing, Richard. Jack will be fine now.'

And Jack was fine, or as fine as he would ever be, and that evening it was an embarrassed Jack who came round to see Richard and apologised for his tears.

'No need to apologise, Jack, none at all.'

'It was just seeing that bag,' Jack said. 'T-Tony was so proud of them flipping marleys. He'd get on my pip sometimes, and the memory of him just sort of flooded in and it just . . .' His voice trailed away and he looked Richard full in the face as he said, 'I'll never have another mate like Tony.'

'I know, Jack.'

'Thank you for the marleys, anyway. I never did say that.'

'That's all right,' Richard said.

'Your mom said that we had to get on with our lives without Tony,' Jack said. 'She said that's what he would want. All I really want to say is I suppose that I'll find it a little easier to do that now.'

In early October it was Sarah's sixteenth birthday. That morning she faced Mrs Jenkins in the shop and said, 'I want to hand in my notice.'

Ma Jenkins stared at her and snapped, 'You what?

Sarah refused to allow herself to be intimidated. 'I think you heard what I said,' she answered politely enough. 'Will a week be sufficient for you or would you want me to work a fortnight?'

'You will work a month, my girl.' Mrs Jenkins said. 'How am I going to fill your place with all the lasses off to war work?'

'How you fill the vacancy is up to you,' Sarah said. 'But I can't work no longer than a fortnight. My cousin has asked for a place for me at the munitions factory where she is, but they can't hold the place for ever.'

Ma Jenkins face took on a look of disgust. 'You're giving up a good job in a shop to work in a filthy factory? I suppose it's for the money. That's all people seem to care about these days.'

Sarah thought that rich coming from her, who was one of the meanest people she had ever met, and then the old woman surprised her by saying, 'I'll increase your wages by an extra shilling a week.'

Which would make the princely sum of ten shillings a week, Sarah thought. 'I'm sorry,' she said. 'It's all arranged now.'

'I bet your mother isn't happy about you working in such a place?' Mrs Jenkins said, and in all honesty Sarah couldn't say her mother had been mad keen, but only because of the danger. Sarah had done her best to reassure her. 'Mary Ellen said they take really good precautions. I mean, she has been there ages and Uncle Pat has, and nothing has happened to them. Siobhan is going next year as well, when she's sixteen.'

However, what Sarah said to Mrs Jenkins was, 'My mother understands why I'm doing this. She'll need more money when my brother enlists next year, anyroad, and in the munitions I can earn three pounds a week.'

'And you'll work for every penny.'

Like I don't work here? Sarah might have said, but instead she said, 'I'm no stranger to hard work. In fact, hard work and I are the best of friends.'

'There's work and work,' Mrs Jenkins said. 'You'll be begging to come back inside of a month.'

'No,' Sarah said, 'I won't.'

Mrs Jenkins saw the steely glint in Sarah's eyes and she said, 'So your mind is made up then?'

'Yes,' Sarah said. 'And I will work a maximum of a fortnight from today to give you a chance to get someone else.'

'But today is only Wednesday. It should run from the weekend at least.'

'From today,' said Sarah firmly.

'Well, get to work then,' Mrs Jenkins snapped. 'I don't pay you to stand here and argue the toss with me.'

Sarah expected her employer to be nasty, and she was all day, making snide remarks and trying to make her look small in front of the customers, but as Sarah told her mother later, she was well able to cope with that, because for spitefulness Mrs Jenkins didn't hold a candle to Grandma Murray.

Despite this, though, Sarah was full of trepidation going to work the next day. She opened the shop door cautiously to find a triumphant Mrs Jenkins inside and, beside her, a thin puny girl.

'You're not calling the tune here, girl,' Ma Jenkins almost spat at Sarah. 'It's my shop and I say who comes and who goes, and right now you're the one to go. Sling your hook, you're not wanted any more. Young Margaret here is taking your place.'

'The poor kid looked frightened to death,' Sarah said to her mother as she explained what had happened at the shop that morning. 'And if she is fourteen I would be surprised. She's so small, and looks as if she's never had a decent meal in her life.'

'Well, she's not likely to get one there.'

'No, and Mrs Jenkins will work her into the ground,' Sarah said. 'And probably for eight bob a week, which is what I started on. Still, that's not my problem any more. I'll go round this evening and tell Mary Ellen I can start on Monday morning.'

Sarah often wondered how her grandmother got to know of things when she hardly exchanged two words with her neighbours, but when she saw her coming up to the house the day before she was due to start at the munitions, she knew somehow she had found out what she intended to do. She was right and Clara started on her straight away. At the end of her diatribe she declared that she would not have a granddaughter of hers working in a factory and that she would be no better than a common guttersnipe similar to their lodgers if she worked in such a place.

'I don't really care what you think,' Sarah hit back angrily. 'I'm starting at the munitions work tomorrow and there's nothing you or anyone else can do to stop me. Personally I can hardly wait.'

Mary Ellen had told her how it would be. 'The girls are a laugh,' she'd said. 'But the best incentive of all is the nice fat wage packet at the end of the week. But the job ain't bad either, and it helps to have *Workers' Playtime* belting out from the wireless and some songs we all join in with. Course, that depends what job you're on. You've always got to remember that if you make a mistake it could cost at least one young serviceman his life.'

Sarah longed to be part of that body of young women all doing their bit, and also to be able to tip up more to her mother, and so what did she care about the warped ideas of a crabbed old woman?

However, Sarah found working in the munitions factory was like entering a different world. To prevent the chance of raising a spark, every bit of metal she might be wearing, like rings or even kirbi grips had to be removed in the cloakroom and given it to the gaffer. She had to put on dowdy, khaki-coloured overalls that buttoned to the neck and reached past her knees, and an elasticated hat that she had to tuck every bit of hair beneath. Strangest of all, she had to exchange her shoes for wooden clogs, which felt very strange.

When she said this to Mary Ellen, she smiled as she said, 'Colm and Chris had to wear clogs when they worked at the brewery, too. You'll soon get used to them.'

Sarah doubted that. The clogs fitted all right, but they felt very stiff and hard, and there was no cushioning of any sort. She imagined her feet might well ache at the end of the day. However, everyone else seemed to be taking the uniform in their stride so she said nothing more and followed her cousin down the iron steps to the factory itself.

'We work in threes,' Mary Ellen said. 'And as

you're my cousin and I've been here ages, our boss, Miss Milverton, said I can show you what to do. It ain't hard. Come and meet Phoebe. You'll be working with her as well.'

It was hard to see what Phoebe really looked like, encased, as they all were, in uniform, but she did have warm grey eyes and a lovely smile. Her accent was strange, though, and she said she came from Doncaster. She had been drafted into Birmingham and, like Peggy and Violet, she lodged with a local family.

Mary Ellen told Sarah they were assembling 303s and tracer bullets. Sarah was to put the casing in, Mary Ellen the lead nose, and Phoebe inserted the brass tube that held the powder.

It wasn't hard work, but it was tedious. Sarah was glad of *Workers' Playtime* to relieve the boredom. But in fact the thing that disturbed her most were some of her fellow workmates. Many of the girls or women working there seemed to have harsh, raucous voices that grated on her nerves, and they all seemed to treat men in such a casual way. Even Mary Ellen did this, which surprised Sarah. She had always got on well with all her cousins, particularly Mary Ellen and Siobhan, because they were near her age and they had been to school together, but this was a side of Mary Ellen she had never seen before.

'What's up with you?' Mary Ellen said as they gathered their things together ready to go home at the end of the first week.

'Nothing.'

'Don't give me that,' Mary Ellen said. 'It's the girls we work with, ain't it? I know it is 'cos sometimes they say summat and I see your mouth go all prissy.'

'It's the jokes they tell,' Sarah said.

Mary Ellen laughed. 'Thought it was,' she said. 'Sometimes you go the colour of a beetroot.'

'And some of them swear worse than any men I've ever heard.'

Mary Ellen let out a peal of laughter and yet she felt sorry for Sarah because she was like a fish out of water. 'Our mom swears and you don't seem to hold it against her.'

'Oh, no, I don't. I wouldn't,' Sarah said. And she didn't, because that was part of her aunt, really, and what she had grown up with. And anyway, she had never come out with some of the words she had heard in the munitions factory.

'Point with you, Sarah, is you have been too gently reared,' Mary Ellen said. 'Your ma has been better since the war began, but before that she was very la-di-da. You've got to admit that she sometimes acted as if she was a cut above anyone else. I mean, you only played out in the street with the other kids when you came to visit us.'

Sarah knew that Mary Ellen was right. Like the twins and Tony, she and Richard had been raised in the garden, and when they had gone to Polly's and there was only the street to play in, the clamour those children made and the lack of restraint in much of their play had unnerved her a little. Many of the people she was working with now were like grown-up versions of those children.

'You haven't had the corners knocked off you, that's your trouble,' Mary Ellen went on knowledgeably. 'You don't have to take no notice of what they say at work. They don't mean owt. They're just having you on, having a laugh. You answer in like vein.'

Sarah, however, still thought their ways were alien to her own and, whatever Mary Ellen said, she couldn't curse and swear the way they did. But after talking her mother into letting her go into the munitions in the first place, how could she go to her mother now and say she had made a grave mistake? She couldn't, and she knew it, so she tried to make the best of it.

Sarah had been there almost three weeks when, leaving the factory one day, one of the women at the front of the queue shouted back, 'Some lucky lass has got a handsome soldier waiting for them.'

There was a chorus of laughter at that, and they edged further forward and then Mary Ellen, a little ahead of Sarah, suddenly said, 'Good God, it's Sam.'

Sarah stood on tiptoe to see, and when her eyes met Sam's, she felt her knees go weak. However, when she emerged through the factory gate she saw Sam had his arm in a sling.

'What are you doing here?' she demanded. 'And what on earth have you been doing with yourself?'

Sam laughed. 'Well, I'd like to say that I was sporting a war wound, but I'm afraid that I crocked my arm up playing football.'

'Oh, Sam,' Sarah said. 'And what are you doing here?'

'I came to meet you, what else?'

Mary Ellen noticed that while he included her in that answer, he really only had eyes for Sarah and she for him. She remembered her mother saying that Sarah had had a fancy for Sam the first time she had seen him, but she had been little more than a child then. Now, unless she was very much mistaken, it looked as if that attraction was still there. And who was she to get in the way of true love?

'I'll have to go,' she said. 'Dad will be waiting.'

'Oh, yes, of course . . .' Sarah said.

'Not you,' Mary Ellen said. 'You and Sam must have plenty to talk about.'

'Oh, but—'

'Come on, Sarah,' Mary Ellen said. 'Haven't you heard the expression "three's a crowd"?'

Sarah was glad of the blackout because she felt the heat flood her face and knew that she would be blushing. ''S all right, I'll square it with Dad,' Mary Ellen said, and she melted into the night, leaving Sarah and Sam alone.

'I suppose you usually go home together?' Sam said.

'Yes, and Uncle Pat waits for us at the tram station. It's only just round the corner.'

'So shall we make for the tram then?' Sam said. 'Or we could walk – it's really no distance? But then what am I saying? You've had a heavy day at the factory so we'll take the tram.'

But Sarah felt as light as air and could think of nothing nicer than walking home with Sam in the concealing dark, so she said, 'No, really, I'm fine and I'd like to walk. The night is a fine one, for all it's cold.'

'Then shall we link arms and be warmer as we walk?' Sam said. 'And thank God that it was my left arm that I damaged.' He took Sarah's arm as he spoke and they walked through the quiet and darkened streets.

'What did you do to damage your arm?' she asked.

'Oh, it was nothing much,' Sam said. 'One of the opposing team tripped me up and then fell on top of me, and my arm was twisted awkwardly underneath me. I've cracked a bone in it.'

'It must have been sore.'

'I haven't come all this way to talk about my arm,' Sam said. 'And the first thing I must say is how sorry I was to hear about Tony. I wrote to your mother at the time because when Peggy wrote to tell me I was very upset. He was always so full of life.'

Sarah nodded. 'He was. And we are getting over it now, because we must, but at home it's always like someone is missing.'

'I really do understand that,' Sam said.

'And now your turn,' Sarah said. 'I suppose you've been given a spot of leave because of your arm.'

'Yeah,' Sam said. 'Seeing that it was my left arm they put me on clerical duties for a bit. I did it more than three weeks ago. Now, they've told me to come home until I have the plaster off, a spot of physio, and then I'll be back into active service again.'

'I bet Peggy was thrilled to see you,' Sarah said, and then suddenly stopped. 'She does know, I suppose?'

'Oh, yes,' Sam said. 'I stopped by the forge and was able to have a word. Your mom knows too because I went there, and they all know that I was coming to meet you from work.'

'And I am pleased to see you,' Sarah said. 'But why did you come to meet me?'

'Well, when I met you last time, you were a young girl,' Sam said. 'But I thought of you a fair bit and I wanted to see you grown up to the grand old age of sixteen.'

'And what do you find?' Sarah asked with a smile.

'That you are not so different at all except maybe more mature, and you have changed your job to one in a munitions factory.'

Sarah sighed. 'Yeah, I have.'

'And why the sigh?'

'To tell you the truth,' Sarah said, 'I think I've made a dreadful mistake.'

'Why's that? Is the work hard?'

'No, though it is boring,' Sarah said. 'But it isn't the work, it's some of the people I work with.' She recounted some concerns that she'd already spoken to her cousin about.

Sam listened without interrupting and eventually Sarah finished, 'I suppose you think me some sort of dreadful snob.'

'Not at all,' Sam said. 'Nor do I think that you've made a mistake. You're doing something the like of which you've never done before with the sort of people that you've never worked with before, and it will take time to adapt. I felt much the same about some of the men I shared a billet with when I first went into the army. They were all so different from me and I had thought we would never get on.'

'But you did?'

'Oh, yes,' Sam said. 'I persevered and now I'm the best of friends with most of them.'

'And you think that's what I must do?'

'I think you should not be so hard on yourself. Just take each day as it comes and in time everything will slip into place. You may find the loudest and most raucous of those woman really has a heart of gold.'

Sam's words made Sarah feel a lot better and she decided to double her efforts to get on better with the women she was working with.

'It's lovely to have someone to talk it over with,' she said. 'I made such a fuss about going into the munitions in the first place, I really feel I can talk to no one at home now about any doubts I might have.'

'You can write and moan to me, if it helps.'

'Write to you!' Sarah repeated.

'Would you mind?'

'No, I don't suppose so,' Sarah said. 'I mean, I write to Dad and I will to Richard next year, so I suppose I could write to you too.'

'We love getting letters,' Sam said. 'Lets us know that we're not forgotten back home. I mean, Peg writes, and the parents – well, my mom really – and sometimes Peter and Daisy scribble a line or two on the bottom of the letter, but some of the men have three or four women writing to them as well.'

'Why don't you?'

'I don't want that,' Sam said. 'But I would like one Sarah Whittaker to write to me.' And then he added sardonically, 'If she would be so kind.'

Sarah had no time to answer, for the twins had been watching for them, and they were barely on the path before Magda had the door wrenched open and the two of them launched themselves at Sam.

'Where have you been?' Magda demanded. 'We've been waiting ages. Our cousin Jack is here to see you as well.'

Sam stayed another two days. He met Sarah every day as she left the factory and they walked home and talked of all and sundry. In fact, by the third day Sarah thought that she knew more about Sam that she had ever known about anyone, and she had confided things to him about her hopes and dreams for the future that she had never given voice to before. Sam listened and never made fun of her. She was very aware of him walking close beside her, which caused her heart to hammer against her ribs so much that she was surprised Sam couldn't hear it. When he linked her arm as they walked along she felt herself tremble all over.

Apart from walking arm in arm Sam never touched her in any other way, though Sarah wouldn't have minded at all if he had. She couldn't say this, of course, because it would be very unseemly, but she was often a little disappointed when they reached home. Had Sarah been able to see into Sam's heart, however, she would have seen how hard he battled with himself not to take their tentative and budding relationship any further.

The way they had talked together as they walked home from the munitions factory until they were as easy with one another as if they were lifelong friends, had convinced Sam that he would have loved to get to know Sarah better, but with the war raging all around them – a war that he would soon be back in the thick of – he felt he had no right to make advances to Sarah in the few days he had here. And on such a short acquaintance he could hardly ask her to wait for him, to be his girl, and so however much he wanted to hold Sarah closer and kiss those luscious lips, he wouldn't let himself. She had agreed to write and that was all he was prepared to expect of her.

Once they reached the house the family would claim Sam's attention, the twins in particular, and though he could no longer do magic tricks with one arm immobilised, he could play most other games and he never seemed to mind being commandered in this way. On his last evening he took Sarah to see *The Philadelphia Story*, though the invitation was extended to Peggy and Violet too. As Sarah sat beside Sam, he made no move to drape an arm around her shoulders, even in a casual way, nor did he take advantage of the darkness of the cinema to hold her hand.

That night Sarah lay in bed and faced the fact that however much she thought of Sam, he definitely didn't feel the same, and she had to accept that. He saw her as a friend and that was all. Her letters to him had to be from one friend to another. This impression was compounded the following morning when he drew Sarah into his arms to say goodbye: his hug was like anyone might give to a friend he was fond of.

That evening Sarah told her mother that Sam had asked her to write to him.

'And are you going to?' Marion asked.

'I said I would,' Sarah said. 'What do you think?'

Marion thought about it. She knew Sam to be a decent young man and she knew Sarah thought a lot of him when she had seen him first, and still more than just liked him, if she was any judge.

However, she was sixteen and maturing in a world with few young men about so there was little chance for her to have any sort of normal life when she would get to know boys in a more natural way. So Marion could see no harm in their exchanging a few letters, and that's what she told Sarah.

TWENTY-ONE

Sarah found that Sam had been right: accepting her work colleagues for the way they were, and doing her best to join in with the banter seemed to make the work easier to cope with. She wrote and told him this. She found it was lovely to write to Sam because she felt she could tell him anything and it was a great help to her to have a friend like that.

Towards the end of November, Sarah had been working at the munitions factory almost eight weeks. At the very end of their shift a few of woman were approached by Mr Baxter, the big boss, who asked them if they would be willing to work in another area on a different job.

Sarah wasn't sure, but Mary Ellen said she had worked long enough at the same thing and Sarah could see her point. She was bored after only a few weeks and she'd hate the thought of doing that job for years and years. When the boss said their wages would rise by five shillings a week, that clinched it for Mary Ellen, and so Sarah volunteered too.

They started the following Monday morning and this time they were sent to an area to the side of the main factory. They hadn't been aware that there was any sort of munitions work going on there because the building was a sort of large semi-underground shed so well camouflaged with grass growing on the roofs and sides that if Sarah had taken any notice at all she would have thought that it was a grassy hillock. She was quite surprised when, once down the steps, it opened up to quite a sizeable area. When Mr Baxter told them all they would be making trench mortar bombs down there, Sarah and Mary Ellen's mouths dropped open for neither had they thought they would be put on jobs like that.

But first they were taken to the cloakroom, where brand-new navy-blue boiler suits were ready for them, made for women. 'Look how fitted they are,' Mary Ellen said, spinning around in front of Sarah. 'They give us a waistline and a bust.'

Everyone saw that for themselves. Even Sarah thought the boiler suits did look quite fetching, and it was nice to wear new clothes and not think half a dozen or more people had worn them before you.

'I don't go a bundle on these bloody turbans, though,' Mary Ellen said, pulling hers over her tousled curls. 'How about you?'

Sarah slipped her turban on too, and wrinkled

her nose as she looked in the mirror. 'They're not very flattering, are they? But then I suppose they're meant to be functional, and at least it keeps the hair in place, especially when we're not allowed to wear grips.'

'Yeah, and I reckon it's going to be a lot more dodgy here,' Phoebe said. 'Have you seen the shoes we've got to wear?'

One of the women picked up a shoe and exclaimed. 'Hey, they've got steel toecaps!'

'My point exactly,' Phoebe said.

'Well, I suppose they know what they're doing,' Mary Ellen said uncertainly.

'Let's hope so,' another woman called out. 'Let's just worry about getting the job done and picking up a big fat wage packet at the end of the week.'

'Yeah,' said another. 'And talking of wage packets, ours will be cut soon if we don't get down on the shop floor sharpish.'

She spoke sense, for by the clock on the wall it was nearly half-past seven. Before they began work every day, the boss told them, they would have to call at the nurse's station where they'd get a small glass of brown liquid to drink, which would keep their lungs clear from the TNT they would be working with. It wasn't pleasant but no one objected. As Phoebe said, 'I don't want my lungs buggered up. My dad had a dose of that in the last war.'

Sarah wondered what exactly she had let herself in for. The first thing they were shown was how to make 'the biscuit', which she found was TNT and nitrate mixed together. They had to carry this mixture in hundredweights and tip it into the ferociously hot boilers, which they had to feed constantly. When it reached the right consistency it went into trays to cool down, while they started making another biscuit. The cooled cooked biscuits were then broken into pieces and put into the bomb casing, and then boiling TNT poured in so that it would fill up between the bits of biscuit inside.

It was hot, heavy and exhausting work. The girls quickly found that they could wear nothing underneath the boiler suits but their underwear, and even then often the sweat ran from them.

Sam's letters, though, bucked Sarah up, though she could tell him nothing about her new job, but she was looking forward to Christmas when she would have the money to buy nice presents for everyone, just as long as things were getting into the shops in the first place.

She was compiling a list on the first Sunday in December, and half listening to *Variety Bandbox* on the wireless when the programme was interrupted by a new's flash.

'Reports are coming in of a Japanese attack on Pearl Harbor, a United States naval base and home of the Pacific Fleet. The attacks were sustained and prolonged, and there are initial reports of much lost of life and destruction on a grand scale . . .'

The report ended and the Whittakers and their lodgers all looked at one another.

'America will be in the war now, I'd say,' Peggy said.

'Can't see how they can stay out of it,' Marion replied. 'Some would say about time.'

'Yes, but I wonder how it will affect us,' Peggy said.

'Well, it will be an escalation, no doubt about it,' Richard answered. 'But on the other hand it is better to have America on our side as not, I think.'

'Yeah, I'll give you that,' Peggy agreed.

'Meanwhile,' said Marion, trying to cut through the doleful atmosphere, 'it is nearly Christmas and it might be Richard's last at home for some time so I think we should all try and enjoy it, especially as it will be just us this year and our first Christmas without Tony.'

That thought sobered them all, and the Whittakers all wished that Peggy and Violet weren't going home for Christmas. The twins in particular were very disappointed.

'Mom said that if I don't go home soon, she'll forget what I look like,' Peggy said.

'And my eldest brother, Bobby, is eighteen just after Christmas,' Violet said, 'so I think I really need to be there this year.'

'Oh,' Sarah said. 'Is your mother upset that your brother will be old enough to be called up?'

'I suppose she is a bit,' Violet said. 'Probably

in her heart of hearts she hoped the war would be over before he was sucked into it.'

'I think most mothers hope that,' Richard said. 'But the reality is every boy turned eighteen is needed.'

'Yeah, Mom sees that. And she tells me in her letters which boys have already been called up from the village and farms around. There only seems to be young boys left at home now.'

'I bet they're all really looking forward to seeing you,' Marion said.

'I'm looking forward to seeing them too,' Violet said, 'for all I will miss you here.'

'And we'll miss you,' Marion said. 'This is something I've been thinking about for some time – when you come back, why don't start going out again, to the pictures or dancing? I know you stopped all this when Tony died, but stopping at home is not going to bring him back and it's more than time you all took up the threads of life again.'

'Wouldn't you be lonely, though, Mom if we went out?' Sarah asked.

'No,' Marion said. 'I'll find plenty to do, don't worry, but it would please me to see you all going out and enjoying yourselves more.'

'All right,' Peggy said, 'but just for now we'll content ourselves with going to the Christmas Dance.'

Richard allowed himself to be persuaded to accompany his sister, Violet and Peggy to the Christmas Dance on 20 December in the Albert

Hall in Chain Walk. Marion watched them all go with pride. The girls had revamped their dresses with lace, ribbons, artificial fur, pearl buttons, and even seed pearls from items of clothing Peggy and Violet had bought from a jumble sale. They had shared the stuff out and worked hard to bring a bit of glamour to tired old dresses, and they all looked so pretty when they set out.

The dance was a roaring success. Sarah knew exactly what Peggy and Violet had meant when they said that dancing to a real band was much better than dancing to records. The obvious enjoyment the smartly dressed musicians got from playing their sparkling brass instruments spurred the dancers on to greater efforts. The only problem was the terrible shortage of suitable men.

'Richard was in great demand,' Sarah said.

'Yes,' Peggy commented. 'No one seems to care a jot about his two left feet.'

In actual fact, Richard had picked up more dancing tips than he realised from the girls, so he had no problem with the dancing that night. It had also given him the opportunity to legitimately hold some very pretty girls in his arms, though he partnered Violet in as many dances as he could and she said nothing about it because no one knew where Richard would be the following Christmas.

On Christmas Eve, Sarah received a package, the first she had ever had. She knew it was from Sam because his writing had become familiar and she longed to open it, but Marion said she had to wait until Christmas Day, like everyone else. And so for the first time in years she was as anxious as her sisters for Christmas Day to come.

The next day, Sam's present was the first one Sarah opened, to reveal dark red gloves, scarf and tam-o'-shanter in the softest wool.

Marion smiled as she said, 'I knew all about Sam's present to you, Sarah, because Peggy told me. Apparently he asked someone's mother to knit it, and she had only dark red wool, but that didn't matter because that will go very well with my present to you.' And she handed Sarah a large parcel.

It was a thick fur-lined black coat, and for a moment Sarah was speechless, and so, it seemed, was everyone else around the table.

When Sarah did recover herself enough to say, 'Ah, Mom, thank you, thank you so much,' her voice was choked with emotion. She leaned across to give her mother a kiss as she added, 'I've never had so fine a coat.'

'It isn't new,' Marion said. 'I looked for new first, for all it would have taken fourteen points, but in these days of utility clothing the winter coats are not warm enough and you need warmth the hours you're standing waiting for trams in the winter.'

'So where did you get it?'

'Well, you know I helped out at the Christmas bazaar at the church?' Marion said. 'They had this second-hand stall, and when I spotted the coat I knew it was just the thing for you.'

'It's lovely,' Sarah said, stroking it almost reverently. 'It doesn't matter how bad the weather is now. 'I'll never feel the cold dressed up in these lovely things.'

At the same Christmas bazaar Marion had been able to buy the twins a new skipping rope each, which they badly needed since their old ones were nearly worn through. And they also had *Alice's Adventures in Wonderland*, which she said they would have to share.

After breakfast Sarah slipped away to her room to read again the back of the beautiful Christmas card from Sam that he had packed in the parcel.

I wish you a very happy Christmas, my
 beautiful Sarah.
I hope you like the things I sent to you.
I like to imagine that when you put them on,
 you will think of me.
With all my love – Sam xxx

It sent a tingle all through Sarah to read those words because he had never written with all his love before. Their letters, until the arrival of that Christmas card, had been as one friend to another, but his words had changed that a little. She could have told him that that she didn't need to wear the things he had sent to think of him, for thoughts of him often fluttered into her mind and would give her a feeling like butterflies in her stomach. Not that she could ever tell him these things – that would be far too forward. But she would send a letter to thank him for the lovely things he'd given her as soon as she could.

After a sumptuous Christmas dinner, Richard offered to play cards with the twins. 'Sorry I can't do tricks with them like Sam can,' he said, 'but I know a few games I could teach you.'

'And where did you learn card games?' Marion asked him.

'At the air raid post. It helps pass the time if it's quiet. They sometimes play at dinner time at work as well, but I steer well clear of that 'cos they play for money. I work too hard for my wages to fritter it away.'

'Quite right,' Marion agreed. 'Your father was never a gambler either.'

'But it's all right to play for a bit of fun,' Richard said as he very professionally shuffled the pack he got out of the drawer. 'Come on, 'I'll teach you rummy first.'

The twins had only ever played snap and happy families, and so were very keen on learning something new. They loved rummy, so then Richard taught them whist, brag and pontoon.

Eventually Magda said, 'I'm bored with cards now. Isn't it a pity that Peggy took the gramophone and records back home?'

'It's only fair,' Marion said. 'She bought it, and

maybe she thought her family would benefit from a bit of jollification over Christmas.'

'Well, let's have our own concert,' Sarah said. They all just looked at her and she said, 'Oh, come on. It's Christmas Day and we all know something we can sing or recite, and the rest of us can join in if we know the words. Remember before we had the gramophone we used to sometimes sing in the cellar?'

'All right,' Marion said, entering into the spirit of it. 'I'll sing you a song from the Great War. I was twelve when it began and I'd been in service then for two years. The poor mistress had four sons and they all enlisted as officers, you know, and only one came back. Sometimes we'd all have a sing in the kitchen of an evening to keep our spirits up, like.'

'Go on then, Mom,' Sarah said encouragingly and Marion got to her feet and launched into 'Keep the Home Fires Burning'.

The children had often heard their mom hum the song and sing a line or two, but that afternoon Marion sang it from beginning to end, word-perfect and from the heart. They all knew that she was thinking of their father so far away from his family that day. Sarah also thought of Sam and hoped wherever he was he would come home safe when the war ended.

There was spontaneous applause at the end, but Magda said, 'Ooh, Mom, that was a sad one.'

'So it was, Magda,' Marion said, 'so it's up to Richard to cheer us all up.'

'That's easy,' Richard said. 'This is jolly enough, although it is another Great War song.' With gusto he began, 'Pack Up Your Troubles in Your Old Kit Bag'.

Everyone joined in and when the song drew to a close, Sarah said, 'I'm going to change the mood again now because I love Vera Lynn's song "We'll Meet Again", but that's sad too.'

It was a lovely song, even though it was plaintive, and it did make them all think what life might be like when the war eventually ended.

When the song was finished, Magda said, 'I had better go last and cheer us all up again because I bet Missie will want to sing something else soppy,' because she knew the song her sister loved.

'"When You Wish Upon a Star" isn't soppy,' Missie protested. 'How can it be? It's from that film *Pinocchio* that Richard and Sarah went to see with Sam.'

'That don't mean it ain't soppy.'

Sarah saw the doubtful look flash across Missie's face and she said, 'Sing it, for goodness' sake. It is a lovely song so don't you let yourself be browbeaten by Magda. She will get her choice after you.'

So Missie stood and sang her song, and very sweetly she did it too, and then Magda brought the concert to a close by a rousing rendition of 'Kiss Me Goodnight, Sergeant Major'.

When she finished, Marion went into the kitchen and came out with a mug of cocoa each and a slice of the eggless chocolate cake she had cooked for tea, and they all looked at her in surprise because generally she didn't believe in eating between meals.

'Now listen,' she said. 'This has been a lovely Christmas Day and I hate to spoil it, but your grandparents will be here in about half an hour's time so I want you to eat that cake and drink that cocoa and wrap yourselves up warmly and then go out. It's a fine dry day, for all it's so cold, and your grandparents won't stay that long because they hate going home in the pitch black in the blackout. If you stay out for about an hour or so you should be just about back in time to say goodbye to them and then I'll do some proper tea for you when they've gone. How does that suit?'

It suited very well, and a walk even on a cold day was much more enjoyable than sitting in a warm room anywhere near their grandmother. They finished their cocoa and cake in double-quick time in case she came in before they left. Sarah put on her new coat, and with the gloves on her hands, the scarf around her neck and the tam-o'-shanter at a jaunty angle on her head, she was ready to be off with Missie to one side of her and Magda to another. They went to the park first, in past the deep pits dug at the edges and the furrowed rows ready to plant vegetables where there had used to be lawns and flowerbeds.

'Let's go down to the lake,' Richard said, ''cos it was frozen over before.'

The lake wasn't fully frozen any more, though it did have great slabs of ice floating in it. 'Look, it's breaking up,' Richard said, picking up a stone from the vegetable beds and hurling it at the largest ice floe. 'It must have got warmer.'

'It doesn't flipping feel like it,' Sarah said. 'Come on, a person would stick to the ground if they stayed still long enough.'

They were not the only ones in the park, by any means. Others were walking off their dinner, and the Whittaker children passed and greeted many people as they made their way round to Aston Hall.

'Dad told us once just one family would live in that gigantic house,' Magda said, looking at the edifice.

'That's right,' Sarah said.

'But why would anyone need that many rooms?' Missie asked.

'It was just the way it was with rich people,' Sarah said. 'They used to have lots of servants to keep it clean and cook and that, but the war has put paid to that, because people have gone into more war-related work now.'

'They haven't a choice any more, anyroad,' Richard said. 'Everyone has to register for war work, and it's far better paid.'

'I bet Peggy and Violet came from a place like that,' Magda said.

Sarah nodded. 'I'd say so. It mightn't have been so grand or large but it was something similar all right.'

'They were more than glad to leave, I know that,' Richard said. 'Violet told me that herself. She said she hated being at the beck and call of someone else, and being looked down on just because they had money and she didn't.'

'And I would,' Magda declared. 'Anyone would.'

'Yeah,' Sarah said. 'So I reckon that even when the war is over, the people who live in these types of houses will find it very hard to get staff to work for them, and a good job too, I say.'

'And I do,' Richard agreed. 'Come on, where shall we go now, because we can't go back yet?'

'What about if we round the park as far as Grosvenor Road and go on to the canal towpath?' Magda said. 'If we follow it as far as Rocky Lane we can go home that way.'

'You and your flipping canal,' Sarah said in mock annoyance. 'It will be freezing down there today.'

'Well, it's not going to be blistering hot wherever we go, is it?' Missie said. 'And I'd rather face a freezing canal any day than Grandma Murray.'

Back at the house Marion was valiantly trying to cope with her mother, who went on and on about Tony and what a tragedy his death was all through tea. It wasn't that they never spoke about him – they spoke about him often, although it had been awakward in the beginning – but Clara's reminiscences weren't like that. She went on and on about the tragedy of losing Tony, though she had taken little notice of him when he had been alive. Yet Eddie, who had got to know Marion's younger son very well, said little, though his saddened eyes spoke volumes. However, nothing Marion said could deflect her mother from her tirade and eventually she would come round to the way that Tony died, and repeat again that she had warned Marion about the gas in the cellar and that if she had heeded her warning then Tony might not have died. Marion could feel the energy draining out of her as she fought the guilt that she was in any way responsible for her son's death.

When the children returned with scarlet faces and tingling fingers and toes, the room was beautifully warm from the fire that Marion had kept banked up. Sarah, though, noticed the lines of strain on her mother's face and she sighed inwardly. She decided to pay no attention to her grandmother and instead began to talk to her grandfather about the walk they had had, with the others chipping in here and there in a way that they knew their grandmother thought unmannerly, but they gave her little chance to say so.

Marion had to hide her smile for she knew that they had found their own way of dealing with their grandmother, and wished that she could ignore her so easily. With dusk descending Eddie and Clara didn't stay long after that, and everyone heaved a sigh of relief when they eventually went back home.

That night, as Magda lay in bed, she gave a sigh of contentment as she said to Sarah, 'Wasn't that the greatest Christmas Day ever? And fancy having dripping toast for tea. It's just about my favourite and I've never had it before on Christmas Day.'

Sarah laughed because it was well known by everyone how much Magda liked dripping toast. She thought it was even better if they opened the door of the range and toasted the bread on the fire using the long toasting forks like they had done that night.

'Yeah, it was a good day,' she had to agree. 'The only thing that could make it better was if this blessed war was to end and Dad was to come home again safe and sound.' And Sam too, she thought to herself, but she didn't share that with her sisters.

The dawning of 1942 didn't fill anyone with enthusiasm, though the young people did take Marion's words to heart and began going out more. They were well used to the blackout now and were very good at using the shielded torches when batteries for them, which were like gold dust to find in the shops, could be obtained. They went dancing every week – Richard was as keen as the girls were now

– but they also loved the cinema. It was as they arrived home after seeing *Citizen Kane* in the second week of February that Marion told them it had been on the news that Singapore had surrendered to the Japanese Army, who had also captured 100,000 servicemen.

It was a big blow and very bad for morale. Yet life had to go on. Rationing began to bite deeper than ever and Marion and Polly often complained about it as most women did.

'Cheese, margarine and tea last year, and points needed for jam, treacle and syrup now,' Polly said one day to Marion as they returned to Marion's house with their shopping.

'I know, and canned meat don't forget,' Marion said, as she filled the kettle. 'I mean Spam don't taste particularly nice but you can always dress it up a bit and make something more or less edible with it.'

'I know,' Polly said. 'There ain't much else. They say even soap will be rationed later this year.'

'Yeah, and sweets,' Marion said. 'Parts of Cadbury's have gone over to putting cordite in rockets now.' She added with a wry smile, 'Must be a bit different from putting soft centres into chocolates. Mind you, clothes rationing gets me down altogether.'

'Yeah,' Polly agreed. 'This make do and mend is all very well if you had plenty of clothes to start with.'

'Yes,' said Marion. 'But even before rationing

some clothes disappeared altogether, or were at the very least in short supply.'

'I thought Father McIntyre was going to organise clothes banks,' Polly said. 'Lots of Churches and Mission Halls have been doing that.'

'Yeah, and by the time he gets around to it, the bloody war will be over.'

'I think,' said Polly, 'certainly before next winter really sets in, you and I might have to take up knitting.'

'You could be right,' Marion said. 'Once upon a time you would never see Ada Shipley at a jumble sale, but now she's a regular, searching for clothes she can adapt or woollies she can unravel and knit into something else.'

'Well, knitting can't be that hard,' Polly said, 'because there's plenty at it, particularly at the moment.'

'Make Do and Mend' was on everyone's lips in the spring of 1942, and to be a squander bug was to be the worst person in the world. In accordance with that, Magda and Missie and all girls of similar age were taught to knit at school. They just knitted squares at first from any spare wool donated, and these were sewn together to make blankets for the homeless. And they taught their mothers how to do it too, for when they learned that clothing coupons were being reduced from 66 points per person to 48, it was all the incentive they needed to get started.

The only place to get wool off ration was at the jumble sale, so Marion and Polly would join Ada Shipley and women like her, doing a little tour now and then to see what they could pick up. In the Whittaker house, everyone became involved. Even the twins became adept at unravelling a woollen jumper and then rolling the wool into balls.

'There's patterns in that magazine *Home Notes*, and tips on sewing too, making things out of nowt sort of sewing,' Polly said to Marion one day when they had the knitting mastered.

'Ah, but it's thrupence a week,' Marion reminded her. 'And thrupence is thrupence when all's said and done. Anyroad, I don't think that magazines like that are for ordinary people. Wasn't it that magazine that recommended making a blouse out of old dusters? I mean, I ask you, what woman do you know buys dusters? Even down this road, a duster is some old bit of rag that really has no more wear in it at all.'

Polly laughed. 'I know. It's the girls buy these magazines, not me. And some of the recipes are good as well as the knitting patterns. I'll bring a few of them round and you'll see what I mean.'

TWENTY-TWO

On the day of Richard's birthday, having already told them at work what he intended, he put on his suit and went down to Thorpe Street Barracks just as his father had before him. He was told to report to the army the following Sunday evening.

Everyone was sorry to see Richard go, but Marion held on to her tears because she knew he would be relatively safer in a training camp than helping in the air raids for the moment. The twins showed no such restraint, because since Tony's death they had leaned on Richard more. He had been aware of it and he was very gentle as he bade them all goodbye.

He hadn't been left long and the family were eating Sunday tea when explosions were heard in the distance. There had been no sirens but as another blast and then another rent the air, it was obvious that a raid was taking place. Marion's heart plummeted at the thought that it was all going to start again, but even as she hauled her shelter bag from under the stairs and began to fill it, all of them point-blank refused to go into the cellar, and instead crowded together under the kitchen table.

The raid went on fast and furious, and though some bombs fell close, they weren't quite close enough to do much damage.

'I think Handsworth is getting the main thrust of it,' Sarah said.

'Whoever's getting it would have been grateful for the siren's warning, I'm sure,' Marion said. 'Got complacent, see, 'cos there has been no raid for a while.'

'Gone to sleep, more like,' Violet said.

Suddenly there was a furious hammering on the door and they all looked at each other in alarm.

'Now who the hell's that?' Marion said. She got to her feet and went out into the corridor. She was back in minutes, followed by an ARP warden.

'It's Grandma,' she told the children. 'She's had a heart attack and has been taken to the General.'

'What about Granddad?' Sarah asked.

'He went in the ambulance with Grandma,' Marion said. 'I shall go straight away.' She turned to the warden. 'My sister, Polly, should know too. She will probably be sheltering in the cellar under Atkinson's Brewery.'

The warden nodded. 'Your father told us that. My mate's gone to tell her.'

'Shall I come with you, Mom?' Sarah asked.

'No, love,' Marion said. 'I'll go with Polly. You'll

401

have to go into work tomorrow and I don't know how long I'll be. Anyway, I need you to see to the others.'

'We can see to ourselves,' Magda said. 'We ain't babies.'

'The best thing you can do for me is to act sensibly and do what Sarah tells you,' Marion said crisply, and Magda said nothing more.

Polly was actually scurrying up the road by the time Marion got to the front door, and the two women hugged each other.

'Do you want us to go with you?' the warden asked.

Marion looked at her sister and then said. 'No, it's all right. You're probably more use here as the raid is still going on. We'll be fine.'

The warden scanned the sky. 'Getting away light tonight, so far, anyway,' he said. 'And I think the trams are still running down Lichfield Road.'

'They are,' Polly said. 'I saw one pass as we came out of the cellar. Thank you for coming to tell us, by the way. It was good of you.'

'Yes, thank you,' Marion said.

Marion and Polly, arms linked, began to walk down the road, glad to have each other. It was late enough to be dark, but the arc light slicing through the blackout lit the sky with an orange glow, picking out the droning planes, releasing their screaming harbingers of death.

'Some other poor bugger's turn tonight,' Polly said, for though they heard the thud and crash of the explosions, they were in the distance, and so were the ack-ack guns barking out their response.

When they reached Lichfield Road, pockets of fire were visible in the distance towards the town, lighting up the skyline and showing up the tram clanking towards them. 'Come on,' Polly urged, 'we'll have a wait if we miss this one.'

'Isn't it awful that we're not more upset about Mammy, that we aren't crying and carrying on, though?' Marion said, as they found seats on the tram. 'The warden that came to tell me didn't seem to hold out much hope for her.'

'I know,' Polly said. 'I feel sort of hollow. I mean, she was never what you'd call a loving mother, was she?'

'No,' Marion agreed. 'I know the pain of losing a child now, and it is without doubt the worst pain I've ever had to endure, but I couldn't give in because of the others. Peggy said her mother lost two children, and it was the vicar or whatever they call him that as much as told her to pull herself together and take joy in the husband and children she did have. I fell to wishing afterwards that something similar had been said to our mother.'

'Maybe it was,' Polly replied.

Marion shook her head. 'No. My bet is she was so upset that everyone made many allowances for her, and in the end she thought that was the right way to behave. And she never gave a thought to the fact that you and I together were clearly told we could not make up in any way for the loss of the others. She never thought how hurtful it was.'

'I never knew that you felt that bad about it.'

'I did. I couldn't help it. I thought one day I would gather up the courage to tell her, but I haven't so far and now it might be too late.'

'I know,' Polly said. 'And may God forgive me, but I can't be sorry.'

'Nor can I,' Marion said in almost a whisper, as if she couldn't bear to say the words out loud.

Eddie was sitting just inside, in the waiting room of the General Hospital, with his head down, twisting his hat between his hands. He looked up as they went in and smiled his slow easy smile, but Marion saw the shadow behind that smile and she was across the floor in seconds. She hugged him tight before she asked, 'Daddy, how is she?'

'She's dead, Marion,' Eddie said. 'When they brought her here, I knew it was no use. When tonight's raid began there was no warning, was there – no siren? And she was giving out about that and she suddenly gave a cry, clutched her hand on her chest and fell to the floor. I hurried up the entry and saw a warden down the street and called to him. He's a decent sort of chap, and he dispatched his mate for the doctor when I told him what had happened. While we waited for the doctor to come he worked on your mother, pushing on her chest. He called it artificial respiration and he'd learned in First Aid. Anyroad, he got her breathing again and then the doctor came and called for an ambulance. I went in with her, and the warden came to tell you, Marion, and his mate went to Atkinson's place. I told him where you'd both be.'

'But you said the warden got Mammy's heart going again?'

'He did,' Eddie said. 'But it stopped again in the ambulance and they couldn't restart it this time. Neither could the doctors here, though they gave it a good try. Anyroad, when they told me she'd gone I thought she didn't need me sitting beside her no more and I came to wait for you two. I knew you'd be along some time.'

Marion saw the lines etched into deep furrows in her father's forehead and down each side of his nose, his crinkled, creased cheeks and rheumy eyes, and felt sorry for him. He looked older than his sixty-five years. It was for his sake rather than her mother's that she'd come pell-mell to the hospital that evening.

So when her father looked up at her with a sad smile and said, 'Do you want to see your mother?' she was nonplussed for a moment and so, she saw, was Polly. Marion had no real desire to see her mother, but she knew, and Polly knew, it would have seemed odd if they hadn't and so they followed reluctantly behind their father.

Clara was laid out on the bed, still and quiet in death as she'd never been in life. Marion was ashamed that the only emotion she felt was relief.

'She was a sad woman, your mother,' Eddie said. 'She never seemed to take a moment's joy in anything.'

'No,' Marion said, 'she didn't.'

'She was packed full of resentment and I should have been the one to have stopped her behaving the way she did, but when the news came in about Michael and she realised that his grave was the ocean, she was beside herself. I was distraught myself but I had to swallow my grief because I thought your mother was losing her mind. Afterwards the tempers she used to get into were frightening. Poor Clara,' he said, and he stroked her cheek gently. 'I can't help but feel sorry for a person who knew such little happiness, even if it was her own fault.'

Pat made all the arrangements for the funeral, as he had done for Tony. The Requiem Mass and funeral were on Thursday of that week, and Marion was gratified by the numbers that turned out. She guessed they had come for her father, who was a well-liked and respected man. Although Marion and Polly had written to the men to tell them of Clara's death, they knew they wouldn't be able to come to the funeral, but Peggy and Violet had time off work to attend to show their support for Marion.

Later that day, Marion broached the subject of Eddie's long-term future. She had assumed that he would stay with them but he said he didn't want to. He had lived in Yates Street for years and wanted to continue to live there.

'But how will you manage?'

'Just fine,' Eddie said. 'Don't you worry about me. Anyroad, I'll be at work all day.'

'You're not retiring then?' Marion said. 'You were sixty-five in March.'

'Yes, but I have no intention of retiring yet. I like my job. Anyway, the Firm has asked me to stay on. I don't do much of the heavy stuff now – I'm more of a supervisor – but I like to feel that I'm doing my bit.'

'Are you sure, Daddy?'

'I'm sure, my darling girl,' Eddie said. 'I'll stay until the weekend, if it's all the same to you, and then move back into my own house ready for work on Monday.'

'That's fine by me, Daddy,' Marion said.

Just over a week later, on Sunday morning, after Mass, Marion said to Polly, 'Our Sarah said that Americans are all they see at the dances these days. Before they landed, there was a grave shortage of young men.'

'Mine say the same,' Polly said. 'And they say these GIs are smarter and better paid than our soldiers.'

'Yes, and talking like men the girls see on the cinema screen, and showering them with nylons and chocolate and chewing gum. You can't blame them entirely for having their heads turned,'

Marion said. 'Thank God our girls are level-headed, as a rule. Yet even Sarah says it seems really funny to be called "Ma'am" or "honey", and she tells me the American boys dance with more energy than she has ever seen. She says British boys are sort of shy of dancing.'

'Oh, well, you'd hardly get a shy Yank,' Polly laughed. 'And our Mary Ellen said some of them are as black as the ace of spades, and they're usually the more polite ones. Some of the white boys don't like them much, according to what the girls say, anyroad. They can get really shirty if our girls dance with them.'

'Sarah says the same. I can't see the sense of it myself. I mean, they're all American, aren't they? And I would think they had their work cut out fighting the Japs, without fighting with each other as well.'

'Me too,' Polly said with feeling. 'Still, that's Americans for you. Now I'd better take myself home. My lot will be sitting there with their tongues hanging out because we all took Communion.'

'So did we,' Marion said. 'But I'm lucky there. Peggy and Violet usually have porridge waiting for us when we get in.'

'Huh, all right for some,' Polly said. 'I bet you bless the day you took those girls in.'

'I do, I admit it,' Marion said. 'And I bless you for giving me the idea in the first place.'

*   *   *

408

Sam Wagstaffe was a worried man. Though his feelings for Sarah had deepened in the time he had been writing to her, he had given her no indication of this, and only poured his heart out in his letters to his sister Peggy.

She advised him to bite the bullet: 'The only thing to do is tell Sarah how you feel and then, if she doesn't feel the same, at least you will know where you stand.'

Sam's answer came by return of post.

I have no right to do that with the war still raging. When the pilots you and Violet were keen on were killed in the Battle of Britain, you said you didn't want to get involved with anyone until the war was over and I agreed with you. Well, I feel the same way about Sarah. At the moment I can offer her nothing but possible heartache, and I feel it would be wrong to tell her of my love for her when I'm in the throes of fighting a war. But, because I feel unable to do this I'm sure she views me only as a friend, although we have become closer since Christmas. But where once she told me all about your nights out at the pictures or the dances, now she talks constantly of the American soldiers. And yes, dear sister, I am jealous because I worry that one of these charmers will sweep her off her feet. And that does happen, even with those

committed to one another – engaged, even –
because many men here have had 'Dear John'
letters giving them the big heave-ho in favour
of one of our Yankee cousins. You can't
blame me for being concerned.

Peggy knew just what her brother meant and felt
sorry for him, but still she wrote and said that
Sarah was doing no harm: 'She's just having fun
and she's entitled to do that because until you
admit how you feel, she is a completely free agent.'

They were all free agents and they thoroughly
enjoyed having the Americans at the dance halls.
They were very glamorous in their blue uniforms.
They had the jaunty American caps on their heads,
under their jackets they wore shirts and ties, and
they had proper tailored trousers. Most strange of
all, many wore white shoes. No one in Britain had
ever seen a man in white shoes. In fact, no coloured
shoes at all except black or brown.

'But they're not army issue,' Mary Ellen said as
the girls made their way home the first night they
had spotted this.

The others giggled. 'I'd say not,' Sarah said.
'One of them was telling me that they have brown
shoes issued, but these are their dancing shoes.'

'Well they put them to good use,' said Peggy.
'Have you seen how they dance?'

'Yeah,' Siobhan said. 'Terrific, ain't they?'

And they were. They jitterbugged in a wild,
unrestrained way that had never been taught in

Madame Amie's Dance Academy, and the music made everyone want to dance, for the American soldiers were not yet war weary. They were free and easy in their ways, and seemed hellbent on enjoying themselves. It was easy to be affected by this, to forget the raids and privations of war in Britain and have a bit of fun. Sarah, like most young girls, thought they were great.

Glenn Miller's dance tunes were the favourite of many and so that's what the band played most of the time. Sarah liked all Miller's songs, but she liked 'In the Mood' the most, and she couldn't seem to stop her feet from tapping whenever she heard it played.

She remembered the first time she had ever danced with one of the GIs, whom she found out later was called Chuck. It was to that tune and he had swept her to her feet. When in the middle of the dance he suddenly shot her between his legs she had been shocked, especially as this was followed by him lifting her above his head. And then she gave herself up to the rhythm and pulsating beat of the dance, and could usually anticipate what Chuck wanted her to do, so she thoroughly enjoyed herself.

Chuck was impressed. When the band finished he threw his arms around her and said that she was 'one mean dancer'. After that, though, Sarah danced with others and showed them the elements of the waltz, the quickstep, and the foxtrot for the slower numbers. But she danced a lot with Chuck because, apart from liking him, they did seem to fit together on the dance floor.

'Me and you could win jitterbugging competitions in the States,' he said one evening. 'Would you consider coming to the States when the war is over?'

Sarah laughed. 'At the moment that's like saying "when the sky falls down". Let's get this war won before we make any long-term plans.'

'I'm just saying.'

'Well, don't,' Sarah commanded. 'Come on, "Chattanooga Choo Choo" is playing. Let's dance.'

Much as she liked Chuck, Sarah was aware that the American soldiers would not be there for ever. These men hadn't been drafted into the army to sit out the war in Britain – one day they would leave – and so she kept her friendship with Chuck and the others light. Some things they said and the compliments they threw she took with a pinch of salt. But however keen they were on the GIs – and they all had their favourites – neither Sarah, her cousins, Peggy nor Violet would even consider stepping outside with any of them because they saw the dishevelled appearance of those that did. Fun and dancing were all very well, but that was as far as they went.

Peggy, however, knew that if Sam had any idea of the way Sarah danced, particularly with Chuck, he would be more worried than ever.

* * *

Sam was not the only one irritated by the GIs' presence in Britain. Richard felt the same. In October he came home for few days' leave. He was barely recognisable from the boy who had strode away in July. Peggy told Sarah that they had all seen Sam's transformation too after a few weeks in the army. Violet told him how handsome he looked, and there was certainly nothing of the gawky and unsure boy about Richard Whittaker the soldier.

The second day of his leave was a Saturday and he was looking forward to going to the weekly hop with the girls, remembering that he had been in great demand before he enlisted. He imagined that in his uniform he would be even more popular.

However, the trickle of Americans that he remembered arriving in Birmingham when he joined the army had turned into a positive tide by October. They swarmed all over the dance floor, far too many for Richard's liking, and he might as well have been invisible because most of the girls ignored him in favour of the American soldiers. He spent most of the evening propping up the bar feeling thoroughly miserable and frustrated.

'I don't know what the attraction of them is,' Richard said to his mother the following day.

'Don't you?' Marion said. 'Maybe that's because you're not a young girl, deprived of the company of young men for a very long time. And then along come Americans, with their silver tongues and money to flash about, and unheard of luxuries like nylons and chocolate. Is it any wonder they like them?'

'But the way they dance!' Richard cried. 'Mom, it's disgusting at times. I mean, I've seen jitterbugging, even done it myself, but not the way they do. They swing the girls round so wildly some of the skirts billow out and you can see their underwear, or lift them in the air, which has the same effect, or shoot them through their legs. Sarah's as bad as any of them.'

Marion hid her smile because she knew what was eating Richard and that was the green-eyed monster. She knew all about the American-style jitterbugging because the girls had described it to her. She wasn't worried what they got up to in a crowded ballroom in front of plenty of other people, it was when young people were alone in the blackout that temptation sometimes overcame them. It wasn't that she didn't trust Sarah – she knew right from wrong; they all did – but she had been young herself once. At the moment their passion was for dancing and they went out together and came back together, and that was how Marion liked it.

'The men at camp think there are three things wrong with the Americans,' Richard said.

'Just three?'

'That's all,' Richard said. 'They're oversexed, overpaid and over here.'

Marion laughed, but she had no wish to argue. She knew that this was probably Richard's embarkation leave and she wanted no bad feeling between them. She also wanted him to enjoy his few days at home and so she told Sarah how he felt, and Sarah told the others. They all agreed he had a point for he had been like a spare dinner at the dance. Violet felt particularly bad about that, for she knew he had really wanted to dance with her. So they went out of their way to make a fuss of Richard and took him off to the pictures a couple of times so that all in all he enjoyed his leave.

Saying goodbye to Richard this time was more poignant. Marion hugged him tight and knew she would worry about him every minute he was away. Sarah hugged him hard, and the twins tried to conquer their tears but didn't quite succeed. Richard kissed them both before turning to Peggy and Violet.

Violet put her arms around him and kissed him on the lips. 'Look after yourself,' she said, her voice husky with unshed tears.

Richard held on to her hands as they pulled apart. 'Write to me, Vi?' he pleaded.

So that's the way the wind blows, Marion thought, as Violet looked into the eyes of the boy become man and nodded.

'Just as a friend? No strings attached?'

'Anyway you want it,' Richard said. 'Will you do it?'

Violet gave a brief nod and Richard, a big smile on his face, kissed her on the cheek. He stopped to wave to them all at the gate and then strode down the street with a lighter heart because Violet had agreed to write to him.

The wintry weather took hold in the city as Christmas approached. Marion and Polly, now they had mastered knitting, began attending a dressmaking course in one of the classrooms at nearby Ettington Road School. It was, Polly remembered, their mother's treadle sewing machine that they had made the blackout curtains on. Eddie had no use for it, so Pat and a few of his neighbours brought the heavy machine from Yates Street to Marion's house balanced on a wheelbarrow.

Just before Christmas, Sarah decided to make a patchwork blouse using all the scraps of material from a pattern she had seen advertised in *Home Notes*. In her letters to Sam she told him about it and how difficult she was finding it, but that she was determined to finish it in time to wear on Christmas Day. His replies were full of encouragement.

On Christmas Eve she received a package much smaller than the one he had sent the previous year and again she was on tenterhooks to know what was inside it.

The next day after Mass, Sarah, wearing her patchwork blouse and a navy skirt adapted from one her mother had bought at the jumble sale, got Sam's parcel from the sideboard where she had left it the previous day. All eyes were on her as she broke through the sealing wax and undid the string. There was a small box inside and when she opened that she gasped in amazement because curled around a pad of silk was a beautiful silver pendant set with a blue opal stone, her birthstone. It was easily the finest thing she had ever owned. She took it out and played it though her fingers, and the twins' mouths dropped agape with astonishment. 'Golly, that's nice!' Missie exclaimed. 'Did Sam send it?'

'Must have,' Magda said before Sarah could answer. 'It would hardly be from Richard.'

Sarah was a little disturbed, though, because jewellery was quite an intimate gift to give someone. 'Oh, it is so beautiful but I really can't accept it,' she cried.

'Why on earth not?' Peggy said. 'It's just a Christmas present, and the sort I would welcome with open arms, I don't mind telling you.'

'Yes, but it must have cost a great deal of money,' Sarah said. She was under no illusions as to what a soldier was paid, having both a father and a brother in the army.

'I wouldn't waste a day worrying too much about that,' Peggy said. 'Sam evidently wanted you to have it.'

'Yes, and all I had for him were the inevitable socks and cigarettes and the chocolate,' Sarah said.

'You don't give a present so you can receive one,' Marion reminded her. 'Let me fasten it round your neck and you will see the full beauty of it.'

417

'It is lovely,' Sarah said, looking at herself in the mirror above the fireplace.

'Yes, it is,' Peggy agreed. 'And if I was lucky to be given a pendant like that I would just say thank you very much.'

'Right,' Marion said, 'and unless we stop discussing all this and get the breakfast things cleared away there will be no dinner made at all today. You know your granddad's coming to our house for it this year.'

'If Grandma was alive, she'd find something horrible to say about that pendant,' Magda said. 'Granddad won't, though,'

'Magda what a thing to say,' Marion said quite sharply, but her heart wasn't in the rebuke because the very same thought had flitted across her mind.

Polly and Pat came round after dinner, Pat proudly carrying the box camera Polly had bought him as a surprise present. Marion had known all about it because she had helped her sister search high and low for it, and Pat said he wanted to take a snap of them all in their Christmas finery. When they learned the story of the pendant, though he insisted on taking a few of Sarah on her own.

'When they're developed you can send a couple to your young man,' Polly said. 'You've made a really good job of that blouse and the pendant sets it off a treat.'

'Thank you, Aunt Polly,' Sarah said. 'But Sam is not my young man.'

Polly said nothing further to her niece but later, in the kitchen with Marion, making tea, she said, 'Who's your Sarah trying to kid? No chap sends a girl a present like that if she's just a friend.'

'I did think that myself,' Marion said.

Polly nodded. 'I reckon he's sweet on Sarah and this is his way of letting her know.'

'Oh dear,' Marion said. 'I don't think she feels like that about him.'

'Maybe she's not letting herself feel that way about him when we are at war. Anyway, it'll do no good us worrying about it, and if we don't take these teas through soon they won't be worth drinking.'

Later that day Sarah wrote a letter to Sam thanking him sincerely for the pendant and promised that she would wear it every day she wasn't at work. In his reply, just a couple of days later, he wrote that he was very pleased that Sarah had liked it so much and that the best present she could give him was the thought of her wearing it next to her heart.

Sarah blushed when she read those lines and she felt as if her stomach was doing somersaults inside her. She folded the letter carefully and put it right at the bottom of the drawer she kept her underwear in, for she wanted no one to catch sight of it.

By the time Sarah was ready to send her next letter to Sam, Pat's photographs had been developed, but Sarah was hesitant to include any.

'But why?' Peggy asked.

Sarah shrugged. 'Dunno really. You don't think it's a bit forward?'

Violet laughed. 'You're a card, you are, sometimes, Sarah. Course it ain't forward. It's even OK these days to tell boys that you like them.'

'Oh, I couldn't do that.'

'No one is asking you to,' Peggy said. 'But to send him a photo, showing him the patchwork blouse and the pendant you were so delighted with won't hurt.'

So Sarah enclosed two of the photos with her letter, and in Sam's response he sent her one of himself. Looking at it, Sarah was surprised at the memories that one small photo evoked, like his mop of dark hair, his deep brown, laughing eyes. She remembered the timbre of his voice and his ready infectious laugh, even the dark hairs on the back of his large square man's hands, and her heart gave a lurch at the danger he was probably having to face.

Maybe because of the pendant and the subsequent photographs, the content of the letters between Sam and Sarah changed and they spoke more about their thoughts and feelings. Sarah always had Sam's picture in front of her as she wrote. Just to think of him sent her heart racing, but she shared these feelings with no one.

In early February of that year a massive defeat and subsequent surrender of the German Army at Stalingrad in Russia cheered everyone.

'Told you Hitler was daft to take arms against the Ruskies in the first place,' Polly said later that day when she popped around to see Marion.

'Well, it is good news, I suppose,' Marion said doubtfully, 'but I don't think that it will change our situation any.'

'It shows the German Army ain't invincible, don't it?' Polly said. 'It's nice to know that the Germans are not having it all their own way and they can be beaten at something.'

In the middle of May, when they heard of the RAF bombing of dams in the Ruhr, morale was high and it continued to rise as they heard of the Allied invasion of Sicily in the summer, followed by Mussolini's disappearance.

In the middle of all this, Jack left school. He had been desperate to go, but as his birthday was in August Polly wasn't sure he wouldn't have stayed on until Christmas, but Pat advised her to get him set on somewhere now.

'I'd have liked him to get a trade behind him,' he said to Marion. 'He's bright enough, but there are few apprenticeships now, with the boys all being called up at eighteen. Maybe after the war there'll be some scheme organised.'

In the meantime HP Sauce had a vacancy, and when they agreed to take Jack on Polly told the education authority and they let him leave in July.

'Mind you, Jack wasn't pleased at first to be working at the Sauce,' Pat confided a few months later. 'He told the gaffer he wanted to do something for the war effort before it was too late. Anyroad, the gaffer had the measure of him 'cos he told him that he was working for the war effort, that they had to put on extra lines for the troops when the war began and that a dollop of HP was a necessity to make the army-issue bully beef and mashed potato edible. Jack could see his point and he's fine about it now.'

'Has to be, don't he, really?' Marion said. 'Can't pick and choose these days. You've got to knuckle down and get on with it. Still, it might be over in no time now that Italy's surrendered.'

'Well, the tide has certainly turned,' Polly said. 'Daddy said the Eyeties' heart was never really in the war. He sees this as the beginning of the end. But I'm not too sure.'

TWENTY-THREE

Sarah thought the beginning of the end seemed a long time coming, and she expressed her feelings of frustration and hopelessness in letters to Sam as the war dragged on through another Christmas and the turn of the year. The optimism of his replies always made her feel better.

Then in mid-February 1944 the Americans disappeared. The girls noticed this first, of course, and Sarah mentioned it to her mother on the way to Mass one morning.

'Disappeared?' Marion repeated. 'Where have they gone then?'

Sarah shrugged. 'Can't answer that. But they're not around here any more.'

'None of them?'

'Well, there wasn't one at the dance last night,' Sarah said. 'And Saturday night was always a big night for them, as a rule.'

'And they gave none of you a hint of this last week?'

'No,' Sarah said. 'But then why should they? They owe us nothing, and maybe they didn't know themselves. If they had known they probably wouldn't have told us anyway. You know, like that poster says, "Careless Talk Costs Lives". The way they go on sometimes it's hard to remember that they're not in Britain to have fun with the British girls and jitterbugging the night away, but they're really here to fight a war. It's a pity that some of the other girls didn't realise the Americans could be whisked away at a moment's notice.'

'You didn't have your head turned then?' Marion said with relief.

For a moment Sarah thought of Chuck and the way they had enjoyed dancing together, and recognised it for what it was: a brief and pleasant interlude in both their lives. She hoped whatever was in store for him that he would make it through the war in one piece because he had been a really nice and kind man. In fact, they had all been kind. People spoke of how good they were to children and wished no harm on anyone. But still she was able to say with honesty, 'Not me, Mom.' Then she checked her sisters were out of hearing before saying, 'Though some girls lost more than their heads. We all tried to warn them not to be so silly. They were the ones doing all the weeping last night, especially Betty Mulligan, who confessed to me that she hasn't seen her period for three months now.'

'Ah, dear God,' Marion said. 'The poor girl will bring shame on the whole family.' And she had a

424

flashback to when her sister came seeking her in the same condition all those years ago.

'I know,' Sarah said. 'I do feel sorry for her because she's not bad, just a bit daft. She said that she told the father last week and he promised to look after her, see his commanding officer and get married by special licence. As if anyone but a fool would believe that. But she swallowed his fairytale hook, line and sinker, as the Americans would say.'

'And now the baby's father is God alone knows where?'

'Yeah, that's it,' Sarah said. 'And what gets me is that they didn't know the least thing about any of these boys. I mean, Betty only knew his name, which he told her was Mitch Stevens, and you never know, that might not even be his real name. The only other thing he told her was that he came from a small town in mid-America and that he was in the Eighth Army, whatever that means.'

'Poor girl,' Marion said, as the church came into view. She did mean that, but she was heartily glad that her daughter hadn't come to her in the same condition. In fact she was glad none of them had – her nieces or Peggy and Violet, of whom she had grown so fond.

'I was talking to Emma Baldrick this morning as we was hanging our washing up and she was telling me a tale,' Polly told her sister and niece one Saturday morning in early April.

'What's that, then?' Marion asked.

425

'Well, seems her sister, Winnie has been having a bit of a time of it, bombed out with two nippers in 1941 and still living in a church hall. Anyway, her nerves have been bad and the doctor has put her off work, sick for a week or so, and with the Easter holiday coming up, Emma suggested she go down south for a real rest where they had an aunt and cousins living. Seems they used to holiday down there when they were children and were always made welcome. Anyroad, this aunt wrote back just the other day and said she would love to help Winnie, but the South Coast was out of bounds to civilians.'

'The whole South Coast is out of bounds?' Marion said.

'Obviously the woman couldn't be more specific,' Polly said, 'but at a guess I would say it's out of bounds because that's where lots of troops are camped – those Americans, maybe, as well as some of our own. And if that's the case they ain't staying there because they like the view.'

'You think it means they're going to try invading France, don't you?' Sarah said.

'Don't you?' Polly responded. 'For the life of me I can't see what else they might be massing there for.'

Marion put her head in her hands. 'Oh God! Another Dunkirk!'

'This won't be anything like Dunkirk, though, will it?' Polly said. 'Then it was just Britain standing alone. This will be the massed Allies.'

Polly's eyes met Marion and Sarah's and they were all thinking the same thing: that their loved ones could easily be part of the 'massed Allies'.

Marion sighed. 'We'll say nothing to the twins about this for now. When we know something definite will be soon enough to tell them anything. Anyroad, if information gets into the wrong hands it could further endanger the lives of many servicemen already putting their lives on the line for us all.'

'Yeah,' Polly said, 'we'll keep this to ourselves for a bit and I'll have a word with Emma and advise her to do the same.'

After Polly had gone, though, Sarah wrote a letter to Sam. Towards the end she mentioned the nice weather they were having and asked him if he could see the sun sparkling on the sea from where he was.

It was after Easter before he replied. She had seen the postman on her way to work and he had passed the letter to her, but it was her dinner break before she had time to open it. When the weather became warmer she had found the heat of the furnaces completely draining, and on fine days Marion would sometimes pack her sandwiches and she would eat them outside, where it was cooler. Her cousins preferred to eat in the canteen and have a laugh with their workmates, but Sarah had never gained that same camaraderie with the other girls. So she went out, sat on the wall and eagerly ripped the envelope open.

Pat spotted her and felt sorry for her being by

herself, and he decided to go and keep her company. He was very fond of Sarah and he seldom saw her to speak to since she had been working on the trench mortars.

She raised her head as he approached and he noted the frown between her eyes and the unopened parcel of sandwiches lying on her lap.

'What's up, young Sarah?' he said. 'You look as if you have the weight of the world on your shoulders.'

'Not really, Uncle Pat,' Sarah said with a rueful smile. 'It was my own fault I suppose. I tried to get an inkling of where Sam is after Aunt Polly came around and told us, you know . . .?' and she looked around carefully to see that she was not overheard, '. . . about the troops massing in the south. I wrote a letter to Sam to try and find out if he was there too.'

'He wouldn't be able to tell you if he was, you know that.'

'Course I know,' Sarah said. 'It was really stupid of me, but I was worried about him.'

'I think you think more of that man that you're letting on,' Pat said, and added with a twinkle, 'and I know I'm right because you are blushing and, do you know, young Sarah, it makes you even more attractive when you do that.'

'Oh, Uncle Pat,' Sarah cried, going redder than ever.

Pat put his arm around her. 'Come on, lass, I was only codding you.'

Sarah looked at the uncle she had always loved, even when he was in the bad books with her mother, and she said, 'Don't tell, will you, but I think you're right about Sam.'

'Well, that ain't nothing to be ashamed about,' Pat said. 'So you love this Sam Wagstaffe, do you?'

Sarah bit her lip. 'I don't know about loving him,' she said at last. 'I mean, how do you know? It's the thing most songs and poems are about, and people say you just know when it happens to you, but how? 'Tisn't as if you have a check list you can cross off.'

Pat gave a roar of laughter. 'Oh, Sarah,' he said, 'you are better than any tonic. Now what did this man that you're not sure you love write in response to your letter? I see the tattered pages on your knee.'

'Yeah, I think he was trying to tell me,' Sarah held the shredded letter aloft, 'but the censor got to it first.'

'Be glad it went no further than that,' Pat said. 'What do you mean?'

'Well, your Sam could be in trouble for even attempting to write a letter like that. Think about it, Sarah. You could be an enemy agent or anything, and the letter could be a front, a way of a serviceman passing on classified information that might help the enemy.'

Sarah gave a gasp. 'Oh gosh! I never thought of that. How could I have been so stupid? I do hope I haven't got Sam into trouble.'

'I would say that it's all right this time.' Pat added with a smile, 'Reckon you would have heard about it by now if they were going to throw you into prison, so no harm's done.'

'Yes, thank goodness, and you needn't worry because I'll never do anything like that again.'

'Glad to hear it,' Pat said. 'Now come on. If I were you I'd eat those sandwiches before the bell goes.'

But neither heard the bell, for at that moment there was a terrific, ear-splitting explosion and the blast from it lifted both Sarah and her uncle from the wall into the yard beyond. Sarah had given one shriek before a flying wooden beam smacked her on the side of the head and rendered her unconscious and she fell to the ground. Immediately she was buried by molten metal, sharp shards of glass, bricks and charred and fractured wooden beams.

When she opened her eyes a little later, she wasn't sure that she had, for the blackness was so intense it didn't make any difference. She was used to blackness, as all British people were then, but this was like a curtain of blackness, and the air was cloying and acrid. Worst of all was the throbbing burning pain she became more aware of as she struggled to full consciousness. It seemed to course through her whole body. It was so acute and agonising that it almost took her breath away and she groaned against it, but when she tried to change position to ease it, she found she couldn't move: she was stuck fast.

She fought the panic that threatened to over-whelm her, though her limbs began to tremble and her teeth to chatter, and she had never felt so cold, or so afraid. She had thought that she had been scared of things before, but that was nothing like this deep primeval fear that she could smell and even taste on her tongue. She thought she might die in that pitch-black stony grave, and she wanted to cry out against that, but the pain was draining her of energy and she hoped it wouldn't take her long to die.

Marion was surprised to see her sister come through the back gate because they had just been shopping together and she hadn't even had time to put the stuff away. Polly's face was chalk white, her eyes red-rimmed, and tears were cascading down her cheeks. Marion immediately thought Polly had heard bad news about one or both of her sons and so she was totally unprepared for what she gasped out.

'There's been an explosion at the munitions works.'

'Oh, dear God!' Marion cried. 'When was this?' She tore off her apron as she spoke.

'Just now, seemingly,' Polly said. 'Pat was in the yard, so though he was injured himself he was able to tell the rescuers where I live and a lad was sent round to tell me.'

'What of the others?'

Polly shrugged. 'The boy knew nothing of

anyone injured but he said the whole place is like one gigantic heap of rubble.'

Pat could have told them of the niece buried beside him, who had uttered no sound but that one terrifying shriek, and his two older daughters, who had been in the factory at the time of the explosion. However, by the time the two distraught women had arrived at the scene Pat had been removed to hospital.

Marion and Polly stared at the sea of devastation before them, mesmerised. They looked at the mangled debris of the main building, bricks, fractured beams, and buckled girders mixed with the mangled mess of sandbags the outside of the factory had been faced with. The force of the explosion had been so great that the yard outside was filled with distorted detritus, and they faced the realisation that their daughters had been in that collapsed building. They didn't see how any of them could have escaped death or serious injury.

Rescuers began arriving to move the bricks one by one, and Marion and Polly went forward to help. They had been working at this for half an hour or so when the ambulance delivering Pat to hospital returned ready to tend any survivors.

The ambulance driver approached the group toiling to release any trapped. 'Is there a Marion Whittaker here?'

Marion felt as if a piece of lead was wrapped around her heart as she straightened up and faced the man, aware that Polly was standing beside her. 'I am Marion Whittaker.'

'The first victim taken to the hospital, Pat Reilly, says he's a relative of yours.'

Marion nodded. 'My brother-in-law.'

'And my husband,' Polly added.

'Well, he said that his niece Sarah Whittaker wasn't in the main building.'

Not in the main building! The words filtered through Marion's brain and her face became alight with joy. 'So she wasn't involved in the explosion? She's safe?'

'No, not exactly,' the ambulance driver corrected her. 'She was with her uncle in the yard and she took the full blast of the explosion while he caught the tail end of it. We know where he was brought out and he said he thinks she's buried under a mound of stuff to the side of him. He heard her give one cry and that was all.' He watched the blood drain from Marion's face and steadied her when she would have fallen. Polly's arms went around her as the man said, 'I'm very sorry to bring you such bad news. Will you be all right?'

Marion shook her head helplessly. She didn't think she would be all right ever again and it was Polly who said, 'Show us the place.'

Two of the rescuers were there already, detached from the main party, and as Marion approached one of the men surveyed the stack of wrecked masonry and scorched roof beams, and said, 'I'd take a bet that all we'll find in there will be a corpse.'

'Shurrup,' the ambulance driver said through gritted teeth. 'That's the mother there.'

'Oh God,' the man said. 'Sorry, missus.'

Marion shook her head. She didn't blame the man; she'd had the same thought herself. Inside she was already grieving for her dead daughter, and with tears streaming from her eyes she moved forward to remove the first brick. Polly joined her.

'This is going to take bloody hours to shift on our own,' one of the rescuers said as they began to help the two women.

'We won't be on our own when word gets round,' the other said confidently. 'But we can make a start, at least.'

The man was right. First Peggy and Violet came, bringing Jack, Orla and the twins with them, and then Polly was directed to help the people search for survivors in the main body of the factory and she went with a heavy heart.

So Polly was there when her daughters were among the first few rescued, and she was amazed and so very thankful when they were pulled out of the rubble virtually unscathed except for cuts and bruises. Marion was so happy for her sister and the nieces she loved so much, and she hugged them all in delight. The girls were going to hospital to be checked over and Polly said that she would go with them, both to be with the girls and check how Pat was. Jack said he would stay and help until Sarah was found.

Marion was grateful to him, and grateful to the others who came in droves – neighbours and, as the time went by, men finishing their shifts who only stopped at their own houses long enough to leave their bags before coming to join the rescuers.

It was dusk before Sarah's face was exposed. Her eyes were shut and she was incredibly still. Marion was convinced she was dead, and the sight of her beloved daughter's face shocked her to the core. It was covered with a film of grey brick dust, but that had done little to hide the blood matted in her hair or the gashes crisscrossed all over her bloated, burned and blackened face.

Marion gave a gasp of dismay and when a rescuer shone his pencil of light into the hollow where Sarah lay, it brought her face into sharper focus and made her look worse than ever. Behind her, Marion was aware of the twins crying and Jack sniffing a lot. Then suddenly Sarah blinked in the light from the torch.

'Good God,' one of the rescuers cried, 'the girl's alive.' He put her hand on Marion's shaking shoulders. 'Soon have her out of there, me ducks. She *is* alive, and you hold on to that.'

Marion took a step back, so stunned was she by what she had seen. Jack put his arm around his aunt and led her away to the distressed twins, who Peggy and Violet were valiantly trying to comfort.

Marion bent down and gathered both girls into her arms. 'Don't cry now. Sarah is alive.'

'Is she really?' Magda asked, scrutinising her mother's face.

'Yes,' Marion said. 'I promise, but she's still covered with rubble and they're trying to move that off her. It may take some time and it would be best if you went home now.'

'No,' the girls protested. 'We want to help.'

'Surely the more you have helping the better?'

Marion shrugged. She was in no state to argue with them, and they all bent to the task again as the darkness settled around them.

An hour passed since that blink of Sarah's eyelids, and there had been no further movement. Marion began to wonder if it had been some sort of involuntary movement, or even if she had imagined it. Obviously, many thought the same, because when Sarah gave a sudden gasp a little cheer went up.

'Maybe we should ask the doctor if he wants to check her over before we go any further,' someone said.

'Good idea,' another said, and work was stopped while one of the doctors working with the injured from the main factory was brought. He climbed into the hole beside Sarah and examined her as gently as he could in the light from a shielded headlight someone had brought.

A few minutes later he climbed out and one of the rescuers directed him to Marion. 'You are the young lady's mother?'

Marion nodded.

He went on, 'I'm going to give her a shot of morphine. She's stuck firmly at the moment, and it might take some time to release her. She might be in further pain when she's free, and I think she's gone through more than enough already.'

Hours later Marion sat on a hard hospital bench in a corridor. The twins had eventually agreed to go home with Peggy and Violet, but Jack had insisted on going with his aunt in the ambulance, though she was hardly aware of him. Her thoughts were with the still figure lifted gently from the rubble and put in the ambulance. There Marion had sat beside her, held her hand and spoken to her, but there had been no response. Once in the hospital they had wheeled her away. It was some time before a young woman in a white coat with a stethoscope swinging round her neck approached them.

'Mrs Whittaker?'

'Yes,' Marion said, leaping to her feet.

'My name is Dr Lancaster,' the young woman said.

Despite the fact that so many women had taken over roles typically taken by men during the war years, Marion was more than surprised that this young woman was a fully-fledged doctor.

'I examined your daughter when she was admitted,'

'Her name is Sarah,' Marion said. 'How is she, please?'

'She is badly injured,' the doctor said. 'We have had to shave a large area of her head to stitch the large cut there and she also has extensive cuts and burns to her face, broken ribs and a fractured pelvis. There is tenderness in the area of her liver so there could well be damage there too.'

Marion, almost reeling from the news, said in a whisper, 'Can I see her?'

'Certainly,' the doctor said, 'though there is little of her visible at the moment and she is of course heavily sedated.'

Marion followed the doctor tentatively. Heavily bandaged, with slits left for eyes, nose and mouth, Sarah lay as still as stone in the bed that had the sides raised on either side so that it looked like a cot. Even Jack was quite unnerved, seeing his cousin in that state.

'I will be transferring her to the burns unit here in the morning,' the doctor said, when they were back out in the corridor. 'Because of the risk of infection, especially once we start the skin grafts, she will be in a private room.'

'But she will recover?'

'In time.' We must be thankful that her eyes have escaped injury.'

'What about her face?' Marion persisted. 'She's only a young girl.'

The doctor nodded. 'I know, and the lacerations will heal. As for the burns, all I can say is that we've learned a lot about dealing with burns from treating servicemen in this war. We will endeavour to do our best for your daughter.'

They could do no more. Marion made for home and Jack took off for his own house to tell them what had happened. Peggy and Violet had prepared a meal for Marion, which she tried to eat, though it tasted like sawdust in her mouth. They were anxious for news of Sarah and plied Marion with questions, which she answered as honestly as she could, though what she said upset them a great deal.

They were all eventually calmer and had agreed to go to bed when Polly called round, terribly shaken by the news Jack had brought about Sarah's injuries. Marion told her about the terrible scarring on Sarah's face.

'That's awful,' Polly said. 'Poor girl, and yet if she had been in the canteen she might have been killed outright because they say the explosion came from the centre of the factory.'

'Thank the Lord that she wasn't then,' Marion said. 'So how come your girls got away so lightly?'

'They were queuing at the hatch,' Polly said, and gave a ghost of a smile. 'Siobhan blames it all on the apple pie.'

'How come?'

'Because they had some on the menu for a change and the girls decided to go for a slice. You know how few and far between puddings are these days. Had they stayed at the table a minute longer they would have been killed.' Then all signs of humour left her face. 'Nineteen women and girls lost their lives today and countless more were injured.'

'Nineteen!' Marion repeated in horror. Yet she remembered the crushed mess of the burning building and thought it surprising there had been so few killed.

Polly, seeing the lines of fatigue etched into Marion's face, kissed her sister and got to her feet. 'Well, I only came to know what's what,' she said. 'And now I'd best be off home. We can go up the hospital together tomorrow, if you like?'

'Yeah,' Marion said, 'I'd like that.'

'See you tomorrow then, bab.'

Marion hardly slept that night, but tossed and turned restlessly on the bed. In the end she was glad to get up, though she felt like a bit of frayed string.

'Are you writing to Bill today to tell him what's happened?' Peggy said the next morning.

'Not yet,' Marion said. 'I'll have to have a long, hard think about any letter I write to Bill because I know he'll blame himself.'

'Why?'

'Because he could have claimed exemption and stayed here,' Marion said. 'If Bill had been here he might well have forbidden Sarah to even think about working with explosives. He couldn't do that when it was him left us high and dry.'

'Do you blame him?'

'Not for Sarah's injuries,' Marion said. 'I was resentful at first when he told me that he wanted to enlist. I thought he wasn't thinking enough about us, but in his mind that's exactly who he was thinking of. I had to see it his way in the end, as that was what he was going to do regardless.'

'Well, you can't carry resentment around for ever.'

'No,' Marion agreed. 'Anyroad, I wasn't the only wife and mother left like that.'

'We'll be late for work if we don't go soon,' Violet warned.

Peggy glanced up at the clock. 'Crikey, you're right. We'll have to get a spurt on.'

'And I must get the twins up or they'll be late for school,' Marion said, but when they had gone, instead of rousing Magda and Missie, Marion sat at the table and poured herself another cup of tea. She dreaded writing to Bill for there was no kind way to tell a father that his daughter was possibly going to be scarred for life.

She got herself together in the end. The twins were still tearful when Marion roused them, and didn't want to go to school. 'You'll do no good staying at home,' Marion said firmly. 'If Sarah is awake today I will ask when she will be allowed other visitors, and that's all I can do for you at the moment.'

* * *

441

Sarah's private room was very bare with just a bed with a chair beside it, and a small wash basin. Even the walls were a nondescript beige.

'Has she not regained consciousness yet?' she asked Dr Lancaster.

The doctor shook her head. 'We are at any rate keeping her sedated for now.'

'Why?'

'Well, if she's kept still and quiet her broken ribs will heal themselves,' the doctor explained. 'And even her liver might do the same, which might save her the trauma of more operations. I will have to operate on the pelvis and then, of course, there will be skin grafts, and all that will be shock enough for anyone.'

'I see.'

'There is something else.'

Marion turned her head towards the doctor but didn't speak and she went on, 'Sarah received quite a crack on the head and then she was unconscious for some time so there is a risk of brain damage.'

Marion felt herself recoil from the doctor.

'It's not a foregone conclusion, Mrs Whittaker. I'm just preparing you for that possibility.'

'Yes, thank you, Doctor,' Marion said.

She left the hospital in a daze and once outside the tears came. Polly found her there later, awash with sadness. Marion clung to her sister and they both wept when Marion told Polly why she was so upset.

'I can't tell the twins any of this,' she said. 'And

I can't write to Bill yet either. The doctor said it wasn't a foregone conclusion and so I must wait and see. Her disfigurement is enough for him to cope with now.'

As one day followed another the twins couldn't understand why Marion hadn't written to their father to tell him about Sarah, and had also forbidden them to write and tell him.

'But why won't you write?' Magda asked for the umpteenth time.

'I will,' Marion said, 'but Dad will be very upset when he hears about Sarah. Richard will be too, of course, but Dad will be especially sad and I wanted to have something good to tell him as well.'

'What sort of good?'

'Well, Sarah hasn't really come round yet,' Marion said. 'At the moment the hospital are keeping her heavily sedated and I really want her to come round fully before I write to tell your father.'

The twins accepted this. Marion visited every day, but it was four days later before she entered Sarah's room to find the sides of the bed down and Sarah lying there with her eyes open. They opened wider and a little light shone behind when they caught sight of Marion, though Marion saw with pity that they were glazed with pain.

'Hello, Sarah,' she said gently.

Sarah didn't answer that, but what she did say was, 'I hurt.'

'I know,' said Marion. 'Maybe the nurses can give you something for the pain later, because you're in hospital now. Can you remember what happened?'

'No . . .'

But as her mother started telling her, it was as if everything slotted back in her mind. She remembered sitting talking with her uncle, and trying to read a letter from Sam and a terrific explosion.

'The factory was an awful mess,' Marion said, but she didn't mention the girls who had died because she and Polly had already decided that Sarah didn't need to knew that. She had enough to cope with.

Sarah touched her bandaged face tentatively.

'Your face and head got a bit knocked about,' Marion said, and she willed her voice not to tremble.

'It's stiff.'

'I expect they had to bandage it up tightly to protect it. Everyone has been asking about you. The twins, of course, and Peggy and Violet, and Polly and her lot, but also neighbours. I have had people stop me in the street or even call at the door to ask after you, and Deidre Whitehead from next door has been ever so good seeing to the twins and all.'

Sarah's eye were closing for all she tried to keep them open, but as Marion got to her feet she said drowsily, 'Don't go yet.'

'I must,' Marion said. 'I mustn't tire you out and I'll be back tomorrow.'

Once outside Sarah's room, though, she set off to see the doctor and told her that she'd had a conversation of sorts with her daughter.

'Yes,' Dr Lancaster said. 'Sarah opened her eyes for the first time earlier today after we stopped the sedation and the first indications are good. We will be running more extensive tests over the next few days and so then we will know for certain if there is any damage to the brain.'

TWENTY-FOUR

It was early May when Marion eventually wrote to Bill and Richard. By then the news about Sarah was at least hopeful. There was no sign of brain damage, her ribs had started to heal and so had the cut on her head. The area around her liver was far less inflamed and tender. The letters took a week to reach Bill and Richard on the South Coast. Bill had been there a fortnight and he had often wished he could have described it to Marion, for he'd never seen so many men, or so many nationalities, gathered together one place. Each day more and more troops were being offloaded from trains and marched down from the station to set up camp.

There were more military equipment and vehicles than he had ever seen in his life, too. Bren gun carriers, lorries, trucks and Jeeps filled fields, and camouflaged tanks lined many of the roads. Most coastal paths were sealed off altogether, while boats, barges and landing craft of one kind and another were holed up in harbours all along the coastline.

He had not met up with Richard since he'd enlisted, but once he realised just how many soldiers were being sent to the South Coast he'd had a good idea that Richard would involved too, and he'd tracked him down in no time. They'd been delighted to see each other.

That day, as Bill was once again on his way to see Richard, he passed the messenger delivering the post, who gave him a letter from Marion, which he stuck in his pocket to read later.

When he got to Richard's tent it was to find him sitting on his bunk reading the letter he had just received from his mother. He looked up as his father entered.

'Terrible news about Sarah, isn't it?'

'What?'

'Haven't you had word from Mom? I had a letter this morning.'

'So did I,' Bill said, withdrawing it from his pocket. 'I didn't take time to read it.'

'I think you'd better read it now,' Richard said, and with a sinking heart Bill tore the letter open. He read of the explosion that had killed nineteen workers and injured many more, including his beautiful daughter Sarah. He read of her many injuries and burns, and that she would in all likelihood be scarred for life.

Tears trickled down his cheeks as he crushed the letter in his hands and his eyes met his son's sorrowful ones as he said huskily, 'This is all my fault and I will never forgive myself until my dying day.'

'How do you work that out?' Richard said.

'If I hadn't joined up then Sarah needn't have gone into munitions in the first place,' Bill said. 'Actually, I wouldn't have allowed her to work in a place like that.'

Richards gave a short laugh. 'You're talking about Sarah, the child you left behind. Sarah will be nineteen in the autumn and has a mind of her own.'

'She would defy me? Is that what you're saying?'

'I'm saying that she would have to do what she saw as right,' Richard said firmly. 'Just as you did. Even if you hadn't joined up, you would probably have been out in the teeth of the raids like I was, doing what you could to help. Would you have tried to stop me, though you knew the work we did was essential?'

'Well, no, I suppose not,' Bill admitted. 'But, Sarah—'

'Dad, Sarah chose to go into the munitions,' Richard said. 'No one forced her. She knew the work she did was dangerous, but in a war some risks have to be taken. And whether you like it or not, Dad, someone has to make the munitions for us. That being said, I am sick to the soul for what has happened to her.'

'And so am I,' Bill said. 'But at least she's alive.'

'Yeah, we've got to hold on to that,' Richard

said. 'Especially after Tony. God, but I missed him after he died. I thought I would just miss his nuisance but I didn't. I missed everything about him. He was a great kid.'

'He was,' Bill agreed sorrowfully. 'And Sarah is another one, though, as you reminded me, she's a kid no longer. Now she's a young lady, who might find a scarred face a great deal to cope with.'

Richard was silent because he knew his father was right and he remembered how pretty Sarah had been.

'I'll write her a letter when I get back and try and think of some way to cheer her up,' Bill said.

'Dunno what you're going to say then,' Richard said, going to the entrance of the tent and looking out at the sea of tents. 'You can tell her nothing about all this. People say we're for overseas.'

Bill nodded. 'More than likely.'

'Fellows I was with say that you usually get embarkation leave beforehand.'

'I think they were trying to keep it all hush hush,' Bill said. 'Couldn't risk anything getting out if every man were to have leave. Anyroad, how *could* they give embarkation leave to this lot?' Have you ever seen so many men in one place before?'

'No, nowhere near,' he said. 'People say whole villages have been commandeered and the villagers have had to live elsewhere. Do you think that's true?'

Bill gazed around and imagined how the lives

of the people who lived there must have been before the army moved in. The ploughed fields that might have been full of new crops had been reduced to a muddy slurry and the lush green meadows that probably once housed placid cows were churned up by so many military vehicles and equipment, packed in wherever they could find space. Once, fishermen would be out on the sea, sparkling before him in the sunshine, but the war had put paid to that.

They had marched through sleepy villages with cobbled streets, old and interesting churches and quaint houses, many with roofs of thatch and ringed around the village green. Places where one generation would follow another and life wouldn't have changed that much in a hundred years or more. He owned that their lives might have been changed somewhat in the carnage of the Great War, they had quite possibly lost sons, brothers and fathers but that war had been finished over twenty five years before and he imagined in this simple community, life would have eventually settled back into an even keel again. Until now that was.

What disruptions it would be to the villager's lives to leave their homes and their livelihood. It would break up their communities and Bill felt suddenly saddened by the thought that life for them would never be the same again.

He sighed before turning to his son. 'I suppose it's true, because I heard the same thing.'

'Yeah, but, Dad, you talk about it all being hush hush and that, but we'll never get all these men and all the equipment over the Channel and into France without being spotted,' Richard said. 'Isn't it madness to even think of it?'

'All war is madness,' Bill said, 'and it was you spoke about the risks people have to take in wartime. I suppose leaders have to take those sorts of risks as well. One thing I'm sure of, though, the Germans will be holding reception committees for us on the beaches. How we respond to that will determine the outcome of the war, I reckon, because there'll be no second chances.'

'It's make or break then?'

'Yes, son, I think it is,' Bill said. He clapped Richard on the back. 'And now I'm away to write my letters because God knows when I'll have the time again.'

'Yeah, you have to grab any time you can in the army,' Richard said. 'I've learned that much.'

'Then you've learned a valuable lesson,' Bill said. Then he asked, 'Have you ever regretted joining up?'

'No,' Richard said. 'I know that I'm in the right place. This is a job worth doing.'

'A job worth doing,' Bill said to himself as he returned to his tent. His daughter, who had thought the same thing, now lay injured and quite possibly scarred for life in hospital. God Almighty! He thought that was a high price to pay.

*   *   *

By the end of May, Pat was out of hospital, with crutches, bound ribs and orders to rest. Sarah was recovering well from the operations on her pelvis.

Marion had received letters from Bill and Richard addressed to Sarah. She popped them in her bag to take in that day.

However she had only just entered the hospital building when she met Dr Lancaster, who told her that as the swelling had gone down on Sarah's face, and the lacerations had healed better than they thought they would at this stage, they would be starting the skin grafts on her face the following week.

'Where will you take the skin from?' Marion asked.

'From the back of the ear, for the facial burns.'

'Does she know?'

'Yes,' said the doctor. 'I popped in to tell her today. When I went into the room ten red roses had just been delivered for her. She has an admirer, I believe?'

Marion smiled. 'A young man called Sam has been writing to her for nearly three years. He's really the only one who would send her flowers. He's a soldier, like most young men these days, and we know him a little because he's the brother of one of my lodgers. Sarah swears he just thinks of her as a friend, but I'm not absolutely sure.'

'I wish I had friends who would send me ten red roses,' the doctor said with a smile.

'Yes,' Marion said. 'His sister Peggy says he's

driving her wild with questions about Sarah that she can't really answer, never having seen her.'

'And that situation can't be remedied yet,' Dr Lancaster said. 'Especially as we are starting the skin grafting. The risk of bringing infection in is a real one, and that's why Sarah will be allowed only a few visitors.'

'But surely you're not banning me too?'

'Oh, no, not at all,' the doctor said. 'Sarah would really go into the doldrums if she were to see nobody. You will probably be instrumental in her recovery. I think we can safely say you and one other.'

Marion thought for a moment and said, 'Oh, well, then, I suppose it must be my sister, Polly, for the others are at work all day.'

Dr Lancaster nodded. 'I'm sure the two of you will do your best to cheer Sarah up.'

'Yes.' Marion pulled two envelopes out of her bag. 'I have something else to please Sarah today: both her father and brother have written to her. I'd better go in now and give them to her, or she'll think I'm not coming at all today.'

Sam had been totally shocked when he heard of Sarah's accident, and it was brought home to him exactly how much he thought of her. If he couldn't have Sarah in his life, he realised, then it wouldn't really be worth living. He had been so distressed that he'd gone to his commanding officer and asked for a few days' compassionate leave so that he could go and see her, but he'd been told all leave had been cancelled.

453

So the letter he wrote to Sarah to explain this was the most ardent that he'd ever sent her. He said that she was very dear and special to him, and she'd blushed when she had read it.

'What lovely roses!' Marion exclaimed when she went in the room.

'Aren't they?' Sarah said. 'I had a letter from Sam this morning as well. It was a lovely letter.'

She felt the heat flood her face as she remembered Sam's words, and she was glad of the concealing bandages that hid her crimson cheeks.

'The roses came afterwards,' she said. 'Wasn't he lovely to think of sending them?'

Marion saw the dreamy looks in Sarah's expressive eyes, and heard her soft voice, and she knew that whether Sarah was aware of it or not, she was in love with Sam Wagstaffe.

'The nurses were impressed as well,' Sarah said. 'They said they'll have to take them out at night because they use up the oxygen or something. But I don't mind about that. I can hardly enjoy flowers at night, can I?'

'No,' Marion agreed, 'and meanwhile the smell in the room is gorgeous. She bent to sniff the petals. 'How are you feeling?'

Sarah shrugged. 'Not bad. But they're starting skin grafts soon, the doctor told me today.'

'I know,' Marion said and as Sarah's eyes looked suddenly apprehensive she went on gently, 'they can do wonderful things today with all the techniques they've learned. The doctor told me herself.'

454

'Yeah,' Sarah said with a sigh. 'But I bet that she never said that they can work miracles.'

The twins were very upset when they heard that they were still not allowed to visit Sarah. 'I don't see how we would bring that much infection in,' Magda said mulishly.

'It really doesn't matter what you think, Magda,' Marion said. 'It isn't my decision, but the Hospital's, and we have to believe that they know best. Sarah isn't happy about it either because she's missing you just as much, and she will probably be sick of the sight of me and Polly before long.'

'We could write to her,' Magda said. 'I'm going to write tonight.'

''Course we could,' Peggy said. 'As long as it's cheerful, positive stuff.'

The result of this was that Marion had a bundle of letters to deliver from the twins and Peggy and Violet when she and Polly went to the hospital the following day.

'Everyone all right?' Marion asked as the two of them boarded the tram.

'Never better,' Polly said. 'The hospital doctor thinks Pat may always walk with a limp, but that won't kill him, will it? Anyroad, he isn't going into munitions again, and the girls have no desire to go back either. They were proper shook up, and they lost friends too, and that takes some getting over. Most of the building is still unusable, in any case.'

'And do the girls like the new jobs Orla got them? GEC, isn't it?'

'Yeah, in Electric Avenue in Witton,' Polly said. 'As you know, Orla's been there since she left school and she was just waiting, she said, till she was sixteen to follow her sisters into the munitions, though she's gone right off that now. Anyroad, luckily they got taken on together and all three are now working in the winding shop.'

'Do they miss the money?

'I suppose they do, but money ain't everything, is it?' Polly said. 'Anyroad, the pay ain't bad, and it's a damned sight safer place to work. Added to that, these are jobs they can probably hold on to even when this bloody war is over and the men come back. Pat's going to look for a job there, or somewhere similar, he says, as soon as they sign him off. Tell you the truth, I'll be glad when they do. I'm used to him going to work now and it gets right on my nerves him being in the house all day.'

'I bet,' said Marion. 'You can get nothing done with men lounging about the place. Come on, this is our stop. Let's go and see if we can cheer Sarah up.'

Sarah first skin graft operation was scheduled for Tuesday 6 June, and Marion and Polly visited her the evening before. They wouldn't be able to see her on the day of the operation. Her head was no longer bandaged – although her face still had dressings over it – and the long vivid scar right across her head was red and angry-looking. The stubble on her head did nothing to hide it.

'Does it look awful?' Sarah asked anxiously. 'The doctor wouldn't let me see yet.'

Marion's heart ached for her daughter and she fought to answer her without showing her own distress. 'Well, whatever it was that hit you did a good job of it. It was a wonder your skull wasn't fractured.'

'I can feel the ridge all the way along,' Sarah said, feeling gingerly with her fingertips.

'It's probably a bit swollen now,' Polly said. 'You know, after they messed with it taking the stitches out and that. Anyroad, your hair will cover any scar that's left when it all settles down. You'll probably have to have your hair cut in a shorter style to sort of match the hair that grows over the gash on your head.'

'I've always had long hair,' Sarah said. 'It's hard to think of it short.'

'Oh, it might make a new woman of you,' Polly said airily. 'Sam will fall in love with you all over again.'

'Aunt Polly, what are you saying? Sam Wagstaffe has never fallen in love with me, and I don't think he would care whether my hair was long or short.'

'Oh, I think he would care very much about anything that concerns you,' Polly said.

Sarah stared at her aunt and her heart began hammering against her ribcage. She wondered if Polly meant what she had said or if she was joking.

But it appeared that she was only having a bit of fun because Marion, seeing her daughter's slight agitation, said, 'Show me a man that hasn't got a viewpoint about anything and everything, because he would be a fairly rare specimen. So rare, in fact, that I have never actually met one myself.'

They laughed together and Sarah was able to relax because no one mentioned Sam again, though they talked of all and sundry, which Sarah knew was in an effort to cheer her up and keep her mind off what she had to face in the morning. She was grateful, because whenever she thought of the ordeal ahead, panic threatened to engulf her.

It was late when Marion got home, and she was having a drink before bed and telling the family how Sarah was when there was the distinct sound of planes in the air and she was thrown into panic.

'Dear God,' she cried. 'After all this time. I have nothing prepared, and there's not even water in the kettle. Peggy, will you carry the blankets down to the cellar? God, it's bound to be damp after not being used for so long, and I doubt I have any paraffin for the stove, and—'

'Marion, they're not German planes,' Violet said, crossing to the window.

'Not German . . .'

'She's right,' Peggy said. 'German planes have a distinctive sort of intermittent sound. God, we should know. We've heard enough of them.'

'And there have been no explosions,' Violet said,

easing the blackout curtain from the window slightly. 'But there are hundreds of planes, all right.'

'And you are sure they're not German?'

'Come and see for yourself,' Violet said.

'I will,' Marion said. 'But I'm going into the garden to see properly.'

'We'll come with you,' said Peggy.

They were not the only ones outside. Many of the neighbours were standing watching as squadron after squadron flew over them, the drone reverberating in the night air. Deidre Whitehead's father, who'd lived with his daughter since he had been bombed out the previous year, called over the fence, 'This is it, I reckon. They're emptying the airfields and the only reason for doing that is so they can protect the invasion fleet.'

Marion felt tendrils of fear trickle down her spine because she knew the old man was right. There could be no other reason for all the Allied planes to be filling the skies.

When the last planes were away in the distance, they returned to the house, but Marion took a long time to sleep. She knew this was it, the make-or-break that everyone was talking about, and she was mortally afraid for all of them.

The following morning Marion still had the wireless on when Polly came in. Marion was not surprised to see her sister.

'Thought there might be an announcement or summat,' she said to Polly, 'though there was nowt on the news.'

'I know,' Polly said. 'I listened too, but, God, all them planes must mean summat's afoot.'

'Deidre's Whitehead's dad said they were emptying the airfields so the planes could protect the invasion.'

'Pat said summat similar.'

Suddenly, there was a break in the programme and then the announcer came on air, apologised and said that the BBC had received an official communiqué from Reuters News Agency which stated that, under the command of General Eisenhower, Allied Naval Forces had begun landing Allied Armies that morning on the northern coast of France.

'That's it then,' Polly said. 'Can't say that I'm that surprised.'

'Nor me,' Marion said. 'God be with them all.'

Sarah was in a great deal of pain when she came round after the operation, a raw and excruciating pain that she had never felt the like of before. In the end, the doctor administered morphine. To all intents and purposes, though, the operation had been a complete success, as Dr Lancaster told Polly and Marion the following day. The burned areas were covered with gauze, and Sarah's eyes were glazed over, for the morphine only blurred the edges of the pain.

Marion, who had seen what Sarah had looked like as she lay in the hole before she was rescued, wasn't completely surprised, but Polly was shocked to the core. She had been told about the battering Sarah's face had taken and that it had been burned in places, but it was one thing being told and quite another seeing it for herself. She realised that she had assumed that when the bandages were off, Sarah's face would more or less be returned to normal.

She was so shaken that she wanted to weep for the young girl so tragically disfigured, but instead of giving way to that she knew she must help her sister dredge up incidents from the family to entertain her. She wasn't entirely successful, and was glad that Sarah was too drowsy to notice her reticence, and she was ashamed of the relief she felt when Sarah's eyes fluttered shut.

'She's asleep, Marion, God love her,' Polly said.

Marion leaned over and gave Sarah a kiss, and the two women tiptoed from the room.

It wasn't only the grafts that were painful for Sarah, but the stinging behind both ears where the skin had been removed, and the smarting saline solution that was applied to both areas, which the doctor explained would help with healing. Sarah hoped that she was right because the skin behind her ears was beginning to feel quite raw, and the grafts often pulled as they tightened.

Every few days more grafts took place, but all were done by the very end of June, though Sarah's face was still protected from infection by gauze pads. Twice a day the whole area was lubricated with special oils that the doctor said would make the grafts bed in better. Dr Lancaster also examined her pelvis and Sarah was very pleased when she said that she could sit up.

'The next thing is walking, I suppose,' Sarah said, 'and then I can go home.'

The doctor nodded. 'We'll start physio next week when your skin should be feeling a lot less tender.'

'Can I see what I look like?'

'Not yet,' the doctor said. 'Some of the latest skin grafts are very raw still. You have to have a little more patience.'

All right for her to say that, Sarah thought when she'd gone. It's not her face. She ran her finger over it gently and then she swung her legs out of bed. The room swum when she tried to stand and she hung on the bed until it stopped. Her legs felt very weak, though, and wobbled alarmingly as she made her way across the room. She knew if any of the nurses on the main ward spotted her they would send her back to bed and so she opened the door cautiously. She was in luck, for the nurses were busy at the other end of the ward, and she slipped through the door.

Sarah had no idea where the bathrooms were and as she stood wondering what to do a nurse came out of a room further down the corridor, carrying a bedpan. Fortunately she turned the other way and didn't see Sarah pressed against the wall. Sarah made for that room as quickly as she could, knowing that there would probably be mirrors and she would see what she really looked like.

Moments later she stood in front of the mirror, gently removed her dressings and looked at herself, only she could scarcely believe that the person looking back at her was herself at all. She didn't know this ugly, grotesque creature, and she touched her face tentatively, unable to believe the evidence of her own eyes. All her imagining what her face looked like had not come anywhere near the reality.

She gave a cry of pure distress and she watched her mouth drop open and her eyes widen as she felt the ridge of the deep cut that had been gouged in her head, which was still visible because her hair was only just starting to grow back. But it was her face that mattered most. Two bright red scars had been scored across her face and the burns on either side of her nose were like a pitted and crazy zigzag mosaic of bright pink skin and normal-coloured skin. The effect was so utterly hideous she could barely look at herself, so she could just imagine how others would react. Suddenly it was too much for her. Her legs gave way and she collapsed on the floor.

She must have lost consciousness because when she came round she was back in her own room, fresh dressings were covering her face and Dr Lancaster's concerned eyes were looking down at her.

'How are you feeling now, Sarah?' she asked.

'How do you expect me to feel?' Sarah snapped. 'You have turned me into some sort of ogre! A freak!'

The tears came then, not any sort of controlled weeping but a paroxysm of grief that shook Sarah's whole body, and Dr Lancaster forgot her professional status and gathered Sarah into her arms.

Even as she held her, though, and tried to give comfort, the doctor knew that the one thing Sarah had to realise was that her face would never look the same as it had before the accident. The damage had been too great. But Dr Lancaster did have a lot of experience – the war had seen to that – and she was convinced that the new skin would weather and the pitting would even out, even disappear. When this war eventually drew to a close and cosmetics were back in the shops, Sarah would be able to do a great deal to cover the scars on her face. However, she knew Sarah wasn't really ready to hear this now because first she had to grieve for the pretty girl she once had been.

Much later Sarah sat in her room and remembered the monstrous face that had looked back at her through the glass. No one would want to know anyone with a face like that, she decided; she would be an embarrassment to be seen with. What she needed to do was get out of hospital as quickly as possible and hide away at home where she didn't have to see anyone she didn't want to see.

As for Sam . . . She felt the pang of loss as she

realised that he too had been a part of her earlier life and she couldn't drag him into this one. He didn't deserve that. She wouldn't be able to bear the revulsion in his eyes if he saw what she looked like now.

Dr Lancaster was waiting for Marion and Polly when they entered the hospital, and she told them what had transpired, and Sarah's reaction to it. Neither was surprised at Sarah's shock as they had expected her to be upset, but when they saw her she was strangely calm, though her eyes looked strangely empty.

'Like the essence of her had gone,' Marion said to Peggy and Violet later after the twins had gone to bed.

Peggy and Violet knew exactly what Marion meant.

'I mean, I tried telling her that her face would look better in time, but she was having none of it. She said under her dressings she looked like some sort of gruesome gargoyle and she could never live and work among normal-looking people again. It was heartbreaking to listen to, because she meant every word, and the hopeless sort of bleak look in her eyes made me want to weep. What Sarah is looking at is the end of her life, and at not quite nineteen years old that is unbearably sad. I don't know what I can do, what any of us can do, to make things any better for her.'

TWENTY-FIVE

Visiting Sarah was a trial after that. She didn't seem to care if Marion and Polly were there or not, and they could talk about very little, for she showed no interest in the progress of the invasion or the family either.

'They all inhabit a world I will never be part of ever again,' she told her mother, and neither Marion or Polly could find an answer to that.

She worked hard at the physio because her greatest desire was to recover enough to go home, where she imagined she would be safe, and by the very end of July she was physically ready to leave the hospital. Dr Lancaster was concerned about her emotional state, but there was nothing she could do about it. Anyway, she reasoned, familiar surroundings and her family around her could work wonders, and she arranged the transport to take Sarah home.

When the ambulance arrived in Albert Road, Marion was so pleased that she lived in a community like that. All the neighbours had been shocked when they'd heard about Sarah, particularly when Marion had told them about her burns. They had asked about her often and knew she was coming home that day. Marion knew more than a few would be watching, but discreetly from behind net curtains, as they had when Bill had arrived home with his crocked-up leg in 1940.

Polly, who had travelled with Marion in the ambulance, was surprised there was no one out on the streets to welcome them home, or shouting encouraging words from their doorsteps. Marion knew that Sarah would have hated everybody gawping at her like that, but Polly saw it as lack of concern.

'We don't live in each other's pockets,' Marion said in defence of her neighbours, 'but they're there if you need anything. Deidre next door is having the twins till we get Sarah settled in, and they'll all be along later to ask about her.'

'Hope they don't expect to see her then,' Polly said, because when they'd arrived home Sarah had said she was tired and had gone straight to her room.

'Well, she did look worn out,' Marion said. 'It was probably a bit emotional for her, and they will understand that, I'm sure.'

'Maybe,' Polly said. 'Or it might be just plain rudeness.'

Marion sighed. 'I don't know,' she said, 'but I admit I was embarrassed earlier when she walked past the nurses that had cared for her, and the doctor that had performed delicate surgery on her, without a word to any of them.'

'Yeah,' Polly agreed. 'I mean, me and you did all the thanking and the shaking of hands and that. Sarah got into that ambulance without a backward glance.'

'I think maybe she didn't want anyone to catch sight of her,' Marion said. 'You know what she's like.'

'I know what she's like now,' Polly said. 'The children and your lodgers will get a shock, and not just over her face and that. I suppose you have prepared them?'

'Course I have. I told them at the beginning how scarred she was and about the painful skin grafts, and how upset and touchy she was about the way she looked. I told Deidre as well, and that's why she offered a hand with the twins.'

'Shall I knock the door as I pass then?' Polly said. 'They're probably champing at the bit to see Sarah.'

'Oh, would you?' said Marion. 'They're ever so excited she's coming home.'

Although the twins had taken on board what their mother had said, and had even, at her suggestion, removed the large mirror that had stood on the dressing table, it was a tremendous shock to them to see how different Sarah was. It wasn't just her face, which Sarah kept semi-covered anyway with the gauze dressings, it was her attitude.

She had always been so kind and gentle with them as they were growing up, and because of that the two girls had often asked her things or confided things that they would hate their mother to hear about, and she had never told on them. She had been a really smashing big sister, Magda and Missie were agreed on that, and they loved her very much. However, the Sarah who returned from hospital seemed completely disinterested in anything they said to her and often didn't say anything at all. And when they lay beside her in bed, it was like sharing it with a plank of wood. It was very strange and unnerving for them because they had no idea what to do about it.

Though the whole family tried hard with Sarah intially – particularly her very worried grandfather, who was terribly disturbed about her – in the end because of her lack of response most of them left her alone, which was what she really seemed to prefer.

Peggy tried for longer than the others. She was getting letters from her brother all the time because Sarah refused to write to him or anyone else either.

'Why won't you just write him a little note?' Peggy said, exasperated with Sarah's attitude. 'It would mean so much to him. He writes to you every week. Surely he deserves some consideration?'

'He deserves to find someone else,' Sarah snapped, though as she said the words she felt as if her heart was breaking. 'Sam is no longer part of my world.'

Well, thought Peggy, Sarah couldn't have made it any more clear that she wanted nothing more to do with her brother. She thought he needed to know that so she wrote and told him, and received a heartbroken reply, but at least he stopped writing letters to Sarah that she didn't even open.

'What does she do with herself all day?' Polly asked when more than a month had passed with no noticeable improvement.

'She reads, or she plays patience,' Marion said, 'or she sits and stares into space. Seems to do a lot of that.'

'God Almighty!' Polly exclaimed. 'No sign of her getting a job.'

'Are you kidding, Pol? There's no sign of her leaving her room except for meals.'

'How are you managing?'

'Well, there's only the twins still at school. Bill sends a bit, and so does Richard, and of course I still have the money from Peggy and Violet. Oh, I will miss them when the war's over.'

'Will they go back home then?'

'I expect so. They'll more than likely have to leave the forge anyway because when the men come back they'll probably want their old jobs back.'

'And Peggy and Violet won't be the only ones turfed out, either,' Polly said. 'There's plenty won't like that. Some of them have had money for the first time in their lives. Mind you, seems to me this war can go on for ages yet.'

'What makes you say that?'

'Well,' Polly said, 'we seem to be going two steps forward and one back. We see the Allies liberating French towns and stuff – I mean, they got to Paris just a few weeks ago – but no one seems to be able to stop these bloody unmanned devices coming over.'

'Yes,' Marion said. 'The ones they're firing now are called V2s, and Daddy said they're worse that the V1s, those bloody doodlebugs that started in June. He showed me the report about them in the paper when he came to dinner last Sunday. Apparently these are proper rockets and can travel at over three thousand miles an hour.'

'Get away!'

'Honest, that's what it said in the paper. And what's more they're completely silent.'

'God Almighty! Just how scary is that?'

'Well, I'll tell you one thing for nothing,' Marion said, 'I wouldn't live in London for a King's ransom.'

Everyone hoped that Christmas 1944 was going to be the last wartime Christmas they would have to endure, and it certainly seemed that way when just after the middle of January the Red Army regained Warsaw. It was also reported the Allies had reached the borders of Germany.

On the last Saturday in February, Peggy got a letter from her mother. That wasn't unusual and she opened it at the kitchen table after breakfast. Suddenly the colour drained from her face.

471

'What is it?' Marion cried, alarmed at the girl's pallor.

Peggy's concerned eyes met Marion's. 'It's Sam. He's been injured.'

Sarah, who usually sat in absolute silence, gave an involuntary gasp as a spasm of pain seemed to grip her stomach. No one noticed, for all their attention was on Peggy.

'Oh, Peggy, that's dreadful news,' Marion said. 'My poor dear girl.'

'How badly is he hurt?' Violet asked.

Peggy shook her head. 'Mom doesn't know. She says from what she can make out it happened a few days ago and he's been in a field hospital and now they're shipping him home.'

'His life can't be in danger then,' Marion said. 'Take heart in that, my dear. Does your mother know where he's being sent?'

'That military hospital in Sutton Coldfield where he was before.'

'When's he arriving? Have they told you that?'

'This weekend, by all accounts,' Peggy said. 'I must go home directly. My mother needs me at home just now. You must give my excuses, Vi.'

'I will,' Violet said. 'Don't worry about that. It's the right time to go, for the work isn't as frantic as it once was and, anyroad, you must have holidays due?'

'I'd say so,' Peggy said with a wry smile. 'Seeing that neither you nor I ever took much time off. She turned to Marion. 'I'm sorry. You do see . . .?'

Marion covered Peggy's agitated hands with her own and said gently, 'You have nothing to be sorry for, and of course I understand that your mother needs you at home for a while. The only thing I'm sorry for is that that fine young man has been injured again. I'm sure we all feel that.'

'Oh, not half,' said Magda.

Missie nodded emphatically before saying, 'We'll help you pack, if you like.'

Although Peggy sent a letter to say that she had arrived safely and that her mother was glad to see her, she didn't write again, and Marion worried that the news was bad. She knew Violet and even Magda and Missie felt the same because she saw it in their eyes, but they never spoke of it.

The next time Marion heard from Peggy was the following Friday morning when she sent a telegram to say that she would be arriving that afternoon. Marion had been alarmed initially at the sight of the telegram, but though she was pleased that Peggy was coming back she felt apprehensive about what she might have to say about Sam.

When Peggy arrived at the door with a case in one hand and a large bag in the other, Marion plainly saw the lines of tension scoring her face, which was as white as lint, and her eyes were very shiny as if she had been crying. She felt her heart turn over in pity as she drew Peggy inside, putting the baggage down in the hall and helping her off with her coat as if she were a child.

'Leave your things where they are for now,' she advised. 'Come into the living room and get warm. It's a dreadful day.' And then she gave a wry smile and said, 'Brass monkey weather, as Bill would say, although it's March.'

It was when they were sitting either side of the range that Sarah sidled into the room and though she sat a little way from them, it was strange that she was there at all. Normally, of her own choice, she stayed in the room she shared with the twins. She seemed to want to be outside the family circle, and anything they did or said didn't appear to affect her at all.

Peggy gave a sudden shiver and Marion leaned forward, gave the fire a good poke and put on some more nuggets of coal.

'I'm not cold,' Peggy said, 'not that sort of cold, anyway.'

'Well, I always think a good fire is cheery in these dismal days.'

Peggy sighed. 'Oh, Marion, it would take more than a fire to make me cheery.'

'Do you want to talk about your brother, Peggy, or will it be too much for you?'

'No, I'll tell you,' Peggy said. 'It's obvious that you will want to know. He's been blinded in an explosion.'

Sarah jerked in the chair. 'Blind?' she cried. 'Did you say blind?'

'That's what I said.'

Suddenly Sarah felt her heart turn over in pity

for Sam and those lovely eyes that lit up when he smiled or laughed. She was at first surprised she even cared, for she had thought her emotions shrivelled up, but this news had shattered through that veneer of indifference.

Marion and Peggy were both aware of the change in Sarah, and then Peggy looked her full in the face and said, 'Mom and I have been every day to visit him. I even broke my journey to see him this morning before I came back here. The hospital gave me special permission to do that. But though he is always pleased when either of us visits, the person he really wants there is you.'

Marion saw that Sarah was flustered and disbelieving.

'No, no. I'm sure you're wrong.'

'I'm not wrong,' Peggy insisted. 'One person I do know is my brother, and I know he loves you dearly. It broke him apart when you refused to write to him, and without a word of explanation.'

'But surely you wrote? You told him why that was?'

'I tried,' Peggy said, 'but it was difficult, because I hadn't seen you either. But I'll tell you what: I've seen some dreadful sights over the last few days when I have been visiting Sam, and most of them young and all getting on the best way they can. Sam was caught in an explosion as you were, and under the bandages he's horribly scarred too, though like you, they said the scarring will heal to a certain extent. But your eyes were saved, his were not. You're not the only casualty of this war, Sarah.'

'That's unfair,' Sarah cried. 'I never said I was.'

'You behave as if you were.'

'I didn't,' Sarah protested. 'I know other people suffered too.'

'But you don't care about them?'

Sarah couldn't answer that because she hadn't cared about other people, not until now, and so she was silent.

When Peggy said, 'Come with me tomorrow to visit Sam?' she gave a gasp of surprise, for it was the last thing that she had been expecting.

Marion was aware that she was holding her breath as Sarah shook her head. 'I can't. You don't know what you're asking.'

'Yes, I do.'

'You can't possibly know how I'm feeling inside.'

'I know how Sam is feeling.'

'Does he ask for me?'

Peggy shook her head. 'No, not now. When you said you no longer wanted him in your life I wrote and told him what you had said because I thought he needed to know, so he thinks that you want nothing more to do with him.'

Sarah's heart gave a lurch and the longing to see Sam again almost engulfed her. And then she stiffened and pulled the shutter up again, and the chill was back in her voice as she said, 'I am really sorry for Sam, but still the answer must be no.'

'Why do you feel you can't come?'

'You know why.'

'No I don't,' Peggy said. 'What I do know, though, is that Sam loved you and probably still does. He told me himself that he carried the photos you sent him around in his breast pocket.'

'Yeah, but that was the old me,' Sarah said, angry that she had been so badgered. 'I bet Sam wouldn't have been so keen on seeing this one.' And with a flourish she pulled the dressings off.

The two women stared at her. Neither had ever seen Sarah's face completely exposed since the operations on it, and though Marion had to admit that there were marks, her skin had bedded in as the doctor had said and was all one colour, and she knew it would get even better yet. At least Sarah would be able to conceal much with cosmetics. All in all, she didn't look half as bad as Marion had expected.

'Why have you been hiding yourself away for months?' Peggy said in genuine puzzlement. 'Your face isn't that bad, and as for Sam, he can't see you anyroad. Come and see him, Sarah?'

Sarah shook her head and put her hands over her eyes. Peggy glanced across at Marion, who gave a small shrug as if there was nothing to be done, but Peggy was made of sterner stuff and she was fighting for her brother's happiness.

'D'you know who you remind me of?' she asked, and without waiting for a reply she went on, 'Your grandmother, who rolled the injustices of her life into a canker of resentment that she carried with her always.'

Sarah gasped. The thought that she could ever be the slightest bit like her grandmother filled her with dismay, and yet she had to admit that there was a nub of truth in what Peggy said.

She had hugged her disfigurement to herself and shut everyone else out, not just because she feared their reaction, but because of the feeling of dejection within herself. Now she was forced to acknowledge that Sam might be feeling much the same way about his lack of sight. So she said to Peggy almost grudgingly, 'All right. I will go with you to see Sam tomorrow if it will make you happy.'

Marion looked absolutely stunned that Sarah had agreed. She realised that the whole family had pandered to Sarah and, almost without being aware of it, made allowances for her behaviour as they had for her grandmother. How wise Peggy was to recognise that.

The twins and Violet were delighted to see Peggy back when they arrived home that evening, though not at all pleased when she told them what had happened to Sam. But they were also very interested in seeing what Sarah's face looked like, for once Sarah had removed the dressings in a fit of pique against Peggy, she decided to leave them off to see the reaction of the others.

However, Marion had done such a good job in telling them how scarred she would be, and in a way Sarah had compounded this by keeping her face semi-protected with dressings, that they imagined that her face would look far worse than it actually did. Magda and Missie lost no time in telling her this.

'She didn't believe them, though,' Marion told her sister the following day when Sarah had set off for the hospital with Peggy. 'Not until Magda ran to fetch the mirror. I saw such a change come over her when she looked in it. God, Polly, it would have brought tears to your eyes. She was touching her whole face, you know, as if she couldn't believe it. I mean, she is changed and there are scars, of course, but she's nothing like the hideous monster that she once thought she resembled. Last night it was like I was seeing little flashes of the old Sarah.'

'Thank God!' Polly said fervently. 'And you say Peggy has bullied her into going to see Sam?'

'Well, if I'm honest I think Sam and his tragic blindness was the lure,' Marion said. 'But it was what Peggy said to her in the end that decided her, I think. She told her that she reminded her of Mammy.'

'Oh, I bet that didn't go down too well.'

Marion grinned. 'It didn't. But she had a point. We were so wary of upsetting Sarah that we let her do as she pleased. Doesn't that sound horribly familiar?'

'Shows you how easy it is to do, though,' Polly said, 'until it becomes a habit.'

'Violet cut Sarah's hair after we'd eaten,' Marion said, 'and made a good job of it too.'

'Well, it had to be done, being all different lengths.'

'I know, but she refused to go to the hairdresser and have it done properly, and wouldn't let any of us do it either. But now she looks a very modern miss with her shorn locks, and the hat I loaned her suits her better with short hair.'

'What hat's that?'

'The one with the small brim and the veil that you can wear over the face if you wish,' Marion said. 'She has the option to do that when she's on the train if she feels self-conscious. Anyroad, the girls freshened it up with steam from the kettle and a soft brush, and then put a new ribbon on it and it looked quite fetching when she set out with Peggy a little while ago.'

'Well, let's hope she can be some sort of comfort to that fine young brother of Peggy's, for to lose your sight must be a dreadful thing.'

'It must,' Marion said. 'I don't think I could bear it.'

'Nor I,' said Polly.

TWENTY-SIX

Sarah never forgot her first sight of Sam that day. She was alone because Peggy said she had to see the doctor, but though she had warned her that Sam had been peppered with shrapnel for the second time in his life, and was heavily bandaged, she was still shocked to see his head swathed like hers had been. She knew how uncomfortable it was to be so encased and, full of sympathy, she crossed the room as quietly as she could, smiling at the three others who shared the room, and sat on the chair by Sam's bed.

Although she had been quiet, Sam heard her and he tipped his head to one side and spoke stiffly because of the confines of the bandages. 'That you, Peg?'

'No,' Sarah said. 'Hello, Sam.'

'Almighty Christ!' Sam exclaimed in great agitation. 'Is that you? Sarah?'

'Yes, Sam. It's me.'

'But what are you doing here?'

'Visiting you, of course.'

'But I thought . . .' Sam began and stopped. 'You do know I'm blind?'

'Of course I know. Peggy told us.'

'Is that why you're here, to pity me?'

'Of course not. What sort of person do you think I am?'

'I don't know what sort of person you are,' Sam said. 'I thought I did. I thought that we knew nearly everything about one another, but then you suddenly stopped writing to me. I sent a letter every week.'

'There were lots of reasons,' Sarah said. 'I couldn't write to anyone at first because I was flat on my back for weeks.'

'I understood that,' Sam said. 'The nurse that wrote that first letter for you telling me what had happened explained that. But afterwards? Peggy wrote and told me that you didn't want me in your life any more. She told me that you said those very words, and I have never known Peggy lie. You broke my heart, Sarah.'

'I nearly broke mine saying those words,' Sarah said. 'And Peggy told the truth because I did say them.'

'But why?' Sam said perplexed. 'I wanted to support you. I know it was only through letters, but that was all I could do at the time. To cut me off the way you did, and not even to try and explain why . . .? I couldn't understand it. I would never had said that the girl I had been writing to for some time had a cruel bone in her body, but that *was* cruel, Sarah.'

Sarah sighed. 'I know it was now. But at the time I wasn't thinking about the pain I was inflicting on anybody else. I was just thinking of myself, although I really did think that you would be better off without me.'

Sam shook his head. 'I can't understand how you would ever feel that way.'

Sarah took one of Sam's arms and held it tight as she went on, 'You need to understand how I was then. How mixed up – still am, to an extent. Peggy had to bully me into coming here.' She felt him stiffen and said, 'That wasn't because of you – I longed to come, yearned to see you once more – but I couldn't face people and I have seldom left my bedroom since I came home from hospital. You see, I sneaked a look in the mirror when the last skin grafts had just been done, the others were only just bedding in and the hair hadn't grown fully over the deep scar on my head. The only word to describe myself then was grotesque. To be honest I couldn't live with the image of myself then and I thought you deserved to have someone better.'

'Better?' Sam repeated. 'You mean less flawed. How shallow you must have thought me.'

'No,' said Sarah. 'I knew you weren't – well, in my rational moments I knew. But I wasn't rational, not to start with. When Peggy told us about you being injured . . . I can't really explain how I felt, and it was strange for me to feel anything because I had cut myself off so much. Then when she came back and said you had been blinded . . .'

'You felt sorry for me?'

'No,' Sarah said firmly. 'I was sorry you have been injured, but it wasn't pity I felt for you. I have never told you this before, but I think I love you, Sam.'

'You think?'

Sarah smiled. 'I know I do. I love you, Sam Wagstaffe.'

'And I you, Sarah Whittaker.'

'Ah, Sam,' Sarah said, and it was as if a hard lump inside her had melted away and set her limbs trembling. She got to her feet and kissed Sam on the lips. 'And my face doesn't matter to you?'

'Not a jot,' Sam said. 'Anyroad, I don't imagine I will be any oil painting when they dig all the shrapnel out of my face. Will that matter to you?'

'Of course not.'

'Well, then,' Sam said, and then he asked gently, 'Can I feel your face? I will be gentle.'

Sarah removed her hat before she leaned forward and Sam gently touched her face so very tenderly. When he felt the slight ridges in her skin, his heart turned over for what she had suffered. 'You've had your hair cut short?'

'I had to have it cut,' Sarah said. 'They shaved my head to stitch the cut on my head and so it was all different lengths.'

484

'Such a lot has happened you,' Sam said, catching hold of her hand. 'I need to know it all.'

And so Sarah held tight to Sam's hand and told him everything from the time she had sat on the wall beside her uncle and tried to read the censored remains of the letter he had sent her.

Much later, Peggy came in to find them both in deep conversation. She had not had to see the doctor at all, she just thought they needed time alone and so she had read some magazines in the visitors' room to give them precious time together.

After meeting Sam again, Sarah felt as if she had been reborn. For so long she had kept a lid on her feelings, because despite the beautiful words he used sometimes when he wrote to her, she thought maybe she was reading too much into them. When she'd first met him she'd been dazzled by him. Meeting him again at sixteen had kindled a love that had matured with her. What she felt for Sam Wagstaffe now was no childish infatuation, but a deep and abiding love, the sort of love that lasts a lifetime.

Marion saw that as soon as Sarah came home. Though the others plagued both her and Peggy with questions about Sam, Marion said nothing because she recognised that Sarah had met her soul mate and she was heartsore for her because she knew just how hard her life was going to be if she saddled herself to a blind man.

'Are you going again tomorrow?' Magda asked.

Sarah shook her head. 'Sunday is really the only

day in the week that Peggy's family can go and visit, but I'll tell you where I am going tomorrow and that is to Mass.'

Marion was so amazed that her jaw dropped open.

'Don't look quite so surprised, Mom,' Sarah said. 'It's about time. And anyroad,' she added simply, 'I want to thank God for bringing Sam into my life.'

Polly and her family were delighted to see Sarah at Mass, and her grandfather had tears in his eyes as he held her close. Many people knew what had happened to Sarah, but though some gave her curious looks, she paid no heed to them. Marion was immensely proud of her.

After dinner was eaten and cleared away Marion went round to see her sister. It was a cold and blustery afternoon and Polly was sitting by a blazing fire. Orla, seemingly the only one home, swept the clutter off another easy chair for Marion and then fetched a bucket of coal and even offered to make them both a cup of tea.

'What's she angling for?' Marion whispered as she went into the small kitchen.

Polly chuckled. 'Oh, you know the measure of Orla all right,' she said in a similar low voice. 'She thinks I don't know, but Mary Ellen let it slip that a crowd of her friends are going to the pictures tonight and she wants to go and she's spent all her money. She's a devil with money – it burns a hole in her pocket. I mean, I give her back the same as the others and she has it spent in five minutes.'

'And will you give her the extra?'

'I expect so,' Marion said. 'If I don't then Pat will, anyroad. Right soft, he is, with the kids and always has been. And don't look like that, our Marion, because I'll tell you something for nothing. I would rather have him that way than the other way.'

Marion nodded. 'Fair enough. I feel the same about Bill.'

Orla appeared then with two cups of tea and Polly waited until she had gone out into the yard before she said, 'Anyroad, you ain't come round here to talk about our Orla, or even the merits of our husbands so out with it.'

'Well, you've seen the change in Sarah?'

'I have and it was lovely to see her at Mass today.'

'Yeah, wasn't it? She told me that she wanted to thank God for bringing Sam into her life again.'

'She's certainly has got it bad,' Polly said. 'Amazing what the love of a good man will do for a girl. So what's the long face for?'

'Well, he is a fine young man and there's no denying that,' Marion said. 'But he has two things against him.'

'Two?'

'Yes. The first is that Sam is not a Catholic, and Father McIntyre will be down on me something fierce when he finds out. But I think it's far more of a handicap that he's blind. I don't want our Sarah throwing her life away like that.'

'Like what?'

'Oh, you know, Pol.'

487

'Are you sure she would be throwing her life away?'

'For God's sake, Polly, how will he ever support her? What sort of life will she have if she goes ahead and marries him?'

'Look, let's leave Father McIntyre out of it for now,' Polly said. 'He's nothing but a sanctimonious hypocrite. And you're more than a match for him, anyroad. So really, your only objection centres on Sam's blindness.'

'Well, yes,' Marion said. 'Isn't that enough?'

'And what would you do if, God forbid, Bill was blinded in an explosion? Would you walk away from him?'

'Of course I wouldn't,' Marion said. 'You should know me better than that. I married for better, for worse, in sickness and in health.'

'It would mean some massive adjustments for you both.'

'Yes . . .'

'Well, all I'm trying to say is that at least Sarah would know what she was going into and they could learn together.'

Marion still shook her head and Polly went on, 'Anyroad loving Sam and being loved in return has certainly lifted your Sarah out of the doldrums.'

'Oh, I can't deny that,' Marion said. 'And she doesn't have her face covered with dressings any more.'

'She doesn't need them,' Polly said. 'I never

would have believed that they would have made such a good job on her face.'

'I know,' Marion replied. 'But she doesn't seem to see what we see, and what really disturbs me is that she might in the end agree to marry Sam because he can't see her. You know what I mean?'

'Surely she wouldn't do that?'

'She just might, Pol,' Marion said. 'And that ain't really a good enough reason to go into a marriage that will have to last a lifetime.'

Sam's parents felt the same way as Marion did when he told them that he intended to marry Sarah.

'Married?' said his mother in disbelief.

Sam heard the tone in his mother's voice and he said almost defensively, 'I have been writing to her for over two years, and Peggy has told you who she is.'

'I know that, son,' his father said. 'But things have changed for you.'

'D'you think I don't know that?'

'Well,' said his mother, 'd'you think you're being fair to the girl?'

'Sarah is no fool,' Sam cried desperately. 'She knows what she's doing.'

'Does she?' his mother asked. 'I thought she wasn't yet twenty.'

The words hung in the air and Sam's parents saw the sudden sag of Sam's shoulders. How could he ask Sarah to throw her life away looking after him? She thought he deserved better when her face was scarred and disfigured, and she certainly deserved better than spending her life playing nursemaid to a blind man.

His father spoke into the silence. 'Was there any understanding between you? Any promises made?'

Sam remembered the declarations of love that they had both made just the previous day and yet he shook his head.

'So no harm done then,' Sam's father said, relieved. 'You'll just have to explain to her.'

No harm done, Sam thought, when I feel as if my heart is shattered. But this is no time to think about myself. If I love Sarah then I must release her. 'Tomorrow,' he said, struggling against the tears that threatened to overwhelm him, 'I was going to ask Sarah to be my wife.'

'And now?'

'Now I see how unfair I am being.' Sam felt as if the words were being dragged out of him. 'I will try and make her see that.'

Sam felt really upset when his parents had left and Peggy, who went in to see him afterwards, saw tears glistening in his eyes and could have wept herself as he told her what he had to do.

'Don't tell her, Peg, will you? This must come from me.'

'I'll not tell her, never fear,' Peggy said. 'But have you thought what you're doing? You will break her heart.'

Sam sighed. 'All I know at the moment is that it hurts like hell, and yet I know it's the right decision. I am releasing Sarah to seek a better life for herself.'

'And what if she doesn't want one? And what about your life?'

'She must be made to see that parting is the best thing for her,' Sam said. 'As for me, I'll only have half a life from now on and that hardly matters.'

Peggy thought he was making a big mistake, but she couldn't dissuade him, though she tried over and over. However, Peter and Daisy were also waiting to see their big brother before visiting time was over and in the end she had no option but to kiss Sam on the cheek and leave him.

When Sarah got to Sam's ward on Monday afternoon she found him in a very pensive mood, but she told herself that he was bound to have off days. Blindness was a lot to come to terms with. And so she sat down by the bed and took hold of his hand as she said, 'Come on, now, I did all the talking on Saturday and now it's your turn.'

Sam heard the laughter in Sarah's voice but his remained grave as he said, 'I've been doing a lot of thinking since then.'

Still in a jocular tone, Sarah said, 'Oh, you don't want to do too much of that kind of thing. Hurts your head, too much thinking.'

'I'm being serious, Sarah,' Sam said. 'It was lovely that you came to see me on Saturday. No, what am I saying? It was more than just lovely, it was amazing, terrific, and I know now that I love you dearly and for that reason I cannot let you throw your life away.'

A cold feeling washed over Sarah and wiped the smile from her face as she asked, 'And how exactly am I doing that?'

'Sarah, I am blind.'

'I knew that on Saturday,' Sarah said. 'Nothing has changed.'

'Everything has changed,' Sam said. 'Can't you understand that? We can have no future together.'

Sarah gasped, 'What are you saying?'

'You know what I'm saying,' Sam said almost harshly. 'Don't make me spell it out, for Christ's sake.'

'Do I get no say in any of this?'

'No, because you are young,' Sam said. 'You would not be totally aware of what you'd be taking on.'

'Yes I would.'

'In time you would begin to resent me.'

'No, I should never do that,' Sarah said. 'We have shared a special relationship for almost three years.'

'And now it is at an end.'

'Oh God, you really mean it.' Sarah was having trouble drawing breath and she felt as if her heart had been shattered into a million pieces. And then she suddenly pulled her hands away from Sam's and got to her feet. 'It's my face, isn't it? Whatever you said to me on Saturday you, Sam Wagstaffe, aren't man enough to cope with a disfigured wife.'

'Sarah, it's nothing to do with your face at all,' Sam cried. 'It isn't even to do with you. The problem is mine.'

Sarah was too distressed to hear anything more, however, and from the door she said, 'Goodbye, Sam,' before fleeing down the corridor.

Afterwards, Sarah remembered walking for hours and hours sobbing until she was awash with tears and yet unable to stop because she didn't know how she would bear this unhappiness and despair. Shafts of pain seemed to pierce her heart and still she trudged on and on till her feet burned.

Eventually, when she had cried herself out and she was a little calmer she wondered what to do and realised she would have to make for home. She didn't really care what happened to her any more, but she knew that her family would worry if she didn't go home, and one way and another she had put them through enough already. This was a pain that she would have to learn to live with, to go through life with this ache in her heart.

However, darkness had descended to blur the streets and she had no idea where she was or how to get to the train station. At last she came upon a road she could just make out was called High Street, and she walked along that hoping that it might lead to Sutton Coldfield town. Eventually she came out at the top of a hill. In the dank and murky darkness she saw a large church to her left-hand side and remembered walking past it earlier that day. Then she knew the station was halfway down the hill and to the right.

It was a busy station, for all it was only small, and there were a good many people waiting for the train. Sarah hid herself as far as possible in the shadows. She felt desolation fill all her being as her vision of the future unfolded in her mind's eye and she bit her lip to prevent crying out against it. Never had she been more grateful for the concealing veil on her mother's hat that hid her ravaged face and wretched eyes from the curious, both in the station and later in the train when it had been impossible to get a carriage to herself.

In Albert Road, Marion looked out of the bedroom window for the umpteenth time that evening before returning to the living room. Everyone looked up as she entered but she shook her head. 'No sign. Where on earth could she be?'

Peggy was more worried than anyone because she knew what her brother would have said to Sarah that day, and how upset Sarah would be. Her innards were gripped by fear. Surely Sarah wouldn't do anything silly. She was a sensible girl, but everyone had their breaking point. Peggy didn't think it would help anyone to share the burden of her knowledge and so when Sarah's key was heard opening the door a few minutes later, her relief matched Marion's and she let out a sigh as Marion opened the door to the hall.

'Where have you been?' Marion asked sharply,

because she had been very worried. Then her voice changed. 'What ails you?'

Peggy sprang to her side to see Sarah lurching from in the hall as if she were drunk and Peggy leaped forward to help her.

'Oh, Peggy,' Sarah cried and even her voice tore at the older girl's heartstrings as she fell into her arms in a dead faint.

With March nearly over and spring fast approaching, Sarah didn't seem to be improving at all. Although she no longer covered her face from the family and didn't hide away in her room she grew more silent than ever. In that austere spring, as the war drew agonisingly slowly to a close, and food was as hard as ever to obtain, Sarah ate less than a bird. It was impossible to find tasty things to tempt her and she grew desperately thin so that her clothes hung on her and her sorrow-filled eyes looked huge in her gaunt white face, the blue smudges beneath them evidence of her disturbed nights.

The twins could have told their mother of the anguished moans Sarah sometimes made when she managed to doze off and the nights she sobbed until her pillow was damp. But they were not sneaks. They knew what she was fretting about, and thought it very bad of Sam not to want to marry their Sarah.

'I don't blame her crying about it,' Missie said one day as she and Magda made their way to school.

'Nor me,' Magda said. 'Don't think we should tell Mom, though.'

'No,' Missie said. 'If Sarah ain't saying nothing then I don't think we should.'

But Marion didn't need the twins telling her exactly how upset Sarah was because it was apparent. Eventually she sought the advice of her sister.

'Don't know why you're all at sixes and sevens about it, anyroad,' Polly said. 'In your heart of hearts, this is the outcome that you wanted.'

Marion didn't deny it. 'All right, maybe I did deep down, but I just didn't think our Sarah would be so upset.'

'Why on earth not?' Polly said. 'She loved Sam, wanted to marry him, despite his disability. She told you that much. What did you expect her to do, go and dance a jig up the High Street?'

'No, but . . . oh, I don't know. Course she thinks her disfigured face put him off.'

'Why would it?' Polly said. 'I mean, quite apart from anything else, he can't see what she looks like.'

'I know, but she told Peggy that first day when she came round, like, that the men sharing his ward had been describing her face to Sam, taking the mickey and that, and it put him off. Peggy said, though, she couldn't see that ever happening. There are so many badly wounded and damaged servicemen there, no one would mock anyone else. They'd probably know that Sarah's injuries were due to some explosion or other.'

'So why did he finish it?'

Marion spread her hands helplessly. 'Peggy told me that it was her parents, who I suppose thought as I did, and told Sam that he would tie her down, that she would be throwing her life away, you know, the sort of things I said to you. The truth is that, probably for the best intentions, Sam's parents succeeded in tearing apart Sam and Sarah and I don't know that Sarah will ever get over it. I daren't even speak the man's name, and she is so cold with Peggy. Now she never speaks to her unless it's absolutely necessary. I suppose it's because Peggy is a link to Sam, who she is trying to rub out of her life, but it makes the atmosphere difficult at home.'

The only one Peggy could speak to about her brother was Violet, so Violet knew although Sam was improving physically, emotionally he was suffering just as much as Sarah. On Good Friday, as the forge was closed for Easter, Peggy had fitted in an extra visit to Sam and found him very despondent.

'I mean, all the shrapnel is out now, and to all intents and purposes he is recovering,' she told Violet, 'but the flashbacks and nightmares I told you about have got steadily worse, and he has even done a bit of sleepwalking. After Mom and Dad visited last Sunday he had to be moved into a private room to avoid disturbing the other patients, and where he could be watched more closely.'

'Ah, Peg, I'm really sorry for you.'

'He told me today he thinks his life is over,' Peggy said. 'He said he can't see the point of going on. Tell you the truth, I'm dreading going to see him again tomorrow.'

'D'you want me to come with you?'

'I would welcome it, Vi, but I never know how Sam is going to be, so better not.'

So Peggy went alone to see her brother. She had just entered the hospital when the doctor called her into the office.

'Your brother's fellow patients told one of the nurses the other day about words your brother had with a young lady just before the nightmares began again. Was it that she couldn't go on with the relationship because he is blind?'

'It was almost the exact opposite to that,' Peggy said. 'Sarah would have had no trouble accepting Sam's blindness, but my parents thought that he should release her to find someone else and convinced him it was the right thing to do.'

'And did she want to be released?'

Peggy gave a definite shake of her head. 'She is broken-hearted. And you say Sam is . . .'

'Without putting too fine a point on it, my dear, your brother's mental balance is beginning to worry me,' the doctor said. 'Of course it must be the decision of the young people themselves, but I would say that he needs that young lady more than ever.'

Peggy soon saw how ill Sam had become. He would start a sentence and lose the thread of it, lose concentration as he jumped from one subject to another, and his agitated manner worried her greatly. Peggy was angry with her parents for coercing Sam into finishing with Sarah. All the way home she thought of her beloved brother and the sadness that seemed to surround him, and Sarah, who was filled with heartache, and decided that enough was enough.

'D'you think I should talk to her, tell her how he is?' she asked Violet.

'Course I do,' Violet said. 'Don't know why you let it get to this stage in the first place.' And then she added, 'Tell you what, if it was Richard I'd do whatever it took.'

Peggy stared at her. 'You and Richard? I thought you were just friends?

'We were when we started writing to one another but I like him even more now I've been writing for a while, of course, I haven't seen him for ages. After the war we'll see . . . But Sam and Sarah are made for each other. It's as plain on the nose on your face.'

'So you think I should talk to Sarah?'

'Yes, I do,' Violet said. 'The sooner the better. And it has to be up to Sarah because Sam can hardly come tripping down to see her.'

So immediately, before she got cold feet, Peggy sought Sarah out. She was in the kitchen helping her mother prepare the evening meal and when Peggy asked if she could talk to her, she saw the wary look flood across her face.

'Talk away,' she said.

'I mean in private,' Peggy said, and her eyes sought Marion's over Sarah's bent head.

So when Sarah said, 'I must help my mother,' Marion said, 'It's virtually done now, just needs to be put in the oven. Go and see what Peggy wants.'

There was nowhere private but the room Sarah shared with the twins, and Sarah followed Peggy up there reluctantly and, once inside, with the door shut, said ungraciously, 'What do you want anyroad?'

'I wanted to ask you how much you love my brother?'

Sarah said stiffly, 'I don't want to talk about that.'

'You must, because both you and Sam are pining for one another.'

'Sam is?'

'I'll say he is.'

'Then why . . .?'

'He thought that he was giving you your freedom to look for another, and my parents helped him reach that decision.'

'It isn't to do with the way I look?'

'Of course not, nothing at all to do with your face.'

Peggy saw Sarah give a deep sigh. 'Peggy, I don't want anyone else.'

'I know.'

'But that hardly matters because he finished with me, so what's the point of all this?'

'Well, if I loved a man like you so obviously love Sam, I would fight for him.'

'And how do you suggest I do that?'

'You could start with a letter telling him exactly how you feel about him.'

'After what he said to me you expect me to—'

'Sarah, he's ill,' Peggy said. 'He doesn't know how much he wants you, but he does need you and the doctor has said that himself.'

'What do you mean, he's ill?'

'He is having flashbacks about the war and nightmares, and now he has begun sleepwalking.'

Sarah remembered her father having that awful nightmare that woke her and the twins not long after he came home from the hospital, and that Mom said he was helped by talking it over with their uncle Pat. She said, 'He doesn't need me, but he will probably be helped by talking it over with someone.'

'Yeah, like you.'

'Not necessarily.'

'The doctor said he needs you,' Peggy said, 'and I would say that he knows what he's talking about.'

'A letter, you said,' Sarah said grudgingly. 'And what good is a letter to a blind man?'

'One of the nurses will read it to him,' Peggy said assuredly. 'I've seen them do that for other patients.'

'That cuts out our writing really personal stuff, like about feelings and that.'

'Will you just write the letter? If you post it

today, even with the Easter Holiday it should reach him by Tuesday.'

'I'll write it,' said Sarah. 'But I don't hold out much hope it will make any difference.'

She began that evening before the twins were sent to bed, and though she hadn't intended the letter to be too intimate and personal because a nurse would be reading it to Sam, once she began the words flowed out like a stream.

She told him of the way her stomach contracted when she just spoke his name, and of the butterflies in her stomach when she'd read his letters, and how the endearments he used often caused the breath to stop in her throat. She told him that she remembered every minute of the first visit he had made to their house and, despite being so young, she believed she had loved him from the first moment she had seen him. That love had deepened when she'd met him again when she was sixteen, and then the letters he wrote just made her love him even more.

She went on to say that when she saw him in the hospital bed, even knowing he was blind made no difference to the way that she felt about him. She would always love him, heart, body and soul till the breath left her body. In fact, she said, she didn't think she could live without him.

TWENTY-SEVEN

The nurses were surprised when Sam received a letter.

'Maybe from someone who doesn't know he's blind,' one suggested.

'Maybe,' another said. 'Anyroad, whoever it's from he'll have to know about it and one of us will probably have to read it to him.'

'I'll do that if you like,' said the first nurse. 'I feel quite sorry for him, to tell the truth.'

'Who's it from?' Sam asked later as the nurse told him he had had a letter delivered that morning.

'I don't know,' she said. 'I haven't opened it yet. Do you want me to do that and read it to you?'

'Please.'

The nurse slit the envelope and withdrew the letter. 'It's from someone called Sarah.'

Sam stiffened on the bed and said through tightened lips, 'I don't want to hear it.'

However, the nurse had scanned the letter and she said to Sam, 'Oh, Mr Wagstaffe, I really think you should hear what she has to say.'

Sam clenched his hands into fists and, through tightened lips and with tremendous trepidation, said, 'Go on then.'

The nurse began tentatively and then grew in confidence. The love that that girl had for Sam Wagstaffe could be lifted off the pages. The words tore into Sam's heart and even the nurse began to cry. When she finished, she crushed the letter to her heart as she said brokenly, 'If I was you, Mr Wagstaffe, I wouldn't let that girl go, because a love like that only comes once in a lifetime.'

For a moment Sam couldn't speak. He struggled to control his shuddering sobs and was aware of tears seeping from his eyes and soaking the dressings covering them. In the end, the nurse, against all regulations, put her arms around him, and when he was calmer and able to speak he said, 'I need to send a telegram.'

'I'll see to it,' the nurse promised.

Later that day a telegraph boy knocked on the Whittakers' door. Only Marion and Sarah were at home, and Marion gave a cry of distress and her hand flew to her mouth when she opened the door and saw the boy there. Sarah, alerted by her mother's cry, had followed her into the hall, her face blanched with fear as her mother took the telegram with trembling fingers.

'It's for you, Sarah,' she said, and Sarah, greatly puzzled, ripped it open. There were only four words: 'PLEASE COME. LOVE SAM.'

Sarah's face was a beam of happiness as the telegraph boy said, 'Is there any reply?'

'No, no reply,' Sarah said, and she shut the door and leaned against it with a sigh of happiness.

'I must go to him,' she said to her mother as she led the way to the living room. 'You must see that?'

'Of course I see,' Marion said. 'I'm not a monster, Sarah. The only reservation I had was because I didn't want you to saddle yourself with a blind man, but I would rather you be with someone of your choosing, whatever his disability, than someone you didn't care for.'

'I would never marry a man I didn't care for,' Sarah said. 'And without Sam my life is meaningless.'

'Then your place is with him.'

'But I won't be able to see him until tomorrow because visiting will be over for today,' Sarah said. 'Oh, Mom, how will I manage waiting until then?'

'I don't know,' Marion said. 'Except by reminding yourself that you have the rest of your lives in front of you.'

'Maybe,' Sarah said. 'I wrote to him, you know?'

'Did you?'

'Peggy sort of asked me to after she went to see Sam last Saturday,' Sarah said. 'She said that he has begun having nightmares and flashbacks and even started sleepwalking. Peggy suggested that I write and tell him how I really feel about him.'

'Ah, these men sometimes suffer far too much,'

Marion said with sympathy. 'I remember your father when he came home to convalesce.'

'So do I,' Sarah said. 'Anyroad, I'll go and see how things are between us, but until then I'd like to keep this telegram a secret, just till tomorrow.'

Marion looked at her anxious daughter, biting her bottom lip in consternation, and with a smile she said, 'What telegram was that, then?'

Sarah was full of trepidation as she made her way to the hospital the next day. She had told no one and so Peggy had not been able to prepare her for what Sam looked like now that all the poking about in his body for shrapnel had been done. His face in particular was pitted and scarred, and his unseeing eyes, now uncovered, were a little unnerving.

When Sarah went through the gates of the hospital she saw that some of the inmates had taken advantage of the good weather and were in the grounds, and she tried to hide her shock at the terrible injuries many men were sporting. There were plenty disfigured in some way, and others with missing limbs walking with crutches, or in wheelchairs, being wheeled in the sunshine by nurses. She also saw a blind servicemen being led outside by a less damaged companion, but there was no sign of Sam.

Peggy had told her how to get to Sam's room and she saw he was aware of her as soon as she stepped inside and he turned his head.

'Sarah?'

She looked at him sitting on the chair beside

his bed and saw the number of red, angry-looking pockmarks and blemishes marring his lovely face.

'What are you doing?' he asked into the silence.

'Studying your face,' Sarah said truthfully, as she crossed the room to sit in the chair placed ready beside him.

'Is it hideous?' Sam asked almost fearfully.

Sarah heard the tone and understood it and so she answered nonchalantly. 'No, it's not bad at all. Looks sore, though.'

'It is a bit, though it's better that they're all out,' Sam said. 'They say I'll look better than this when the scars are all fully healed and start to weather in.'

'Hospitals love those words "weather in",' Sarah said, and let her eyes meet Sam's. It was hard to believe that he could see nothing, for those dark brown eyes looked just as she remembered them. She felt so sorry for him that never again would he see the world around him, nor would his eyes sparkle as they used when he laughed or smiled. But she kept those sad remembrances to herself. What she said instead was, 'Mind you, they sometimes get it right. My face definitely looks better than it did.'

Sam fumbled for Sarah's hand and, when she grasped it, he said hoarsely, 'I prayed you would come.'

'Of course I would come when you asked me to,' she said with a smile. 'Even if your manner of summons did almost send my mother into an apoplectic fit.'

Sam gave a rueful smile because he could well understand why the sight of the telegraph boy would strike fear into a person's heart. 'I'm sorry, I couldn't think of any other way of contacting you quickly. I needed to know if you meant all those things you wrote in that letter.'

'Every word.'

'I don't know what the future holds for me.'

'None of us knows what the future holds,' Sarah said. 'And maybe it's as well. But whatever the future, isn't it better to face it together?'

'Are you sure? Absolutely sure?'

'Yes I am. Of course I am.'

Sam's voice was still full of doubt. 'You're very young. My parents pointed that out to me as well.'

'Does that mean that I feel any less?'

'No,' Sam said. 'I don't mean that, but I am many years older than you. I'm twenty-seven.'

'Well, neither of us can help that.'

'No, I know.'

'Sam, will you stop fretting?' Sarah said. She leaned forward and gently touched his lips with hers before saying, 'Old or young, blind or not, none of this matters. What does matter is the love I have for you that is unshakeable. You talk of the future – well, mine is meaningless without you in it. If I lost you, as I thought I had, I didn't really care what happened to me then. I didn't really want to go on.'

'Neither did I,' Sam admitted. 'I felt that I was doing the right thing for you. But when you were gone from me my life seemed futile and I began to wonder why I'd been spared in that explosion. I was the only one, you know.'

'Were you?' Sarah's voice was sympathetic. 'That must have been hard to take.'

'It was hard to cope with the fact that they were dead at all,' Sam said. 'I know that all soldiers are at risk, but we had been through so much and we were a tight group, just six of us and such good mates. Do you remember the roses I sent you?'

'Of course.'

'Well, they came from one of those men. See, all my mates felt sorry for me when I explained what had happened to you. One of them was having a pleasant little dalliance with a florist in Dover, and when he told her about us and what had happened to you he asked her if she could help and she donated ten red roses from her private stock.'

'How kind of her,' Sarah said. 'They were the most beautiful roses. And how lovely of him to think to ask her.'

'That's the kind of men they were – kind and generous, every one of them – and we were laughing and joking just minutes before and then, bang, and five men lay dead.'

'What happened to you?'

'I was a little to the side and that probably saved my life,' Sam said. 'I was knocked unconscious, though, and fell into a pit. It was assumed I was dead and might have been if I had lain on the frozen ground much longer. It was the soldier detailed to remove the dog tags from the others that noticed I was breathing. I knew none of this, of course. First I knew, I was in some field hospital wrapped up like a mummy and shouting like a lunatic.'

'Was that because you couldn't see?'

'I didn't know I couldn't see then,' Sam said. 'The shrapnel hit my eyes, but there was a lot of blood in and around the eyes and so they had pads on them. No, it was because of the memories pulsating through my brain. It was when they were changing the pads that I realised I couldn't see either.'

'That must have been a shock.'

'It was. But in a way I felt almost guilty that I had survived. Because I'm blind I can do nothing to fill my time, to try and forget, even for a short time, what has happened. And I'm afraid to go to sleep because of those horrific nightmares. I mean, D-Day, the invasion, was hailed as a success and I know it had to be done, but the cost in human life was colossal.'

'Was it very bad?'

'Bad enough.'

'Tell me?'

Sam shook his head. 'No. You don't want to know.'

'I want to know anything that involves you,' Sarah said. 'Don't you know that?' And then she grasped his hand tighter and urged gently, 'Tell me, please?'

When Sam began to talk about nearing France that morning in the landing craft with the bombers circling overhead and the machine battery pounding them from the beaches, Sarah remembered how her aunt Polly said once he must be an Irishman underneath because he was a born story-teller, and he was doing it again, painting pictures in Sarah's head.

She saw in her mind's eye Allies blown out of the water before they had even reached the beaches their bodies, or sometimes only parts of bodies, floating in the water, one a man that Sam had shared a cigarette with before they had set out. She heard the mournful tone in Sam's voice as he told her of the planes wheeling and diving, flak flying everywhere as the RAF sought to protect the hundreds of men trying to make their way through the water to the beaches with their guns raised about their heads. They were facing the clatter of machine guns, the booming guns on the ships, the whine of bullets and the crump and crash of the exploding bombs.

'It sounds like hell on earth,' Sarah said. 'It must have been dreadful.'

'Maybe I shouldn't have told you so much.'

'Oh, no. I think that you did exactly the right thing and I feel privileged that you did.'

'I've been having those terrible nightmares again recently,' Sam said. 'That's why I'm in a private room, but I suppose Peggy told you this?'

'She did, and I'm not surprised. But now I'm

here and you can unburden yourself.' And she heard Sam sigh as he put his arms around her.

'Your father would never tell me things like that,' Marion said to Sarah later that evening as they sat around the table and she had told the family where she had been and some of the things Sam had shared with her that afternoon about his impression of D-Day.

'Sam hasn't got anyone else,' Sarah said. 'There is no handy Uncle Pat to take him for a drink.'

'And he would never burden Mom and Dad,' Peggy said. 'Nor me either when I only really get to see him on Saturday, and sometimes Sunday when I share him with everyone else.'

'Don't you mind hearing it all, Sarah?' Magda asked.

'It is harrowing listening to it,' she admitted, 'but then I tell myself that Sam actually experienced it, and that has to be far worse. I am going to write down what he tells me while the memories are still fresh in my mind because he tells them in such a vivid way I could see all he was describing in my head almost like snapshots. I shall try to recapture that style when I write his accounts down because what he has seen and experienced should never be forgotten.'

The following day, Sarah took a notebook to hospital. Sam was more than pleased to have her visit.

'Ah, Sarah,' he said with a sigh, and he kissed her lips. 'You are good for me. I slept like a top last night.'

'That's maybe because you talked about the things getting between you and sleep.'

'You could be right.'

'Well, it's just that sharing his troubles helped my father. Uncle Pat took him for a drink and got him to talk about the things haunting him because he wouldn't discuss them with Mom.'

'And I worry about telling you.'

'Don't,' Sarah said reassuringly. 'I have broad shoulders. Anyway, it was different for Mom because when Dad was better, he had to go back into the fray. You won't have to. For you, the war is over.'

'I should think it will soon be over for everyone.' Sam said. 'We were in Germany by January and it's the fifth of April today. Anyone but Hitler would have surrendered by now.'

'He'll never surrender, not him.'

'In a way I hope he doesn't. Then I'll take great pleasure in hearing that he has been hanged by the neck from a very long rope.'

'That will please a lot of people,' Sarah said with a laugh. 'But how did the ordinary German people treat you when you reached their country?'

'They were very subdued,' Sam said. 'Can't blame them, I suppose. They knew they were on a losing wicket; totally different to the attitude in France . . .' And he was off again and Sarah felt

513

as if she were one of the French, lining the streets, cheering a welcome to the advancing Allies freeing them at last.

'There was so much relief,' Sam said. 'Some of them were nearly starving. The military handed out chocolates and sweets to the children.' He smiled. 'You should have seen their faces. And we had tins of meat for the adults. Those were the good experiences, the ones you keep in your head to remind yourself what you're fighting for.'

'I can see that.'

'Now, enough of this war talk,' Sam said. 'You and I need to talk about things.'

'What sort of things?'

'Well, the first thing is this,' Sam said, and he slipped off his chair and onto his knees on the floor.

'Sam!' Sarah cried, alarmed. 'What are you doing?'

'Damn this blindness,' Sam said. 'I'm trying to get on one knee to propose to you and I'm not sure that I'll be able to balance.'

'Oh, is that all?' said Sarah, with a giggle as she kneeled down beside him and put her arms around him. 'That's the conventional way of doing things. Let's be a little bit different. Now what did you want to ask me?'

Even Sam smiled. 'You are great, Sarah. Do you know that?'

'Yes,' said Sarah cockily, 'though it is nice to be told on a fairly regular basis. But I'm sure that wasn't what you were going to say.'

'No, it wasn't,' Sam said with a laugh. Then he said, 'Sarah Whittaker, will you do me the honour of becoming my wife?'

'Yes, yes, and a thousand times yes,' Sarah said, and the passion of their first real kiss took them both by surprise and nearly had them both over-balancing onto the floor.

Flushed and slightly breathless, Sarah helped Sam back on to his seat and he said, 'I'm not the same religion as yourself. Will that matter?'

'Not to me.'

'But your mother? The priest?'

'Mom has always known you aren't a Catholic, but I don't think she sees that as a major problem.'

'Will the priest have something to say?'

'Undoubtedly. He has an opinion on anything and everything, and his views are usually at vari-ance with everybody else's, but Mom can cope with him. She did it before when Richard missed Mass when he had been out fighting the fires the night before in the Blitz, and she will do it for me. She was more worried about your blindness.'

'Did she think you were throwing your life away, like mine did?'

'Maybe a bit at first,' Sarah admitted. 'Though I think she was mainly concerned with how I'd cope and that. But then she said to me that she would much rather I marry a man of my own choosing. That's when I told her that my life would be nothing without you in it, and then she sort of sent her blessing to both of us.'

Sam sighed. 'That's a big relief. But I still think that we must wait for the war to be over before we can plan our wedding.'

'That could be ages,' Sarah protested. 'Why must we?'

'It won't be that long,' Sam said. 'Really, it can't now, and we must do this right. I must have your father's permission.'

'We could write to him.'

'We could, but no father worth his salt is going to give a blind serviceman he has never met permission to marry his daughter, especially when there is no reason for haste. It might be different if I were being posted somewhere, but we have all the time in the world.'

'And you have your Captain Sensible hat on.'

Sam laughed. 'If you like. One of us has to. And,' he continued, adopting a mock pompous tone, 'you still have the impetuousness of youth.'

'Yes, and this impetuous youth might just brain you in a minute.'

'Don't do that,' Sam said. 'This is much nicer,' and he took hold of Sarah's hand and pulled her onto his knee, and this time when their lips met it was as if a fire had been lit inside them and they gave themselves up to the pleasure of it.

Sarah came home ecstatically happy to find that no one was a bit surprised at her news, though Peggy said, 'Doesn't mean we are any the less pleased just because it was semi-expected.' And then she kissed Sarah and added, 'And there is no one I'd rather have as a sister.'

'And you'll be good for Sam, and make him happy, because you're made for one another,' Violet said.

'I'm so glad that you came to live with us,' Sarah said, catching up the hands of both girls.

'Many times I have said that,' Marion said. 'And we'll all miss you when you're gone.'

'We might not be gone very far, though,' Peggy said.

'I thought you would be going back home?'

'There's nothing for us there,' Violet said. 'Anyroad, we like it here. I mean, I know that we will have to leave the drop forge. There's little enough to do there now, and the men coming back will likely want their old jobs back And we know too that we'll be competing with returning servicemen and -women for anything else, but we still think we've a better chance of getting something here than back home.'

'The only stumbling block was finding somewhere to stay,' Peggy said. 'Then last Sunday, when you were washing up in the kitchen, your dad said we could stay with him,' Violet said. 'He has that big attic and that would suit us down to the ground. We'd be company for him too.'

'Oh, you're right, that would be just perfect!' Marion cried. She knew that the girls would look after her father as well, and as he got older she did worry about him living alone. 'But,' she said, 'my father's house is only back-to-back. It opens directly onto the street, but there's no indoor toilet, and no bathroom at all.'

Peggy laughed. 'And what sort of house did you think we had in the country? Lap of luxury, this was to us, when we came here. But whatever job we get we won't be getting the money we got in the drop forge and so we'd have to find a cheaper place than this. Anyroad, you'll want your own house back when Bill and Richard come home.'

'Just now, though, we have a wedding to plan,' Marion said, putting her arm around her daughter. 'I am so happy for you.'

'Are you really, Mom?'

'Yes,' Marion said emphatically. 'That isn't to say I won't worry about you, or wish both for your sake and his that Sam wasn't blind. I won't tell you either that love conquers all, because it wouldn't be true. Sometimes marriage has to be worked at. But I will say that neither are you happy apart from one another. You belong together and so I'm happy for both of you.'

'I am so glad about that,' Sarah said. 'There is no rush to plan anything, though, because Sam says he has to ask Dad's permission, and in person.'

Marion laughed. 'So why the long face? It's the way things are done. It just shows that Sam has manners.'

'Mom, we don't even know when the war will end, never mind when Dad will be demobbed.'

'Well, that's just the way things are,' Marion said with a shrug.

'And meanwhile you can write down Sam's memoirs,' said Peggy with a laugh.

'Plenty of time to do that, though,' Sarah said, ''cos I can't visit tomorrow.'

'Oh, yes,' Peggy said. 'They're doing some work on his eyes.'

'Seeing if there's any point in operating, is how Sam put it,' Sarah said. 'It's all to do with how much of the cornea was burned off in the explosion.'

'Nice if he could see something, however slight?'

'It would be great,' Sarah said. 'I think he just doesn't want to get his hopes up.'

'Mind you, you haven't got many notes written,' Violet said, skimming through the notebook that Sarah had tossed on the settee.

'I don't need it really,' Sarah said. 'I only take the notebook in case Sam says something specific so that I would be accurate. When Sam is telling me something I become so engrossed that I would probably forget to take notes anyway, but I don't forget what he says 'cos it sort of becomes engrained on my mind. Like, the other day, he was telling me about liberating the French towns and that, but today he said outside of the towns the roads are often booby-trapped with land mines, or there could be snipers placed to pick them off one by one.

'Just before the explosion he was talking to one man who was really shaken up. He was a despatch rider. They have motor bikes and are used like scouts to check the roads and areas ahead, often working in twos. Well, this man and his mate were riding along through a German forest and, before retreating, the Germans had stretched thin wire between two trees on either side of the road and it had sliced this man's mate's head clean off. He managed to duck in time.'

'Ugh, that's horrible.'

'It is, and not likely to be easily forgotten.'

'So are you going to write that down?'

'Yeah,' Sarah said. 'I'm going to write down everything he tells me as long as he doesn't mind.'

When Sam told Sarah and Peggy that the doctor said there was no point in doing any operation or further treatment for his eyes, Sarah was sad for him and thought it was wise of him not to have raised his hopes up. Peggy, however, knew her brother well and guessed that wasn't the whole story, but that he would say nothing unless she got him on her own.

He was tickled pink, however, that Sarah had written down the things he had told her about.

'So you don't mind at all?' Sarah asked.

'Mind? Why should I mind? I think it's a jolly good idea to have some form of record. One day I hope we might have children. If my son should ask me what I did in the war I can show him what you've written down. No, you go ahead with it if you want to.'

Sarah was glad to hear that assurance from Sam though his reference to children embarrassed her a little in front of Peggy. But she told herself not to be so silly and the rest of the visit passed off really well. Peggy thought Sam nearly back to his old self and, despite his blindness, looked better than she had ever seen him. She left about fifteen minutes before the end of visiting time to give Sam and Sarah time alone, but she still wondered what the doctor had actually said to Sam. There had been no opportunity to ask him, and she never got much time with him on Sundays. She would have to have patience but she was determined to get the truth out of him at the first opportunity.

The doctor popped in to see Sam that day just after the women left, and he picked up the hand-written pages Sarah had left and asked what they were.

'Sarah asked me to talk about my war experiences when my sister told her about those horrific nightmares and flashbacks I was having,' Sam said. 'She thought it might help because when her father was traumatised after being rescued from Dunkirk, talking his experience through with a relative eased his nightmares.'

'Well, something has helped yours, all right,' the doctor said, 'because they were becoming a nightly, sometimes a twice nightly, experience and you haven't had one at all for a few days.'

Sam grinned. 'I know. I've been sleeping like the proverbial baby.'

'I'm glad you made it up with your girl anyway,' the doctor said. 'You had words, didn't you?'

'How do you know that?'

'Oh, no secrets here,' the doctor said. 'Some of the others on the ward told one of the nurses, and they told me.'

'Well, it was me being stupid,' Sam said. 'And I was so miserable without her that I often wished I had died alongside my companions. It was Sarah writing to me that brought me to my senses and now I have asked her to marry me and she said yes.'

'Oh, congratulations,' said the doctor. 'That's wonderful news.' And he remembered Sam's sister saying that the girl that Sam had once thrown over would not care a whit that he was blind. It seemed she was absolutely right.

'Course, we can't make plans to marry yet,' Sam said. 'I want to do the job right and ask her father's permission, and he's in the Forces.'

'Will he give it?'

Sam made a face. 'I don't know. He's bound to have misgivings, as any father would, and that's another reason why I want to become as independent as possible before I leave here. Being blind is a bugger, and I don't want Sarah having to run around after me. I want a wife, not a nursemaid, and I want her father to see that too. As to the future, well, I don't know what's going to happen there.'

'Then you are in the same boat as the rest of us,' the doctor said. 'But in the meantime your Sarah has written down your experiences very well.'

'She said when I told her things it sort of painted pictures in her head,' Sam said. 'And she tried to remember exactly what I said so that it was my voice and not hers. She just said she thought things that I'd experienced shouldn't be forgotten.'

'She's right,' the doctor said. 'And I have an idea. I have a man in here who has lost both legs and he's very depressed.'

'Understandable, I'd say,' Sam said. 'Poor sod!'

'Of course it's understandable,' the doctor said, 'but unless his depression is controlled, he will never recover totally. His wife told me, though, that he used to be a really good artist, just pen and-ink stuff, but I haven't been able to get him interested enough to do anything. If you don't mind, I'll get these typed up and give them to him to read, and see if that will stimulate him. The starkness of pen and ink will be the perfect background to the things you describe.'

'Do what you like, Doc,' Sam said. 'And if it helps the poor bugger, all to the good.'

TWENTY-EIGHT

Sam said nothing to Sarah about the doctor's proposal, thinking it might fizzle out to nothing in the end. As part of his own therapy over the following week he explained many battles to her and even told her his own account of Dunkirk. Sarah became dearer to him as each day passed and he was glad that his parents eventually realised that.

By Saturday Sarah had saved some of her sweet coupons to buy some bull's-eyes for Sam as Peggy said they were his favourite. Not finding them in Aston, they decided to look in Sutton Coldfield before making their way to the hospital. Peggy glanced at her watch. 'It's nearly the start of visiting time,' she said. 'Shall I go up to the hospital and keep Sam company till you get there?'

Sarah knew that Sam hated her being late. It was hard for him to pass the time and he looked forward to her visits, she knew, but then Peggy got little enough time with him on her own and so she said, 'Yes, if you like, Peggy. Tell him I'll be up as soon as possible.'

It was the opportunity that Peggy wanted and she hurried as fast as she could to the hospital.

'Where's Sarah?' Sam asked when he realised his sister was there alone.

'Buying sweets for you,' Peggy said, 'so we haven't got long. She'll be here in a minute, so tell me quick, what did the doctor really say about your eyes?'

'God, Peg! Are you some sort of witch?'

'No, I'm just a concerned sister who knows you very well.'

'Well, the whole thing was absolutely bizarre,' Sam said. 'Apparently, there's nothing wrong with my corneas at all.'

'Then what . . .?'

'I know, I'm really as confused as you,' Sam said. He ran his fingers through his hair, a sure sign that he was puzzled. 'The doctor said it was something they call hysterical blindness. I tell you, I wasn't very pleased. It sounded as if I was making it up. Either that, or I had some form of madness. I mean, hysterical, I ask you?'

'What does it mean?'

'Well, he said it was something that happens sometimes after a great shock or trauma. But whichever way you look at it I can't see, and yet there's no physical reason why I can't.'

'God!' Peggy said. 'But does that mean that you might regain your sight one day?'

525

Sam shrugged. 'The doctor said he doesn't know. Some do, others don't. In the meantime I'm going on with rehab for living life as a blind man, which I am at the moment and might always be.'

'And why don't you want to tell Sarah, because it's obvious you don't?'

'A number of reasons really. The first is because I feel a bit of a bloody fraud, to tell you the truth. And then there is the fact that it might give Sarah false hope that I might be able just to wake up one day and be able to see. And she is still touchy about her scarred face, for all the assurances I give her that it will make no difference to me. If she thought that one day I might miraculously be able to see, it could easily make her nervous or unsure of herself. She doesn't need that, especially as the chances are it won't happen, and I'll never be able to see any better than I can at the moment. Can you understand what I'm saying?'

'I can,' Peggy said. 'I've never heard of this before and cannot understand it any better than you can, but Sarah definitely doesn't need to know. In fact, I think that we should keep this information entirely to ourselves.'

A week after the doctor had first taken away Sam's papers, he returned them. 'You certainly fired up Mike Malone, the chap I was telling you about,' he said. 'Said it brought all his memories back as well and he has completed some absolutely amazing drawings. It was great to see his enthusiasm return, and his wife is delighted at the change in him. Anyway, the upshot of this is that I showed a couple to a newspaper friend of mine yesterday, and he's going to run a column detailing your experiences and illustrated by Mike in the *Sutton Coldfield News*.'

'Really?'

The doctor smiled. 'Really. The man said it will be in on the twenty-seventh of April, next Friday's edition.'

'It's just that things like this don't happen to me,' Sam said. 'To people like me, I mean.'

'Well,' said the doctor with a smile, 'they have now.'

That afternoon Sam was bursting with excitement, and Sarah thought it no wonder when she heard the news.

'Wait till I tell them at home,' she said. 'They'll be over the moon. We'll have to get the paper and have a look. Maybe some good news will cheer us all up, with this flipping war dragging on and on.'

Sam nodded. 'It should have been finished ages ago. I listen to the wireless in the day room, and the Allies have reached the outskirts of Berlin, and so have the Red Army from the North. Hitler hasn't a chance now. He must know that.'

'It's awful,' Sarah said. 'And what about those horrendous death camps the Red Army and now the Allies are finding?'

'Yeah,' Sam said. 'Makes you wonder how many there are altogether.'

'Sometimes,' Sarah said, 'I can hardly bear to read about them, and the pictures of the stick-thin people make me cry. There was a picture in the *Despatch* yesterday and it just showed mounds of earth and the reporter said the earth covered the bodies of hundreds of people and some bodies had just been piled up and set fire to. You'd like to think that it's one awful dream but this really happened to families like mine and yours, all because they're Jews. Why did the Nazis pick on them?'

'I've no idea,' Sam said.

'Imagine the evil thoughts that have been tumbling round inside Hitler's head for years, and the people who could administer such cruelty. It's a wonder that they can live with themselves,' Sarah added.

In the end the family bought lots of copies of the paper because everyone wanted to read Sam's account and see the illustrations. They were very impressed.

'You've written this really well,' Polly said.

'Thanks,' Sarah said, 'but I can take little credit for the content. I just wrote most of it as Sam told it to me.'

'Well, I remember that he could tell a good enough tale when he was here before,' Polly said, 'but these accounts – well, you almost feel that you're there alongside him.'

'Poor Sam,' Magda said. 'I would just hate being blind.'

'So would I,' Sarah said. 'It's heartbreaking sometimes to see him like that. But he's always so positive.'

'He wasn't like that before,' Peggy said. 'That's 'cos of you.'

'It's a bit scary thinking that one person is responsible for another's happiness.'

'It's the price you pay when you love someone,' Marion said. 'You suffer with them like you are now with Sam, and yet the good times should make it all worthwhile.'

Sarah thought about her mother's words that day as she made her way to the hospital, taking the paper with her. When she saw Sam in the grounds she called to him. He turned, and a delicious feeling of warmth flowed through her at the sight of him. She was proud also as she watched him walk towards her with confidence, playing his stick in front of him. She hugged him as he reached her and their lips met, but it was a fairly chaste kiss as they were not the only ones taking the air that day and, as it was, a slight cheer from some of the other soldiers made Sarah's face flush crimson. She was glad that Sam was unable to see it.

As they walked arm in arm across the lawn back to the hospital, she felt Sam give a sudden jerk.

'What is it?' she cried. 'What's the matter?'

'Nothing,' Sam assured her. 'Nothing to worry about, anyway. Just felt a little chill.'

Sarah was puzzled, for the day was a warm one

with only a light breeze, but she didn't argue though she knew that something *was* the matter because after that Sam was quiet and subdued. She thought he might tell her what was so obviously troubling him when they got inside, but he didn't and when she asked him he said he felt fine. Still Sarah knew there was something wrong. It put a damper on her visit and she returned home very worried.

Sam wasn't ill. In fact he was rather excited. In the grounds the sunlight had penetrated the blackness that he had lived with since the explosion, and he had asked to go inside to see if he had been imagining things. Once inside he found the blackness had receded to grey, and he could see vague forms in front of him. He was thrilled even to have such limited vision, but could hardly share that with Sarah when any moment he imagined it might be snatched away from him again.

That night he was almost afraid to go to sleep, certain that he would be totally blind again when he woke up. However, next morning, the vague indistinct images that he had seen the night before were sharper and more defined. He would have asked to see the doctor dealing with him but the man was having a well-earned day off and Sam didn't want to go to anyone else.

Peggy came with Sarah that day, as it was Saturday. Sam was in the day room, and as soon as they were positioned beside him he said, 'Did you hear about the Italian partisans that found where Benito Mussolini was holed up and took him out and hanged him?'

'Yes,' said Peggy. 'It was on the wireless and personally I think hanging is too good for him, and Hitler too. But I'm more interested in you because Sarah said you were acting very strange yesterday.'

Sam burst out laughing. 'I've never felt better and I'd say a man is entitled to act a little strange once in a while.'

He smiled in Sarah's direction as he spoke and she felt herself go weak at the knees. Sam looked better than she had seen him for ages. There was a lightness about him, somehow, and she felt silly for making a fuss.

'I was probably overreacting,' she said, 'especially as Sam is fine now.'

'I was fine then,' Sam protested. 'I told you that when you asked, but I'm sorry that I worried you.'

'It's all right,' Sarah said, and she leaned forward and kissed him gently on the lips.

'Would like me to go out for a bit?' Peggy asked.

'No, I'll go,' Sarah said. 'You two have a few words together and I shall take a nice walk around the grounds.'

When she had gone Peggy looked at her brother straight and said, 'OK, as our American cousins would say, out with it. There's summat up with you, and don't even try denying it. So what is it?'

Peggy's tone implied she would stand no nonsense, and anyway Sam wanted to share what had happened to him with someone. So he said, 'All right, then, though you will hardly believe it.' He leaned forward and said in a sort of awed whisper, 'I can see.'

It was the last thing Peggy expected Sam to say, and her mouth dropped open in astonishment as a large lump formed in her throat and tears stung her eyes. 'Oh, Sam,' she said when she was able to speak, 'it's what I have hoped and prayed for, and yet never thought . . .'

'I can't see properly,' Sam said. 'I can just see outlines. Like I can see that clock, but not the hands on it. But that is an improvement because yesterday I was in the grounds coming back into the hospital with Sarah, and we were facing the sun, and suddenly I saw a muted shaft of light. It hurt a bit and was so unexpected that I jumped and realised that the blackness in front of my eyes had been replaced by blurred grey images. This morning it's better still.'

'Will it get better than that?' Peggy asked. 'What did the doctor say?'

'I haven't seen the doctor,' Sam said. 'He isn't here today and he's always difficult to see on Sundays, so I don't know what he thinks.'

'And you don't want to tell Sarah?'

Sam shook his head. 'Nor the parents. Nobody, really, because I want to see that this improvement is going to last, or get better before telling everyone.'

'Sam, this is just such marvellous news,' Peggy

said as she put her arms around her brother. 'And I couldn't be more pleased for you, but I will have to tell someone or I'll burst. Can I tell Violet?'

'Oh, yes,' Sam said. 'I don't mind Vi knowing. Just make sure that no one overhears you.'

'I'll be careful,' Peggy said. 'And now we must talk of something else because Sarah will be on her way back.'

The following day, though, there was further improvement in Sam's ability to see. Faces were sometimes still a bit blurry, so he wasn't able to see the troubled eyes of his parents, his mother in particular, but her heard the apprehension in her voice. He felt a wave of sympathy for her wash over him because she had hardly got over the fact that he had been blinded.

He would ask the doctor about his recovery as soon as he saw him the following day.

The doctor was both amazed and delighted when Sam told him of the changes to his eyesight and he took him into his surgery and shone the pen light into the back of his eyes.

'What do you think, Doc?' Sam asked.

'I think, Mr Samuel Wagstaffe, you are one very lucky young man.'

'D'you mean that I will regain my full sight?'

'It's impossible to say with certainty,' the doctor said. 'You could, or it could stay the same as it is now, though the fact that you say each day it improves is a hopeful sign.'

'It does,' Sam said. 'This morning, for instance, it's like a film has been removed from my eyes, and I could see the fingers on the clock on the wall as soon as I woke up.'

The doctor nodded. 'That's the sort of thing that can happen and it's not all that surprising, really, because you lost your sight as a result of trauma or shock. But now your life is much better and, most importantly you have the lady you love by your side. Good gracious, I bet she's over the moon?'

'I haven't told her, Doctor,' Sam said. 'And I'd rather you didn't, not just yet.'

'I won't say a word, don't worry,' said the doctor. 'It's not my news to tell.'

'But I won't have to stay here any longer now, will I?' Sam said. 'I mean, I don't need rehab any more.'

'Oh, can't wait to leave us now, eh?' said the doctor with a smile. 'Just leave it another few days, till the weekend, and we will have a better idea of how good your eyesight is going to be.'

Sam saw the sense of that and he prepared himself to see Sarah's face clearly for the first time since the accident. His hearing had become much keener since he'd lost his sight, and as he sat on the chair by his bed he was listening out for her. Eventually he heard her footsteps in the corridor getting closer and he felt as if a ball of excitement had unravelled inside him. Then Sarah was framed in the doorway.

He was prepared for her to be scarred. Heavens,

he had been shocked enough when he'd seen his own pockmarked face for the first time that morning. However, Sarah had a smile that nearly split her face in two and caused the light to dance behind those beautiful eyes. Her discoloured blemishes were no longer unsightly and didn't really seem to matter. She was his own dear Sarah, whom he loved with a passion.

Had Sarah not had news of her own, she might have been puzzled at Sam's preoccupation with her face, but she had barely sat down before she said, 'We hadn't heard a word from Dad for over a fortnight. Remember me telling you that?'

Sam nodded. He knew how worried Sarah had been, and even Peggy had expressed concern.

'Well, that was because he was in hospital,' Sarah said. 'He had developed a fever and so was sent to a fever hospital in France where they spoke little English. He said that no one seemed to know where he was for a while. Anyroad, in the end they tracked him down and the military doctor that examined him discharged him from active duty. He said the fever had damaged his heart slightly. It isn't serious as long as he's careful, but he's not fit for fighting any more and so he's being shipped home.'

'Oh, I bet your mother is pleased,' Sam said. 'When's he due?'

'This Saturday. I won't be able to visit on Thursday or Friday because Mom wants a hand getting the place spruced up.' And at this she gave a wry smile. 'As if Dad will even notice. Mom did want to welcome him home with a party but he doesn't want one. He says the end of the war, which will have to happen any day now, is time enough to celebrate and he wants to have a few quiet days at home with family. We haven't seen him for nearly five years.'

'I think he's right,' Sam said. 'He's going to see a mighty change in all of you.'

'I'll say.' Even the twins will be thirteen in June. The Americans call them teenagers and it so describes that age halfway between an adult and a child.'

'Oh, yes,' Sam commented wryly. 'We have much to thank our American cousins for.'

'Yeah,' said Sarah with a giggle. 'According to your Peggy that includes GIs and nylons.'

'That sounds like Peggy all right.'

'Are you sure you don't mind me not coming in for a few days?'

'Of course I don't,' Sam said. 'I really do think that you all need time together as a family.'

It actually suited him very well. He was being discharged on Friday, and then on the following Monday he had an interview with the editor of the *Sutton Coldfield News*, which the doctor had arranged. After that he would go to see Sarah and surprise her with the fact that he could now see again. He put his arms around her and said, 'We must make the most of the time we have.'

On 2 May the Red Army found the burned remains of Hitler and his mistress, Eva Braun, whom he had married just days before. They had both committed suicide. Inside the same bunker were the bodies of Goebbels and his wife and six children, who had been poisoned by cyanide.

Still the fighting continued.

On Friday Sam said goodbye to the hospital. Although he was happy to leave he left behind some good friends, specially Mike Malone. Sam knew how much he owed the doctor and nurses and thanked them sincerely for what they had done for him. He made for home and hoped that he wouldn't be that much of a shock for his poor mother because he had not told his parents he was being discharged, nor that he could now see. Peggy advised him to write first and tell them because the surprise he wanted to spring could upset their parents.

In the end, though, it was just as he imagined it would be. He walked from the station, for there wasn't a bus for an hour or two, enjoying the exercise because he had grown sluggish in hospital. He took pleasure in the walk, seeing the beauty of the countryside around him as if for the first time.

When he had walked at a good pace for little over an hour he could see his home in the distance and two figures, whom he knew would be his father and his younger brother, Peter, toiling in the fields. He skirted the fields, however, and made for the house. He knew his mother would be in the kitchen and he lifted the latch and walked in. She was cooking something at the range and, thinking it was her husband or younger son come back to the house for something, didn't move until Sam said, 'Hello, Mom.'

Almost in slow motion she turned her head slowly to see her elder son as she never thought to see him again, standing straight and tall in her kitchen, and she blinked as if unable to believe the evidence of her own eyes. 'It is me, Mom,' Sam said, 'and I'm completely better. I can see.'

Before the words were out of his mouth his mother was across the room and had his face in her hands. 'You can see?'

'As well as ever I could.'

'Oh, praise God!' she said fervently, with her arms wrapped tight around Sam, though tears ran down her face in a flood of thankfulness. 'Oh, praise God!'

Sam's father too was amazed, and enfolded his elder son in his arms in a way that he hadn't done since Sam had been a small boy, and Peter was awed by the whole miracle. Then things moved with speed. Daisy, in her last year at the village school, had to be fetched, and so had Violet's parents. The news ran round that small community like wildfire, and in those days of flux, when the war was not yet officially over though everyone thought it ought to be, it was wonderful to have good news. Everyone wanted to see this man blinded by the war who could now see again.

Sam could never remember a time when he had been hugged and kissed and cried over, nor had his hand pumped so many times. He was a hero, no doubt about it, and a miracle into the bargain. There was a sad moment when he caught sight of the parents of two of his mates killed in the blast that had temporarily blinded him, and saw their eyes still clouded with grief.

He approached them awkwardly. 'There are no words to say how sorry I am,' he said. 'They were the very best mates for a man to have and we had been through so much we thought we were invincible. For some time after their death I felt bad to be alive, and I still wonder why I was saved when five good men died alongside me that day.'

'You mustn't feel responsible in any way,' one of the fathers said, laying a hand on Sam's shoulder. 'We are delighted to see you hale and hearty, for we have known you since the day you were born. Just take joy in your life, for it's a precious gift to have. And this is a day to celebrate that fact, and one our son would have approved of.'

'Hear, hear,' the other father said. 'You must never feel guilty that you are alive. My son's death was not your fault.'

Sam felt humbled by the courage of the fathers who had lost their sons to a war now slowly grinding to a halt, but he was glad he had spoken to them and he shook them both warmly by the hand.

TWENTY-NINE

After a relaxing weekend with his parents Sam went for his interview at the *Sutton Coldfield News*, thinking it was to talk about more articles. However, the doctor had told his editor friend that Sarah had virtually copied what Sam had told her and he had wanted to see this. So after a chat with Sam he gave him a number of news items to write an account of, putting his slant on them and when he had completed these the editor was so impressed that he offered him a job on the paper there and then.

Sam was stunned. He had thought he would revert to work on the land when the war eventually ended, because that was all he knew, and he was astounded that such an opportunity had been offered to him. Even though the paper had accepted the articles that Sarah had written up on his behalf he had never imagined that it would lead to any sort of employment, and the starting wage of five pounds and five shillings as a cub reporter was a good wage – far more than he could have earned ploughing a field.

However, though he accepted the job, he was seriously worried that he wouldn't be able to do it. When he admitted this to the editor he said he could quite understand Sam's trepidation at starting something so totally different from anything he had done before, but to have confidence because he could write very well. The editor assured him that he would soon settle into it and he would help him all he could.

Even so, Sam would have liked to have talked it over with Sarah, but even as he was thinking this the church bells began to ring and a young man burst through the doors and cried, 'The war is over. Germany has surrendered and old Winnie has declared tomorrow a day of celebration.'

Sam wanted to make for Sarah's but he stopped himself. Sarah had told him that their father wanted to celebrate when the war was over so in all likelihood that would be that night. It would be a family affair and maybe he shouldn't intrude, so instead he decided to return home and tell his parents the good news about the job that he still could scarcely believe he had accepted.

That same evening Bill acknowledged that he was a lucky man. He had a wonderful wife, whom he still loved as much as the day he'd married her. He'd been so worried when they told him his heart had been affected by the fever, thinking his days were numbered, but the doctor was quick to reassure him.

'There is no reason for you not to have a long and happy life if you're careful,' the doctor said as he was getting ready to leave. 'There is no need to think of yourself as an invalid either.'

'I'm very glad to hear that.'

'What line of work are you in?'

'The brass industry,' Bill said, 'but I was in a supervisory role when I enlisted, and they said the job would be waiting for me when I got back – if I got back, they meant, of course.'

'So there is no lifting, or heavy work?'

Bill shook his head, 'Not now. That sort of work is for the young fellows, younger than me, at any rate.'

'Then there's no reason why you should not return to it.'

'And what about marital relations, Doctor?'

'Sex, you mean?' the doctor said with a grin on his face. 'Good for body and soul. As long as you don't go at it like a bull at a gate. But that is really the prerogative of the young. You have years of a healthy sex life ahead of you.'

And that is what he had told Marion as they snuggled in bed. Marion was glad the lights were out because she was embarrassed and a little frightened, though Bill had assured her there was no possibility of pregnancy. Marion would have preferred to turn over and sleep, but she heard the longing in Bill's voice and acknowledged that he had been away for five long years. Surely she could do this one thing for him, though she didn't expect that she would get much enjoyment from it herself.

However, Bill took his time. He had waited years and to wait a little longer could only bring sweeter pleasure, he knew, as he removed Marion's nightdress for the first time and began caressing her body, gently at first and then more firmly. She was not at ease with that initially, but made no move to stop Bill, and very slowly the sexual feelings she had repressed for so long she had thought them dead and buried began to steal through her body. She felt them pulsating through her veins and seeping into her very bones so that she couldn't help her little moans of passion. Then for the first time in her life she found herself crying out, 'Now, oh, please now . . .'

Bill had a smile on his face as he entered his beautiful wife, and waves of pleasure seemed to rise higher and higher in Marion until she felt almost consumed with desire.

Afterwards, as she lay in sated contentment, she thought it was the only time that she had experienced such exquisite joy in making love to her own husband for all her married life. She had been frightened all the time that it might result in pregnancy, so much so that they had not enjoyed any sex at all since the twins had been born.

'Can you see how what we have just enjoyed has anything to do with the Catholic Church?' Bill asked her.

543

'No, I can't.'

'Then bugger the lot of them and their rules on contraception, I say.'

'Oh, Bill!' Marion said.

'"Oh, Bill!"' Bill mimicked. 'Come here, woman.' And he gathered Marion into his arms. 'I love you, Mrs Whittaker.'

'And I am quite fond of you, Mr Whittaker.'

'Only fond?'

'Oh, Bill, I love you heart, body and soul, and you know that,' Marion said.

Their lips met and the kiss seemed to seal the pledge. Then they slept entwined in each other's arms.

Oh, yes, Bill thought, he was a very fortunate man. He even had a job to return to that he enjoyed and that paid a good wage, and many had far worse. But he had missed so much of the children's growing up and he bitterly regretted that. The twins had grown out of all recognition, almost teenagers now and had been little more than wee girls when he had gone away. However, they had missed their father very much and hugged him tight and shed happy tears that he was back and would never have to go away again.

The loss of Tony, now that Bill was home, seemed more acute than ever. It was as if there was a space where he should have been. A desolate look sometimes lurked behind Bill's eyes and when Marion saw this her heart was sore for him, but she knew that time eventually would make the pain more bearable for him as it had with her. Life had had to go on, for the sake of the others as well as her own sanity, and eventually Bill would realise he had to do the same.

Bill also felt a pang when he looked on Sarah's face. It had given him a bit of a shock, because despite the letter telling him of the scarring, in the picture he had carried in his head Sarah had flawless skin and her long hair was tied up in a bun to match her mother's.

'If I'd been here I would have fought you going in the munitions,' he told her. 'I am so sorry about your face.'

'I'm sorry about my face too, Dad,' Sarah said, 'and I'd be lying if I said anything different – like I'm sorry for all the victims of the bombing and the war. But the work I was doing was vital to the war effort and though I knew the risks I never thought anything would happen to me. You never do. If you thought that, no one would ever do anything.'

Bill could only agree. Richard had been right: Sarah the young girl had gone for ever and left behind a stalwart and principled young woman. Once he had accepted that, he had to admit her face wasn't that bad at all and her bobbed hair quite suited her. What he couldn't accept, though, was this Sam Wagstaffe, whom she wanted to marry. He knew that he was a brother of Peggy's and that he was probably a decent enough chap but he was blind. Bill was sorry for him and all that, and he knew it would be a terrible affliction for a young man, and he knew that probably Sarah felt sorry for him too, but she didn't have to be sorry enough to marry him, for God's sake. There was no way on God's earth that he was allowing his daughter to saddle herself with a blind man, and he was amazed that Marion had let it go as far as it had.

Still, there was no need for him to argue the toss with his daughter straight away – not that night, at least – for the war was over for them all and soon Richard would be home too. Sarah would give up this foolhardy idea of marrying this Sam Wagstaffe and life would get back to normal . . . Bill gave himself up to enjoying the celebrations.

They had all made inroads into the food and drink and the atmosphere was a jolly one, helped by the big band music belting out from the gramophone, when there was a knock at the door.

'Wonder who that can be,' Marion said, getting to her feet.

'Probably your neighbours to complain about the noise,' Polly said with a grin.

'I hope not,' said Marion. 'It's hardly late yet.'

'Stay here,' Bill said. 'I'll go.' Marion knew that it was Bill's way of establishing himself as the man of the house again so she let him.

Outside the door, Sam wasn't sure that he was doing the right thing, but his parents had insisted when they learned that Sarah didn't even know

Sam could see again, let alone that he had left the hospital and had got the job at the newspaper.

'And even without those things,' his mother said firmly, 'you should be with the one you love on this very special day.'

'I don't want to butt in,' Sam said. 'It'll be a family celebration.'

'Yes, and a family you will join if you marry Sarah, as you say you want to.'

'If her father gives his permission.'

'Well, why don't you go and ask him?' Sam's father suggested.

'Now? You really think I should?'

'I think there is no time like the present.'

And so Sam Wagstaffe was standing outside the Whittakers' door, and Bill saw the man was slightly discomforted, though he looked respectable enough. His face was open, though he had a fair few shrapnel burns. His eyes were very dark and there something vaguely familiar about him.

'Can I help you?' Bill asked.

Sam guessed that this was Sarah's father and so he met his gaze levelly and said, 'My name is Sam Wagstaffe and I'm here to see Sarah.'

Inside, Glenn Miller's 'In the Mood' had come to an end and Sarah was pensive as she removed the record and wondered whenever she would get to see Sam again. Her mother sort of expected her to spend time with her father, especially as she was at home all day, and even her father said that he didn't want her to be running off to the hospital every five minutes. She did love her father dearly and knew that he had been parted from them for years, but she ached to see Sam. She found the most frustrating thing about being with her father was that he didn't discuss Sam with her at all, yet Sam was the very person she wanted to talk about. If she tried to tell him amusing or interesting things that Sam had said or done her father would change the subject.

Sarah was thinking this as she sorted through the records, deciding what to put on next, and above the ensuing chatter, Sarah heard the incredulous tone of her father as he said, 'But I thought you were blind?' She went to the door into the corridor to see who he was talking to.

When she saw Sam at the door, she couldn't quite believe it. She had thought him still in hospital, and then he lifted his head and smiled at her, and those eyes she'd thought sightless fused with hers and she saw the love light shining in Sam's as her hands flew to her mouth.

'Sam?' she asked tentatively.

'Yes, Sarah,' Sam said firmly, 'I have recovered my sight.'

Sarah gave a shriek before running down the corridor to Sam, and he caught her up in his arms. Then she drew him inside under Bill's surprised nose. 'Come and see the others,' Sarah commanded, tugging him towards the room. 'They'll all want to see this.'

'We'll Meet Again' was belting out from the

record player, and Polly and her mother were dabbing their eyes, Sarah saw, as she dragged Sam into the room. When they caught sight of Sam, however, there were shrieks of surprise, and when he told them that he was able to see again everyone one wanted to know how it happened. Peggy and Violet had to admit that they had known about it but had promised not to say a word until he was fairly certain that his recovery was permanent.

Bill watched all this in dumbfounded surprise.

When Sam had answered everyone's questions, he faced Bill and, still holding Sarah to him, said, 'And you are Sarah's father?'

Bill gave a brief nod. 'I am.'

'Well, then,' Sam said, 'I would like your permission to marry your daughter. I love her with all my heart and soul, and will do so until the breath leaves my body. I will do all in my power to make her happy.'

Bill was impressed by the sincere way Sam had spoken, but before he could speak, spontaneous applause broke out from the family, who had crowded all around Sam and Sarah.

Bill looked at them and then turned to Sam. 'You seem to have the support of everyone here, but Sarah is very dear to us. Until a few minutes ago I thought you were blind, and what I want to know is, will you be able to support her?'

'If you had asked me that question yesterday, sir, I wouldn't be able to answer you so definitely,' Sam said. 'However, today I was invited to the offices of the *Sutton Coldfield News* where I was interviewed by the editor and given a short test and as a result of that I have been offered a position as a reporter.'

'You have?' Sarah asked.

'I can scarcely believe it myself, Sam said. 'I went back afterwards to tell my parents and I was having to pinch myself on the train. They could scarcely believe it either. And to think that this all came about because of all my experiences that you have been writing down.'

'What's this?' Bill said.

'Sam already has a weekly column in this paper,' Sarah said. 'It's detailing his experiences in the war. They're illustrated by another patient called Mike Malone. I'll show you. We've kept the papers.'

'Well, I never,' Bill said, astounded.

'So what about it, Mr Whittaker?'

'Well, Bill?' asked Marion.

Bill looked at the two young people still clasped together and almost felt the love sparking between them. He knew he was looking at something precious and very beautiful. Sarah was young yet, but had he the right to deny her happiness? If he had been asked, he would have said all he wanted for his children was that they found someone to share their life with that they loved as wholeheartedly as he did his Marion and he knew in Sam Wagstaffe Sarah had found her soul mate.

'I risk being lynched by this mob if I say no,'

he said to Sam with a smile. 'So I suppose I must say yes.' He put out his hand. 'Welcome to the family, Sam.'

Sam was staying the night, as he had before, and later, when Polly and Pat and their brood had gone home and the house grew quieter, Sam told Bill all about losing his sight because of the shock of the explosion. He showed Bill the columns in the papers and told him how that had all come about. However, Bill was learning much more about Sam by noticing how he was with the other members of his family. Even the children were easy with him, and everyone seemed to like him, which boded well for the future.

Much later and unnoticed, Sam and Sarah slipped out of the house and went for a walk hand in hand.

'Look at the stars,' Sarah said, 'and the half-moon. It's a rare sight to see such things in Birmingham's smoky air, though it was even worse when the bombs were falling and incendiaries setting the whole place alight.'

'At least that's over,' Sam said.

'Yes,' Sarah agreed. 'It was a terrible war, and yet if it hadn't happened we would probably never have met.'

'Perish the thought,' Sam said. 'And I would still be a farm hand.'

'I wouldn't have minded being married to a farm hand.'

'I know. I'm just saying without the war these sorts of opportunities wouldn't arise.'

'Yes, I suppose so,' Sarah conceded. 'You tend to think nothing comes from war but death, destruction and tragedy.'

'There is plenty of that too,' Sam said. 'But I think that we owe it to those that died to live life the best way we can, and to be honest I think my life would be incomplete if I hadn't got you in it.'

'Well you have, don't worry,' Sarah said, and in the darkness, with no one to see them, the passionate kiss they shared was the promise of good things to come.

AUTHOR'S NOTE

I do hope that you enjoy this novel about a family called The Whittakers who lived in Aston, Birmingham during the Second World War. It tells of how an ordinary family dealt with deprivations of war; rationing, blackouts, terrifying raids, the tragedy enacted all around them, and how it all touched their lives. At the end of it all everyone is changed, the children are children no longer and the dynamics, both for them and their relatives the Reillys, have altered. Life will never be the same again, but there is peace at last and they look forward and begin to rebuild themselves.

While researching this book I came across 'The Birmingham History Forum' website, which I found a hugely valuable tool. If I was searching for more information about anything, I would post a request on that site; the response was always phenomenal. I received all the answers I could wish for, reams of information sometimes, even accompanied by photographs! Conversations about 'games we played as kids', 'Brummie sayings', or 'the kind of sweets we used to eat' would often jog my memory too. Thank you to all you amazing fellow Brummies who have helped me so much.

I must also mention too some books I found very informative, *Catholics in Birmingham* by Christine Ward-Penny. *Britain at War: Women's War* by Martin Parsons, gave me an insight into the type of work that women undertook during the war. *City at War: Birmingham 1939–1945*, compiled by Birmingham Museums and Art Gallery and edited by Phillada Ballard gave an excellent insight into Birmingham's industries, the raids and the Home Front, interspersed with real life accounts and advertisements from the period. Carl Chinn is a marvelous man, who has been such a help to me over the years. He is a true Brummie, as anyone in Birmingham would probably know, and his reference books are superb. I used two of his books, *Homes for People* and *Brum Undaunted* (Birmingham through the Blitz) to aid me with the historical detail. I also checked facts in my old copies of the *Birmingham Evening Mail* through that period to add authenticity.

Finn Sullivan couldn't understand his family. They had been aware of the rumblings of an unsettled Europe and so why were they surprised when Britain declared war on Germany on 4 August 1914? When the news filtered through to them, via the postman, in their cottage in Donegal, Finn's eldest brother, Tom, went to Buncrana, their nearest town, and bought a paper so that they could read all about it.

'England has declared war on Germany because they invaded two other countries,' he said as the family sat eating their midday meal.

'Well, if that's about the strength of it,' his father, Thomas John, remarked, 'it's a wonder that no one can see the irony.'

'What do you mean?' Finn's brother Joe asked.

'Well, isn't that what England has done to us?' Thomas John said. 'They invaded us, didn't they? Who rules Ireland now?'

'Not the Irish, that's for sure,' Biddy, Finn's mother replied. 'It's England has us by the throat.'

'Aye,' Thomas John said, 'and that means anything that involves England automatically involves us too.'

'You mean the war?' Finn asked.

'Of course I mean the war, boy. What else?'

Finn coloured in anger. He hated being called 'boy' by his father now he was over eighteen.

'So you think there will be call-up here?' Joe asked.

'Don't see how we will get away without it,' Thomas John said.

'Maybe they are hoping for volunteers,' Tom said. 'After all, young Englishmen are volunteering in droves. The recruiting offices are hard-pressed to cope with the numbers who want to take a pop at the Germans. So the paper says, anyway.'

'And why would Irish boys volunteer to fight for a country that has kept them down for years and years?' Thomas John demanded.

'The carrot that they are holding out might have something to do with that,' Tom said.

'What's that?' Joe asked. 'Have to be some big bloody carrot, for I would not volunteer to lift one finger to help England.'

'The paper claims that the government will grant Ireland independence if they get Irish support in this war.'

'Let me see that,' Thomas John said, and Tom passed the paper to his father, who scanned in quickly. 'That's what it says all right, and I don't believe a word of it. To my knowledge, England has never kept any promise it has made to Ireland

2

and the Irish. For my money they can sink or swim on their own. We will keep our heads down and get on with our lives. It's no good seeking trouble. In my experience it will come knocking on the door soon enough.'

Finn couldn't believe that his father thought their dull, boring lives would go on totally unaffected by the war being fought just across a small stretch of water.

To Finn, war was new and exciting. He knew that in the army no one would look down on him because of his youth and no one there would call him 'boy'.

He didn't share these thoughts, but when his young sister Nuala came in from her nursemaid's job at the Big House and was told the news later, she noted the look on Finn's face and the zealous glint in his deep amber eyes, and she shivered and hoped that her impetuous brother wouldn't do anything stupid.

War dominated the papers and Finn read everything he could about it. After the first weeks there were pictures of the first troops to go overseas waving out of train carriages, all happy and smiling. They would soon kick the Hun into touch, the papers said, and be home by Christmas with the job done. Finn looked at the pictures and ached to be there amongst them.

The following Saturday morning, he tripped getting up from the milking stool and spilled half a pail of milk over the straw on the floor of the byre. Thomas John, suddenly angered by the mess, gave him such a powerful cuff across the side of his head that it knocked him to the floor, although he had never raised his hand to any of his children before.

No one helped Finn to his feet and he was glad, because he would have hated his brothers to see the tears he brushed away surreptitiously.

'Don't worry about it, Finn,' Tom said quietly as they walked back to the house. 'You know Daddy's temper flashes up out of nothing and is gone in an instant. He will be over it in no time.'

But I won't be, Finn thought, but he said nothing.

When he set out for Buncrana later that morning with Tom and his mother, he was as angry as ever. This anger was increased as Biddy took out her purse as they pulled into the town and, dropping some coins into Finn's hand, told him to go to the harbour and buy some fish for their dinner.

Finn never got to the harbour, however, because as he turned down Main Street he heard a military band and saw the line of soldiers at the bottom of the hill. In front of this company was a tall officer of some sort, in full regalia, and so smart, even the buttons on his uniform sparkled in the early autumn sunshine. He held a stick in his left hand.

Suddenly the band behind him began to play and the officer led the soldiers up the hill to the marching music, the beat emphasised by the young

4

drummer boy at the front. The officer's boots rung out on the cobbled street, the tattoo of the soldiers' tramping feet completely in time.

Shoppers and shopkeepers alike had come to the doorways to watch the soldiers' progress. As they drew nearer, though, Finn was unable to see the officer's eyes, hidden as they were under the shiny peak of his cap, but his brown, curly moustache fairly bristled above the firm mouth in the slightly red and resolute face.

Finn felt excitement swell within him so that it filled his whole being. Tom, brought out of the Market Hall to see what was happening, saw the fervour filling his brother's face and he was deeply afraid for him, but the press of people made it impossible for him to reach Finn.

And then the company stopped, and while the soldiers stood to attention the officer talked words that were like balm to Finn's bruised and battered soul, words like 'pride', 'integrity' and 'honour' to serve in the British Army, whose aim was to rid the world of a nation of brutal aggressors. The army would crush the enemy who marched un invited into other counties, harassing and persecuting innocent men, women and children, and they would deal swiftly and without mercy to any who opposed them.

Many, he said, had already answered the call and now he wished to see if young Irishmen had what it took to join this righteous fight. He wanted to see if they felt strongly enough for the poor people of Belgium and France, their fellow human beings, who were prepared to fight to the death for freedom. Any who felt this way should step forward bravely.

At the time, freedom and liberty were what many Irish people longed for, and so those words burned brightly inside Finn. And if he were to join this company, like he saw more than a few were doing, then Ireland would gain her freedom too; wasn't that the promise given?

His feet stepped forward almost of their own volition and he joined the gaggle of young Irish men milling around, unsure what to do, until the company sergeant came forward to take them in hand.

'Finn, what in God's name are you doing?' Tom cried. He had broken through the crowd at last and now had his hand on his brother's shoulder.

Finn shook him off roughly. 'What's it look like?'

'You can't do this.'

'Oh yes I can,' Finn declared. 'You heard what the man said. They need our help and if enough Irishmen do this, Ireland will be free too.'

'This is madness, Finn . . .'

'Now then,' said the sergeant beside them. 'What's this?'

'I want to enlist,' Finn said firmly. 'My brother is trying to prevent me, but I am eighteen years old and the decision is my own.'

'Well said,' the soldier told Finn admiringly. He

turned to Tom. 'As for you, fine sir, you should be ashamed at trying to turn your brother from what he sees as his duty. As he is eighteen he can decide these things for himself. It would look better if you were to join him rather than try to dissuade him.'

Finn shot Tom a look of triumph, then said rather disparagingly to the sergeant, 'Tom can't join just now, for he has an urgent errand to run for our mother.' And he dropped the coins their mother had given him into Tom's hand. 'I'm going to be busy for a while, Tom, so you must get the fish for Mammy.'

He turned away before Tom could find the words to answer him and followed behind the sergeant to find out what he had to do to qualify to join the battles enacted on foreign fields not that far away.

If Finn were honest with himself, he had joined more for himself than for anyone else. He was fed up being pushed around, barked at to do this or that because, as the youngest boy, he was at the beck and call of everyone. Yet he couldn't seem to do anything to anyone's satisfaction and he never got a word of thanks.

Even if he expressed an opinion, it was often derided and mocked. His father in particular seemed have a real downer on him, and then to knock him from his feet that morning for spilling a bit of milk – it was not to be borne.

According to the army he was a man and could make a decision concerning his own future. He was pleased when he saw that his best friend, Christy Byrne, had enlisted too. They had been friends all through school and they were of like mind. Both lads wanted excitement and adventure and were sure that the army could provide it.

By tacit consent, Tom never told their mother what Finn had done. Later that day Finn looked at his family grouped around the table eating the fish Tom had bought in Buncrana. He loved his father, whose approval he had always sought and seldom got. He loved his elder brothers too. He saw Tom was nervous because he knew what Finn was going to say and he hated any sort of confrontation and unpleasantness. Joe, on the other hand, was eating his dinner with relish, totally unaware of the hammer-blow Finn was going to deliver, and Nuala was at work. He wondered how his mother would react. She was often so bad-tempered and unreasonable, about little or nothing, and sometimes no one but his father seemed able to please her.

Still, he knew he had to get the announcement over with. There was no point in beating about the bush. 'I joined the army this morning,' he said, as soon as there was a break in the conversation. 'I enlisted,' he emphasised, in case there was any doubt. 'I'm in the Royal Inniskilling Fusiliers, and I am to report in the morning.'

Biddy and Joe sat open-mouthed with shock,

but Thomas John leaped to his feet, his face puce with anger. 'Are you, begod?' he snapped, thumping his fist on the table. 'Well, you are not. You will not do this. You are just a boy yet and I will accompany you tomorrow and get the matter overturned.'

'This is the army, Daddy, not school,' Finn said loftily. 'And I am not a boy any more, not in the army's eyes. I signed my name on the dotted line of my own free will and there is not a thing anyone can do about it.'

Thomas John sat back in his seat defeated, for he knew that Finn spoke the truth.

'But why, Finn?' Biddy cried out.

'I am surprised that you can ask that, Mammy,' Finn said, 'for nothing I do pleases anyone here. And I began to ask myself why I was working my fingers to the bone anyway for a farm that one day will be Tom's. I shall have nothing, not even a penny piece to bless myself with, because it seems to be against your religion to actually pay us anything like a wage.'

'Finn,' Biddy rapped out, 'how dare you speak to me like that? Thomas John, haven't you a word of censure for your son?'

Thomas John, however, said nothing. He knew he no longer had any jurisdiction over Finn, whom he loved so much, though he was unable to show it. Well, it was done now. The boy had stepped into a man's world, only he had chosen a dangerous route and Thomas John knew he would worry about him constantly.

9

His brothers had a measure of sympathy for Finn, although Tom expressed concern for him.

'Why worry?' Finn said. 'They say they fight in trenches, and a French or Belgian trench, I would imagine, is very like an Irish one, and those I am well familiar with. And if I pop off a few Germans along the way, so much the better.'

'You don't know the least thing about fighting.'

'Neither do any of us,' Finn said. 'We'll be trained, won't we? And after that, I expect I'll be as ready as the next man to have a go at the Hun. And there's something else, Tom. They say the French girls are very willing. Know what I mean?'

'Finn!' Tom said, slightly shocked. 'And how do you know, anyway? Just how many French girls do you know?'

'God, Tom, it's a well-known fact,' Finn said airily. 'Don't get on your high horse either. A fighting man has to have some distraction.' And Finn laughed at the expression on Tom's face.

Much as he could reassure his brothers, though, Finn dreaded breaking the news to Nuala when she came home. He had missed her when she began work, more than he had expected and more than he would admit. She had always listened to him and often championed him. She did the same that day in front of her parents, but later she sought Fin out in the barn.

'You will be careful, won't you, Finn?'

'Of course I will. I have got a whole lot of living to do yet.'

'Will you write to me? Let me know that you're all right?'

'I will,' Finn promised. 'And I will address it to you at the Big House. That way I can write what I want, without worrying about Mammy possibly steaming it open.'

Nuala nodded. But she said plaintively, 'Finn, I don't think I could bear it if anything happened to you.'

Finn looked into his sister's eyes, which were like two pools of sadness. He took hold of her shoulders. 'Nothing will happen me. I will come back safe and sound, never fear. And it's nice to have someone even partially on my side as I prepare to dip my toe into alien waters.'

'I'll always be on your side, Finn,' Nuala said. 'You know that.' She put her arms around her brother's neck and kissed his ruddy cheek. 'Good luck, Finn and God bless you.'

The next morning, Tom told his father he was going with Finn as far as Buncrana. When Thomas John opened his mouth as if to argue the point Tom said, 'He is not going in on his own as if he has no people belonging to him that love him and will miss him every minute till he returns.'

'As you like,' Thomas John said. 'But remember that the boy made his own bed.'

'I know that, Daddy, but it changes nothing.'

'So be it then. Bid the boy farewell from me.'

'I will, Daddy.'

Tom watched his father and Joe leave the cottage for the cow byre before going to see if Finn had all his things packed up.

Finn was ready and glad that Tom was going in with him and Christy, for his insides were jumping about as they set off up the lane.

'This is real good of you, Tom,' he said.

'Least I could do for my kid brother,' Tom replied easily.

Christy was waiting for them at the head of the lane and the two boys greeted each other exuberantly and then stood for a few moments to look around them at the landscape they saw every day. The September morning had barely begun. The sun had just started to peep up from behind the mountains but it was early enough for the mist to be rising from the fields. In the distance were rolling hills dotted with sheep, and here and there whitewashed cottages like their own, with curls of smoke rising from some of the chimneys, despite the early hour.

Finn knew soon the cows would be gathering in the fields to be taken down to the byres to be milked and the cockerel would be heralding the morning. Later, the hens would be let out to strut about the farmyard, pecking at the grit, waiting for the corn to be thrown to them just before the eggs were collected, and the dogs in the barn would be stretching themselves ready to begin another day.

It was all so familiar to Finn and yet wasn't

that the very thing that he railed against? Didn't he feel himself to be stifled in that little cottage? Maybe he did, but, like Christy, he had never been further than Buncrana all the days of his life. As he felt a tug of homesickness wash over him he gave himself a mental shake

Christy was obviously feeling the same way for he gave a sigh and said, 'I wonder how long it will be until we see those hills again?'

Finn decided being melancholy and missing your homeland before you had even left it, was no way to go on. He clapped Christy heartily on the shoulder.

'I don't know the answer to that, but what I do know is that joining the army is the most exciting thing that has ever happened to me.'

Christy caught Finn's mood and he gave a lopsided grin. 'I can barely wait. People say that it's all going to be over by Christmas and all I hope is that we finish our training in time to at least take a few pot shots at the Hun before we come home again.'

'I'd say you'd get your chance all right,' Tom said as they began to walk towards the town. 'And maybe before too long you'll wish you hadn't. War is no game.'

'Sure, don't we know that,' Finn commented. 'When we decided to join up, we knew what we were doing.'

Tom said nothing. He knew neither Finn nor Christy was prepared to listen, and maybe that was the right way to feel when such an irrevocable decision had been made. The die was cast now and it was far too late for second thoughts.